BREAKERS

BREAKERS, BOOK ONE

~

EDWARD W. ROBERTSON

Cover art by Stephanie Mooney

ISBN: 1479395226
ISBN-13: 978-1479395224

To Caitlin, for letting me get lost in other worlds

I:

PANHANDLER

1

If he'd known the world had already started to end, Raymond would have kept the drugs for himself. At least that way he wouldn't have to lie to his wife about it. It wasn't the drugs themselves that were the problem — they were casual smokers, Mia would greet the pine-skunk scent with a smile — or the amount, two ounces of weed, no more than he'd handled in college whenever he needed a few extra bucks. Instead, it was what the drugs meant: very soon, they would be out of money.

He turned away from the overgrown back yard, the wood of the deck creaking beneath him, and finished his lie. "We can even get a dog soon. Isn't that what you've been wanting? To clean stains out of the carpet five times a day?"

Mia's dark hair fluttered around her chin, the breeze bringing with it a whiff of salt. "I want to get a great big one. A wolfhound. Something big enough to eat you if you kick it."

"You think I'd kick our dog?"

"People get up to all kinds of bad things when no one's looking."

He smiled back. "Gotta run. Interview in Beverly Hills."

"Look at *you*."

"I won't be coming home in a Porsche. The guy just wants some cover art."

She cocked her head, brown eyes questioning. "He needs an interview for that?"

"Psychologist," Raymond shrugged. "Don't ask me. But if it works out, he's got some other projects he wants me for." He leaned in and kissed her before she could say anything more. She tasted like fresh peaches, lip gloss sticky as melted sugar. "If I get the gig, we'll go out for Indian."

Inside the bungalow, he grabbed his wallet and hustled out the front door exactly as if he had a traffic-filled 90-minute drive into the city ahead of him. Wilting heat breathed from the door of his '96 Altima. From the outside, all looked good: crisp white paint, sunroof. Inside, the left turn signal didn't work, the speedometer crapped out half the time, leaving him to estimate his speed by RPMs, and the AC took a solid five minutes to quit blowing hot air. He was sweating before he left the cracked driveway.

It was a lie, but not one he felt particularly bad about. The details might have been bullshit, but the basics, those were whatever the opposite of bullshit was. Grass, maybe. Or a fine, aromatic meal. Probably not a productive line of thought.

He *did* have an interview. Of sorts. In any event, he would soon be handing over $400, borrowed from Kelsey, which he would exchange for two ounces of wholesale weed. He could flip that to his friends and friends' friends for $800. With Mia's part-time, $800 would get them through the month. If he hadn't picked up any extra design work by then, he'd give these guys another call and repeat. Clean. Simple. Low-risk. As loose as LA weed laws were, he doubted he was even committing a felony.

With the city waiting uselessly to the north, Raymond swung south on the Pacific Coast Highway, cruising past the Thai massage parlors, organic grocers, and colon hydrotherapy salons of the South Bay. Lukewarm air flushed the swelter from his open windows. On the cliffside hills above him, smooth white manors contemplated the ocean, protected from the syrup-thick traffic by winding residential roads, gates, and the inborn social understanding that you have no business there. The lesser hill of the PCH dumped him into Torrance.

Strip malls and chain shops bordered the boulevard. When he idled at long red lights, exhaust and the smell of hot asphalt poured through the windows. He swung off the PCH, passing a bowling alley, liquor stores. He'd written himself directions from Google and drove in the far right lane, peering for street signs. Pastel bungalows lined the side streets, two-bedroom joints that still appraised at $500K despite the bubble and recession. Not that anyone was buying. When he'd poked around his options for selling the house his mom had left them in Redondo, every realtor in town advised him that unless he was desperate, he should just rent and wait it out for a year or three until the rebound catapulted the old home back up into low seven figures. But Mia had always considered herself a California girl at heart, and from 1000 miles away outside Seattle, finding new jobs sounded perfectly simple, something normal people do every day. They'd moved down.

Nine months later, Mia was lucky to get 15 hours a week at the clinic. He snagged odd jobs on Craigslist, ebook covers and logo design for website startups, but biddings-wise it was a race to the bottom. In a lucky month, he could cover the utilities and gas for the car. His checking account had died a slow bleed. He didn't even have a credit card. He was reasonably certain they could mortgage the house, but he didn't even rightly know what a mortgage *was* besides something he couldn't pay. What happened with the electric company in three months? What happened when their bank account was as empty as their fridge?

He parked in a weedy lot behind a beige rectangle of apartments. When he'd left Redondo, it had been comfortably warm, just a few degrees above cool, but the Torrance heat was almost painful. The difference between coast and inland, separated by no more than five miles of six-lane avenues and CVS pharmacies, could be a twenty-point jump on the thermostat. Transitioning between the two always made Raymond feel insane, as if he'd left not just his hometown, but his entire reality.

The blacktop shimmered. He closed his door, yanking his hand away from the scalding metal. A couple blocks away, traffic whooshed like surf. A crow cawed, was abruptly silenced by the bleat of a child's whistle.

Two ounces in broad daylight in an empty parking lot. Bobby had set this thing up for him, and he'd been buying from Bobby since bumming him a cigarette outside a bar on the pier three months back, so it's not like he was worried, exactly, but that wasn't exactly how he planned to do business himself. Ideally, he'd deal out of the house, but Mia was back by 1:30 in the afternoon. He'd have to drive to clients, set his phone to silent to disguise his sudden popularity. On the other hand, why not tell his customers that if they weren't at his house by 1 PM, they'd be out of luck? Telling stoners to be up and at 'em by early afternoon was a little like lecturing a dog to chew with its mouth closed, but he'd be the one with the pot. The power. It'd be his way or the dry way.

At the mouth of the lot, a gleaming black sedan turned off the road, bass thudding so hard Raymond could feel it in his chest. The car eased into the spot next to his. Engine idling, the passenger window slid down, washing Raymond's face with icy air. A skinny white guy with a shaved head leaned across the seats.

"You Raymond?"

He patted his pocket for the envelope of bills. "Are you Lane?"

"Get in."

Raymond popped the door and inserted himself in the passenger seat. Cool air rushed over his arms, raising his fine blond hairs. Lane stared at him like a bald basset hound. "Money?"

"Yeah. Two ounces, right?"

Lane nodded. Raymond squirmed the envelope from his pocket and passed over the last of his cash, most of which had been borrowed. Lane lifted the flap with one finger, shook the envelope up and down. "Cool."

"So?"

The man smiled like a kindergarten teacher. "You never done this before, have you?"

"Everybody does it their own way."

"Our way, you pay me the money, I send you to Mauricio. That dapper gentleman up there." Lane pointed to an apartment balcony across the way. Behind the black rails, a fat shirtless man sprawled in a lawn chair, a silver beer can propped on his gut. "Nobody's straight-up trading money for shit. Anything happens, we're all protected."

"Sounds like a good system." He raised his eyebrows. "When I sell this through, can you get me more?"

"There's always more." Lane stuck out his knuckles for a bump. Raymond fumbled for the door handle. Sunshine smothered him; Lane's car backed up and swung for the lot exit, gleaming. Raymond swept sweat from his hairline and scanned for the stairs. Heat roiled from the pavement. Sweat tickled his ribs as he jogged up the balcony to Mauricio.

"What's up?"

The fat man dragged a damp cloth over the folds of his neck.

"Sup?"

Raymond gestured at the empty lot. "Lane sent me up."

Mauricio's shoulders lumped together. "I don't know any Lane."

"The guy in the car. Shaved head. We were just down there."

"I saw him. Don't know him."

"He knows *you*. What is he, your stalker?"

The man wriggled upright in the lawn chair, grabbing his beer before it splashed over the concrete landing. "Look man, I don't go into this stuff. I'm an upstanding citizen. But that guy, I think he ripped you off."

Raymond's face prickled. "You'd be in a pretty good position to know that, wouldn't you?"

Mauricio spread his blunt palms. "I've just been sitting here. If they made that illegal, I need to go on the lam, man."

"What if I call the cops?"

The man's belly shook. "About how you were trying to buy weed? With intent?"

"I'll tell them Lane robbed me." He blinked sweat from his lashes. "Give them his plate."

"I wouldn't do that, bro."

"He's got my money."

"I just wouldn't do that. That would be rude. But mostly it would be a very bad idea."

"That was all I had left."

"Seriously?" Mauricio smiled past his beer. "My first lapdance tonight is going out to you."

The parking lot's heat thudded over Raymond's skin. He drove off on autopilot, lighting a cigarette—he usually only smoked when he drank; the battered pack of Dunhills had been in the glove box for weeks—sweating, face burning, swearing at everyone who switched lanes without a signal, which was fucking half the population of Los Angeles. The AC pumped hot air into his face. He drove past the turn to his house and parked two blocks from the pier where there were no meters to feed.

The coastal breeze was a cool hand. He scuffed over the time-fuzzed boards of the pier, past bars and fast food stands and the seafood places with the live crabs clambering over each other in the windows. At the far end, Asians and Hispanic guys lobbed lures into the waves beyond the breakers and waited for a bite.

Could he do that? At least they'd have food. It's what his great uncle had done during the Depression—once a week, he and his brother and sister and parents would go to the creek and catch their limit, forty trout apiece, two hundred trout in total, and they'd eat trout until the next week rolled around and they did it again. His uncle had died unable to eat fish ever again, but they'd made it through. How would Mia feel about fish?

But he couldn't put fish in his gas tank or in the envelope to the water company. Besides, all the time he'd spent down on the pier, he'd never seen anyone catch a single fish. The Depression was another world. There were too many people to live off the land. That was the lesson from the parking lot. This America, you made money or you died.

Mia had been saving a couple hundred dollars towards a laptop that didn't crash three times an hour. She'd have a paycheck at the end of the week. If they ate beans and rice and left the heat off, he figured they could last about two months. Maybe enough time to find a real job. This economy.

Gulls bobbed on the swells. A pelican drifted ten yards above the water, then dropped like a feathered stone, tucking its wings the moment before it shattered the surface. Kelp and fish guts mixed in the breeze. He'd moved here for Mia—if they'd just sold the house, even at the current market, neither of them would have had to work for a decade. But she'd wanted the sunlight. The palms. The ocean. A place where winters were only a memory. He'd wanted her to be happy—for them to be happy together. It was time to stop hiding, to give up the dream of design freelancing, or at least put it on hold for a while. It was time to come clean to Mia and work it out together. They were supposed to be there for each other. If he kept trying to go it alone, he'd destroy them.

He texted Mia to get ready for dinner. He watched the waves a while longer, drove home, changed, and took her to the Indian place down the street. She waited until the naan arrived, then, over the smell of garlic and coriander, asked him how it had gone.

"I didn't get it."

She reached across the table, lips forming a concerned O. "I'm sorry, cutie. Next time."

Raymond nodded, rallying his nerves. Reminded himself that, no matter what happened next, all he could control was his reaction. He took her hand. "What if there isn't?"

She snorted. "Like what if an earthquake kills us tomorrow? No! I haven't even chosen a cemetery!"

"We're out of money." He stared at their hands on top of the red table. "I *owe* money. I don't know what to do."

2

In the city that prided itself, quite wrongly, on being the center of the universe, Walt Lawson moaned and carefully returned Vanessa's breakup letter to the drawer where she kept her theater tickets.

A letter. How like her: dramatic, elegant, and perfect. Slyly impersonal, too, another symptom of her actress' ability to make everyone and thus no one the full center of her attention. Worst of all, it was permanent. A decade from now, he'd still have to read the same words he'd read minutes ago. If she'd told him face to face, even a phone call, his self-defense systems could have gone to work, distorting his memory, convincing himself, day by day and month by month, that her words had been selfish, crazy, bitchy. Enough time, he might even have been able to make himself believe he'd left *her*. But a letter? That was a preemptive strike. He couldn't interrupt, he could only listen to a decision that couldn't be swayed. And her side was on record. His side, if she'd been able to deploy her handwritten sneak attack before he'd stumbled on it (quite innocently; he'd just wanted to check what she'd seen last night, catch up on the reviews), would be jangled, panicked, shameful. Every time he'd reread that letter, he'd be reminded of his own tongue-tied response, supporting evidence of the very inadequacies her carefully regretful sentences had cunningly accused him of.

Of course, she knew he wouldn't be able to throw it away.

Six stories below the window, cars and cabs raced and weaved, the perfect combination of mass and aggression to smash out his brains and lungs. Or should he go somewhere higher — the Empire

State Building? Shouldn't his last action be a big one? His last seconds strange ones? There should be more to it than simply dying. He didn't want a neighbor recognizing his face. He wanted *obliteration*. The kind a gun couldn't provide (besides, he didn't have one) or he could count on from the currents and fish of the Upper Bay (nor would he trust himself not to kick for shore after the first salty gulp). The plain truth, a truth he'd faced several times a day for the four years they'd been together, was he'd rather not exist than be without her.

Traffic banged over the metal plates welded over the holes in the asphalt. He was six stories up, but the roar was such the cabs and delivery trucks may as well be driving straight through his bathroom. He crossed to the window and shoved it open, smelling exhaust, kebabs, and humidity. Did he feel small because he lived in New York? Or did he feel small because he *was*?

He hated those metal plates. He could sleep through horns, car alarms, drunks shouting from ground-floor bars, but each time a truck crashed over one of those plates, he woke with a heart-yanking jolt. Instead of laying a thunderous iron plate over the potholes, *why didn't they just fix the fucking holes?*

Walt withdrew his head from the window. So Vanessa thought she was leaving. She thought he was a pothole. What if he could create a plate for himself?

Not in the sense of something to be run over. In the sense of a temporary fix with the illusion of permanence. The letter had once more mentioned her gauzy desire to move to LA, implying it might not be so much that she wanted to leave *him* as that she wanted to leave New York. And she hadn't actually given him the letter yet; there existed the possibility she didn't intend to — *straw-grasper!* — or, less unlikely, that she was waiting for a particular time to hand it over. Assume the possibility he could alter the destiny she intended for him. How could he convince, trick, or strongarm her into staying?

He quickly rejected several alternatives. If he left this instant on a days-long trip, she would have no address to deliver his letter to, but that would only cement her perception of him as unreliable. Nor could he take her on a breathless tour of romance, hansom cab rides and dinners in Little Italy, a balloon ride from his parents' place in Long Island. Being such an expert herself, she had a nose for manipulation. He could make a visible display of renewed effort on the novel he'd been working on for months (and, counter to her epistolary claims, he *had* been working, even when it didn't look like work; at times he suspected the cliche of "the rudderless, irresponsible writer" had poisoned her opinion of his ambitions), but that could easily backfire. Much easier to dump a person who has something to keep them occupied through the upcoming period of mental anguish. Hell, great art came from pain, didn't it? To her, leaving might spur him to a literary success that would console his broken heart.

He smiled, cold as a Kubrick flick. He would pretend to be sick. It would take a person of intense cruelty to inflict breakup-level emotional pain on someone already suffering physically. Especially when she could be confident she'd have to wait no more than a few days, at most a couple weeks, before he cleared up. Once healthy, she could deliver her letter guilt-free.

Walt knew it wouldn't be enough to restore her love, but spooning someone chicken broth could hardly be more intimate, could it? He could call off work at the bodega, too. With all those free hours, he could plot out a more permanent plan, something to forestall the letter forever.

Vanessa came home on a breeze of lavender and fresh sweat. He sat up from his couchside nest, blinking, remembering to cough. What time was it? Ten? Midnight? She slung her coat on a hook and pulled the pencil from her swept-up hair, loosing her locks over her shoulders.

"How was your day?" he croaked.

"Don't ask," she laughed, splaying the fingers of one hand. "Don't even ask. By the time I finished someone will be dead."

"Preferably neither of us."

"So okay. Mark hardly knows any of his lines. No, that's being too kind—he doesn't know *any*. He's got fewer lines than a baby's ass. He thinks he'll be ready next week?"

He cleared his throat. "Is that where you were all this time? Mark's?"

She stopped teasing out her straight dark hair to give him a look of dying annoyance. He didn't like that look. It said: *Calm down: he won't be here much longer*. "What, we're going to rehearse in the park? Get stabbed mid-soliliquoy? I know, we could practice on the platforms at Union Square. Treat the commuters to a sneak preview."

"It was a question, not a snake. Don't get so wound up."

"It's not the question. It's the tone."

"Sorry." He cut himself short with a coughing fit. "Got the flu or something. Voice sounds funny."

She frowned. Disbelief? Concern? "You *don't* sound good. Need some water?"

"Tea?" he tested.

This time, her smile was as soft as her skin. She clicked to the kitchen while he watched from the couch. She ran the teapot under the faucet, leaning over the sink, breasts hanging against her shirt. He was already half hard. In ten or twenty years, Vanessa might be as fat as her mom, but at 25, her swollen tits and musical hips drove men's imaginations to feverish degradation. He'd possessed that body for four years now, touched it thousands of times, fucked it hundreds, but he still couldn't go swimming with her without wearing a jockstrap under his suit to bind his erection. She caught him staring and smiled over the stove. So what if she privately hated him? She lived to be looked at.

She handed him a steaming floral-print cup. "Maybe you should see a doctor."

"A doctor?"

"You know, one of those guys who pats you on the head until you feel better?"

"I'm familiar with the word. I didn't know *you* were."

She shrugged, breasts rising. "I don't want you to be sick."

He sipped. He didn't even like tea. "And normally you'd be pestling up some herbs right now. Doing the Dance of Good Humours."

She rolled her eyes. "Please."

"Thanks for the tea." He reached for her thigh, squeezing its springy muscles.

"De nada. I'm going to take a shower. I stink."

She rose, leaving him on the couch. The bathroom door snicked. He frowned over his tea. She didn't believe in doctors for anything short of cancer. Suddenly she was ready to ship him to the waiting room? Was he onto something with his ersatz illness? Would she strike as soon as he improved? And what about the Mark factor? She wouldn't leave him, Walt, unless she had someone else to go to. He knew better than that. That's how he'd gotten her himself, after all, prying her away from a high school boyfriend she'd been looking to leave since getting to NYU, some sad-sack future electrician who'd eventually agreed to an open relationship rather than dumping her like he should have. That had been the dude's death-knell. She'd told her good friend Walt the news on a Friday; Saturday night, he'd talked her into bed.

Ten minutes into her shower, he stripped down and snugged into bed. The shower hissed and splattered, muffled by the door. He closed his eyes and imagined the soap slipping down her skin. He wanted to *be* the soap, clinging to her curves and folds, touching all of her at once—but he already was the suds, wasn't he? Slipping away from a body he could no longer hold onto. Rinsed down a drain into darkness and shit.

Twenty minutes later, she slid in beside him, kissed him once, and turned her back. A truck banged over a metal plate.

In the morning, he let her overhear him scheduling a doctor's appointment for that Friday. He shuffled around the apartment, sipping tea, a sheet wrapped around his shoulders. When she left to read lines with Mark, he walked up to Washington Square Park and bought a falafel. Old men of all races played chess on the boards at the park's corner. Tall, thin black guys cruised through the cool spring sunlight, hawking drugs with their one-word mantras. College kids, mostly white, smoked cigarettes in the dry fountain and watched the skateboarders tricking on the asphalt hills.

After a couple hours, he went back home to ensure he'd get there first. She wasn't back until 11:37 that night.

Thursday, when she left to meet Mark for more work, he followed.

He watched her hips roll from a half block back. He was dressed in a sweater he hadn't worn in years and a knit cap he bought yesterday. The morning was cold and steam drifted from the corner grates with a smell of laundry and sewers. Vanessa only looked back once; he'd ducked into the gap between two parked cars, heart on fire. At the Bleecker Street station, she jogged down the stairs for the 4-5-6 trains. He swiped his card and pushed through the turnstiles in time to see her descending to the uptown 6 local.

He went home. The next day she had a shampoo audition; he

ate soup and a sleeve of saltines, claiming an upset stomach. She bought him ginger ale and vitamin C. He left for the "doctor's" and wandered all the way down to Bowling Green, where he watched the gray waves of the Atlantic.

Whenever he tried to think about how to hang on to her, he found his mind mired in sick, hesitant hate for Mark (what were they doing together all those long hours? He was an actor, too—did he look like one?) and sick, overwhelming love for Vanessa. That love was a boulder, an anchor, a devouring cancer that had eaten a hole through the man he'd used to be (another part of him said: the hole had always been there, he'd just let himself forget that). At first he'd been faking, but now he grew nauseous whenever he thought of her, unable to put down more than cereal and chicken soup. He felt infected, hot, dizzy. The world looked like a puked-up joke, unstoppable, crashing.

She had another meet-up with Mark that Sunday. When she left the apartment, he donned his sweater and cap. When she cut east for Bleecker, he sprinted north, then jogged parallel for Astor Place. The train pulled in as he hit the platform. The doors bonged, closing. What would he tell her if she caught him? The doctor's appointment? A call from an agent uptown?

He didn't have to worry. He pressed his nose to the scratched glass until he was certain she wasn't in the next car, then crossed forward, rocking on the narrow platform between cars. As usual, Vanessa was at the very front of the train. One car back, he slouched down in a seat. She detrained at 86th. Uptown.

The street smelled like bread and rain and Chinese chicken. She stopped in front of a brick walkup less than a block away. On the stoop, a man stood. His grin looked permanently installed in his jaw. His jaw looked like it spent the day breaking rocks. Vanessa grinned back at him, gave a tight, waist-high wave. He leaned in, kissed her—lips? Or the cheek? Typical overfriendly actor-greeting, or the hello of newly-minted lovers? They disappeared inside the building.

Walt found himself cold and half-lost in Central Park. He bought a soft pretzel, chewed down half, tossed the rest in bits to pigeons. Was she already gone? Then what the fuck did it matter what he did? He could propose to her, burn down her apartment, hold her mom at knifepoint. It wouldn't matter. She was gone.

He sat down in the grass. The dew seeped into his jeans. If he had a box with a button that could erase his existence, he would have pushed it.

This same park had been the start. In another sense, the year and a half of NYU classrooms and dorm rooms and Village bars where he'd dogged her had been the start, but *the* start, the start that had launched their first movie together, their first night of moany, eye-buzzing sex together, their first morning-after when he'd descended to a gray and silent Sunday AM in a city so empty it could have been built just for the two of them—all that had sprung from this park.

How had he talked her into coming here? He could no longer remember. He suspected it wasn't the particular words that had finally convinced her to a date with him, but rather his steady, undaunted presence. His persistence. So on that cool Saturday afternoon in spring, spurred, perhaps, by the dying of her last shreds of respect for the future electrician, she'd agreed to hop the train up to the park, where they walked around the paths before lying down in the grass on a quiet hill where she rested her head in his lap and he touched her hair above her ear and felt he'd never need to be anywhere else. They didn't move for an hour. It probably wouldn't sound that special to tell someone about. Everyone, at some point, sits in the grass with the person they love.

But after a year and a half of fruitless and corrosive pursuit, fueled by a desire his roommate Ajit kept calling "obsessive," it had been perfect. How often do you get to realize a dream? To put your hands on the exact thing you've always wanted?

Now that he was losing it, what wouldn't he do to keep it?

As if it had always been there, he had his answer. Stolen right out of *The Royal Tenenbaums*, which she'd seen, too, but tweaked just enough to elude notice. Smiling the unweighted smile of a man who's staked everything on the turn of one last card, he went back to the subway station, rode home to their apartment in the Village, and practiced his worried-face in the mirror. When Vanessa got home, it took her two minutes of how-was-your-day talk until she noticed.

"Everything okay?"

"The doctor called."

"What've you got? The flu?"

"There's a problem." He looked down at the carpet. It was a

nice carpet, so thick your toes could get lost in it. He'd miss it if she kicked him out. "With my heart."

She reached for his shoulder, gaping, horrified. Her fingers never felt so good. "Your *heart*? Are you going to be okay?"

"I don't know. They want me back tomorrow." He covered his eyes with his hand, shoulders shrinking. "I'm scared."

3

Across the desk from Raymond, Lana Englund turned from her monitor, the wrinkles around her eyes highlit by the Santa Monica sunshine spilling through her great glass window. "We have a problem here. Our ad specifically asked for a *degree* in Communications."

"I minored in it."

"And maybe if you'd minored in English you'd know words have meanings."

He cocked his head. "The ad said experience would be the key factor."

"So it is. Your resume mentioned web work. Can you elaborate?"

"I've designed graphics for a half dozen different sites. I've been designing and writing my own blogs since before there was a word for them. I had a popular one that covered art supplies—pens, brush brands. I think that will carry over here."

She frowned, round cheeks puffing. "Traffic?"

"For my site?"

"No, for the 405. I was thinking of running out for some tapas."

"Before I moved on, I was drawing about 1500 unique visitors a month." Raymond's mouth twitched as Lana literally rolled her eyes. He'd been trying to keep things pro. "Is something the matter?"

"Something? No. Some *things*? Take your pick." She ticked off her points on her fingers, bending them back until the knuckles cracked. "You don't have a BA in the field. No direct experience writing copy. The best you can muster is a website that wasn't even a blip on the screen and has been dead for years. What I'm not understanding is who cleared you for an interview in the first place."

"I know my resume isn't a knockout. That's because I'm the only guy in LA County who doesn't lie on it. That's what I'm offering: honesty. I can do this job."

"I don't need a guy who'll tell me when my ass is looking big. I need a guy who can write me crisp, compelling copy. You're not that guy."

Raymond stood. "Fuck you."

"Excuse me?" She drew back in her chair, chin disappearing inside her high collar.

"You're talking to me like you never expect to see me again. So fuck off."

"Security's going to squash you like a toad." She reached for the phone and they probably would have, but he'd already left, walking down the sidewalk in a wrap of sunshine, smelling salt from the shore and grilled carne asada from the truck down the block. He hadn't told her to fuck off out of anger, but more out of the conviction that if you don't make a habit of standing up for yourself in the small moments, you'll never be able to do it when the big ones rolled around. Well, that and some anger. Anyway, it would make a better story for Mia.

Mia, when he'd told her they were out of money, that unless something changed, within two months they'd be living out of his car or, with luck, a spare room at one of his siblings', had been exactly the woman he'd married: concerned but forgiving, miles from petty, focused on nothing but making it together. She'd reached across the table and taken his hand and said they'd be okay.

He'd fully resolved to put his graphics career, if he could use the word without stringing quotes around it, on hiatus. A man on a mission, he'd replied to every feasible want ad on Craigslist. Most hadn't replied. A handful scheduled interviews. Lana Englund had been his first.

Mia smiled when he relayed his day. "Nowhere to go but up."

"Or postal."

"It's one interview."

"Maybe I should stop wasting time on the ambitious positions. I can worry about liking my job after I've stopped worrying about starving to death."

"You know what?" She grabbed his waist, shaking him like the beautiful thing you're compelled to destroy. "We should do something fun."

"You look like you already are," he said, voice rattling as she shook him.

"We should go live on the beach this weekend. I mean with tents and vodka-canteens and public urination."

"All of that is illegal."

"Who cares?" She released him, tugged open the crumbling curtain that overlooked their wild backyard, the lemon trees and wildflowers and the fifty-foot magnolia tree with its red, corn-cobby buds. "If we have to leave soon, why not have some fun? Enjoy the damn place? This is Southern California. Let's love it while we can."

He had to smile. "Of all the things you have to choose from, you want to go camping three blocks from your house?"

She put up her dukes, hopped forward, and tapped him in the gut with a fist. "It's free, isn't it?"

He couldn't argue with that. In between emailing his resume around and clipping coupons, he went down to the basement, a half-finished space cluttered to the point of unnavigability by books, tools, jars of screws, camera lenses and developing fluid, and half-painted, rough-sawn wood scraps from his dad's old projects. Decades ago, before his birth when they too had been too poor to do much else, his parents had been campers. Between two sawhorses and beneath a layer of dust thick enough to write your name in, Raymond dug up a tent, metal stakes, some tarps, canteens, and a tackle box that still smelled like bait, plasticky and fishy.

Saturday morning, they drove to the beach. He left most of the gear in the trunk until dark. They made up some rules: no leaving the beach unless a) the bathrooms were closed or b) to stow the tent in the mornings. When smoking weed, make sure no one could see the fire. Bag up all their trash. And absolutely no talk of money.

The sun bounced off the water and the sand; within an hour, Raymond had to break the first rule to go buy stronger sunscreen. It was late March and he knew the water in the bay had carried down the coast from Alaska, but he waded to his knees, coaxing

Mia out into the curling surf until the soles of their feet went numb. They combed for shells, smelling salt and kelp and warm sand. On the rocks at the south end of the bay, where the mansions of Palos Verdes clung to the cliffs on eighty-foot stilts, small black flies swarmed in thousands over brown mats of drying kelp. He overturned stones, searching for crabs.

"I've been down here two dozen times and I've never seen a single fish," he said. "How hard can it be to find a fish in an *ocean*?"

"Maybe they just don't like you," she smiled. They'd been swigging warm vodka from a metal flask.

"Then they must know something you don't."

"Or vice versa. I've seen you naked."

"Maybe we should educate them."

After midnight, drunk and grinning, they carried two towels down to the tideline, laid one beneath them and one over them, and made love amidst the sand, the moon, the waves. Once they finished and Raymond had caught his breath, he popped up, naked, and faced the sea.

"Get a good look, fish. One night only." He plopped down on the towels, pawing in the moonlight for his underwear. "Why can't I shake the feeling this is a trial run for how we'll be living a few weeks from now?"

She waggled a finger in his face. "No money-talk, remember?"

"Who said anything about money? I'm talking about bindles and cans of beans."

"We'll have to memorize the train schedules."

"I think a barrel with two straps would look very flattering on you."

"We can't go homeless when we have a home, can we? Maybe we can get a thing. A lien."

"No money talk!" She sprung from the sand in a flash of light brown, her skin speckled with the darker spots of her nipples, belly button, and the gap between her legs. She tackled him on his back and smushed a towel into his face. "Gonna follow the rules? Or do I have to smother you?"

They woke sticky-mouthed and sunburnt, hungry and hungover. Between a couple covert puffs, packing the tent in the trunk, and a walk through the not-quite-cold morning, the fog lifted from their heads, the poison washed from their flesh. Just past the breakers, dolphins paralleled the shore, sleek gray fins shedding seawater.

When they drove the half mile home on Sunday afternoon, Raymond felt no less charged and refreshed than if they were on their way back from a trip across the Pacific. An interview request waited in his inbox. Wednesday morning, a video store just a few blocks up the street. Part-time clerk position. He didn't care. Low stress and more time to build his freelance career.

"Good luck," Mia kissed him. "You'll do great."

He walked, meaning to save gas and pick up some exercise. Besides, the weather, as usual, was glorious, a clear-blue day with the typical breeze tousling the towering palms. He, like everyone, had heard about Los Angeles weather before moving here, but after living through a fall, winter, and the early part of spring without feeling any temperature below 42 degrees, he still had a hard time believing that on any given day he could walk outside in a t-shirt—that in the middle of November, it had been too hot to do anything but jump in the ocean. Cars grunted down the PCH. A young Hispanic woman with a smooth belly trotted after a gasping dachshund. By the time he reached the video store, a light sweat filmed his back.

He nailed his interview. He was roughly the same age as the long-haired guy who questioned him and was able to make him laugh repeatedly, finding common ground over the greatness of *Dead Alive* and *Repo Man*. When they discussed Raymond's post-college two years with a UPS store, the guy had flat-out said it sounded harder than his own job. He promised to let Raymond know by the end of the week.

Raymond walked out feeling good. Like he had a chance. He knew he shouldn't count on it until he walked in for his first day, and that it was almost certainly a tedious job, one he'd be sick of six months in and ready to quit two years later, but it meant he'd be okay. He'd eat. He and Mia would sleep and wake in their own house. Miles from rich, but in exchange for five hours of his day, five days a week, he could continue a reasonable approximation of an American existence. Strange how fast everything changed. A couple weeks ago, he'd been concerned about their very ability to go on eating from non-Dumpster sources, and sending out dozens of resumes and getting back virtually nothing in response had done nothing to dam his rising tide of fears. Yet an hour at a video store had reduced those worries to a placid ebb.

Up the block, a beefy bald man in a blue suit spilled out of a Thai restaurant, clamped his hands to his knees, and vomited into a strip of grass.

Raymond jogged forward. "Hey, you okay?"

The man heaved again, yellow noodles mingled with bright red fluid—curry sauce? Raymond held up a few feet away, reached for his cell. The man straightened, pale as a page, swaying like a palm in a coastal storm. Red tears dribbled from his eyes.

"Sir?"

The man waved one thick hand, groping for something that wasn't there. Viscous reddish drool gleamed from his chin. He panted in shallow hitches, head bobbing with each breath, as if he were slamming it to a punk show beneath the stage of the Whisky A Go-Go and not puking, mid-afternoon, on the sidewalk of Redondo Beach.

"Run," the man said. Blood trickled from his eyes. Without warning, he fell straight backwards, stiffly awkward, head cracking the sidewalk like a bottle wrapped in a blanket.

Raymond took a step backward. A siren shrieked up the PCH. Under the warm California sun, the stranger's blood sunk into the sidewalk's spidery cracks.

4

Walt was glad to see Vanessa sick. *Real*-sick, not fake-sick, be it his forced coughs or some nebulous notion of a weak valve that could collapse on him at any time. Which, incidentally, had cut both ways. On the one hand, she cared again. She didn't stay out so late. She replied to his texts within minutes instead of hours/never. Brought soft tacos from the Ecuadorian place down the block. Held his hand while they watched movies on the couch. Even fucked him, after a two-week drought, gently and apologetically and with an earnestness that let him believe they were back on track.

But she couldn't keep her mouth shut, telling his parents about his "condition" even after he'd asked her not to. They had, in usual fashion, scheduled an appointment for him with one of their own specialists on Long Island.

So when *Vanessa* got sick — well, there was a sweetness to that. A little payback. It kept her in the apartment, too. She depended on *him*. She just felt too weak, she said, and seeing the way she coughed, one hand clenched to her mouth while the other waved as spastically as if she'd swallowed a moth, well, he could believe it. She wasn't the type to take sick days. After the report of the death in Idaho, that limb-curdling cough worried him, undercutting his pleasure, but then he'd bring her a mug of green tea and she'd smile at him, a smile he hadn't seen in months, that summed up her simple beauty like the green flash of the last second of a tropical sunset, and he'd remind himself people died of the flu every year, especially old people who lived in Idaho, and that she'd be fine in a few days.

But as improved as things seemed, when she went to the bathroom and he checked the drawer where she kept her ticket stubs, the letter was still there.

Three days later, she couldn't sleep from coughing. He paced to the window, considered the traffic. "I'm calling a doctor."

"No doctors," she said, ensconced in the comforter, voice ragged with phlegm.

"You were fine with them when *I* got sick."

"And you came back thinking you could die at any moment."

"You'd rather I dropped dead without warning?"

"I'd rather you lived to forever and had a spout that dispensed tea."

"That would require a lot more doctors." He sat down on the bed. The heat of her body felt strong enough to cook breakfast. He reached for her hand. "We're going to make a deal. If you're not better in two days, I'm making you an appointment."

She frowned, wrinkling the corners of her glassy brown-green eyes. "That sounds more like an ultimatum than a deal."

"So your fever still hasn't zapped your thinking. I'll have to wait until you're delirious to ask you to change your will."

She rolled her eyes but laughed, thick barks that morphed into a wet and gloomy cough. Two days later, she was no better; sometimes she had to lean on him on her way to the bathroom.

His doctor was booked for the next two weeks.

"That won't work," he told the receptionist over his cell. "In two weeks she'll be better."

"Then what do you need a doctor for?"

"In case she isn't."

"Then we'll see what we can do for her at that time."

"Say it's something serious. Do you know how many times a person can die in two weeks?"

The man sighed. "What's she got? The flu? Just like everyone else? Plenty of water, some orange juice, a decongestant or three, hey. All better."

On the off chance the receptionist was currently operating a telescope, Walt scowled uptown. "Is that your professional opinion?"

"As a state-licensed, Hippocrates-sworn nobody? Absolutely."

"Look, what if she were growing a third hand? Or had blood squirting out of her belly button? There must be a protocol for vaulting the queue."

"Go get her some NyQuil," the man spat. "If she's improved before you're scheduled to come in, please cancel the appointment in advance, will you?"

"Anything to help." Walt hung up. The corner bodega was out of anything resembling NyQuil, Advil, Cold-Eeze, or Flintstones chewable vitamin tablets. Up at Yukio's, where he wasn't due in for another four hours, he fared no better.

"Walt?" Behind the counter, Yukio pushed his white cap to the back of his head. "You're early, man. Like, by most of a day."

"My girlfriend's sick, but apparently we're no longer concerned with profiting off the illnesses of others."

Yukio grinned, ducked under the counter, and flipped a green NyQuil bottle at Walt, who promptly fumbled it, allowing him, as it skittered across the shoeprinted tile floor, to discover the bottle was plastic.

"Been saving it," his boss said. "We sold out days ago. Make it last—we're supposed to get more next week, but the way this city's coughing right now, I'm doubting it."

Walt tapped the bottle in his palm. "Thanks. See you tonight."

He brought the bottle home to Vanessa, then went back out to hit up every bodega, grocery, and Duane Reade he could find. He wasn't a scaremonger—after 9/11, every grocer south of 14th Street had run out of bread, milk, and everything else with an expiration date by the day after, which only made him roll his eyes and swear about having to walk up to Midtown for a fucking bagel—but unlike most of these surgeon-mask-wearing dipshits stocking up on cold medicine and face masks, Vanessa actually *needed* it, and given his proximity to her, he probably would soon, too. In the grocery stores, the white ladies wore transparent plastic gloves. An empty circle appeared around anyone who coughed. He tried three more pharmacies before he found a Walgreens with a single bottle of aspirin. The selfishness of it floored him. Unless the entire goddamn city was sick, no way that should be happening.

But the whole city *wasn't* sick. A lot of coughing, yeah, a handful of pale faces and people resting against street signs while they waited to jaywalk, but for the most part, you still had your same old hustling crush of pedestrians. Middle Eastern guys still sold fruit from sidewalk stands, and behind them, the Gristedes and Cafe Metros and Chinese joints still saw a constant flush of customers. That meant people were hoarding. Preemptively stealing resources out of the fear there might not be any left if they ended up needing them later on, thus *guaranteeing* people went without them now. It made him feel like knifing somebody. Several somebodies. After buying up all the Band-Aids in town.

The squeak and clunk of his shoes on the hardwood woke Vanessa. She squirmed upright, rubbing yellow gunk from her eyes, tucking her greasy hair behind her ears.

"Brought you some aspirin." He rattled the bottle. "Had to go to like eight different places. Half the city's sick and the other half's a bunch of assholes."

She smiled, a beacon beneath her patina of illness. "You're so sweet to me."

And he was. Whatever his faults (and Walt presumed he had a few), whenever someone close to him needed something, he gave without complaint or hesitation. At times it was practically a compulsion, so reflexive Walt didn't always consider it a virtue. Nor did he resent sacrificing his time or money or self-interest. If someone needed, they deserved; if he could give it, it was theirs.

Vanessa, though, sometimes she forgot it was a sacrifice. She felt entitled. Partially, he blamed it on the acting: when you come to expect eyeballs on your every word and gesture, pretty soon you start to expect the hands and brains behind them to start giving as well. Whatever the case, it had been weeks? months? since she'd expressed more than bare thanks when he did the dishes, took her clothes to the laundromat, or made vindaloo, her favorite, spiced so ruthlessly it made their noses run.

Hearing her now, he almost had to turn away. "It's nothing. People who love each other go to eight million stores for a stupid bottle of aspirin."

"I'm not sure. A hell of a lot of people treat each other like servants who can't even remember which side of the toast the butter goes on." She sat up further, pressing her fingers to her sweat-damp chest. "I hate getting sick, but a part of me loves it. It's the only chance I get to slow down. It's easy to miss what's in front of you when you're always flying past at 90 miles an hour."

He smiled. Vanessa and her aphorisms. "Just remember this when I catch whatever you've got."

"No such luck. I'll dump you down in the boiler room and

lower in some water twice a day."

"Twice a day? Ritzy."

He went in for his shift at the bodega, where people bought bread and disposable gloves and herbal supplements that hadn't moved in months. Three days later, with Vanessa more or less the same, he left work at two minutes after midnight and walked down a Broadway that was deserted even by the sparse standards of the hour. As with the hoarding, he hadn't seen Broadway this empty since 9/11, when he'd been able to stand smack in the middle of the street at ten in the morning to take pictures of the buses lining both sides of the street like a hollow aluminum fence. He didn't see another pedestrian until he crossed 8th Street and entered NYU territory, where freshmen smoked on dorm steps and argued books from the benches in Washington Square. The tower-channeled wind smelled as cold as it felt. He stopped for takeout at the Indian place on MacDougal, bombarded by cumin and cardamom. Where decongestants failed, a vindaloo might be the only thing to knock down the wall of phlegm inside her sinuses.

He buttoned his coat collar before returning to the street. From a stoop, a white guy with a shaved head jerked his chin at Walt. "Hey."

After nearly a decade in the city, Walt could have ignored a man dressed in nothing but a trumpet codpiece. He went on by.

Feet scuffed the sidewalk behind him. "Hey, you got a quarter?"

Walt did pass out change to out-and-out bums, no matter how obviously insane or drunk; if anyone deserved a plastic bottle of booze, he figured it was the homeless. Besides, he considered it a karmic investment on the not-insignificant chance he someday ended up streetside himself. But when a guy like this asked for change, a guy in clean jeans and a black bubble jacket without any stains or tape-mended tears, that hit Walt's obnoxious-button. It felt unsavory. Shameless. It wasn't about deserving, it was about demanding.

"Hey, I'm asking you a question. It's an easy one. All you gotta do is stick your hand in your pocket."

Walt glanced back, giving the guy the chance to catch up and circle around in front of him. Walt shifted his takeout to one hand, dug into his pocket, and tried to keep his inner scowl from touching his face. "Yeah, I think I got something."

"That's great. I was gonna go to Gray's, you know, some fruit juice to wash down my dogs, but then I remembered their special went up."

"Yeah." Walt retrieved four of the ten-odd coins in his pocket and jangled them in his open palm, making sure there was at least one non-penny in the bunch. "Hope this helps."

From under his bubble jacket, the man removed a short and shiny blade. Almost sadly, he smiled under the never-dark of the streetlights. "You know what's next."

"What? Come on, man."

The man gestured with his knife. "Exactly. Come on and hand over your shit and we can both go home."

Slowly, Walt reached for his wallet. "There's like five bucks in there. Can't you go rob somebody on 86th Street instead?"

"Know what, I wasn't lying about the hot dogs. I'm fucking starving. Give me the bag, too."

Walt reached up to rub his eyes. The guy feinted at him with the blade, freezing him. He raised his palms. "It's for my girlfriend. She's sick."

"So's my grandmother. Buy her some chicken noodle, not this spicy shit." The shaved-headed man pocketed the wallet, snatched the bag, and raised his eyebrows. "We cool?"

"Totally. Want to go play some pool when you finish eating?"

"Don't be a dick," he frowned. The knife flashed, pointing the way. "Get on home now. Your girlfriend needs you."

Walt turned, stone-faced, and crossed the empty street. His cards, his cash, even his *food*...but what, you're going to get stabbed over five bucks and a curry? It was insane, when you thought about it, how easily the things you owned could be taken away, be it via knife or foreclosure. Incontrovertible proof the whole thing was a sham, wasn't it?

It wasn't so much the physical loss that bothered him. Literally just a few bucks. He could cancel his debit card, order a new one and a new license with a few minutes of phone calls. Could probably call the bank that night, in fact. The wallet itself was some black fake leather knockoff. Finding another in Chinatown would be easier than finding wet in the shower. Aside from that, he'd lost little more than a bunch of useless receipts, unnecessary rewards cards, and expired phone cards he should have thrown away years ago as soon as he got a cell. The only thing he truly regretted losing was a worn-edged photo of a bikinied Vanessa grinning on the shore of Brighton Beach, but knowing her, she'd have plenty more self-photos stashed somewhere.

Two things troubled him. The powerlessness, of course, an itching raw thing that had him imagining himself going back in time, taking the man's knife away, and slipping it so far inside the man's guts Walt could feel the warmth of kidneys on his hand. Still, after years with Vanessa, he was used to feeling that—the powerlessness, that is, not the kidneys.

The worst thing of all was very simple: the disruption of the illusion of safety. That if you were a good person who worked hard and stayed within the law, you'd always be okay. Every time he was reexposed to the truth, the whole city looked different. Hungry. Predatory. And utterly, terrifying indifferent.

He thought about turning back for another curry for Vanessa until he remembered he had no way to get more money. At least, not without resorting to violence himself. He thought they still had some soup in the cupboard. He wouldn't tell her about the curry; no need to worry her, to disappoint her with what could have been. To make himself look weak.

It was nearly 1 AM by the time Walt got home. On the good chance she was sleeping, he slipped the bolts home as softly as he could, easing over the hardwood floor toward the bedroom. By the time he hit the doorway, he could no longer deny the stink: wet and sour, metallic and hot, so thick he could have stirred it with a spoon.

"Vanessa?"

She lay in bed, a silent lump under the shapeless down comforter. One foot dangled off the bed's edge. Her dark hair splayed across the pillow. Walt called her name again. Beyond the windows, traffic clamored against the ceaseless rush.

5

"There's someone outside."

"Probably a possum." Raymond didn't open his eyes. Beside him, Mia sat up, pulling the covers away from his bare chest.

"That scraping is shoes. What kind of possums wear shoes?"

"Possum marathon runners."

"What?" She grabbed his shoulder and shook. "Go look before we got shot!"

"If I'm going to be shot, I'd rather do it in my sleep." Directly below their bedroom window, the backyard gate clicked. Raymond sat up so fast the sheet billowed around his waist. "Oh shit."

"I guess that's just a six-foot-tall possum? With hands?"

"Lock the door behind me. Call the police. I'm going to get the gun." He swung out of bed, naked except his boxer-briefs, and scrabbled through the closet for his keys. He crept into the dark hall. Mia locked the door with a metal snick. The buttons of her phone beeped softly.

Past the kitchen, he heard the low creak of the deck steps leading to the back door. The loose step near the top scraped against the stucco. Splinters snapped. Something heavy thudded to the wood. A man swore.

Raymond ran into the spare room, panic tickling his skin like hot ants. Years before his dad had left the house and their lives, the old man had kept a couple pistols stashed around the house, ostensibly to protect them from all the burglars who would rather rob a 1940s bungalow than the 4000-square-foot imitation Tuscan villa neighbors. After the death of his mom, he and Mia had moved down to a house of clutter and relics. Cleaning it out took weeks. In the drawer below the oven, hidden beneath a stack of greasy casserole dishes, Raymond had found an old six-shot Smith and Wesson revolver. His dad had brought him shooting enough times as a kid for him to know he didn't want to leave it where anyone, self included, could get to it without a hassle, and locked it in the closet of a room they always left closed.

Wise, except for the part where it was about to get him killed.

At the back door, metal skittered on metal. Raymond tried three keys before the closet's lock turned. The revolver rested in a leather holster, a stag carved on each side of the yellowed faux-ivory grip. The piece felt unnaturally heavy, old and fearsome. He thumbed open the cylinder catch. In the gloom, all six chambers were dark. Loaded. He snapped it shut and clicked back the hammer, drawing the trigger back with it.

It felt good. Solid. More real than it looked. More real than the dark house around him.

From the living room, the fish tank's filter splashed through the darkness. Raymond crouched behind the kitchen doorway, right arm leveled at the door, left hand gripping his forearm. The lock clunked, sprung. The rubber lining the door's lower edge huffed over the tight carpet his parents had inexplicably glued to the kitchen floor decades earlier. A man's silhouette filled the back door.

"Don't move," Raymond said, regretting his decision to cock the revolver early; it would have made the perfect exclamation point to his command. "I have a gun. The police are on their way."

"Bullshit," the man said. He dropped his lock pick and reached for his belt. Raymond's heart thumped. He jerked the revolver up and squeezed the trigger. His hand flew back. The boom clapped from the kitchen's tight walls. The shot chunked through the ceiling, showering the carpet with paint and plaster.

"Five left," Raymond said.

Wordlessly, the man leapt back out the way he'd come in, screen door snapping shut. Stairs rattled and thumped. Raymond shouldered the door closed. He set the lock, the bolt, and the three small hinge plates spaced between the top, middle, and bottom of the door that he'd been too lazy to bother to close since two months after moving down. The bedroom door cracked open.

"Ray? Are you all right?"

He flicked on the light, standing in the carpeted kitchen in his underwear and a grin, the heavy old S&W pointed at the ceiling. "There was a burglar!"

"Did someone get shot?"

"Just the house. Don't worry. It had it coming."

"Jesus. Jesus!" She barred her arms over her t-shirted chest. "We could have been killed. What's going *on* out there?"

"Some guy is running off to tell his friends I'm the dirtiest dude in town."

"A town with very strict gun laws."

"Right. Right." He closeted the gun, washed his hands, dressed. By the time he finished, his head was halfway back to normal. "So where the hell are the cops?"

Mia shrugged, shoulders rising under her thin white tee. "Twenty minutes, they said."

"Do they think burglars are running around with muzzle-loading muskets? *Twenty minutes?*"

"That's what they said."

Raymond's adrenaline-charged exultation slowly soured to a wearying, worrying fear. The police showed up over an hour later, an older white guy with a buzz cut and a uniform-straining gut and a tall Hispanic man about Raymond's age.

"Hi," Raymond said. "What took so long?"

The older cop made a line of his mouth. "Kid, half the town's booked it for their ranches in Montana. You're our third B&E of the night."

He had Raymond give him the rundown, then sent his partner out to the deck while he continued rehashing the details. The man's pale blue eyes settled on the fresh hole in the ceiling.

"Who fired the shot?"

Raymond nodded. "The burglar. Would-be burglar."

"He breaks in, takes a shot, and then leaves empty-handed?"

"I was yelling at him. From behind the bedroom door. I told him you guys were on the way. I don't think he expected anyone home." He gestured to the living room with the bulky old TV, the Super Nintendo, the rickety wooden chairs surrounding a scratched dining table layered with paperwork. In one corner, half-empty boxes stood stacked to shoulder height. "Anyway, you see anything worth stealing?"

The cop closed one eye, squinting at him with the other. "Lot of old stuff here. If that included an old firearm, maybe one so old everyone forgot to register it, well, the new residents might want to do something about that."

"So I'd imagine," Mia smiled. "Can I make you some coffee?"

The cop rubbed the bristle on the back of his neck. "Only if you want me to propose."

They didn't stay long, leaving Raymond with a desk number and another hardly-concealed warning about the criminal penalties for unregistered pistols. He left the porch light on as they drove away.

"Think that was a good idea? Lying to them about the gun?"

Mia frowned over her coffee. "Is it registered?"

"My mom left it under a casserole dish for fifteen years. So yeah, the registration's probably under a cookie sheet somewhere."

"They could have arrested you. Or confiscated it. Then what do we do when the next guy's breaking in and they're an hour away? Retreat to the Bat Cave?"

"Well," he said. "You know where it is. You know where the key is."

"I'm just glad you're safe."

He fell back asleep sooner than he expected, which was nice, because his cell woke him earlier than expected. "Hello?"

"Raymond? This is John. From Choi's Video."

"Hey. Hi." He sat up, rubbing sleep, heart racketing at the long-haired clerk's voice. "What's going on?"

"Just dying a little inside every time somebody rents *Transformers 2*. You?"

"The normal. Waving revolvers at criminals."

"Sure, sure." John cleared his throat. "So, look. Your interview went great. You're obviously overqualified, but that never stopped anyone else from working in a video store."

Raymond squeezed the back of his head. "But?"

"But Mr. Choi won't hire anyone without meeting them himself, and right now Mr. Choi's sick. So, I don't know. You won't starve if I can't get you in to see him until next week, will you?"

"Sure. Two weeks, though, I hope you can speak skeleton."

Raymond closed his phone and set it on the end table and picked up a glass of water. Call it two weeks until he started. Two weeks after *that* to see his first paycheck. Cutting it close (they were already eating the heels of bread, preparing dinners like spaghetti with pepper and oil, and rooting around the basement for old metal, bottles, and print they could drag down to the recycler's), but four weeks, that could work. He wandered to the living room, meaning to put on a Bourne movie or something, but Mia was tucked into the recliner, feet tucked beneath her, scrolling through the Netflix titles.

"No work today?"

"Huh uh. Between everyone getting the flu and everyone else leaving town, we've had about 75% cancellations. They're running a skeleton crew until things pick back up."

"Um," he said. "I think I'm going to go look for more jobs."

"Heard anything back from the video store?"

"Yeah, but I don't think we can count on anything right now." He showered, clothed himself, gelled his hair, laced his shoes, and still felt underdressed. He wandered into the bedroom, snagged the extra set of keys. When Mia went to the bathroom, he went to the closet, snapped open the revolver, replaced the spent casing with a heavy, blunt-headed shell, and ran it out to the glove box of his car so she wouldn't feel it in his waistband when she hugged him.

Just having it close made him feel better. It was getting strange out there. Like the old rules had begun to bend.

Traffic on the PCH was light enough for the surgeon-mask-wearing pedestrians and dogwalkers to jaywalk at will. Raymond cruised north, flashing past darkened shops with handmade signs printed on neon paper hung beside their "CLOSED" signs. Northward and inland, smoke hung over the sprawl, drifting eastward on the ocean winds. Faraway sirens burbled through his open windows. He hadn't had much luck jobhunting in the upscale, mostly residential Beach Cities, so he swung inland, where the $1.5 million imitation Spanish plantation-houses quickly faded into condos, apartments, and bungalows no bigger than his own, replaced, in turn, by warehouses and office buildings. Spotting a fish and aquarium store that didn't look too bad to clerk, he pulled into the same kind of dingy but shoppable strip mall he'd seen in every corner of the country.

From the Ralph's on the other side of the lot, a white guy rushed from the entrance, pushing his shopping cart in front of him like a game show contestant. Blue bottles gleamed and clanked from his cart. A navy-jacketed security guard raced behind him.

Raymond popped his glove compartment, stuffed the revolver under his belt, and stepped into the sunshine.

At the automatic doors, a second shopper sprinted into the parking lot. Raymond jogged forward. The guy with the liquor bottles stopped beside a pickup with rusty wheel wells, yanked down the tailgate, and got tackled to the ground by the security guard. Raymond crossed into the sweetly air conditioned store.

Cashiers continued to ring up shoppers while the shoppers watched in shock as other patrons ran down aisles flinging food into their carts. A bottle of spaghetti sauce smashed across the tile. Loose cereal crunched under shoes and rickety wheels. At the cigarette counter, a bulky manager yelled into a phone. A middle-aged woman in platforms pushed past Raymond, cart loaded with Saran Wrapped steaks.

He'd already reached his decision. The city cops were overstrained, incapable of showing up to a fucking *armed break-in* in time to do anything more than harass Raymond about an 80-year-old revolver. Around him, people screamed while others shoveled armloads of food into their carts. The scene was already far too chaotic for one security guard and one well-muscled manager to do a damn thing about. Load up, get out, drive home. In five minutes he could secure two weeks of food for himself and Mia. That would be all the cushion they'd need. Anyway, it was just one chain store. They'd be insured. And what if this was just the start of a trend? What if, by the time they could afford groceries, there weren't any left?

He grabbed a cart and jogged toward produce, loading up potatoes, bananas, bell peppers. As screams kicked up from the front of the store, he rushed down the cereal aisle, sweeping cardboard cartons into his cart, then swerved for the breakfast meats, where he pitched packages of bacon three at a time. Others clogged the aisles, ignoring each other as they snatched up frozen pizzas, 12-packs of Coke, plastic rings of peeled shrimp. Trampled bags of chips spewed greasy crumbs across the floor. In dairy, a bald man tore a half gallon of creamer from another man's hands. The victim cocked back his fist and punched the bald man into a display of taco shells.

Raymond skidded through a slick of strawberry soda, grabbing at pasta and bottles of alfredo, then swung around to the opposite aisle to top his cart with bagels and bread. It was a good thing, he reflected on his way to the doors, the chains stuck to such ironclad, marketing-bolstered floor plans; with a layout nearly identical to the Ralph's down the street from him in Redondo, he'd wasted almost no time tracking stuff down.

He flew for the doors with tight-chested glee. A faint guilt, too, but he'd hardly been the only one plunging into the chaos. And you know what? He highly doubted anyone in that store was a month away from potentially starving. They weren't taking because they *needed* it. They were taking because everyone else was and they feared there might not be anything left tomorrow. They were taking because they were scared a few old people had died barfing blood. They were taking because talking heads on NBC predicted billions of dollars could be lost to sick days, potentially cratering the recession into outright depression, while talking heads on FOX claimed the flu pandemic was directly attributable to government involvement in the American medical system.

Right then, Raymond didn't really give a shit. He just wanted to get his stuff home, stick it in the freezer, and sleep a little easier knowing that if Mr. Choi took three weeks to get back to business instead of two, he and Mia would still have something to eat.

Sirens roared. Sunlight struck his face, even brighter than the store fluorescents. Sweat glued his shirt to his back. Shoppers scattered across the parking lot, bound for their cars or homes. At the turn-in to the lot, a police cruiser skidded in hard; two officers sprinted for the looters, reaching for their batons.

Raymond broke left for his white Altima. Soles slapping the asphalt, he weaved around a broken case of beer, glass shards bright amid the hoppy-smelling foam. He pulled up to his car, shopping cart clunking into his bumper. He popped the trunk and started dishing food inside.

At the exit fifty feet from his Altima, two more cruisers screamed into the lot, one weaving toward the Ralph's while the other swung in to block the exit. An officer unloaded from the passenger side, unholstered his sleek black pistol, and sunk in behind the car door. He pointed his gun at Raymond.

"Hands up!" he screamed.

Raymond reached for his gun.

6

Walt walked to the bed, pulled the comforter away from Vanessa, and shuddered, groaning. Half-dried blood weighed down the sheets, clinging to her cheeks and pooling around her neck, a stinking, chunky flow of red and phlegm and chunks like ground beef. He reached for her mucky chin. It was slick and room-temperature. Her mouth sagged open without resistance. Her bruised tongue oozed, sluglike, past her lips. Her glassy eyes stared through a question they couldn't form.

He called 911, sat on the floor, and cried. They'd take her away this night, wouldn't they? Would his last sight of her be at her funeral? Would her parents even invite him? He struggled to his feet, lurched to the bed. Paled by sickness, crusted with blood and spittle, her beauty hadn't been completely masked and erased— the lines of her cheekbones were graceful as ever, her lips soft and wide, her nose small and straight and freckled. He would never see or touch or hold her again. Numbly, he reached forward, palmed her heavy left breast, and squeezed.

He raced for the bathroom and heaved until the paramedics buzzed up.

They asked him quiet questions and he gave them clipped answers, replying even when they asked if he'd tried to get her in to see a doctor.

"Just like that," he said. "She was fine. I left. She died."

The paramedic pressed his fist to his forehead. "She's not the first. Girlfriend?"

"We'd turned things around. We had a future."

"Hey, kid, you still got one. Hang on."

Walt didn't see much point to that. He didn't see much point to anything. The paramedics left with her body. He got drunk and called her parents. He couldn't remember falling asleep.

Time became strange. He spent his days glued to his computer, combing the news for NYC death toll updates: dozens, then hundreds, soon thousands. The trajectory was mirrored around the nation, the world. Governments advised people to stay indoors, wash their hands, and handle their own food. Wash their hands! Three-quarters of the country was sick and they were telling people *Remember: soap exists*. Face in his hands, Walt laughed. He was glad they were dying. They deserved it. This was what everyone deserved.

Walt threw out the comforter. The sheets. Hauled the mattress to the curb and slept on the couch. He got a temporary debit card so he could drink Jim Beam straight from the bottle like the worst of cliches. He didn't care.

His parents called to ask him to come back to Long Island. He said no. Unless they floated off in one of their balloons, there was nowhere they could go where people weren't barfing up blood.

He'd never been religious. Not past 7, anyway, when he'd asked God for a bike. A couple weeks later, at the Unitarian church his parents brought him to, Walt left Sunday School and saw the feathery pulp of a baby bird ground into the sidewalk by strollers and well-shined shoes. No one else bothered to look down. He never got his bike. Instead, he believed in the goodness of man, their natural rights and inherent dignity.

With Vanessa's body somewhere under a hospital, Walt watched the LA riots with a smile. He nodded in satisfaction at the twelve-fatality trampling in the London tubes. The reverend Frank Phillips preached on TV about Revelations. Two days later, his cough forced him off a live broadcast mid-sermon. Walt set up a Google Alert for his obituary.

Four days after Vanessa's death, he decided to hunt down his mugger and stab him to death before the plague could get him.

A cold spring wind blew off the bay. Sunlight glittered like ice. Uptown was supposedly a ghost town, but the Village was still reasonably populated with its native artists, transgenders, college students, and professionals who imagined they were still cool, unaware the entire neighborhood hadn't been for at least a decade. Walt crossed the narrow streets with no particular pattern, jiggling the butterfly knife in his pocket. He knew there was no real chance the man with the shaved head would be in the coffee shops or cafes (the ones that were still open, anyway), but checked regardless, nauseated by the smells of espresso and fried plantains and kung pao. On the sidewalks, people lifted their surgical masks to talk quietly on their cells. Others hurried past, coughing into their fists, driving oncoming pedestrians to the other side of the street. Walt walked until his toes blistered, until his nose numbed in the wind, until the sun went down, then he bought a new pint and walked until he couldn't. He sat on the stoop where the man had sat and leaned against the iron rail that lined the stairs.

He woke sometime before sunrise, stiff, hungover, colder than stone. He dragged himself home and slept on the couch deep into the afternoon. The apartment still smelled like blood and the gritty blue cleaning powder he'd used to scrub it out.

He put down some water, whiskey, and toast. Before he'd managed to dress, he heard chanting in the street. A clump of protesters marched north, parkbound, clapping gloved hands, waving signs that said "VACCINES KILL" and "WHERE'S THE CURE?" and "SICK CROPS, SICK PEOPLE."

Walt brought his coat, a bottle, the knife. Washington Square swelled with students, middle-aged women in glasses, gray-haired men in corduroy vests. The drug dealers retreated to the shadowy, tree-thick corner, hands in the pockets of their black hoodies. Walt circled the fringes, hunting for bald white heads. A woman with a frizzy ponytail descended to the center of the dry fountain, propped up a picture, and lit a candle. Notes and photos appeared as if conjured. Walt smelled wax, incense. The standard protest sights: a bearded kid slapping his bongos, 2-4-6-8 anti-government cheers, short-haired 50-year-old women yelling into megaphones. A squad car rolled to a stop alongside the arch on the north entrance of the park. An officer swung his legs out the door, leaned against the car, and muttered into his radio.

The crowd chanted, made speeches, told anecdotes about crowded hospitals and delayed appointments and insurance discrimination. People poured into the park by twos and fours, clogging the concrete around the fountain. On the south edge, a column of kids in red and black filed into the park, circled A's painted on their signs and sweatshirts and masked faces. They carried plastic shields and black batons. The cop near the arch grimaced and leaned into his car. Back by the swing sets, a man with a shaved head flagged down a college kid and bummed a cigarette.

The mugger lit up, squinted, spat smoke between his teeth. Walt walked over, hand in his pocket.

"Hey."

The man closed one eye. "What's up?"

"How was the curry?"

The man cocked his head, confused, then grinned slowly. "Tasty, man. I gotta go back to that place."

Three more squad cars joined the first up by the arch. Inside his pocket, Walt unfolded his knife. "My girlfriend died."

The grin seeped from the mugger's eyes. "Yeah, well, she's not the only one."

"If you hadn't stopped me, I might have gotten home in time."

"To do what? Suck the poison out? Cast a spell? I lifted your wallet, not your fucking medical license."

On the south side of the park, a man barked like a drill sergeant. The anarchists formed four orderly lines. Some belted riot masks under their chins while others raised transparent shields. Sirens squealed up on 5th Avenue.

"Maybe I'd have seen her."

The anarchists jogged forward in formation. Protesters shouted, deserting the square, shoving onlookers into the fountain. Someone screamed. By the arch, two mounted police clopped behind a knot of NYPD holding tasers and batons.

"She died," the man with the shaved head said. "Ain't nothing worse than your girl dying on you. But if you're trying to blame me for that, you need to get yourself some fucking grief counseling."

Wordlessly, the anarchists broke into a sprint. The outnumbered cops held their ground. The two mounted units trotted forward. The front line of red-and-black anarchists raised their riot shields above their heads, the curved plastic tonking under the horsemen's batons. The second line of anarchists rushed forward, surrounding the horses, and yanked the two cops out of their stirrups. Their own batons rose and fell. Sirens yowled over the screams. The horses reared. A kid in black collapsed, convulsing. From the arch, a policeman charged for the downed mounties, pistol drawn, emptying his clip into the anarchists beating the two downed cops.

Walt lunged forward, slashing at the mugger's face. The man shouted and threw up his hands. The knife cut a deep red line across his fingers. He swore, stumbling back a half step, then crouched low with his hands extended. Walt jabbed for his ribs. The mugger grabbed his wrist, folded it, wrenched away the knife. Walt smelled the man's sweat, heard the whuff of his breath. A bright point of pain burst through Walt's gut. Two more followed. The man drew back. Walt collapsed. Metal clattered on the concrete. Walt moaned, dry-mouthed, wet-handed.

"You fucking idiot," the mugger said. He turned and ran. Walt rolled on his back and clutched his stomach and thought: *I want this.* A bearded face poked into the narrowing tunnel of his vision. Words he couldn't understand. He saw Vanessa smiling, lying on her back in a field in Central Park.

"Get up. Hey, Stitches. Time to get up and go home."

Walt shook his head. Something tugged his nose, pinching. He pawed at his face. A strong hand grabbed his wrist.

"Let me take care of that for you. Don't want you losing any more blood."

The pressure on his nose increased, then disappeared. Something pinched his forearm instead. A black guy in scrubs stood beside his bed, winding thin clear tubes with strange, sharp smells of plastic and antiseptic.

"Can you walk? The answer better be yes."

"I'm in a hospital?"

"For the next five minutes, maybe."

Walt eased upright. "What kind of hospital wakes a stabbing victim up to kick him into the street?"

"One with two thousand sick people hacking their guts across the parking lot."

He leaned forward, wincing at the stitches tugging his stomach. "Am I...in trouble? Police-wise?"

The nurse pushed out his lower lip. "Officer came by a couple days ago, but you were out. Now they're a little busy with the fire up in Midtown to give a damn about whatever earned you a knife in the belly."

"Which hurts exactly as bad as you'd think getting stabbed

hurts. At least give me some painkillers. The sick people don't need painkillers, do they?"

"Just a bed and someplace to die."

Walt laughed. The nurse didn't. "You're serious."

"Kid, if you're not sick yet, the last place you want to be is a hospital."

"You're talking like we're all going to be wearing tires and spikes by next Tuesday."

"All I know is I haven't seen one person bounce back." The nurse peeled back his sheet. "Get dressed. I'll get you those pills."

Walt had to lean across a chair to pull on his pants without stretching his stitches. The nurse opened the door, flipped him a rattling bottle, and gestured him out. As soon as Walt shuffled into the hall, the nurse rolled a second bed into his room. Walt went to the drinking fountain and swallowed a pill.

Patients in gowns slept on benches and coughed from chairs, dabbing blood from their lips. The air stunk of copper and warm raw meat. Walt hobbled to the receptionist, holding his stomach with one hand while he signed out with the other.

"I don't have any insurance."

She gazed at him over her glasses. "Then it's a good thing you didn't get stabbed a week ago. Get out of here."

He ran a hand through his greasy hair. "Since when could you walk out of a hospital without paying a pound of flesh?"

"Feds have suspended hospital billing until the Panhandler's finished," she explained, obviously not for the first time.

"Panhandler? Like a homeless guy?"

She snorted. "You been in a coma or something?"

"Maybe?"

"They traced it back to some wheat farmer in the Idaho panhandle. Thus—"

"Idaho doesn't have a panhandle. It's vertically oriented. More like a bottle neck."

"What are you, a cartographer? Just pretend somebody's holding the pan down by their side."

The front doors flew open, disgorging a pair of paramedics wheeling in a young girl vomiting blood onto the white tile. The receptionist stood, yelling questions; the medics yelled back.

Walt hobbled for the door. Vanessa was dead.

Ambulances clogged the front drive, lights whirling in the

dusk. A queue of cabs let out coughing passengers who stood on the sidewalks, swaying, until a panting nurse emerged from a side door to escort them inside. Dozens of tents bivouacked the parking lot, overseen by dark-eyed doctors and a small patrol of soldiers in camo and gas masks. Walt got out his discharge papers. Nobody bothered to ask.

A block from the hospital, the firehose of traffic reduced to a drippy faucet. He crossed Second Avenue without breaking his slow stride. The sidewalks glittered under his feet. Metal bars shuttered storefronts on both sides of the street. Faraway laughter echoed between the towers. Walt limped down the stairs to the 28th St. 6-train. Two young guys waited on the opposite platform. His was empty besides a dead woman and a tacky pool of blood.

A breeze blew down the tunnel, carrying the scent of cold wet laundry. At least the trains were still running.

Home, first thing he did was get in front of a mirror and tug up his shirt. Three inch-long sets of stitches tracked the left side of his stomach, looking sickeningly like ingrown hairs, but deliberately placed, as if he'd been plowed and seeded. He let his shirt fall back into place.

Online, he learned he'd missed Vanessa's funeral. Google alerted him to the death of the Reverend Frank Phillips, 72, infamous picketer of soldiers' funerals, dead of the Panhandler virus. MSNBC.com estimated the American death toll in the hundreds of thousands, with more by the minute. Millions worldwide. His mom had left five messages on his phone. She and his dad were sick.

She didn't answer his call. He stuffed some clothes in a backpack, washed a hydrocodone down with some whiskey, and caught the subway up to Grand Central, where he bought a ticket to Long Island. A towering black cloud rose from Midtown, spilling out over the Upper Bay. His fellow passengers—a dozen or so, three of whom, like him, showed no sign of the cough or watery, bloodshot eyes that formed the virus' early symptoms— watched in silence, detraining one by one in the quiet Island townships. He got off in Medford a little after eleven. His mom still wasn't answering her phone.

Though he'd quit a few months back, he bought a pack of Camels at a Shell station that, by the look of it, was the only open store on the street. On his way to the exit, he turned around and bought three packs more. After so long, the smoke tasted ashy and bitter. The way nonsmokers smell it. His head went tingly and light. If he hadn't had to slow down to keep his balance during the head rush, he would have tripped over the body sprawled on the sidewalk.

Walt crossed to the far sidewalk. Crickets chirped tentatively from dark lawns. TV screens threw pale flickers on closed curtains. A dog whined from behind a chain link fence. The windows of its house were black. Walt crossed the yard, dew dampening his Converse, and knelt in front of the small black dog, which waved its thick tail and battered at the fence with heavy white paws. He fed it Bugles from the bag he'd brought with him and scratched its ears. He barely felt his stitches; his breathing felt good. He told the dog it was good. He drank from his pint of whiskey, glass glinting in the darkness. The base of his throat burned but his stomach felt warm.

"Good dog."

The dog whined, licking his hand as hard as if he'd been swimming through butter. He had another drink. He was delaying. He stood, stomach tugging, and walked on.

He let himself inside. His parents' house smelled the same as his apartment the night he'd come home from work. His mom was a bloody thing in her bed. He found his dad crusted to the wheel of his Jaguar. The car was off and the tank was still a quarter full; probably, he'd died of the virus instead of exhaust.

Walt took the money his dad kept above the bookshelf, found a butcher knife and a steak knife, then gathered up the bottle of scotch his dad had been saving since Walt had been born. He sat down on the front porch and had a drink from the scotch and lit another cigarette. Once he'd smoked it to the butt, he called the police and walked back to the train station. He fell asleep watching cartoons on his apartment couch.

While everything else began to shut down—schools, local governments, Taco Bell, commercial airlines, the borders— television stayed strong. Amidst Wile E. Coyote and Marvin the Martian blowing themselves up, Walt heard sirens, gunshots, screams. While Stimpy gave Ren a sponge bath, Walt smelled smoke and tear gas and burning meat. When the news informed him an estimated 35 million Americans had died, that an estimated 90% of the remaining populace showed signs of infection, with similar incidence rates worldwide, Walt got up, roamed the apartment, and reread Vanessa's letter.

At least she'd never actually broken up with him.

Maybe she'd never intended to. He had no way of knowing. Maybe she'd written it to see how it would feel, to see if she believed it. Vanessa was gone now. The letter, her rehearsals with Mark (had he died, too? Walt hoped so, that hard-abbed prick), Walt's hopes for another day with her like their day in Central Park, those were nothing but lost possibilities, could-have-beens rendered moot by an invader too small to see. Walt sat down on the bare box spring that had held the mattress where Vanessa had died. He didn't see a future where the rest of mankind didn't die with her. Whatever Obama said, with three quarters of a billion dead just three weeks after the first case and with no cure in sight, Walt figured an average cricket match would outlast civilized society. But the Panhandler didn't just mean the extinction of people. It meant the extinction of dreams.

Walt had wanted to write books. He'd never finished one, had never seen his works go to print where they'd shout *This is how I feel. If you feel like me, that means we're not alone.* He supposed it wouldn't matter soon. Soon, people wouldn't be using books to find understanding. They'd be using them for kindling.

His parents had been talking about retiring soon. Scaling back, at least, to pilot their balloons on trips of their own, challenging records, touching down in Greek islands where the seas were as green as skinned avocados. They'd died having worked their whole lives. And honestly enjoyed it, by and large. But they'd wanted, expected, and deserved more.

Vanessa had wanted to move to Los Angeles, to see if she could make the leap from stage to screen. She'd never made it out. He supposed he was partly to blame: whenever she brought it up, he said little and changed the subject readily, not wanting to leave the city that had become his home, fearful that removed from his environment, adrift among the millionaires and fakers of LA's shallow social seas, he would lose her to a producer in a Mercedes, a confident fellow actor-on-the-up. What was so great about the place, anyway? Along with Woody Allen's arguments, which were irrefutable, weren't they coughing up blood and bleeding out their eyes the same in LA as they were in New York? All the sea breezes and sunny weather in the world couldn't combat *that*. Vanessa's letter had once again declared her intent to move there. What had she expected? To be carried into town by a parade, delivered at the feet of Steven Spielberg, and be cast on the spot as the lead in *The Woman So Beautiful All the World Loved Her Forever*? Delusions. Delusions and ignorance, most of it willful. The second time she'd brought it up, maybe he should have agreed to go with her, just to prove there was nothing magical about the place, that plenty of people more talented than either of them had failed and starved there on the edge of the Pacific, that it doesn't matter *where* you are, all that matters is *who*.

But she was dead now. The dinosaurs had all died, too, along with their dinosaur dreams. A world capable of such genocidal indifference didn't deserve its own existence. Walt wanted to watch it wither, to crumble into shit and dirt, fertilizer for a future that would one day crumble itself.

He decided to walk to Los Angeles. He intended to die along the way.

7

Under the afternoon sun, Raymond touched the warm metal revolver. Sweat slipped down his temples. Lights whirled from the cruiser's roof.

"Get your hands up and step away from the car!" the officer shouted.

Time became something that happened elsewhere. Raymond could see the silvery snaps on the cuffs of the officer's sleeves. The sight at the end of his pistol. A mole on the side of his neck.

"I'm just here to feed my family."

"Hands up or I spread you like mustard!"

Half hidden behind his car, Raymond eased out the revolver, slung it into the far corner of the trunk, and raised his hands. They'd find it. He knew that. He just wanted to introduce deniability. He took a slow step from the car. The cop sidled from behind his door, relaxing his elbows, black pistol swallowing the sun.

From the front of the Ralph's, three quick shots spooked a flock of screams. Raymond flinched down, shoulders scrunched against his head. The cop twitched his gun, following him, then aimed it upright and charged across the sunny lot. His partner spilled out of the car and followed on his heels. Raymond pawed the rest of the groceries into his trunk, slammed it, squeezed in behind the wheel, and pulled out. Shoppers ran past, covering their heads and ducking, pinging erratically across the asphalt. Raymond swung around a woman carrying a kid in her arms. A shopping cart banged off his bumper. The abandoned cop car stretched across the exit. He rolled up beside it, left tires shuddering over the concrete-bordered strip of grass that ran alongside the lot, then jolted back down into the road with a harsh metal screech. Back at the front of the Ralph's, gunshots popped in the humid air. Raymond finally registered the upcoming light was red and stomped the brakes, his car bucking stopped six inches from the rear bumper of an Expedition.

Hands shaking, he waited for the light to turn.

His senses returned homebound on the PCH. It had happened so fast, shortcircuiting his rational thought. The cop with the gun, had he known or suspected Raymond of looting? Had he been stopping everyone to sort it out? Had Raymond seriously considered, however briefly, pulling his gun? Had he intended to bluff, or try to shoot his way out, envisioning arrest for armed robbery, an impossible bail, years without Mia? On the other hand, why not?—but maybe for a lesser crime. Was it better to go to jail than to go broke?

He didn't know. All he could remember was the glint of the officer's buttons, the small black brick of his pistol, the sense his world was about to slip beneath the breakers. Yet he'd thrown down the gun. A stranger had fired his own instead. Raymond's future had popped above the waves, taken a juddering breath, and resumed paddling.

He pulled into his driveway. Time to recohere. You become what you pretend, so pretend to be something good.

In the trunk, he hid the revolver under an old coat and started hauling groceries. Mia smiled at him from the recliner. "How went the job hunt?"

"Riotous."

"At you? Or with you?"

"Literally." He set down an armload of cereal and tomatoes and shook his head like they were discussing a 6-year-old dragged under by a shark. "I'm picking up some applications at this strip mall, right. So I see the Ralph's is having this big sale. Go inside, load up my cart, and all of a sudden everyone starts looting the place."

Mia sat up, plunking her elbows between her knees. "Looting? Really? Did the Lakers win again?"

"I think people are afraid."

"Should we be?"

"Do you feel sick?"

"No." She smiled then, chin tilted. "So you robbed the place blind, right? How much bacon did you get?"

He looked up, thinking. "About five packs?"

"Wait, you *did*?" She glanced to the side, as if seeking the support of an unseen audience. "Does this mean I'll finally realize my lifelong dream of sleeping with a felon?"

"Possibly. Will you still be turned on if it turns out I'm just a misdemeanist?"

"So what *happened*?"

"One minute I'm piling up the rice and things, the next minute everyone's screaming and stampeding for the door. Somebody had a gun, was waving it at the checkout lines. I just got out of there."

"And the groceries got with you."

He shook his head again. "It all happened so fast. I didn't have time to think. Do you think I should take them back?"

"I don't know." She tapped her teeth. "I think if you go back, you're confessing. Places like that have insurance, don't they?"

"I think so." He jerked his thumb toward the door. "Want to give me a hand?"

Mia unfolded from the recliner. "What, and be an accessory?"

Which was exactly why he hadn't told her the truth. He waited for a knock, a call, a radio crackling from his back steps—he had to protect her from those consequences. He went online to see what the news had to say about them and found his looting had been the third of the day. A Best Buy in Long Beach, the usual steroes and TVs carted out through broken windows by brown people, but also a Sprouts in Torrance, blonde mothers clinging to their kids with one hand and stuffing organic heirloom tomatoes into their purses with the other. Watts caught fire the next day, smogging the valley. At night, sleek black SUVs rolled down the curvy lane. Glass shattered down the street; later, Raymond rose for a glass of water and saw his windows painted by the spinning lights of a cruiser. Two young Hispanic guys lay facedown on the sidewalk, hands cuffed behind their backs, a potbellied white cop shouting at them as he paced. Raymond could see no obvious evidence of a crime. He moved the revolver to a drawer in the bedroom.

Craigslist blossomed with security-wanted ads. Raymond embellished his resume, added a paragraph about his home invasion defense experience. He got a call later that day for an interview up the street in Palos Verdes.

While Mia, still home from work, researched mortgages and liens and applied for credit cards (both of them had somehow made it this far in life with nothing more than debit cards), Raymond drove up the winding roads into the ocean-gazing hills, his dusty Altima conspicuous among the glassy-bright Benzes and Porsches, and pulled onto the long driveway of a Tuscan-style manor fronted with whip-thin, forest-black pines. From the third story of its wide-windowed turret, a curtain fell closed.

A middle-aged Asian man in suit and glasses answered the bell. Raymond's sneakers squeaked on the stone floor. Should have worn something black and shiny as a beetle's back. Oh well, regrets were no use: Just do better next time. The servant led him to a well-lit study of thick white carpets. A fresh marine breeze slipped through the slats built into the wall. From behind a glass desk, Kevin Murckle picked at a stain on his wash-worn t-shirt, looked up, and snugged his surgical mask into place.

"Frankly, I'm looking for someone bigger. Possibly blacker. A shaved head helps."

"Sure," Raymond nodded. He wasn't surprised; he was 5' 9", 155 pounds, with arms that neither popped nor wilted. "But try squeezing one of the big guys into the air ducts when your daughter's kidnapped."

Murckle laughed, creasing his tanned face. "You've seen my movies."

"I'm smart. I've got my own piece. I can start today."

"Your experience is a little flimsy. Some might compare it to a greasy Fatburger wrapper."

Raymond leaned back in his wireframe chair. "Why haven't you skipped town?"

Murckle waved at the ocean sparking below his window. "I live here."

"And two or three other places, right?"

"Five."

"Everyone else in your tax bracket has fled for a ranch in Wyoming or a mountain in Colorado. You've got something you want to protect — your house, your business, your girlfriends."

"Something like that."

"I've got something I want to protect, too. She's ten minutes away. You find yourself with an emergency, that puts *me* ten minutes away from providing backup. Day or night."

The man stuck out his chin, scratched his thumbnail along the salt-and-pepper whiskers lining his neck. "We'll get back to you. Show yourself out, will you?"

Raymond kept putting in applications. At night they smelled the smoke from Watts. The news started running death tolls: first hundreds nationwide, revised to thousands by the next day. The warble of ambulances yanked them from sleep. Murckle called him three days later.

"Swing by tonight."

"Great," Raymond said. "What tipped the scales?"

"You were the only applicant without a criminal record."

"Sure. I'm a clean-cut guy."

"I don't consider that a positive. But I need *some*body with a clean record. Now get over here so my doctor can stick a needle in you."

The middle-aged man in suit and glasses led him to a dustless garage where two other men waited, one big bald black guy and one big bald white guy, both in their underwear. Small metal instruments and syringes rested on a glass table.

Raymond raised one hand hello. "What's up?"

The white guy elbowed the black guy. "Bet you fifty when the doc draws his blood he collapses like a used condom."

"That's disgusting," the black guy said.

"Remove your clothes, please," said the man who'd answered the door. He waited in perfect stillness while Raymond tugged off his shirt and dropped his pants, then took them away before Raymond had a chance to look confused, folding them with crisp snaps of his wrists. Raymond thought he heard him sniff. An old guy with a laurel-leaf of white hair fringing his head walked through the door.

"Okay, boys," the old man said, tugging the hems of his jean jacket. "A little jab, a quick physical, and we'll send you on your way."

The white guy gave the other man another elbow. "That's the same line you use on the dudes, isn't it?"

"Christ."

The doctor drew their blood, checked their breathing, prodded the glands around their throats. "Naturally, if you are ill, you will not be invited back. I will call with your results tomorrow afternoon."

Raymond turned out clean. So, apparently, did the other two. He met them the next afternoon in Murckle's sun-splashed foyer, their arms folded, bulging in their tight black suits.

"You will wait here," the doorman said. His footsteps echoed up a curled flight of stairs.

"We better be on the clock," the black guy mumbled.

They stood in silence a couple minutes, shuffling, eyeing the airy living room, red couches on white carpet, lurid old movie posters framed on the walls. When he couldn't take it, Raymond introduced himself, earning a handshake from Bill, the guy who'd spoken a minute earlier, and a nod from Craig.

"You guys done this kind of work before?"

Bill gave him a wry smile. "So it says on our resume."

Craig tipped back his head, eyes slits in his beefy face. "You packing?"

"Of course," Raymond said.

"Let me see your piece," he beckoned. Raymond handed over his revolver butt-first. Craig cracked the cylinder and cackled. "Yo, check this out."

"You steal that thing off a Confederate?" Bill said.

"Sure. Everyone knows they can't fight back."

Craig shook his head. "You're in here in street clothes packing some John Wayne cap gun and we're supposed to feel good you got our backs. What kind of desperate-ass times are these?"

"I know how to use it," Raymond said.

"Sure. Just aim and run away." Craig tipped the gun and tapped the cylinder, clattering shells over the stone floor. Raymond held out his hand. Craig sniffed and passed it over. Raymond held it a moment, feeling its reassuring weight.

The doorman cleared his throat, scowling from the top of the stairs. Craig gazed back placid as a cow. The doorman descended, planted himself in front of them, and folded his hands behind his back.

"I am Mr. Hu. Naturally, Mr. Murckle will not risk himself to exposure when he has no idea where you go home to each night. I will therefore introduce you to the facilities and function as the go-between when Mr. Murckle has tasks beyond keeping the grounds safe from burglars, looters, and assorted ill-wishers."

"How are we supposed to guard his body when we can't even see him?" Craig said.

"By ensuring no one else is able to see him, either."

Bill chuckled. Craig socked him in the arm as soon as Hu turned his back. Hu showed them the entries, the ground-level windows, the yards, the cliffside deck where a mild fog speckled Raymond's face, the security pads (but not how to work them), the panic room, the control room and its nine TVs, where Raymond toggled cameras like a pro while Craig struggled to zoom. Straightforward enough: watch the monitors, prowl the grounds if anyone showed up, be ready to use your weapon. Could you really just hire a man off the street to use deadly force while on your property? Would he even be able to pull the trigger on another person? He wasn't at all certain of either. He was all but certain, however, that it didn't matter on either count. There wasn't going to be any house-to-house looting or roving bands of harm-doers burning down hillside manors and running off with the jewelry. This bodyguard thing was just an absurd fad. One he would take advantage of to earn a few bucks while he waited for the video store to officialize his hiring.

Hu told them their schedule—Craig had first shift—then showed Bill and Raymond to the porch. With the evening sun pouring over the Pacific, Bill jiggled a Marlboro from his pack and lit up.

"I feel like we're into something strange here."

Raymond squinted. "Yeah?"

"So this dude is looking to hire himself some security." Bill glanced at the windows, lowered his voice. "Somehow none of the three guys he hires has any direct experience?"

"Everyone's got the flu. Anyone who isn't is probably tending to their own family."

Bill shrugged his thick shoulders. "Look, you seem like an all right guy, you know? Watch out for yourself."

He went home to bring Mia the good news. A frown fought a smile for her face. "I'm glad you're working. I was starting to get scared about moving out. But now I have to be scared for you at work instead?"

"It's not a big deal." He clicked open the cabinet under the microwave, snagged the bottle of Captain Morgan Private Stock she liked. "It's sitting behind a desk in a little tech room watching screens."

"And getting shot like a redshirt if something goes wrong."

"The guy's Hollywood. If something goes wrong, he'll have a SWAT team in three minutes."

She mashed her lips together and absently accepted his celebratory rum and Coke. "Don't get hurt, okay? If anything happens to you, I'll run away with the mailman."

He woke before his alarm, rolled up to the manor eight minutes early. Craig met him on the porch, blear-eyed.

"Have fun, kid. I was too bored to beat off."

He learned quickly what Craig meant. For all the break-ins, looting, riots, and fires around Los Angeles County, none of that manifested itself on Murckle's quiet cliffside street. He had the nine closed-circuit screens to watch, but except for the constant soft sway of the fronds, he may as well have been watching nine still lives of palms. He tried to find an internet radio feed for the Mariners and discovered the games had been postponed. For the Mariners, that was probably a mercy.

He wandered the grounds. A light fog clung to the cliffs, dewing the grass and the planks of the deck. He went back inside. The radio reported riots in a park in New York, three deaths and a couple dozen injuries, armed anarchists clashing with police over accusations the disease was an escaped government project. In Atlanta, crowds had been forced away from the CDC with live ammunition.

Bill clapped him on the shoulder that afternoon. "Anything go down?"

"Just my heart rate."

"Guess them crooks haven't figured their way up to the hills yet."

Before he left, Hu asked him to drop off a box of files in Hawthorne. The windows of the looted Ralph's were dark, gaping, glass glittering on the asphalt. Men stood on their front porches eyeing pedestrians and traffic, baseball bats and golf clubs dangling from their hands. At a Spanish bungalow with an iron fence around its rooftop barbecue, Raymond handed off the box of files and got home an hour before dark.

"I made $96 to sit in a room and watch a bunch of TV screens," he told Mia. "I think we'll be okay."

She gathered her long dark hair behind her head, sticking out her lower lip. "No one tried to break in?"

"It was so quiet I could hear the mice in the walls plotting their heist."

So was the next day. When Bill showed up to relieve him, Hu handed Raymond an address. "Mr. Murckle has some files he needs delivered to Torrance. Do you know Torrance?"

"Enough to get around."

"When you arrive, knock on apartment 218 and return to the car. When the man comes downstairs to the car, pop the trunk. Do not speak to him. Once he accepts the files, return here and see me before you begin your rounds."

Down the hill in Torrance, tarps fluttered from smashed windows. In the Sprouts parking lot, cops stood over a line of men cuffed and laid out on their bellies. Ambulances howled down the PCH, shepherding the thinned traffic to the sides of the road. Raymond turned off, passing a bowling alley, liquor stores. He parked in a weedy lot between two beige stucco apartment buildings, stepped out into an afternoon as warm as a dog's breath, climbed the stairs, knocked on 218, and returned to the car.

A minute later, a skinny white guy with a shaved head and the long, drooping jaw of a basset hound jogged down the steps, reached into the open trunk, and pulled out a briefcase.

Raymond drove back to Murckle's. Hu opened the door before he could knock. "Everything went well?"

"Perfectly," Raymond said. "Hey, I think I left something in the control room."

Hu nodded and gestured him upstairs. Raymond took them at a walk. In the control room, Bill clasped his hands behind his head and gazed blankly at the ceiling. Raymond knocked on the open door and Bill flailed to keep from falling from his chair.

"Christ, man, I'm trying to goof off in here."

Raymond closed the door. "You were right. We're into something strange."

Bill glanced at the door and leaned forward, suit drawn tight over his shoulders. "What's up?"

"I think we're dealing drugs."

8

Walt wanted to die, but he didn't want it to be easy. He packed extra shoes, a toothbrush and toothpaste. He packed as many lighters and matchbooks as he could find and then went to the nearest open bodega to buy more. He packed six pairs of his least-worn socks, a flashlight and extra batteries, his fuzzy-cornered copy of *Catch-22*. He packed the aspirin and cold meds he'd gotten for Vanessa, a mostly-full box of Band-Aids, some old rags, a tube of Neosporin, an extra pair of jeans, and two shirts. He packed his rusty old jackknife and a half-eaten bag of beef jerky and a box of saltines. He moved to a second backpack, filled it with a small pan, scissors, paperclips, three pens, two more pairs of socks, a pair of gloves, a windbreaker, some vitamins, a plastic water jug, a sleeve of bagels, a legal-sized notepad. Because, well, fuck it, he combined his remaining whiskey, vodka, and rum into a single handle and jammed that into the first pack.

Then he sat down, because his stitches hurt, and he dug out his handle of mixed business and poured a drink and thought some more. He decided to wait until he'd recovered enough to walk without pain. He didn't want to die midway through the Bronx or Jersey City, dropped by blood poisoning or because he couldn't hobble away from some thug with a crow bar. He could only die once. He wanted to make the most of it.

But he did want to die. The urge was like a hand pulling him below the soil, as if the dirt were water and his feet were covered in oil and all he could do was sink and drift and fall, a voiceless lump plummeting through the lightless caverns beneath an empty sea, alone and lost. Vanessa's lavender scent hugged the couch pillows. Her cursive handwriting graced the fridge lists and the end table beside the bed where she logged her dreams, inspirations, and performance notes. By comparison, the death of his parents was a small and sighing thing: he'd accepted long ago they'd die before him. All he'd wanted was to be with Vanessa until the far-off day one of them winked away.

Nothing seemed worthwhile—why work when the woman he'd worked for was gone? Why move, why watch, why breathe? Walt ate listlessly, cramped by constant nausea, microwaving canned soup and buttering toast. He left his apartment once the day after his return from Long Island. He bought things that would last: beef jerky, canned beans, alcohol. He didn't know whether the whole world was ending or just his own. Either way, money no longer mattered; instead of plastic jugs, he bought handles of Crown Royal, the fat bottles like fantastical potions. Anyway, the couple liquor stores still open had run out of the cheap stuff.

He watched the city from his window. Ambulances painted their lights on apartment walls, idling while pairs of men in biohazard suits dragged lumpy black bags down to the street. At sunset, a speeding SUV slammed into an oncoming sedan, smearing the sedan's driver over its hood and catapulting the SUV's into the middle of the intersection, where he lay, moaning, until he bled to death. At midnight, a yellow pickup braked behind the wreckage. Two big dudes got out, failed to start the SUV, and finally tried to push it out of the way. As they sweated in the cold, a taxi swung around the corner, tires screaming, and plowed into the remnants of the sedan, jolting the SUV backwards over one of the two men and pinning him under a tire. As his blood filled a black pool in the street, his friend ran screaming. The cab driver got out and approached the pinned man. Moans filtered through the window. The pinned man stretched a bloody arm across the pavement, pawing at the cabbie's shoelaces. The cabbie skipped away, vomited into the gutter, and jogged away down the street, wiping his mouth with his sleeve.

By morning, the street was impassible, a rubble of abandoned cars and hovering flies. A rat crouched on the pinned man's corpse, eating his nose. From his window, Walt took this for a sign. The ultimate metaphor for what happened when you tried to do good.

It rained that night, a steady beat that washed the blood and debris into the drains. Maybe the fish would get sick, too. Gunshots popped every few minutes, dampened by the mist. On the sidewalk below, a man shuffled forward, dropped his umbrella, and collapsed to his knees, phlegmy blood dangling from his mouth in strands.

Jets rattled his windows that morning, jarring him awake. The pain of his hangover felt right—the stabbing temples, the slow crush of his stomach, the sluggishness that made everything look less real than it already did. Heavy squeals and metallic shudders echoed between the buildings. Walt leaned out the window. Upstreet, a platoon of camo-wearing, rifle-swinging soldiers jogged across the intersection. With a rumbling, ear-wrenching shriek, a tank followed them down the street, pluming exhaust.

They came for him the next day.

The door pounded. His head did, too; he sat up from his blanket-nest on the couch, gum-eyed, parch-mouthed. "What?"

Quick, muffled talk from behind the door. "Open up! U.S. Army!"

Walt rose, naked except his underwear, and draped a sheet over his shoulders. He leaned his mouth against the door. "What can I do for you?"

"We're here to take you to a safe place."

"I'm pretty safe in here."

"What about your family? Any roommates?"

"I think they're pretty much dead. Let me check." Walt sniffed, gazing dumbly at the floor. "Yeah, all dead."

"Sir, I need you to step outside and come with me. In the event of noncompliance, we are authorized to break down your door."

"Authorized by who?" He unbolted the bolts, unlocked the locks. A pair of armed soldiers stood in the doorway, helmeted and vested, protected by gas masks and rubber gloves. "I appreciate your belief that you can keep me safer than I can keep myself, but I'm doing fine here."

The taller soldier shook his head. "We're authorized to round up all the survivors."

"The fact we are survivors might just imply we don't need your help."

"Sir, we don't have time for this. Come with us or we'll drag you down the stairs."

"Doesn't sound like either of us would enjoy that," Walt said. "Just tell them nobody was here."

The shorter soldier passed his rifle to his partner, grabbed Walt's wrist, and twisted until the bones rubbed each other sideways. Walt wilted to his knees. Stitches tugged his gut. The soldier clamped his wrists together, tying them tight with a plastic strip-cuff.

"Drag him out."

"I'm in my underwear here," Walt said from his knees.

"There's no time."

"At least put on my shoes. You expect me to walk through fucking New York City barefoot? People were shitting, bleeding, and puking in the street. And that's *before* the Panhandler."

The soldiers exchanged gas-masked glances. The one who'd hogtied him swore. "Where are your shoes?"

They let him pull on some pants and his Converse, then draped his coat around his shoulders and fitted him with a surgical mask and thin, transparent gloves.

"What's this about?" he asked on the way down the cold stairwell.

"Rounding up the survivors to keep you safe," said the soldier who'd cuffed him.

"Brilliant, gather us all together. The best way to guarantee that if we *can* get sick, we *will*."

"Has anyone told you you stink like whiskey, sir?"

They exited the building to an overcast noon. The streets smelled of smoke and blood and sour biology. Walt thought about running—he doubted they knew New York any more than he knew whatever non-New York backwater they'd coagulated in, and if they truly intended to scour the entire goddamn city for survivors, there was a fair chance they wouldn't waste time coming after him—but then again, they had guns. And tanks. And troops on the corners. Helicopters ruffled the clouds overhead. The soldier led him to a high-roofed truck and gestured him up a ramp. Twenty-odd other survivors sat on the truck bed, surgical masks in place, eyes bored rather than glassy or watery, no coughing or blood staining their masks. Only two of them were handcuffed. Walt sat down and leaned his back against the truck's side, glad for the shade. His stomach twisted, wringing itself like a beery old sponge.

They sat there a long time. The soldiers brought down an old woman in a black coat and led her into the truck, then a scruffy bearded guy around Walt's age. The soldiers cracked a can of paint, splashed a bright red X across the door, and moved on to the next building.

A woman asked to go to the bathroom. The soldiers told her to hold it. She asked again and a soldier glanced down the street, smashed in the door of a Starbucks with the butt of his rifle, and gestured her in. Walt napped, woken constantly by the truck bed jostling with new arrivals, by the whirr of choppers and the sky-tearing sound of jets, by people sobbing, the crackle of radios, the squeak of tank treads, by his own headache. Sometime midafternoon—he'd left his cell beside the couch—the truck grumbled to life and weaved slowly down the street, dodging abandoned cars, sprays of glass, sometimes a body.

Earlier, he'd asked a soldier where they were headed and gotten a vague non-answer. He didn't bother asking the other passengers. They rocked in the truck bed, staring blankly, as unresponsive to the contact of their neighbors' shoulders and knees as if they were down on a cramped 4-train to Yankee Stadium. The truck hooked south down Lafayette and rumbled through Chinatown, where shutters barred the stalls and seafood markets and t-shirt shops. Goods carpeted the sidewalks—shirts, wallets, belts, toys in cheap bubble plastic, sunglasses, squashed bananas, trampled cabbage, crushed crabs, some still waving their claws from the gutters. It stunk like old fish and rain-sodden greens. The truck turned down a street Walt didn't recognize and stopped cold. Radios squawked from up front.

Truck doors thumped. Boots hit the sidewalk. Ahead, metal scraped asphalt. Men swore, chattered over radios.

Out past the tailgate, three strangers wandered toward the truck, a slow shuffle punctuated by coughing jags. They wiped bloody fists on their pants and continued closer.

"Stay where you are," a loudspeaker blared from the truck.

"We're sick," a tall, thin man called from the trio. "We need help."

"Wait on the corner," the soldier replied. "Help will be sent as soon as it's available."

"You're the third truck that's told us that!"

Windows opened from a handful of apartments. Two more

people turned the corner, leaning on each other for support, and joined the trio. Up front beyond Walt's sight, something heavy and hard grated over the pavement. He took shallow breaths. He'd been thinking he might throw up for a while now. At least the truck was canvas-topped, open around the sides. Fresh air.

Down on the corner, the crowd grew to a dozen. Five minutes later, with the soldiers still struggling to clear whatever was blocking the road, and Walt wondering why they didn't just take a different street, the gathering of the sick swelled to more than thirty, shivering, coughing, spitting wads of blood on the sidewalks.

"Where are you taking them?" a squat woman shouted. "Do you have medicine?"

"My apartment's full of fucking corpses," a hefty guy hollered in a Brooklyn accent. "How about you show us a place to sleep that doesn't smell like a Red Lobster's Dumpster?"

"Help is on the way," the soldier said. "Stay where you are."

"Like hell!" The hefty guy started forward. After two steps, the crowd followed in one of those strange mass movements, muttering, shouting, crying for answers and aid.

"This is a quarantined vehicle. Stop where you are and turn around."

Two soldiers ran to the back of the truck and knelt, raising assault rifles to their shoulders. The hefty man sneered and limped on.

"You're taking them to the cure!"

"Please don't leave us!"

From the advancing crowd, a thin blonde woman staggered away, hugged a lamppost, and sicked blood across the gum-dotted sidewalk. Someone in the truck moaned.

"Stop now or we will open fire," the loudspeaker blared.

Fifty feet away, the man laughed and broke into a run. Others lurched to keep up.

"Oh fuck," one of the kneeling soldiers said. Gunfire battered Walt's ears. The hefty man's chest puffed in three places, blood misting the people to either side of him. They fell alongside him, holes in their foreheads, chests, legs. Those in back screamed over the gunshots. One woman froze, clamping her arms to her face. Holes burst in her elbow, the back of her hand. The others turned and ran, stumbling and shrieking, disappearing around corners and through open doorways. The gunfire stopped dead. A dozen bodies lay bleeding on the pavement, some gurgling and clawing the asphalt, others as still as the streets beyond. Pale faces watched from windows. In the truck, people moaned, scrabbled their feet on the floor and pushed their backs against the walls, gagged, prayed.

"Shit," the first soldier to fire said.

"Hold your fire!" A man with stripes on his shoulder jogged from the side of the truck.

The soldier stood, shouldering his rifle. "Sarge, they charged us. Another two seconds and—"

"I know." The sergeant leaned in, grabbed the younger man by the neck. "You followed the protocol. You remember that tonight. Those people were already dead."

"Key word *people*," Walt called, dazed, tingly, jarred free from himself. "Not some goddamn zombies."

The sergeant turned on the truck, vaulting up onto the bumper. "Who said that?"

Walt shrunk against the side of the trunk, suddenly paternalized, pinned down by the authoritarian bark of a teacher quick with the detention. Across the truck, a dark-haired woman pointed him out. The sergeant clambered in over the tailgate and stuck a finger in Walt's face.

"Listen up. People are dying out there. You want us to leave you with them, just say the word."

Walt lifted his cuffed wrists. "This look like I volunteered?"

The sergeant grabbed him by the belt and frogmarched him to the tailgate, where he shoved Walt's front half over the ledge and planted a boot on his ass. The pavement waited below. "Just say the word!"

"At least cut my cuffs!"

"Say the word. You know how many bodies I seen the last week? Say the word and over you go."

"Okay," Walt said. "Please set me down. Please, officer."

"I'm not a fucking officer."

The man shoved him aside and jumped out the back. Walt eased himself back against the truck's side, stitches tingling. He flushed, furious. Why not jump? He was cuffed in the front; he could run home, get inside, find a knife to saw through the plastic. The truck juddered to life, pulling forward. But what if he snapped his wrist in the fall? Cracked his head? Were there any hospitals left? He hadn't kept up with the news. The city had fallen overnight, becoming a cemetery instead, its dead memorialized by the mausoleums of skyscrapers, the catacombs of the subways, the island-tomb of the unknown citizens. The military's plan, that was dead in the water. What would they do, ship everyone to Antarctica to trade stocks from their igloos? The plague had already taken the world. It had come too fast, spread too far to be stopped now. Everything else was delusion.

If he knew that much, why hadn't he jumped?

The truck rolled into a broad garage with red axes and thick fabric hoses strung along the walls. The soldiers waited for the doors to creak shut, then offloaded the civilians, split them by gender, and shuffled them into two locker rooms. An armed soldier ordered them to strip and deposit their clothes in a wheeled canvas cart.

"What are you doing with them?" a chubby guy said through his thick black mustache.

"The same thing we're about to do to you," the soldier said. "Now get in the showers."

"Oh Jesus," said the lanky young Jewish guy next to Walt. A soldier clipped Walt's cuffs. He showered, got dusted with a sharp-smelling powder by two anonymous people in full rubbery biosuits, then got ordered to shower again. In a tight benched room, a soldier passed Walt a pair of sweat pants and a loose white t-shirt that billowed past his waist. After he dressed, a man in a mask and a lab coat called the captives one by one into a room that until recently had been a personal office; photos of somebody's daughters hung on the walls, with bowling trophies occupying a corner shelf. The doctor drew Walt's blood, checked his breathing, his pulse, pressed his fingers to the side of Walt's throat and made him swallow, examined his stitches and told him they looked good.

"What's going on?" Walt said.

"We're seeing if you're sick."

"I wasn't before I got hauled onto that truck. Couldn't tell you for sure *now*."

The doctor smiled with half his mouth, skin crinkling around his eyes. "If you aren't already ill, chances are you never will be. Besides the cold, the flu, and cancer, of course."

"If we're doing fine, why scoop us up at all?"

"In the hopes you can help those who aren't so lucky."

"I can think of safer places to base the world's salvation than an old fire station in downtown Manhattan."

The man laughed, tapping his nose. "That's why we're shipping you to Staten Island. We've already disabled the bridges." He flicked his fingers apart. "Kablam!"

A short man with angry blond brows led him in silence to a small dorm and locked him in. Walt paced the tiles, fuming and muttering, castigating himself for not asking the doctor why they needed so many subjects, for not pulling the old man's lab coat over his head and punching him in the back of the skull. If Walt didn't want to be here—and he'd already begun to consider clocking his head against the wall until it or he cracked—why hadn't he done *anything* to get himself out? Were the solutions to his desires supposed to manifest themselves by magic? Did he expect, when he silently asked the universe to return him to his apartment, it would give him a thumbs-up, a grinned *Heyyyyy*, and poof him back to his ratty couch?

The blond man brought him a plate of hamburger and rice. Walt chewed sluggishly, forcing himself to swallow. He couldn't finish. The man returned for his plate, exchanged it for a glass of water and a bucket.

Walt tried to sleep on the sheeted twin bed. Instead, he remembered Vanessa. He remembered how long it took him to tell her he loved her. He remembered wanting to ask her about Mark. He remembered sitting next to her in a theater in college before they started dating, their arms resting so close on the arm of the seat he could feel the warmth of her skin, the brush of her tiny translucent hairs, and he wanted to put his hand in hers and smile at her, but he was afraid she'd pull away, that she'd say no, that the time wouldn't be right, that he'd never have a chance to find the moment that was. She'd kissed him, finally, two months later.

He'd lost two months he could have spent with her. Lost the better part of their junior year to a fun-but-light relationship he couldn't properly enjoy for always wanting more. When she'd started practicing lines with Mark, he'd lost weeks to gut-crushing anxiety.

For all those worries, here he was trapped in a room, shitting in a bucket and waiting to be shipped to a quarantine island.

Vanessa was dead. He'd never have another minute with her again.

The labs came in the next afternoon. Walt was released from his room. The cafeteria smelled like sweat and Lysol and boiled meat. Walt counted heads. Three missing. He asked around. No one knew where they'd gone.

The doctor drew more blood. Soldiers sentried the exits like gas-masked gargoyles. At dinner, driven by the instinct they were no safer here than they'd been on their own, Walt sat down across from a girl with rows of tight black braids and asked about the missing men.

She frowned, spoonful of mashed potatoes halfway to her mouth. "You say there were three of them?"

"I counted on the ride in. A few times. I do things like that."

The girl chewed potatoes. "They killed them."

Walt glanced at the door. A soldier scratched the mask strap beneath his neck. "How do you know that? Did you see the bodies?"

"My room's got a window looks over the courtyard. Last night I heard three shots—pop pop pop."

"Maybe they were popping champagne to celebrate their upcoming non-execution."

The girl smiled. He noticed she was pretty. He went to his room and closed the door. That night he dreamed of wrestling the soldiers' rifles away, of leading a charge for the exits to a city too bright to see. But when he faced down the last guards between himself and freedom, he raised the rifle to his shoulder and couldn't pull the trigger. The people around him fell and died, eyes blacked out by bullets, shots connecting dots across their chests. The world faded to something he wouldn't remember when he woke.

He stared at the wall. Cinderblock. Painted white. No windows. That was clearly a fire code violation. He went to the cafeteria, tried the double doors that led out into the halls where they'd been showered down and prodded by the doctor. A chain rattled from the other side. Across the room, a masked soldier pushed off from the wall and closed on Walt.

"Please step away from that, sir."

Walt tried the other handle. "What if I told you to unlock this and get out of my way?"

"Sir, I would try not to laugh."

"I'm not a beanbag chair. I'm not a beagle. I'm not your property."

"Orders say we keep you here." The mask muffled the soldier's voice as thoroughly as it did his face. "They think we can break this thing. It's time for all of us to step up."

Days crawled by, as foolish and horrid as a half-crushed spider, as divorced from life as a button on a calculator, marked by blood-draws and meal times and the morning/evening lights-on/lights-off. Without notice, Walt was rousted by a heavy knock four days later. He dressed in darkness, angry and sleepy, and joined the others in the garage, where they milled for most of an hour before a pair of soldiers ordered them into the truck.

The truck blew through streetlights that kept changing despite having no one to change for. Walt rocked as they turned southwards. Cold wind cut through the gaps in the canvas and he snugged his loose clothes to his body. Once, he thought he heard a gunshot; another time, a scream. The truck strolled along, weaving irregularly. Out the back, in the dimmest light he'd ever seen in downtown Manhattan, Walt saw bloody bodies in the lanes, charred shells of burnt-out cars. Despite their sluggish pace, the drive didn't last long.

To Walt, the port looked how he imagined the rest of the world would look in another fifty years: dingy and abandoned, a useless leftover of the dead. Grime marred the grout between the time-beiged tiles that covered the floor and the lower half of the walls. High-backed wooden benches lined the terminal, the wood's grain fuzzed by salt air and the asses of countless passengers. The room smelled like mold and salt and far-off sweat. The soldiers marched them up a ramp where a massive orange ferry idled alongside a palisade of sea-soaked logs. The wind ruffled Walt's hair, stinging cold, and he was glad for the two-week stubble shielding his face. Out in the bay, lights speckled the black lumps of islands.

A pair of soldiers shepherded them over to the gently rolling ferry and up the flight of stairs to its top deck. Another pair brought up the rear, posting up at either side of the staircase. The survivors fanned out, taking seats on the plastic benches, gazing silently across the dark bay. Across the two rivers that bracketed Manhattan, the towers of Jersey City and Brooklyn stood dark, pricked by sporadic lights. Boots clunked on the lower deck, just audible over the burbling grumble of the engines. Staten Island. And they'd blown up the bridges. Walt had ridden the ferry there once in college just to see the fifth borough. He'd been shocked to find suburban neighborhoods complete with lawns and wooden fences.

The engines growled up, churning water and foam. The ferry pulled off with a neck-swaying jerk. The four soldiers watched the two dozen survivors with dispassionate professionalism, rifles slung from their necks, pockets bulging with gear. Beyond the windows, the rails of the observation deck painted dim orange lines over the silhouette of Brooklyn.

Walt's heart beat so fast he was sure the soldiers would be able to count his pulse by the throb of his carotid. He breathed slowly, inhaling through the nose, exhaling between his lips. That only helped so much. He had no intention of getting hauled to Staten Island just to get locked up there, too.

He thought he might die. He had resolved to risk it. A large part of him welcomed it. But he still feared — what? The irrationality of death? Even those who thought they had all the answers, the right Reverend Frank Phillips, for instance, well, those answers made no fucking sense. If there were a heaven, which there wasn't, how could it possibly function? His heaven would be with Vanessa; he had no delusions hers would include him, at least not in any capacity greater than an awkward semi-friendship. How could the two paradises coexist? In his perfect heaven, would his Vanessa be just a specter, a perfect simulacrum, while the *real* Vanessa spent eternity in her own separate bliss, charming men at parties, chugging champagne without hangovers, her face on every cloud? Yet how could it be perfect if he knew the woman he was with wasn't the real thing? Was heaven then a series of parallel paradises, each one honed for its individual inhabitant, no more or less real than any of the others? If so, what about the alternate-Vanessa forced to inhabit *his* heaven? Wouldn't he effectively be raping her? The alternate-her wouldn't even know the real her would never share his bed. So either Vanessa would be forced to be with him, or he'd be forced to be without her. Either way, one would suffer. One wouldn't know heaven.

He knew the out: in the divine hereafter, earthbound romance would seem irrelevant, a gravel-crumb's worth of joy beside the mountain that is His Truth. That, above all else, proved it was all a sham.

Hell was more laughable yet, a ghost story meant to scare kids from stealing toy cars at the supermarket. Reincarnation was pointless because, with no knowledge of your past lives, you may as well never have lived them in the first place. Heavens, hells, rebirths—what else was there? The great crushing nothing, the permanent mute button? Too absurd to dissect. If there were nothing, you wouldn't even know it when you began to experience that nothing. Regardless, that nothing, he believed, was the truth, but—

Outside, the ferry cut east, putting more space between itself and Brooklyn as it vectored to Staten Island. He was out of time.

Walt raised his hand. "I need to go to the bathroom."

"Hold it," a soldier said.

Walt didn't really have to piss—just a bluff, a pardon to get up and walk around—but something about being denied the base right to go to the bathroom made him want to choke the soldier until vertebrae cracked free of the man's skin like ice cubes from a tray. Walt stood and sprinted for the doors to the deck. A soldier shouted behind him. He slid the door open and rushed onto the concrete platform. Sea winds buffeted his face, stealing his breath away, wetting his eyes with tears. He sprinted down the deck toward faraway Manhattan, thumping the metal floor.

A soldier spilled out the open door and leveled his rifle. "Stop right there!"

Walt laughed madly. "I didn't kill my wife!"

The soldier stepped forward. Walt thought: *I love you*. He vaulted the gut-high rail, palm slipping on the spray-damp metal, and plunged headfirst over the side. The ocean roiled above him, the liquid sky of an upturned world.

9

How did you keep upright when the ground kept sliding away beneath your feet? Two days after Raymond discovered his ostensible boss Kevin Murckle was a drug dealer, which meant Raymond himself had been unwittingly slinging, Murckle dispatched Hu to call him and Bill into his office. Raymond stuck a smile to his lips and nodded.

"I'll be right there."

It was one thing to have wanted to sell a couple ounces of weed to his friends. Murckle deceiving him into delivering bricks of God knows, coke or heroin or meth, that could get him locked up for years. It was the lie as much as the crime that bothered Raymond. Murckle could've hired any number of couriers who'd have no qualms making dropoffs for a payday. Instead, he'd turned to the desperate, exploiting them for twelve bucks an hour. Raymond walked into the office ready to resign.

From the far side of the sun-bright room, Murckle held up his palm. "You two just stick right there, why don't you." The white of his surgical mask stood out from his tanned orange skin. "These carpets are too nice for me to start upchucking blood on them."

Bill smiled tightly. "What's up?"

"I've got something here that needs to be in the city. Here isn't the city."

"My goodness."

"That's what I said. But then I thought, Hey, I've got you two. You two can take it into the city for me."

"Today?" Raymond said.

Murckle wagged a finger. "Tonight. The recipient is a night

person."

"I have plans with my wife."

"Do those plans include explaining how you got fired less than a week after you got hired?"

"That would be a crummy idea of a date."

"Then take her out tomorrow instead. Problem solved." Murckle shook his shaggy head. "See why I get the big bucks?"

He turned to his computer, tilted back his head to see through his reading glasses. Bill and Raymond shared a look and saw themselves out.

"What do you think?" Raymond murmured in the hall.

Bill rubbed the stubble on the back of his head, lips pursed. "Nighttime delivery to east LA? Can only be one thing: bibles."

"What do you think he'd do if we said no?"

"Fire us for sure. Possibly frame us. Or hire some boys off Craigslist to shove a boot up our ass."

Raymond frowned at the abstract painting down the hall, as if expecting to spot Hu's eyes blinking behind two holes in the bright splashes of color. "Maybe we should think about calling the cops."

"With my record, man? We might as well cut out the middleman and drive straight to Lompoc." Bill folded his thick arms. "Look, guys like Murckle, you don't walk out on them with a handshake and well-wishes for your future endeavors or some shit. You got to leave with enough leverage so they don't hit back."

"So we take pictures of where we're going and who's picking it up."

"For a start. I'm going to let Craig know what to do if we don't come back."

"Does he know?"

Bill's chest bounced with laughter. "You kidding? If Craig knew the details, he would kill that man. Not over the dirtiness of the deed, mind you, but because Murckle's not giving us our cut."

Raymond came back that night with the revolver and a digital camera. Hu pulled a seal-sleek black sedan up to the gates and repeated the address. Bill got in behind the wheel, grinning as he closed the door.

"What do you bet this thing's registered to somebody's grandma in Arizona?"

Raymond shook his head. "I'm so far out of my element right

now I'm expecting to see fish any minute."

The ocean roared in the dark behind them. Bill wound down the cliffside road, city lights twinkling from Malibu to Long Beach, and cut through town to the 110. The freeway was wide open as Montana, sparsely dotted with headlights. Abandoned cars gleamed from the shoulder.

"I never seen it this empty," Bill said. "Place is deader than my dachshund."

"I heard they're mobilizing the National Guard."

"What do you think? This the end times we got here?"

"During World War I, an outbreak of the flu killed like fifty million people."

"Jesus. We're talking about like the Black Death here."

"The thing about diseases is the deadly ones burn themselves out." Raymond fiddled with the camera, checking the zoom, its light levels. "A strain can't pass itself on if it kills its host too fast. AIDS used to kill people in months. Now nobody dies from it."

In the dim light of approaching headlights, Bill smiled with half his mouth. "Not here where we got money. But tell that to Africa."

He switched lanes, peeled down an offramp. Two- and three-story apartments crowded the lots. Silhouetted men crouched on stoops, metal glinting in their hands. In an Albertsons parking lot, people slept on rows of cots under plastic tarps, attended to by men in masks and white coats. While Bill idled at a light, a man pulled a windowless van into the lot, hopped out, and snapped a pair of rubber gloves past his wrists.

Bill whistled. "Be grateful you live in your little beach world, kid."

"What's going on out here?"

"If some too-big-for-its-britches flu can kill fifty million people before we put a monkey into space, why can't its great-great grandson take out a billion?"

Sirens bayed. Raymond gripped the camera in his lap. A cop car tore down the boulevard, whooshing through the intersection. The light changed and they rolled on. Chain link fences bordered weedy lots. Smashed windows gaped from storefronts, some covered by taped-down tarps. Garbage spilled from corner bins. Upstreet, a man jogged across the empty lanes.

Bill swerved around a burnt-down couch, cursing under his

breath. Debris caltropped the outer lane, toppled chairs and busted bottles and sharded plates, funneling the car to the turn lane. Ahead, a metal gate stretched across the middle of the road.

"What the hell is this?" Bill slowed. Beyond the gate, a man in a leather jacket stood with his feet apart, a rifle angled over his shoulder. "You got your piece?"

Raymond touched the bulge in his waistband. "Maybe we should turn around."

"Hang on. Stay frosty."

The car rocked to a stop. The man strode around the gate, keeping the rifle shouldered, and approached the driver's side. From five feet away, he bent at the waist and rolled his hand in the air. Bill cracked the window a couple inches.

"What's up?"

The man leaned closer. "What's your business in the neighborhood?"

"My business?" Bill cocked his head. "I got a delivery for one of your villagers, man."

"Who you going to see?"

"I'm just a pizza boy, I'm not the Godfather. I got his address."

The man glanced past the gate while Bill recited their destination. He nodded absently. "You get in and you get out. Any problems, don't expect to leave."

He strolled toward the gate. A radio crackled on his hip. He mumbled into it, eyeing the car, and swung the gate back with a rusty creak. Bill edged forward. Raymond smelled smoke. Two blocks on, a bonfire gushed flame and smoke in an empty lot to their right. Beside it, two men with white rags over their mouths swung a long, heavy bag between them, building momentum, then chucked it into the fire and stumbled back. Plastic melted away. An arm flopped between the timbers. The men walked to a pickup with its tailgate down and hauled another body off the bed.

Bill leaned forward and squinted through the tinted glass. "Should be that apartment block up there."

"You mean the one with the skull and crossbones spraypainted on the doors?"

"That's the one." Men watched from the opposite sidewalk as they pulled into the lot. Bill let the car idle, glancing front and back. "This is a dumbass plan. Just *sitting*."

"Repeat after me: twelve bucks an hour. Twelve bucks an hour."

"Take this shit for ourselves. Find some palace on a lonely Mexican hilltop until this thing goes away."

Raymond unbuckled his seatbelt. "Why haven't you left town?"

Bill shrugged his big shoulders. "Where am I going to go? At least here I know my way around."

A man walked out from behind the apartment block, hands in his jean pockets, shoulders drawn tight. Raymond sat upright. "Suppose that's him?"

"See if he responds to Murckle's Bat Signal." Bill flashed the headlights, twice short, once long. The man bobbed forward and leaned down to the window, toothpick tucked in the corner of his mouth.

"Yeah?"

"Yeah what?" Bill said.

"You my guys?"

"Guess so. Stuff's in the —"

Raymond elbowed Bill in the ribs. "He wasn't supposed to speak to us."

Across the street, a man hollered, "Don't you open that door! You keep your sickness in there!"

"What?" Bill said.

"He's supposed to go straight to the trunk," Raymond said. "That's the routine."

"We got a problem?" the man with the toothpick said.

From the apartment stoop, an old man with a crown of white hair waved his fist at a small crowd that had pulled up in the middle of the street at a safe distance from the plague-house. The man gritted his teeth and took a gingerly step toward them.

"Not another step, old man!"

"What did you say your name was?" Bill said to the man beyond the window, one hand drifting toward his waistband.

The toothpick-chewing man beat him to it. The streetlamps gleamed on the sight of his black semiauto pointed at Bill's face. "It's Mister Hand Over Your Fucking Shit."

Raymond's heart roared. Bill slowly raised his hands. "It's cool, man. Stuff's in the trunk."

"So open it before I open your skull."

"I have to reach for the button. Be cool."

Flame sparked from the street. Two men jogged toward the old man, burning bottles in hand, and slung them through the ground-floor windows. With a deep whoomp, fire blossomed inside, lighting the faces of those in the street. The man with the toothpick flinched, glancing toward the flames. Bill swept out his own pistol. The window shattered; three ear-cracking bangs roared from the gun. Raymond smelled spent gunpowder. Beyond the broken window, the man with the toothpick stumbled back, air leaving his lungs in compressive grunts, and dropped to the grimy asphalt.

From a dark window on the third floor, a gun flashed and popped. The people in the street screamed and scattered. Two retreated in a crouch, going for guns, firing back. Smoke gushed from the downstairs windows. A young couple piled out the front door dragging two young girls behind them, their free hands pressing bloody handkerchiefs to their mouths. Gunfire erupted from the far sidewalk, pummeling the family down in the doorway.

"What the *fuck*," Bill said.

"Go!" Raymond found his revolver. His hand shook too hard to aim. The car jolted backwards, tires whining. Something ripped into the rear door with a great metal clunk. "They're shooting at us!"

"Get your fucking head down."

Glass sprayed inward from the rear window. In the street, a young man in a white wifebeater went down hard, spurting blood. The car chunked over the curb, jolting Raymond's spine. Smoke clogged the street, lit by irregular flashes of gunshots, pierced by screams and sobs. Bill tore down the middle lane. Before the gate, he swung right, hunched over the wheel, hunting for an unblocked route back to the freeway. Beyond terse directions, neither of them spoke until they were back on the wide empty lanes.

"I am not one to pass judgment lightly," Bill said, knuckles clinching the wheel, "but *fuck* that."

"That was crazy. That was more East Berlin than East LA."

"I'll tell you this. Murckle's smarter than he looks. He saw the writing on the wall."

Raymond shoved the revolver back in his waistband. The cold metal stung his skin. He wanted suddenly to be away from it, to pitch it out the window. He'd been pretending at this for reasons he didn't completely understand—as if he needed to prove he could be as scary as the world was quickly becoming—but now all he wanted was to be home.

"I'm not coming in tomorrow. I'm not a guy who shoots people. I thought I could do it to protect myself, but that family on the stairs—"

"I am a man who'll shoot a man, and *none* of us are coming in tomorrow." Bill wiped sweat from his chin, glaring past the steering wheel.

Raymond leaned his elbows on the glove box. "I just need the money so bad."

"You got a family?"

"A wife. We're about to go under."

"We'll get paid. This is no time to be broke."

Raymond sat back and took a long breath. "What about you? You got a family?"

"Yeah. I got someone."

"She's lucky."

"And jealous," Bill grinned. "So don't start crying on me. Those types can smell the tears, you know."

They flew down the barren freeway. The meaning of the violence at the apartments eluded Raymond, as half-glimpsed as the dim cars left along the sides of the roads. And who decided to walk away from their cars mid-freeway? Had their drivers left them in the midst of a jam to be hauled off the road by the city? Where had all the passengers gone—the sunset? Had some of them died, coughing and puking, blood dribbling from their tear ducts, behind the wheel? There was no longer any sense that Raymond could see.

But sense was what you made it. That was the lesson of life, repeated in every tragedy, every windfall, every mystery of a long-lost city or a whale washed on the beach. He would get his money. If Mia was the only thing that mattered, the only plan that made sense was to go home to her and stay with her until things got better.

On the PCH, he could smell the sea blowing in through the empty window. Bill snaked up the steep cliffside to Murckle's estate. From inside the control room, Craig rolled open the gate, then met them at the door. One look at Bill and he cocked his big stubbly head.

"What happened out there?"

Bill glanced upstairs. "Where's Murckle?"

"Out. With Hu."

"Establishing an alibi." Bill bared his teeth. "Murckle's slinging."

Craig snorted. "He's a fucking Hollywood hack."

"You think that makes him *less* likely to be in the shit?"

Craig leaned forward, brow beetling, and sniffed Bill's shirt. "You fired a gun."

"Damn right. I'd be dead if I hadn't." In quick, specific strokes, he relayed the relevant details, starting from Raymond's trip to the Torrance parking lot, where he discovered he was couriering drugs, to their eastside delivery-turned-battle. Craig paced the room, face red as raw steak. By the end, his hands dangled by his side, still as a dog that's heard a distant bark, his back turned, ears burning, a vein squiggling on his neck.

"Still got your piece?" he said softly.

Bill nodded. "Going to need to ditch it, though. Murder weapon."

"You." Craig jammed a thick finger at Raymond. "Get up to the control room."

Raymond glanced at Bill. "What's going on?"

"Shut it off. All of it. Cameras, alarms. I want this house as dumb as a dropped baby."

"I'm about to be involved in a crime. How about you at least let me know what it is?"

Craig stepped so close Raymond could smell the musk of his skin. "Heavy burglary and vandalism, all right? Now get your fucking ass upstairs."

Raymond jogged up the cushily carpeted stairs and installed himself in the sterility of the control room. Things were happening too fast again. As fast as the looting at the grocery store, the shootout at the apartments. His fingers pounded the keyboard, shutting down cameras. The screens winked off one by one. He unplugged what he could, then wiped the keys down with the hem of his shirt and ran to the landing. In the foyer, Bill tapped his palm while Craig shook his head, skin bulging on the back of his neck.

"Cameras are down," Raymond said. "Still don't know how to shut off the alarm."

"It's okay," Bill waved. "We'll be out before they're back."

Craig strode straight for the paintings, shoes thumping tile. He yanked the frames from the walls, spraying paint and plaster, tiny nails clicking off into corners, and leaned the pieces beside the front doors. Bill hefted a bronze statue of a stylized penguin and set it in the foyer with a tile-chipping clunk. He raised his black brows at Raymond at the top of the stairs.

"Come on, kid. Steal till you can't steal no more."

On moving to the house in Redondo, Raymond had imagined he'd be able to build a fat financial cushion selling off his mom's old things. After a few weeks of cleaning, sorting, and combing the internet, he sold a box of long-limbed, creepy-eyed boudoir dolls for $100. Drunk with Mia, he'd rifled the silverware drawers, peering at the backs of his grandmother's Depression-era spoons and forks for the names of their manufacturers, grinning like a fool when he found the silver alone was worth thousands, that a set of the right sterling could hold them afloat for a good six months. The next morning, he called an antiques dealer. Scheduled a visit later in the week. Inside their living room, the dealer pursed his lips, mustache fluffing, and told him it was nothing but plate.

In the house of Kevin Murckle, Hollywood producer, drug-runner, Raymond went straight for the kitchen.

The silverware disappeared into his double-layered trash bags with an avalanche of screeching metal. He twisted the bags' necks, tied them off, walked them up front. Craig and Bill lifted the flatscreen from the wall, sweat beading their brows, and deposited it by the door. Raymond bounced upstairs, heart racing, and opened Murckle's bedroom door.

He could hear the breakers curling in the dark, their breath-like advance and retreat on the rocks below the cliff. He clicked on the light. The bed was a round red lozenge, maroon silk sheets puddled at its foot. Bamboo shades covered the windows, flanked by vents that let in the smell of salt and seaweed. In the teak dresser, Raymond found gold watches that weighed as much as his foot. Small gem ear studs. Rings of a strange deep silver. He stepped back, pockets sagging. Was it okay for him to take this just because Murckle was an asshole? Amendment: an asshole who owed him money. And had put his freedom and life at risk without informing him of those risks. Too, some unknown quantity of the man's money was earned through drug sales. Like

Raymond's dad had said, when you try to take advantage of someone, you open yourself up to be taken advantage of.

He rubbed three of the five rings off on his shirt, returned them to the drawer. Replaced all but one of the watches. His pockets felt lighter.

A man shouted from downstairs.

Craig and Bill held guns on Murckle and Hu. Around them, the foyer and front room were piled with paintings, electronics, statues, upturned cushions, toppled chairs, bunched rugs, strewn papers.

"I'll tell you what's going on here." Craig's voice echoed through the vaults, the fine glass of the chandelier. "You hired us on to watch the place, then used us to deliver coke."

Murckle laughed. "That's anything new to you two?"

Craig muscled his pistol into Murckle's face. "How about a new hole through the back of your head?"

"No, I don't think so. My stylist is out of town."

"I only want to hear two more things out of you: where's your money, and where's your stuff."

Murckle laughed again and rolled his eyes. "If I had money, you think I would hire you three?"

Hu watched, stony as the cliffs below, while Craig leveled the pistol at the assistant's face. "Give it up or he gives up the ghost."

"Go ahead," Murckle shrugged. "Would you be kind enough to shoot him in the chest instead? I always thought I'd have him stuffed."

Raymond started down the steps. "Craig—"

Craig clicked back the hammer. "Give it up, you inscrutable fuck."

Hu flinched, lips pulled back in a silent snarl. "There is a safe beneath the third stone of the path in the back yard."

"You son of a bitch," Murckle said through a disbelieving grin.

Bill pointed the gun at the ceiling. "What's the combo?"

"36-24-36," Hu said.

"I'm taking anything they steal out of your pay," Murckle said.

Craig swiveled the gun to Murckle's face, his triceps swelling like an incoming wave. "You think you can take and take and take and the money will keep you safe. You know what the best part of this is? Everyone's too busy dying to give a fuck."

Murckle's jowls sagged like a shirt in need of a wash. The crash of the gun pounded from the high, bare walls. Murckle's head snapped back, exit-blood fanning the white carpet, a limp stream gushing from the hole in front. His legs folded beneath him with a wet pop. Raymond tried to step backwards, caught his heels on the stairs, and thumped to his ass. Hu shuddered away, blinking and licking his lips. On the floor, Murckle's left hand wiggled like a shoelace being drawn across a carpet.

Hu let out a long, shaky breath. Craig turned and shot him three times in the chest.

Bill threw up his hands. "Craig!"

"What? He was Murckle's right hand here. Guilt by association."

Bill shook his head at the floor and put away his gun. "What if he was lying about the safe combo?"

"Oh. Shit." Craig wiped his nose, jerked his chin at the piles of paintings and TVs and laptops. "Well, we'll still have all that."

Bill considered the paintings. "Least it's abstract. They won't even notice the blood."

The step creaked under Raymond's descent. Craig's shiny scalp swiveled. "Where you going?"

"Home." Raymond's chest felt filled with motes of painless light. "To my wife."

Craig shook his head. "See, the problem is I can't let you do that."

"It's all right." Raymond took another step. Craig raised his pistol.

"What the hell you doing?" Bill said. "You think he was in on it, too? He's the one who tipped me off."

"I know he's fine on that. I also know he witnessed us kill three men tonight."

Raymond gave his head a tight shake. "I'm not judging."

"That's comforting, but you know who will? The *judge* you're put in front of."

Bill lifted his hands to his waist, palms down. "Craig."

Craig's eyes flickered and his jaw hardened. "I'm keeping us safe, Bill. It's all right."

"You shoot that boy, I will leave you. This is no joke."

Craig's mouth drooped open, slow as a sunset. "You kidding me?"

"I just explicitly said it wasn't a joke. Do you ever listen to me?"

His jawbone bulged the thick skin beneath his ear. "You're willing to put us at risk over this guy?"

"Murckle could have landed me in jail," Raymond said. "He almost got us killed tonight. You think I care if he's dead?"

Bill smiled with half his mouth. "I wouldn't say there's any 'if' about it."

Craig craned back his neck, teeth bared, and stuffed his gun in the back of his pants. He closed on Raymond. His stubble looked like it could scour pans. "Your word. Give it to me."

"It's yours."

"Come on, kid, convince me. Tell me you won't tell a soul. Not your wife. Not Jesus Himself if he took you out for a beer at Dodger Stadium."

Raymond raised his right hand. "No one."

Craig drew back, giving Bill a look. "This lands us in jail, I'm finding me a nice Aryan boy."

"Thanks," Raymond blurted. He stepped over Hu's silent body, smelling copper and feces. "I'm going home. Good luck."

Bill waved. Craig stared at nothing. Raymond opened the front door. Fog wisped from the ocean, slicking the rails along the porch steps. On the way to his car, Raymond had to fight to keep from running. He drove downhill at a crawl, lights blooming the fog, imagining his brakes would fail at every stop. He parked at the esplanade and took the ramp to the beach where he watched the breakers until his shoulders quit shaking.

"Where have *you* been?" Mia said when he stepped through the door. She grinned from the recliner, lit only by the pale blue light of the television. "It's past midnight."

"The boss kept me late."

"Hunting the undead? You look like you've seen a ghost."

"No," he said. "But I may have seen a few get made."

She grinned again, mistaking it for a joke. As he stood silent, she covered her elbows with her palms. "What are you talking about?"

"We just needed money so bad."

"What happened?"

He closed his eyes. "I don't want to tell you. But if I don't, that will it easier for me to make the same mistakes again."

He gave her the broad strokes—the inadvertent drug-dealing, their plan to extricate themselves, the chaos in LA and then in the mansion in Palos Verdes. Confessing felt like a breeze through his body, like the events he described had happened to someone else.

After he finished, Mia stared at her hands for several seconds. "But you didn't kill anyone?"

He shook his head hard enough to dislodge a tooth. "No. Of course not. I was just there."

"That's crazy. That's crazy, Raymond."

"Should I have done something to stop them?"

"What could you have done?"

"Gone to the police. Or quit going in to Murckle's before it got that crazy. We could have picked up and driven to Albuquerque. I could have done a million things different."

She sniffled, steepling her fingers over the soft point of her nose. "It's different when you're living it, isn't it? I think it's a lot easier to know what you should have done after it's happened."

"Yeah," he said: but wasn't that just another excuse? He felt better, though, like he always did when he spoke up, when he confronted feelings and doubts; he always felt stronger, capable of grappling any problem; if nothing else, of resolving to do better next time. And Mia, she still loved him. She stared at the TV a minute before unpausing it. A cartoon kid made a fart joke.

She glanced at Raymond. "You know what I read today about how it got its name? The Panhandler?"

"What's that?"

"It nickel-and-dimes you. Drop by drop—your blood, I mean. Once it's weakened you far enough..." She spread her hands in front of her in a gushing motion.

He told her he needed to go to bed, but he thought maybe that was how you lost yourself, too: bit by bit, by nickels and dimes, until one day you look inside and there's nothing left at all. But money, you could always earn more. If you lost what was inside, could you save it back up?

Like his long night at Murckle's, the end of the world came too fast to know what to do.

The city burned. Raymond and Mia stayed indoors, curtains drawn, and followed the news on their laptops. When that grew exhausting they watched horror movies over the Xbox with the lights turned off and the sound low enough to hear footsteps in the driveway. When they went to bed Raymond placed the revolver in the dresser and locked the bedroom door. Sirens dopplered down the PCH night and day.

Ambulances and cop cars came to their formerly quiet street as well, double parking in front of Cape Cod manors and haciendoid mansions while the paramedics gathered up the bodies and piled them in back.

Raymond's email overflowed with mass-mailed funeral notices, with scared and sentimental goodbyes from friends he hadn't seen since high school, with strange, fevered queries from total strangers. At first he read each one; later, he skimmed; later yet, he deleted them unread. Mia's parents pleaded for them to come back to Washington, but nonessential flights had been grounded to try to limit the spread of the disease. Trying to drive the thousand-plus miles struck Raymond as beyond suicidal.

Anyway, it looked like there might be hope. The power stayed on. The water stayed on. The garbage collectors missed their pickup, which Raymond was glad for; he pulled the empty juice and soda bottles from the recycling and filled them with water and stored them in the basement. He and Mia began rationing food, shifting most of their meat to the freezer and eating crumbled bacon over rice they fried in the bacon grease. On the news, reports of cures shriveled away, replaced by increasingly vague international death counts presented with little commentary and by federal advice to stay indoors, minimize contact with the infected, and to report household deaths immediately.

"I don't think it's going to get better," Mia said softly during the end credits of *A Nightmare on Elm Street 2: Freddy's Revenge.*

"I don't know, I'd say the credits are a big step up from the rest of the movie."

"Not that." She sat in the recliner with her knees to her chest, eyes bright in the TV-washed darkness, staring at the wall as if a cryptic threat were written on the dirty pink paint they'd never gotten around to redoing. "The world."

"Oh. That." He leaned forward, shoulders hunched, room tilting. "Just the world we know, right? Not the Earth itself."

She drummed her bare feet against the floor. "Yep. Still there."

"And so are we."

Mia smiled through the shadows. "Don't say that's all that matters."

"Isn't it?"

"Will life be worth living without ice cream?"

"Who says it's the end of ice cream? We'll still have cows. We'll still have snow." He stood, crossed to his laptop. "Guess we'd better start downloading survival guides before the internet disappears, huh?"

"See if there's anything about how to sew tires into coats."

He smiled. The days passed same and strange; locked in the house, he could almost pretend he was in the midst of a long weekend, happily isolated, with and wanting no one but his wife.

The moment they made plans, that illusion was shattered. They decided they would wait for the Panhandler to die down, only leaving the house to forage when they were down to a few days' food. They'd take the car, grab canned food, water, pasta, rice, and anything else that could be cooked simply over a fire or in boiling water. Longer-term, they'd find out whether any of their neighbors were still alive and in residence. Try to find walkie-talkies, as many batteries as they could carry, establish some sort of neighborhood watch. Keep the radio tuned to emergency channels. Put together a couple survival packs and be ready to move in minutes if things got worse.

The sirens thinned day by day. Within a week, they stopped altogether.

Raymond woke one night to the beeping keen of the smoke detector. He burst from bed and grabbed the revolver; but it was useless against the smoke and fire beyond the door.

10

Walt knifed feet-first into the water. An icy fist closed over his head. The cold of the water crushed him, clamping his muscles; he gasped, plastering his palm across his mouth and nose. He thrashed his feet but couldn't tell which way was up. His head throbbed. He burst from the water just before his lungs began to sear.

Behind him, the ferry's slow bulk drifted away, engines gurgling and rumbling and burbling. Walt slipped below a wave, gasped, and kicked out of his shoes. They sank unseen into the sea. Wonderful: shoeless in Manhattan. If he didn't die by drowning, he'd die of gangrenous AIDS-feet.

Paddling, he forced his shallow pants into long, regular breaths. Muscle by muscle, he willed himself to relax. He started kicking for the dark towers of the city.

Shouts carried over the water behind him. A minute later, the searchlight of a small vessel bobbed on the water just past the ferry terminal. Walt laughed bitterly. The docks of Brooklyn looked a zillion miles away. He swung right anyway, angling away from the direct line between the ferry and the boat dispatched to track him down, pacing his kicks. He'd always been a strong swimmer, taking lessons at the country club when he was five, then transitioning to a beach rat a few years later, talking his parents into driving him to the shore every weekend he could. Things changed in his late teens when a mounting dread of the creatures lurking beneath the foamy waves drove him back to their backyard pool. He hadn't been over his head in a lake, river, or ocean since he was 19.

The bay yawned beneath him, a miles-wide mouth of cold black water.

The ferry chortled into the distance. Walt swam on, salt in his mouth, limbs clumsied by the cold. His neck strained from tipping back his chin. His loose shirt billowed in the swells, caressing him like a supple, grasping hand. The scattered lights of Brooklyn waited. How far? A mile? A mile he could walk in 15 minutes. How long would it take him to swim? Half an hour? Was that another way of saying he might have as little as thirty minutes to live? Like a man out of a precognitive sci-fi story, he knew more or less the precise time he would die, but the information was totally useless. He wasn't in position to make the most of his dwindling minutes by hopping on a roller coaster or the classiest hooker in the yellow pages. He would spend his final minutes swimming, skin frozen while his muscles and lungs burned, salt dripping in his eyes, pitched by swells.

Roughly halfway to shore, he was certain he wouldn't make it. His arms felt like overcooked ramen. He couldn't catch his breath. Salt seeped down his nose into his throat, sickening and thirsting.

He kicked and stroked and swam. He swam until his arms and legs seemed like the property of another body. He swam until he couldn't think of anything besides keeping his head above the waves, of riding the inward ebb of the current, of inhaling when the water dropped away and exhaling when its icy hold clambered up his neck to his mouth.

He swam.

And with the pilings rising and falling from the water some three hundred yards away, he decided he'd come too far to die. Maybe the hypothermia would get him shivering on the docks. Maybe he'd be eaten by rats or starving survivors. But he wouldn't drown. Not with Brooklyn so close. Drowning now would only prove what he already knew: jumping from the ferry had been the stupidest idea of his life.

He kicked and paddled, nose blowing bubbles in the waves. In the moonlight, a dark, tilted slab stood on narrow wooden pilings a few feet above the water; beside it, a tall steel dock rose twenty feet above the soft waves, skeletal and pitted. He pushed for the slab. His muscles felt like ten thousand ants withering in a fire. His breath gushed out of him in ragged huffs. The pilings swung close enough to bash his brains out. He reached out, plunging beneath the water as he lifted his arms, and grabbed the slippery wood. Splinters and barnacles shredded his palms, a dull burn beside the total pain of his body. He hugged himself to the piling and rested there in the motionless cold until he found the strength to lift his arms above his head. The plank above him groaned under his weight. Arms shaking like they were ready to fall apart, he hauled himself up to the platform's lip, wormed his weight over its edge, and flopped onto a pile of loose, fish-stinking boards. He shivered there for a while.

A breeze swept goosebumps across his skin. The night wasn't that cold — if he hadn't been carrying 900 gallons of seawater in and on his skin, he could have survived in a light jacket — but he felt like he would die if he stayed there and slept. A narrow gangway led to an ocean-rotted wooden ladder up the side of the metal dock. He yanked on the rung above his head. It held. He climbed hand over hand, resting both feet on each rung before moving on. Rust clogged his nostrils. Corroded metal rods projected from the dock's rectangular frame. At the top, Walt crawled across the gappy planks to a crumbling factory. Glassless windows stared dumbly out to sea.

He walked inside to a grimy concrete platform. His shirt was wet. He needed to be not-wet. He peeled his shirt off, shivering hard enough to snap his neck. On his bare stomach, his closed knife wound was hot and pink and ticked by stitches. Walt grabbed the shirt at its hem and strained, trying to tear it in half, but his biceps quivered like a scared dog. He took the hem in his teeth and yanked. It gave way with a wet rip.

He stuck a foot inside each sleeve and knotted the sopping fabric around his ankles. They weren't good shoes. In fact, they were shit. Cold, wet shit that threatened to fall off his feet just a few steps into the dark factory. He reknotted them and shuffled on. On a dusty shelf, he found a pile of burlap sacks. The corners shredded easily. He stuck his arms through the holes and crouched down in a ball until he stopped shaking.

The front doors were held by a heavy iron chain. He swung his legs out a window and dropped down to the street.

Graffitied, rust-colored factories flanked a wide, weedy street. Walt ducked through a hole clipped through the chain link fence, scratching his ribs on a sharp wire. He straightened, gritting his teeth. A dog trotted down the street, nails clicking, tags jingling. It had been days since the world stopped working. Had the pet tasted blood yet?

Down the block, Walt opened a newspaper dispenser and stuffed his burlap shirt with wadded pages of the *Village Voice*. Metal shutters sealed the corner bodega. He swore, dropped to the gutter, and scooped his palm into the stagnant, cool water there. It tasted like dirt and sweetness and life. He allowed himself three palms full, then gargled out the last of the salt.

He walked on. Smelled decay and bad meat. A lumpy, blanketed body sprawled from the stoop of an apartment. Brown blood crusted the top step. The paint around the door handle had been scraped down to the wood. Walt lifted the burlap over his nose and untied the dead man's running shoes. He smelled death, sour and rotting and hot as a sleeping baby. When Walt pulled the second shoe free, a glistening tube of foot-skin gave way with a wet slurp.

He scrabbled back and vomited into the street.

The right shoe fit. The left, he couldn't squeeze over his heel. He tied his shirt back over his unshod foot and limped on.

He hadn't had much of a plan till then — "Don't drown or freeze to death," yes, but given that was high on everyone's daily goals, he didn't think that counted. He was somewhere on the western shore of Brooklyn. The bridge into Manhattan would be a few miles north; his apartment a couple miles further up from that. He knew there was an R-train around here somewhere. With luck, it would still be operational, and he could ride into the Village, grab his stuff out of the apartment, take another train up into the Bronx, and start the long march west. With no luck, or rather the standard of luck to which he'd become accustomed in the last few weeks, he'd have to hoof it the whole way.

He didn't know if he could handle that just now. He'd made it the few blocks from the docks on a cocktail of I-almost-died adrenaline and the need to get moving and warm. He could feel the weakness, though, the worn-out tremor of his calves and thighs. He'd need to rest soon. Somewhere warm. Somewhere with clean water.

Thin clouds skeined the sky above the silent streets. Drapes flapped from open windows. Black gum spots stained the sidewalks. The cars clung to their parking spots, motionless, forgotten. If Walt had come from another time, he might have mistaken them for cramped metal huts.

Beneath a raised highway, Walt could actually hear the traffic light click from red to green. His shirt-shoe squished across the asphalt with wet, irregular tracks. He walked past a VFW, a sporting goods store, a Greek cafe, one- and two-story storefronts with hand-lettered signs and exhaust-grayed paint. He didn't know where he was. Without the towers of Manhattan to guide him or the Citibank skyscraper rising in blue glass loneliness from the middle of Queens, he could have wandered away into Long Island.

There was a logic to New York, though, one that ran deeper than its numbered grid. Live there for a few years and every neighborhood starts to feel familiar. Walt may not have known precisely where he was going; the wrong turn, and he could easily stumble into a block of weedy lots, blank brick walls kudzued by old graffiti, and suspicious-eyed locals who looked teleported straight out of Soviet Russia. But soon enough, Walt would get where he was going. At times, the city felt like a dreaming giant. Walk through its mind for long enough, and it starts to tell you where to go.

He spotted the subway station two blocks later. The marine green rails, the black board with the bright yellow alphabet of the routes, the hole in the sidewalk to the platforms that, under normal circumstances, smelled pleasantly of laundry and unpleasantly of urine.

Now it smelled like death.

Walt waited at the top of the steps for the better part of a minute. Faint, buzzing light illuminated the grimy steps. He didn't know what he was waiting for: the rumble of a train, the crank of a turnstile, or maybe just a wise vagrant to pass by, roll his prophet-bright eyes, and warn him to move on. Finally, it came to him. A weapon. You don't descend into dark underground places without a weapon. He glanced down the street. A few spindly trees bordered by tight black iron fences. Wire trash can chained to the traffic light. Hamburger wrapper. More gum stains. Parking signs. A shuttered fried chicken joint. Out front, a green sandwich board resting on its side, white chalk lunch specials half-erased. He shuffled over, grabbed one of its legs, and yanked. He gave his three-foot club a swing, lashing the air, enjoying the hiss. Would probably break the first time it hit anything of person-level density. Still. Better than nothing.

The handrail along the stairs was greasy with humidity and the ongoing touch of thousands of passengers. Crunchy, rusty stains tracked a thick line down the center of the stairs. The stench had been gaggable at street level, but halfway down, he had to draw his burlap shirt over his nose again. It didn't help. He breathed shallowly through his mouth, burlap scratching his lips. The glass of the token booth was spiderwebbed with cracks. A fluorescent bulb buzzed, casting flickering pale light over the concrete and turnstiles. If he'd had the energy, he would have jumped them just for kicks; instead, he scuffed along through the wide-open metal-banded door to the platform.

The air was still and close and hot, so thick with stink it felt like it would coat his skin and stick inside his throat. Flies whined. He swallowed down warm bile. Something rustled in the mud and puddles along the dimly gleaming tracks. Walt raised his stick and edged out onto the platform. To his left, fat black bags mounded the platform to shoulder height.

A viscous brown puddle collected around the pile's base. The bags on the lower strata looked like proper thick body bags, but those on top were black plastic garbage sacks. Arms and bloated yellow faces protruded from the rips and holes. Brown blood smeared split lips and blackened noses. Dozens of bodies had spilled from the pile onto the tracks, a rotting landslide of the dead. A second mound rested on the opposite platform, stretching away into the darkness.

Walt backed away, gagging. He banged his hip into the metal door and collapsed on his ass. He scrabbled backwards until his palm skidded through a crusted smear of brown slime. Hastily, he wiped his hand on the tiled wall and ran up the steps to the damp, cool air of the street. He ran around a corner and slumped against an apartment block until he no longer smelled the sludge of former people.

Eight million people had populated New York City proper. Most—90%? 99?—were now dead. They'd had to store the bodies somewhere.

He didn't know when the last semblance of law had left the city, but he guessed it had been right around the same time they started stuffing the subway tunnels full of corpses. Yet as desolate as the streets looked, he knew he wasn't alone. *He'd* survived the virus. So had the dozens of survivors the military had cooped up and ferried off to Staten Island. There had to be others out there. He had no intention of spending the night anywhere but his home.

The corner bodega was locked but unshuttered. Walt bashed in the glass door with his stick. Spilled couscous gritted the floor. Jars of pickles lay smashed across an aisle, the briny juice smelling like a withered sea. The shelves had been stripped of everything but a few candy bars, some freeze-dried lunch noodles, scattered cans of off-brand soda. Walt ate a Snickers in big chewy bites and walked to the back where "I HEART NEW YORK" shirts and hoodies hung from the wall. He stripped naked and toweled down his damp crotch and thighs, then pulled a t-shirt and a hoodie over his chest. He found the extra-larges and stepped into a shirt, pulling the sleeves over his legs, then did the same with a navy blue sweatshirt, his balls dangling in the hood. From a third sweatshirt he reeled out the drawstring and belted it around the loose fabric at his waist. Dressed, if rather unfashionably, he cracked a fizzing can of soda and chugged until the last drops slid from the can's mouth. He crumpled it and dropped it on the tile. A series of belches foamed up his throat.

The dried salt still scummed his skin and hair, but he felt refreshed, capable of at least attempting the trip back. Briefly, he considered trying to steal a car, but nobody in this city would have left their keys in the ignition, and besides, on the empty streets, it would be an awful lot of attention. He'd take a bike if he found one.

He wasn't banking on that, though. He found a canvas bag behind the register and filled it with sodas and 3 Musketeers and jars of peanuts. He found a baseball bat there, too, but no guns. Just as well. All he knew about guns was they had a trigger and they went bang.

He still wasn't too jazzed about his shoes. He had something like 3000 miles of walking between himself and Los Angeles. He didn't much feel like ruining his feet before he'd left Manhattan.

The door to the four-story walkup beside the bodega was locked. Walt circled around to the side where a chain link fence walled off a small garden. He scaled the fence and dropped into the yard. A rake leaned against the back porch. He used it to unhook the fire escape and snag its lower rung. The stairs swung down with a metal creak. On the second-story landing, he smashed in the window and crouched out of sight. After a minute of silence, he cleared the jagged glass with the baseball bat and clambered inside.

After the stink of the subway, the rot inside the apartment was a nasal Sunday drive. A fat body moldered in the bed, yellow underwear clinging to its crotch. Walt opened the closet. The dead man's loafers were three sizes too big. Walt slipped on three pairs of gold-toed socks. The loafer fit.

In the kitchen, he took a paring knife and a box of matches and climbed back down to the street. He saw his first person five minutes later, a short, thin figure that scooted across the asphalt a block ahead. With the Brooklyn Bridge bobbing above the walkups, something growled from a stoop. Walt jumped back, bat in hand. A German Shepherd's eyes glinted in the gloom. Walt backed away and walked on.

He was used to a New Yorkerly rush, but he forced himself to stick to a light pace that barely upped his breathing. A door slammed and Walt hid in the shadow of a tree. Far off, a car engine purred, followed by a single gunshot. He passed a body every few blocks. Some sat upright in alcoves; two lay in the middle of the sidewalk; others rested behind car wheels or slumped against apartment windows. For the most part he didn't see them at all. He supposed most had died in their homes, or been gathered up and burned or stored in the subways. As fast as the Panhandler had flashfired through the world, it hadn't struck people dead on their feet. It had given them just enough time to hide away.

A rhythmic whapping echoed down a side street. Walt got out his knife and snuck forward. A man leaned over the hood of a car, pants around his ankles, hem of his shirt halfway down his pale, tensing buttocks. Beneath him, legs and arms lolled across the car's hood. Slapping flesh echoed from the brownstone fronts. Walt moved on.

Lacking his cell phone, he wasn't sure how long it took him to reach the base of the spidery Brooklyn Bridge. A couple hours, he guessed. Long enough for his feet to hurt. Blister on his left pinky toe, he thought. His shoe was too tight. He stopped for another candy bar, a couple handfuls of peanuts, a soda. His teeth felt fuzzy. He must remember to take a toothbrush with him.

Dead cars scattered the lanes below the footbridge. He leaned up the curving ramp. Cables webbed him in on either side. The twin gates of the bridge loomed ahead, silhouettes of skyscrapers rising behind them. He had a bad feeling. Manhattan was an island. If you controlled the bridges, you controlled Manhattan — for whatever that was worth when there was nothing left to control.

The white line dividing nonexistent bike traffic from nonexistent foot traffic carried him to the tall brick gates. Walt paused where the boardwalk split, meaning to pop off his shoes and give his feet a rub. The waves of the East River capped and rolled. Walt heard a metal click.

A thin man in a leather jacket moved sideways from the huge stone pillar. He held a black pistol. The pistol pointed at Walt's head.

"Your money."

"Does it look like I've got any money?" Walt laughed, surprising himself. "My balls are in a fucking hoodie."

The man stepped forward. A thin brown beard fuzzed his cheeks. "Nobody crosses the bridge without paying the troll."

"Trolls are supposed to live *under* bridges."

"Trolls with guns live wherever the fuck they want. Drop the bat and put up your hands."

Walt let the bat go. It clattered, wood on wood, and rolled toward the steel cables at the side of the bridge. "I'm just trying to get home here."

The man flicked his gun in a come-on motion. "Give me the bag."

"Fine. Hope you like candy bars."

Walt lobbed it at the man's feet. The man knelt down, keeping his gun trained on Walt's chest, and pawed open the plastic sacks. Silver wrappers winked in the moonlight.

"This is all you got?"

"I had to take a swim across the bay earlier tonight. That meant leaving my gold bricks at home."

The man switched his gun to his left hand, biting his lip. "Take down your pants."

"Are you fucking kidding me?"

"I said take down your pants or this bullet will take *you* down."

"Just because the world's over doesn't mean we have to turn

into a pack of rapists!"

"One more chance. Then I shoot out your knees and make you get down on them."

"No." Walt took a step. The man jerked his gun to aim between Walt's eyes. "You will take nothing from me. I'll die first." His hands shook. His heart felt divorced from his body, a crated dog hurling itself against the bars.

The thin man edged back. "I can make that happen."

"Promise me you will."

"I solemnly swear."

The tip of his trigger finger twitched. Walt ducked and bowled forward, plowing into his ribs. The gun crashed. They staggered back together, reeling over the boards. Walt jammed him into the steel cables with a hard jolt. The pistol fired again, stinging the side of his face and dazzling his ears. He wriggled his elbow against the man's neck, grabbed his belt, and toppled him over the side.

The man screamed. The gun fired a third time, the bullet whirring crazily as it ricocheted from the bridge. The man hit the road below with a thick squelch, gun flying one way, guts another. His arm raised, wavery as a puppy, then collapsed against his smashed chest.

Walt spit over the edge. To his surprise, he felt no guilt. Just a vague sense of disappointment he pinned down at once: he was still alive.

That and a tug on his side from his old stab wound. He lifted his shirts. Saw no blood. Just a warm pink line. Once his heart and breathing slowed, he walked on.

The bridge dropped him into a downtown as deserted as Brooklyn. The steeple-like crown of city hall rose above the darkness. Red X's crossed the doors of apartment buildings and hotels. On the corner, a scorched Humvee rested on its side, dead soldiers slumped behind its cracked windshield. A block further, the stench of corpses roiled from a subway entrance. He tucked his mouth below his sweatshirt hem and crossed the street. Ten minutes ago, he'd killed a man. His own life—no different than before. The event may as well have never happened. What did that mean? That if a tree chopped down another tree in the forest and no one was around to see it, the first tree didn't have to feel sorry? If emotions were created for social creatures, did they cease to exist as soon as society disappeared?

He got home without incident. Past the front door's red X, the lobby's smell of dust was a welcome change from the putrefying meat of the street. Walt stripped naked and lowered himself to the couch. From nowhere, he began to cry. Vanessa was dead, and he wanted to be.

He woke with late afternoon sunlight slashing the dust motes in front of the window. He showered and soaked his feet in saltwater and bandaged his blisters. His apartment had gone untouched; his bags of food and gear were still ready to go. He moved with a cold momentum, in no particular hurry, stiff and sore, intending to keep out of the streets until after sunset. To his bags he added two paring knives, a long meat knife, tennis shoes and sandals, three pairs of shoelaces looted from Vanessa's old shoes, a second box of Band-Aids, a printed Google map of the United States, and a metal bowl. He guessed anything metal would have great utility from here on out.

A couple shots of whiskey passed the time. He added a few more to his stomach's collection and opened the window to listen to the silent city. When the sun faded to nothing, he put on his coat and slung a backpack from each shoulder.

He descended to the building foyer, opened the front door, and stepped outside.

The humidity had him sweating three blocks later. He didn't see another living person until he reached Washington Square, where a man on a bench stirred beneath his blanket. Walt drew his knife and came up close.

"What are you doing?"

The man blinked and sat up straight, tugging his blanket around his neck. "I don't want trouble. I'm not bothering anybody."

Walt gestured at the red brick walkups lining the north of the park. "You think anyone lives there anymore? What are you doing sleeping in the park?"

The man scratched his black beard, wrinkling his forehead. "Being stupid, I suppose."

"Good luck." Walt walked on. The man waved and stood up.

Every few blocks, silhouettes stirred behind windows; a couple times an hour, shoes scraped the pavement, dark figures ducking into doorways or behind parked cars. In total, he saw evidence of a couple dozen survivors between the Village and the hotels of Midtown. No doubt more were hiding or had fled. Still, how few did that leave throughout the city—five thousand? Ten? On 53rd Street, the white walls of a tower were scorched black. Beyond, the charred rubble of a skyscraper mounded the street, wafting the faint smells of smoke and cooked meat. Walt made a quick detour, then cut north at a light jog. On the south front of Central Park, a horse lay in a stiff-legged heap, still reined to its hansom.

He leaned against a glass-faced storefront and scanned the park. Water. Arable land. Would it become a co-op farm? Or a tribal battleground, its waist-high stone walls converted into perimeters, the plaza above the lake raised into a keep? He wouldn't see it, would he? After nearly a decade, the full run of his adult life, he was leaving New York. Even if his foolish quest succeeded and later that year he found the cool Pacific washing over his ankles, he doubted he'd ever see his city again.

In one sense, that was already true. If he stayed, he'd never again stand on a subway platform and feel the warm, moist breeze of an incoming train. He'd never taste the flag-like pizza slices with their sweet marinara; the absurd, delicious fusions of curried lamb BLTs with cumin mayonnaise; the endless pots of tea, perfect for a hangover, before and after his kung pao at Suzy's. He'd never again see the sidewalks that glittered like the open sea on 3rd Avenue. Never sneak down from the nosebleed seats during a Mets game. Never get woken up by those fucking trucks banging over those fucking metal plates.

And rather than the devouring sadness of the loss of Vanessa, the sadness of this loss felt sweet. He'd had good times. He'd known a place. Now, that place was gone. For all he hadn't done— the Statue of Liberty, closed since 9/11; a Jets game, too far in Jersey—he couldn't have asked for more.

He rested on the corner of the park, listening to the wind shuffle the leaves and eating a bagel that had grown hard in the days since the army had extracted him from his home. He wished it had lox. He'd probably never taste lox again, too.

He walked through the white baroque facades of the Upper East Side, the brownstone walkups of Harlem. The bridge to the Bronx was clogged with empty cars. Walt slunk along the gnarled, bolted metal girders. His feet were sore again and so was pretty much the rest of him. The train tracks lifted from underground to elevated rails; beneath their shadows, he smelled urine and decay. No trolls this time.

Alongside the flags at the front of Yankee Stadium, a woman's body dangled from a light pole. Walt was glad he'd never had kids.

The air took on the warm, moist smell of approaching morning. Walt hurried for the George Washington Bridge, resolving to steal a watch at his next opportunity. Dawn broke across his back in the suburbs of New Jersey. Between townships, he tromped a few hundred yards into the woods, plunked down beneath a tree, and discovered he'd done something very stupid: forgotten to pack a blanket.

A blanket. A watch. And something to eat besides these damn bagels. He had a lot to learn.

He rose the next afternoon, thighs and hips and feet sore, toes and soles blistered. He shadowed the road to the outskirts of a town, then waited for darkness to sweep over the quiet green streets. The lights stayed out. On the far edge of town, the blank white walls of a Wal-Mart stood like a modern castle in the black moat of its lot. Walt clicked on his flashlight and stepped over the broken glass carpeting the entrance. He wandered past baskets of blue-fuzzed tomatoes and bins of spinach and cilantro collapsed in their own deep green juices.

In sporting goods, he found a large duffel bag and filled it with the contents of one backpack. The battery racks were bare of AAs and Cs, but he found some by the registers. He bypassed the digital watches in favor of an analog—digital didn't feel right anymore. He wandered back to the sports aisles and stuffed the duffel with a lightweight sleeping bag and a crinkly emergency blanket. He grabbed a few sleeves of Pringles, a plastic bottle of orange juice, the last bag of beef jerky in the store, and as many tins of almonds and cashews as he could fit in his backpack. On his way out of the dark store, he turned around and replaced a couple jars of peanuts with a couple rolls of toilet paper.

Walking gave him something to think about besides Vanessa. When he had to stop to rest or pop a blister, he remembered her smile, the way her nose wrinkled when she laughed, her easy elegance whether sheathed in a black dress or lounging in a pair of cutoff jean shorts. He'd always have those memories. Then why bother with this journey at all? Even if he made it to Los Angeles, what would he do then—shoot himself? Why not cut to the chase?

Every day he woke up, thought the same thoughts, packed up his camp, and walked on.

The endless townships of Jersey gave way to open, empty forests of short pines and broad-leafed oaks. Somewhere in eastern Pennsylvania, following the highway along the rolling hills, with the daytime humidity lending soft edges to the ridges and skies, he ran out of food.

He wandered off the highway into the woods, roughly paralleling the road as he searched for—well, he didn't know. Something that looked like it could sit in his belly without being violently ejected a few minutes later. That ruled out mushrooms. But walnuts, strawberries, wild carrots? Would he know a wild carrot if he saw it? He didn't think he would.

A gunshot cracked the sky, echoing among the hills. Walt shrunk down, hand scraping the rough bark of a tree. He counted down a minute before rising.

"Got to be around here somewhere," called a high, rasping voice downhill. "What do you want to do with 'em when we find 'em?"

"Leave him on the border," replied a clear baritone. "Let everybody else know to stay the hell out."

11

Smoke whispered along the ceiling. The alarm screamed from the hallway. Raymond pulled on his clothes, leaving his shoes unlaced. He threw their emergency bags in the back of the car by the time Mia dressed. Flames whipped along the roof, fed by the night breeze and by weeks without rain, pouring gray smoke into the black sky. The neighbor's house burned, too; across the street, half the block crackled and roared, spitting sparks, turning the street as bright as dusk. Raymond heard no sirens.

"What now?" Mia asked from the sidewalk.

"There's a hose around back." He dashed down the side yard, fumbling with the latch on the back gate. Hot smoke tickled his lungs. He opened the spigot far as it would go and stuck his thumb over the hose nozzle to jet water at the flames. Fired from two floors below, the spray mostly spattered the wall and the open bathroom window. What little reached the roof disappeared into the shifting wall of yellow and red.

"The whole block's on fire," Mia said from the gate. "We have to get out of here."

Raymond bared his teeth, face heated by the flames. "I can't just leave it."

"The rest of the street's being redecorated as ash. Even if you can save it with one hose, do you know how to patch a roof?"

"It can't be that hard."

"Raymond!"

He turned. Her brown face was paled by the flickering light. The hose drooped in his hand. "It was my mom's."

"And the last thing she'd want would be for you to die trying to save it." She touched his shoulder and lowered her voice, barely audible over the rumbling, snapping fires. "There are other houses out there."

He let out a long breath. Dropped the hose. Water soaked his untied shoes. "Is there anything you need inside?"

"Yeah. But I'll live without it."

Out of habit, he closed the gate behind them. "I know where we can go."

Fires burned along the hill, throwing wavering light on the clouds of smoke above the city. Raymond stopped at the red light on the PCH, frowned, looked both ways, and pulled through. Down by the esplanade, the sea air was cool and soft and damp. The city had rebuilt the sidewalks just a couple months earlier, installing upscale stone trash bins and planting cacti and flowers amidst the fresh cement. Without maintenance, how long before the upgrades washed away?

He swung south, wound his way up the cliffside road to the dark manor where he'd fled a murder, and parked outside the gates.

"What do you think?"

Mia squinted at the pillars flanking the front porch. "Is this where you were working security?"

"Pretty, isn't it?" He nodded to the high white walls and their whip-thin pines, the circular window near the top of the four-story turret, the all-glass extension to the left of the house complete with reflecting pool. "Gates, cameras, even a panic room."

"And a body in the living room."

"Wrong."

"I thought you said they killed the owner?"

"*Two* bodies in the living room."

"Damn it." She slapped her palms to her thighs. "At least we know the owner won't be coming back."

"Unless this turns out to be a zombie thing."

"Don't even joke."

Raymond scaled the wall, punched in the gate code, and pulled the car into the quiet drive. Far down the hill, a yellow blanket of fire smothered their old home. The door to their new one stood open. Raymond could smell the nauseating cloud of death from the front steps.

"Oh wow," Mia said. The bodies had bloated, blackened and reddened, become swollen-fingered things that looked like God's failed lab experiments. Rusty blood caked the carpet. The paintings, statues, and TVs were all gone, hauled off by Bill and Craig or any other looters who'd come through in the meantime. At least that made it easier to get around.

"I'll go get the cleaning stuff," Raymond grimaced. "Want to bring in our gear and find us a bedroom?"

She shook her head, black ponytail metronoming. "I'll help. We have to start getting used to the bodies sometime, right?"

He found bleach, towels, rubber gloves, trash bags, air freshener. Murckle's limp arm squished when he grabbed it, releasing a fresh bloom of old meat. Raymond fell back, gagging.

Mia nodded at the trash bags. "Maybe we should wear those ourselves."

"Wish we had some goggles. And boots."

"Or one of those power suits from *Aliens*."

They tore holes in the bottom of two bags and slid them over their heads. Static lifted strands of Mia's hair into a black halo. Sewage leaked from Murckle's clothes when they swung the body onto a layer of plastic bags. Learning from this, they pulled bags over Hu's head and legs and rolled him into another layer of black plastic. Mia crinkled her nose and fitzed copious sprays of air freshener into the high-ceilinged foyer.

"What now? Raymond said. "Fling them off the cliff?"

"No way. You want a bunch of rotting bodies below our beautiful new home? How am I supposed to eat fish when I know they might have been nibbling on these guys?"

"Could bury them if we can find a shovel. Bet Murckle's the kind of guy who hired out all his yardwork." Gloved hand covered in goo, he wiped sweat from his forehead with the back of his arm. "The lighthouse."

"You're not a sea captain. I am not living in a lighthouse."

"It's out on that big point. We drop the bodies off the cliffs there, they won't wind back up in the bay."

She nodded. "They'll make your car smell worse than it already does."

"So steal us one that doesn't offend your delicate olfactory sensibilities."

"Maybe I will. Go pop your trunk."

His grin lasted until they hauled Murckle's body out to the car. Mia's grip slipped on the steps and he let go, too. The corpse smacked the top step and thumped down to the walk.

"Hang on, will you?" he said. "These aren't the groceries."

She gave him a look, but held tight until they manhandled the body into the trunk. They dropped Hu's in beside it without any problems. Raymond peeled off his gloves and trash bag before getting behind the wheel. The road spooled along the cliffs down to the silent lighthouse. Lights pricked the shore of Malibu to the north. They dragged the bodies to the cliff's edge, spray misting their faces.

"Should we say something?" Raymond panted.

"They sounded like jerks," Mia said. "Maybe it'd be better to say nothing."

Instead, they rolled Murckle's body over the edge, then Hu's. The trash bags flapped in the wind on the way down, disappearing into darkness.

The house stunk as bad as when they'd left. Mia poured bleach over the stains, covered them in towels, and walked over them to soak up the residue. Raymond opened windows and the shuttered vents beside them. The sun rose. Clouds rolled in from the sea, gray and low. Rain spattered the windows as they went to bed.

The rains extinguished the fires. They seemed to extinguish the city, too. A few times a day, Raymond heard the crack of gunshots, the moan of engines. Once, a helicopter blatted across the sky. Besides that, everyone had disappeared.

Murckle's house didn't have much in the way of food. The Ralph's up the PCH had been hollowed out, but they came out with rice, soda, crackers, fruit juice, eggs, potatoes, green peppers, and a couple loaves of Wonder bread. They continued on to a CVS and loaded up on soap and shampoo and deodorant and razors, on floss and toothpaste and batteries, on chips and tequila and candy bars. Mia hopped the pharmacy counter and, reading off a list cobbled from the internet, bagged up antibiotics, birth control, painkillers, and cough syrup.

"We should go to Home Depot," she said.

"Oh, did you want to redo the master bathroom? I thought it looked a little cramped, too."

"They have that huge garden section. The food in the stores won't last forever."

"I'm so glad you've got a brain to match your ass."

"Be more glad I'm taking that as a compliment."

They went everywhere together. That was the deal. He carried the revolver, she carried a knife; if she was keeping guard while he gathered supplies, they switched weapons. From Home Depot they took baskets of seeds and two flat orange carts loaded with seedlings and cuttings for raspberries, bell peppers, basil, orange and lemon and avocado trees. They took seed packets of cilantro and mint and carrots. They took shovels and pots and soil, filling the car, and spent the rest of the day weeding and planting and fertilizing, sweating through the afternoon, cooled by the steady inward breeze off the bay.

They adapted faster than Raymond would have guessed possible. In a way, the Panhandler had been too big to grapple with its subtleties, had struck too fast to deny. Like their old house, the world had burned down overnight. It hadn't rotted for years while Raymond shrugged off the mold in the walls and the termites in the foundation. It was *gone*.

So what use was it to pretend otherwise? Between driving and looting and cleaning and planting, Raymond barely had five minutes at night to be saddened with thoughts about lost friends and relatives. In a strange way, his life with Mia was hardly any different than it had been for the last six months—the two of them, together, building something they meant to last. Most of the time, he was happy.

In part, it was the house. The approximate size of everywhere else he'd ever lived put together, it had stone floors, lush carpets, a four-story turret, spiral stairs with a gleaming black iron rail, a deck on the second floor and on top of the roof, and, most stirring of all, floor-to-ceiling windows facing the ceaseless sea. He'd loved how close the water had been to the house in Redondo—he could walk to the beach in five minutes if he hurried, which he usually had—but from the deck of the old house itself, he'd only been able to see thin strips of blue between the condos on the horizon. Late enough at night for the blatter of cars to fade away, if the wind and surf had been right, he'd been able to hear the breakers whomping the shore, a cacophony like titans tearing down the walls around them.

From the house on the hill in Palos Verdes, he could hear the surf in his sleep, the seals arping from the empty marina, the harbor bell clanging forlornly. If he opened a vent, he could smell the salt. If he opened a curtain, he could see the waves stretching until the Earth curved away. It was where he'd always wanted to live. Mia found him there on the back deck, just watching, all that sun on all that water. He wiped a tear.

"What's wrong?" she said. "Just too beautiful for you?"

He shook his head. "I miss baseball."

"Jesus. Seven billion people die, and you're sad because a few of them were baseball players?"

"We used to be so safe. So prosperous. We paid money to spend three hours watching men mill around on a grassy field."

"You remember what made that world possible? A handful of men who let millions starve so they could buy homes like this one."

"Yeah," he said. "But they're all dead now."

A few days after they moved in, Raymond woke and found the toilet didn't refill when he flushed. The sink spat air and a few fizzing flecks. The lights wouldn't flick on; the clock by the bedside showed a blank black face.

There was no longer anyone at the controls.

12

Walt leaned in against the trunk of the tree and reached for the knife on his hip. Downhill, boots crunched through leaves. A man chuckled. Walt didn't hear any dogs, which seemed like a stupid oversight if these yokels were at all serious about tracking down and stringing up strangers in the middle of a forest that could have been straight out of Middle Earth. If *he'd* been killing interlopers, he'd have dogs. Big baying ones that would put the fear of God in his quarry. With these fools, all he had to do was wait for them to pass by.

He smelled chlorophyll. His stomach growled. A leaf fell, clicking through the branches. He saw nothing but leaves and dirt and creeping vines. Leaf-crunching footsteps faded downhill. Walt edged out from behind the tree.

"You take one more step, better make sure you enjoy it," a voice said from the trees. "Because it will be your last."

"What are you guys?" Walt froze. "The spirits of the woods? What do you care if I'm out here?"

"Disease can't spread if everyone stays put." The man raised his voice. "Mark! Harold! We got our little bunny."

"You guys have been out here too long. The virus is done. Everyone's dead."

"You shut your mouth and keep it shut."

A bearded man with a puffy green coat and a rifle crunched up the leaf-strewn hill. He leveled his gun at Walt from ten feet away. "What do you think you're doing out here, kid?"

"Going to Los Angeles."

The man's beard ruffled in a grin. "You gonna be a movie star?"

Walt shrugged. "I'll probably have to do porn first."

The tree beside the bearded man shook and rustled. A leg jutted down from the screen of branches. A bald man with glasses swung onto a low branch, dangled his legs, and dropped to the ground.

"Just let me go," Walt said.

"No, I don't think so," the bearded man said in his high rasp. "On top of putting all our lives at risk with sickness, you been trespassing. And when there's trespassing there's stealing. You hang a thief, pretty soon the other thieves quit thieving."

"Either that or, feeling threatened, they gang up and eat you with rice and sliced ginger."

The man with the beard shook his head. "Lewis, will you tie this punk up already?"

The bald man knelt and rifled through his backpack. Cold anger slithered through Walt's veins. "Let me go or I will kill you. I'll leave your bodies in the woods where no one will know you died."

Lewis emerged with a rope and a grin and wrestled Walt's hands behind his back. Rough fiber sawed over his wrists. "You hear that, Harold? What should I tell your wife? Wait, my God! I'll be dead, too!"

Harold smiled through his beard. "You're soft, kid. Soft like mud."

As Lewis bound Walt's hands and took away the knives on his hip, a chubby teenager—Mark, presumably—hiked up between the trunks, huffing.

"What took you so long?" Harold gestured to his bags with the barrel of the rifle. "Grab his stuff."

"Who's the thief now?" Walt said.

"Just taking back what's ours."

"The only thing I have of yours is the dirt between the treads of my shoes."

Harold leaned in and slugged him in the gut with the butt of his gun. Walt doubled over, gasping, tears oozing from his eyes. Rage roared over his pain.

Lewis snugged the ropes tight, jerked his wrists. "All set."

"I'll kill your son, too." Walt nodded at Mark as the kid hoisted his bags over his round shoulders. "Right before I kill you. Not over some bullshit about apples and trees, but because it's what you deserve."

Mark's bulging chin dropped.

"Christ," Harold growled. "Let's get him back to town before I shoot him before we can hang him."

Lewis shoved Walt in the back, sending him stumbling downhill. Afternoon sunlight trickled through the colander of branches. Harold lit a cigarette, the smoke trickling back to Walt's nostrils. He wanted one. He slipped in the loose leaves. Down on the road, they shoved him into the back of a pickup truck and slung his bags in behind him.

"You too, Mark," Harold rasped. "I don't want to waste gas chasing him down if he decides to hop ship."

"I hate riding in back," Mark said. "It's so windy."

"Get your ass up there or I'll strap you to the hood instead."

Mark mashed his lips together and clambered up into the pickup bed. Walt stared at him, the folds of skin on his neck, the plump softness of his wrists. The three men piled into the front. The engine rumbled alive.

"Harold's your dad?" Walt said over the wind and the rattle of the truck on the road.

Mark nodded, eyes slitted at him. "Sure is."

"Your dad's a bad man."

"He's just trying to keep us safe."

"Do you think I'm a threat?"

He shrugged. "You said you'd kill us. I don't consider that something a civilized person would say."

Walt snorted. "Nobody's civilized when men with guns are planning to hang them."

"Well, maybe you shouldn't have broken the law."

"How the fuck was I supposed to know there *were* laws? Do you have 'No Trespassing' signs posted in the middle of nowhere? Are you doing flyer campaigns? Sailing around in a blimp with a sign saying 'STAY OUT! WE'RE CRAZY AS SHIT' flapping from the tail?" The truck jolted, clacking Walt's teeth together. "If I had a couple friends and a couple guns, I could declare it illegal to walk down the street without doing a little jig, and if you didn't jig, by God, I'd spackle the walls with your brains. I could declare—"

"Shut up!" Mark kicked his heel into Walt's shin. "You're crazy. I don't have anything to do with this. Just be quiet."

Walt stared at him across the jouncing truck bed. The sun

drifted below the hills. The wind blew cold on his skin. The truck pulled into a Shell station on the edge of town. From the blank streetlight, a body twisted from a rope, toes transcribing half a circle as they slowly rotated right to left, left to right. The truck doors creaked open. Harold popped the tailgate down and gestured at Walt with the rifle.

Walt smiled. "You want me to help you kill me?"

"All right, then." Harold handed his gun to Lewis, hopped up in the truck, grabbed Walt's bound hands, and dragged him out the back. Walt scrabbled; his ass clunked hard on the bumper. He dropped into the gravel, knees stinging. Harold yanked him to his feet. "Can you walk on your own, big boy? Or you want me to drag you around until I'm carrying the stubs of your arms?"

Walt got up. Harold jabbed the rifle into the middle of his back, marching him beneath the street light.

"Hey Lewis, get the rope?"

Lewis pushed his glasses up his nose. "What rope?"

"The one we're gonna wrap around this boy's neck, smart guy."

"I don't have a rope."

Harold planted his fists on his hips. "How the hell you going to hang a person without a rope?"

Lewis spread his palms. "How was I supposed to know we were gonna be doing any hanging? I don't walk around with water skis just in case somebody shows up with a boat and a river."

"Christ on the cross." Harold flung an arm at the gas station. "Mark, you take him in there and you watch him till we get back." He quirked his mouth at Lewis. "We're gonna need two ropes, you know. Second's for you."

"Hell," Lewis said.

"You're going to leave me alone in there with him?" Mark said.

"He's all tied up," Harold said. "What's he going to do, shoulder you to death?"

"Well what if someone else comes by?"

"Oh, for Pete's—Lewis, give him your pistol, will you? Will that keep the boogeymen away?"

Lewis patted his coat pocket. "Why don't you give him your gun?"

"Because I'm not the fool who left the rope at home." Harold folded his arms. "Get a move on. It's getting dark."

Lewis did some grumbling and handed over a silvery automatic to Mark, who held it at arm's length and thumbed the safety on and off. "Thanks, Lewis."

"We'll be back in a jiff," Harold said. "You just stay in that gas station till then."

The truck door slammed. They pulled out, spitting gravel from the tires. Mark flicked the pistol's barrel towards the dark station. "Well, come on."

"You should let me go," Walt said.

"So you can kill us?"

"I was angry. I didn't mean it."

"Come on," Mark said. "I don't want to have to shoot you."

"You don't have to shoot me." Walt started across the asphalt. "You don't have to help your dad hang me. You don't have to do anything anymore. You never did. It's just more obvious now."

Mark held the door open, then locked it behind them, staring out on the empty highway and the trees going black in the dusk. Inside, the shelves and counters stood grayly in the gloom. Mark flipped on a flashlight and set it light-up on the counter.

"Now we wait."

Walt lowered himself carefully to the floor. "Both my parents died."

"So'd my brother."

"I lost my girlfriend, too. I was going to marry her. She died in our bed. One of the first."

Mark wiped his nose, glanced out the door.

"The bed was covered in blood," Walt said. "I mean, I could have wrung out the sheets. She was all I wanted. She was so beautiful—her face wasn't striking like a model, but there was a light in it you could get lost in. When she died, I wanted to, too." He lowered his head, squinting at a stain on his jeans. "I still do. When I'm walking down the highway, I hope a BMW will zoom by and smear me across the lanes. I hope when I'm up in the hills I stumble off a cliff and crack my skull like a big pink egg. You know what I see? A hole. A great black hole in everything. My girlfriend wanted to try to make it in LA. When she died, I decided to walk there, but no matter where I go that hole's still there."

"Sounds like hanging you would be a favor."

He nodded ploddingly. "But when I think of my ghost after

this, I think he would be angry."

Mark tilted his head. "You believe in ghosts?"

"No. Or in justice or fairness or any of that. But I know I don't want to die being hanged over nothing."

Mark set the pistol on the counter with a soft metal click. "Are you hungry?"

"Let me go."

"If I do that, my dad—"

"Tell him I untied myself. That I jumped you and stole your gun. He'll blame Lewis."

Mark stared out across the empty lot. Crickets whirred in the night.

Walt strained his ears for the rumble of the truck. He gave it a couple minutes before pushing again. "Do you think I should die?"

"No."

"Then what are you doing?"

The boy grimaced. "Promise you won't hurt anyone."

Walt looked him in the eye. "I promise. I'll be long gone before they're back."

Mark circled behind Walt, knelt, tugged ropes. Fibers chafed Walt's wrists. Dusk deepened beyond the window. He'd be out his bags, all his stuff. He thought no particular thoughts, just a dull red roar that thudded in his ears like tribal drums.

Mark fussed and fiddled for minutes. Finally, the ropes fell away. Walt rubbed his wrists like any prisoner—not because they hurt, but more as if to reassure himself they were no longer bound.

"Thank you." He rose, eyes locked with Mark, and took the pistol from the counter, then two packets of peanuts from the ransacked shelves. Headlights peeped down the highway. Walt smiled. He stepped outside and pressed his back against the pumps.

Mark stood in the gloom of the doorway. "What are you doing?"

"It's too late to run."

The headlights poured over the parking lot. The truck ground to a halt. Harold cut the engine and jumped into the twilight, laughing; Lewis got out from the other side, rope in hand. Walt clicked off the safety of the pistol.

"Dad!" Mark screamed.

Harold reached into the truck. Walt rolled out from behind the pumps. He pulled the trigger, shattering glass over Harold, the crash of the shot crackling between the hills. Harold came up behind the door and fired a wild shot from the rifle. Walt strode forward, pumping shots into the door. Harold swore, wrenched open the bolt, jammed another round home. Walt fired again and the man's head snapped back. Blood gleamed black in the moonlight.

Lewis had frozen on the other side of the truck, knees bent, shoulder stooped. "Don't shoot, man. I'm unarmed."

Walt smiled and circled around the truck. "What's that in your hands?"

The man glanced down as if he'd forgotten the weight of the rope coiled in his arms. He met Walt's eyes, mouth slack. "It was Harold's idea. He just wanted to keep us safe."

With his left hand, Walt pointed to the corpse hanging from the street light. With his right, he pointed the pistol at Lewis' flannel-covered chest and squeezed off three shots.

The rope thumped the pavement. So did Lewis' body. His hands twitched on his chest, tendons so tight they looked like they'd tear through the backs of his hands. He gurgled wetly and went limp.

Mark moaned from beside the pumps. Walt whirled on him.

"You promised," Mark said.

Walt sighted down the silver weapon. His jaw clenched so hard his teeth ached. He flipped on the safety and stuck the gun in his waistband. He took the rifle from Harold's hands. His bags waited for him in the back of the truck. He slung them over his shoulders and started down the dark road.

"Where are you going?" Mark hollered. "What am *I* supposed to do?"

"Whatever you want," Walt said. "It doesn't matter now."

He walked for an hour, waiting for headlights to rush up behind him and Mark to leap out rifle in hand, but he hadn't seen another car by the time he dropped off the shoulder into the woods to eat some peanuts and unroll his sleeping bag. He felt calmer than a pond, as if he'd spent the day reading Zen or napping on the beach. He examined the pistol until he figured out how to eject the clip, then thumbed out the shells. Three left. The rifle had a catch beneath the bolt to release the magazine, which had four rounds of its own.

He didn't think seven shots would hold him all the way to LA.

Before he went to sleep, he resolved to pick up more ammo and find something that didn't require any. A big steel sword. Possibly an axe. Something that would never jam or misfire or run dry.

He smashed in the window of a house in the woods and ate cold SpaghettiOs. He added cans and a can opener to his duffel along with a bag of dried bananas, a jar of cashews, and two new knives to replace the ones the men had stolen from him. Water bottles grew dusty in the garage. He drank two, used another to shave his beard, and added five more to his backpack. With no bodies in the beds, he decided to stay there overnight.

In theory, he'd go thirty miles a day. That had been his original goal. It hadn't seemed farfetched: eight hours a day at a fairly easy pace of four miles per hour. That would leave him another eight or so hours a day to forage, rest, and nap. Los Angeles was around 2800 miles by road from New York—rounding up for diversions, call it an even 3000—thirty miles a day, a hundred days of walking. Even at a 20% margin of error to account for injuries, detours, and the like, he'd planned to enter the city limits in four months, which was amazing when you thought about it. In April, he'd been swimming in the Atlantic; by August, he could be paddling around the Pacific.

In practice, he got blisters. He got tired. Sometimes he had to spend hours combing hills for a stream and then precious minutes more gathering kindling to boil his water. Four miles per hour was doable on a flat road, but when the asphalt sloped up or he had to hike through woods and fields to avoid the towns, hampered by his swollen heels and toes, he found himself reduced to half that pace. Counting by highway mileposts, he managed ten to twenty miles a day.

Along the road, flies clouded bodies lying gape-mouthed in cars. He drank when he could find it, which was often. Dogs barked behind dark windows. Their owners made no appearance. Except, perhaps, when the dogs licked their blood-dirty muzzles.

His mind was often numb. When it wasn't, he experienced his hurt from a remove, as if he were isolated outside the fence of a park while inside a man struck a goat with a cane until it bleated and bled. And sometimes it all hit him with a shock as icy and total as when he'd jumped into the Upper Bay. Then he lost track of his own steps, mumbling to himself, ears ringing in the silence, a black stricture tightening around his neck, fingers tingling with the cold of it all. And if his thoughts were trite—indifference was universal; everyone would die some day; no one would get what they want—that was just a reflection of the world's own triteness, an existence where dogs ate their dead owners only to starve in the locked house that once kept them safe.

He walked on.

A cough laid him up in a white house in an Ohio suburb. He waited for flecks of blood to show up in his phlegm or to seep from the corners of his eyes, but after three days he felt well enough to keep moving. In a quiet parking lot, hundreds of VW Bugs had been arranged in a snaking conga line. The black, quartzlike Sears Tower thrust from the skyline miles beyond. On the plains, he saw men in chains dragging plows and hacking hoes into the soil while two men with guns watched from chairs at the end of the field. Walt ducked into a ditch on the far side of the road and crawled forward until his jeans clung to the rubbed-raw skin of his knees. An hour later, he almost went back for them, but it was getting late and he was tired.

When he passed in and out of the cities, he looted houses for canned food and dry goods; many had already been broken into, windows shattered over living rooms, kitchens littered with spilled coffee beans and moldering bread, but enough had gone untouched to keep him alive, if bored, on a diet of all the unwanted things families donated to canned food drives: beans, carrot soup, cream of mushroom. Outside the cities, he walked across dusty farms, plucking carrots from the dirt and tomatoes and soybeans from the vine. He'd picked up some ammo back in the green hills of eastern Pennsylvania—most houses he'd broken into there had a gun collection somewhere—and sometimes when he was off in the woods and fields he shot at squirrels and rabbits. Once in a while he even hit them. He ate these roasted on sticks over fires lit with lighters, inured to the greasiness of the meat and the occasional tendon or small bone missed by his clumsy butchery.

His feet grew calluses so thick he couldn't feel it when he poked them with a knife. He slept in the grass and listened to the wind. It couldn't tell him where it had been, but it seemed to carry other secrets, a wistful sadness of the constant traveler that sometimes exploded into the righteous gales of the wronged. Birds twittered, too, and screamed at each other or themselves to hear anything besides the rustling wind. He heard cars no more than once a day; once, a single-engine plane buzzed like a fly beyond a window; another time, the chug of a lawnmower blatted from somewhere in a wooded village.

During a muggy and miserably rainy summer day in Missouri, he left the road, shoes squelching, and climbed a low rise to change his socks; they wore harder when they were wet and he was down to three pairs. Rain lashed the forest canopy, thumping his hat with thick drops. He stripped off his soaked socks, rubbed his feet, drank some water.

Down the way, the road bent around the hill. Some two hundred yards along, four cars had been parked lengthwise across the lanes.

He put on clean socks and his shoes and picked up his pistol and the rifle. He left his bags beside a broad-leafed maple and crept downhill, keeping a screen of trees between himself and the road. He knelt beside a trunk and fitted his eye to the scope of the rifle. The cars were silent, empty. Beyond them, a man climbed up the road's shoulder, rifle in hand, and stared down the way Walt had come from.

Walt backed away and crept a couple hundred yards through the woods along the road, now grateful for the rain that pattered the leaves and obscured their crackles. The road wound around the hill, hiding him from the man with the gun; he cut across and circled back, peering between the dripping branches. On the slope above the cars, smoke stagnated in the soupy air. Two men sat with their backs to a tree, cigarettes in hand, rifles propped beside them.

Walt didn't need a pile of skulls to know what they were. He lined his crosshairs on a forehead, waited for his breathing to slow, and squeezed the trigger. The scope jolted as the stock shoved into his shoulder. The man's head snapped into the tree and rebounded forward. He slumped, drooping between his sprawled legs. His partner grabbed his rifle and bounced to his feet, sweeping the trees. Walt's shot took him through the right lung. As he lay gasping in the damp brown leaves, Walt aimed, waited, and shot him through the head.

Discarded wallets littered the ground beneath the tree. The men wore gold rings on most of their fingers, heavy watches on their wrists. The rain washed the blood down their bodies.

The old masters said if you met another Buddha on the road, you should kill him. All reality is an illusion: if you think you've found the incarnation of enlightenment, destroy that illusion on the spot. But the real world is real. Therefore, if you meet a bandit on the road, you should kill him. Anyone who seeks to make a bad world worse is a monster and an alien. You don't hope they'll come around for the same reason you don't hope the weeds in your garden will realize the error of their ways and convert to a life of cornhood. To lock these men up or threaten them would be no more effective than imprisoning the milkweed or shouting at the kudzu.

So the universal tendency is to entropy and chaos. Most of the universe is cold, airless, bereft. The first step to reversal is to eliminate anything aligned with prevailing universal philosophy.

Walt flung the bandits' rifles into the woods, stole their food, went back for his bags, and moved on. He slept when he was tired. He ate when he was hungry. He walked when he could. There were few days now he didn't cover twenty miles. Once he went two days without water, lips cracked and skin burning, until he left the road for the wooded hills and scouted the draws until he found a creek. For the most part, water wasn't a worry—he gorged himself when it was plentiful, rationed when it wasn't, checked any gas stations and houses and canals he found.

At times the walk grew hypnotic, the slow unspooling of a land he'd never seen. Cornfields, the morning gold of the Mississippi, and town after town after town. Other times, the outer world was lost to him. Instead he swam in a dim memory-sea of Vanessa's face, of the taste of falafel and vindaloo and pierogies with sour cream, and of his dream, now pointless, of writing literature so powerful it could lift hearts and inspire readers to right wrongs. Frequently, he walked miles with no memory of what he'd just seen.

13

"No," Mia said when she tried the shower, a clean reach of dark slate and cool tan travertine. The faucet stood silent. "*Noooooooo!*"

"I don't think we should count on that coming back any time soon."

Mia sunk to her knees, laughing ruefully. "Well, it was fun while it lasted."

"There's fog here like every day. Look how green it is compared to Redondo."

"Do we have tarps? Buckets?"

They found several of both in a shed bracketed by lemon trees in the back of the yard. They tied the tarps to the bottom of the deck, funneling the lower ends to waiting buckets. That night, stirred by the silence, Raymond wandered the house, candle in hand, and found a radio. They sat in the couch in near darkness and twiddled the dial. Static ruled the FM side from start to finish. On the AM, a garbled voice quoted scripture. A few ticks on, a sleepy-sounding kid DJed sets of electronic music. Mia got up and swung her arms in the Monkey. After sitting through a set, Raymond dialed on. A springy man's voice rose from the static.

"...steer clear, it's Bakersfield, where armed gangs are reported to be enslaving other survivors and putting them to work on the farms. As if you needed one more reason to stay out of Bakersfield! The tourism board is going to have problems this year. In the meantime, for the first time in its history, Los Angeles has stopped burning. As the I-5 remains permanently clogged, visitors are advised to arrive via foot, boat, or flying machine. This has been your daily travel report with WTFN news."

"He's going to get in trouble," Mia said. "Callsigns that start with W are reserved for stations *east* of the Rockies."

"Where's he getting his info? This could be crucial if we ever go anywhere."

"Where are we going to go? Our summer home?"

"What if I decide to steal a yacht for our anniversary?" He shrugged. "It would sure be useful to know the South Pacific's swarming with pirates before I sail you to Tahiti."

The tarps worked just well enough to keep them alive. They drove back to Home Depot, loaded the car with dozens of orange mixing buckets which they left in the yard to gather rain. At the old house in Redondo, they found a burnt-out shell with black stakes rising from the foundation. Somehow, the basement had survived; amongst ashes and old books, Raymond rooted out a camp shower to hang from the deck alongside the tarps. They gathered up loose sticks and branches and leaves and hauled them in a stolen truck to their new house, where they stashed the kindling in the shed in the back yard and used it to barbecue hot dogs and boil water for rice and potatoes and drinking.

Cilantro sprouted beside the green onions and mint. They sowed artichokes, potatoes, tomatoes. Mia suggested restricting candles to the back of the house where they couldn't be seen through the front windows. Cars crept by a couple times a week. From a sporting goods store with smashed-in display cases, they took two more pistols, a .308 with a scope, heavy boxes of ammunition, a bow and scores of arrows. They wrote lists of goods and made weekly trips to the grocers and pharmacies. After a month, most of the shops had been emptied out. Meat rotted in black piles. They listened to Josh Jones' hourly show on WTFN every night, heard about the growing colony in Portland, where hundreds of survivors policed a few square blocks from looters and gangs, and the fires that reduced Phoenix to a charred wasteland. Jones relayed theories on where the Panhandler had come from: accidentally released from the CDC labs, stolen from Russian facilities by Middle Eastern terrorists, a naturally lethal mutation of the flu.

"Remember, folks, in our brave new world, dogs are no longer man's best friend," Jones declared over the sough of the surf. "It's potatoes. An acre or two of potatoes can keep a man alive for a year. Plant 'em early and often and you won't be eating each other come winter. Have you ever tasted human meat? Much too fatty in this country. You'll die of cardiac arrest before you get the chance to die of good ol' fashioned cholera. God may not be watching, but with all those eyes, you can be sure the potatoes are."

Weeks went by in a soft blur of gardening, gathering, and jury-rigging the house for the long haul: filling the garage with extra jugs of water collected during heavy rains, testing the fireplaces for the couple weeks in winter when they'd need them, digging a proper firepit and lining it with stones taken from the walk of the home next door. After another dinner of rice and beans, Raymond crumpled his paper plate and dropped it into the firepit.

"I miss meat," he said.

"I miss ice cream."

"Let's get some meat."

Mia nodded. "Let's get some ice cream first."

"I'm serious. We should get chickens or something. We can have eggs. Grow more chickens and eat those chickens."

"Look, we can't just go 'get' chickens. We'd need things. Cages. Chicken food. It'll be work."

"And with these high-stress jobs of ours I'm sure we can't find the time." He plopped down on the couch they'd dragged out to the back porch. "There used to be this place on the PCH that was like a bulk pet store but for farm animals. I doubt anyone's looted that."

"We could use dog crates for coops." Mia frowned in thought. "So where are we going to find the chickens?"

"The Chicken Depository should have a few."

"Of course." They picked up crates and heavy bags of seed from the supply store. In their free time, they parked in the valley in the middle of the peninsula's hills and roamed the silent yards. It had been a horse-heavy community, with crossing signs posted on many of the main roads, and Raymond had hoped that some of the people who'd been willing to husband animals as big as horses would have raised some chickens as well because why not, but over two weeks of searching they only found two coops. Both were closed. Inside, mounds of feathers ruffled in a breeze of faint decay.

Once they saw a curtain swirl in a window. Another time, while they tramped up a grassy ridge, a car pulled up alongside theirs. Mia watched through the scope of her rifle as two men tried the doors, exchanged a few sentences, and drove off.

Summer arrived. They left the windows open at all hours, retiring to the shade beneath the deck during the afternoons of a week-long heat wave. As the garden wilted, they tapped the jugs in the garage to keep their food alive; when the jugs dwindled, they drove to the ocean, filled them with seawater, and boiled huge pots under tarps slanted to catch the steam. Raymond wiped ash from his hands, sweat tickling his ribs. How did plants turn water and sunshine into bananas and peppers and blueberries? It was magic. True-life alchemy. Every day, Raymond played apprentice to this sorcery, watering the spreading leaves, plucking thorny weeds. He learned the difference between a thistle sprout and a budding cilantro or basil plant.

Mia talked him into driving to a surf shop on the PCH, where they grabbed a few boards and a couple wetsuits. On days when the work was light, they walked down to the beach and taught themselves to surf. They grew tanned, lean, taut-muscled, bobbing on the breaks. Dolphins paralleled the shore, dark fins cutting the water. Pelicans tucked their wings and splooshed into the waves. They fished from the shore. Often they caught nothing. When they brought home a catch, they fried it over a fire lit with eyeglass lenses, eating the fish skin and tails along with the meat.

"Rumors have flowed from New York for weeks about a secret government vaccine," Josh Jones reported. "And isn't it just like the feds to slam the barn doors after the horses have run off? First, they made us take off our shoes in airports after a single failed shoebombing that would never be repeated. Now, they funnel their resources into a cure for something that's already killed everyone who could die from it. Do they even know how viruses work? Do they think infections just chill out when their hosts die? Wrong. Wronger than a Noah's Ark carrying two of each wrong. When the host dies, the virus dies. Oh, the Panhandler was a great virus, all right: it got everyone. Not one in a hundred was immune. But it was a very stupid virus, too. It burned down every house it could possibly live in. Now it's gone. If, God forbid, you pop a kid out into this wasteland, you can sleep easy knowing that whatever else the little tyke has to face, he won't have to worry about the Panhandler.

"Well, that's all moot now. The government hideout on Staten

Island got blowed up. Witnesses report soldiers fleeing in lifeboats and helicopters. They were not headed in the same direction. Are there other government holdouts out there somewhere? Oh, no doubt. But if you're waiting on them for salvation, well, you better be wearing comfy shoes."

"Because you've got a long walk ahead of you?" Mia said. "That doesn't really make sense."

Raymond stretched his sore legs. "I am not sure this man is a professional."

Mia kept track of days on a kitchen calendar. On August 13, on a trip to the rambling homes near the south of the hills, Raymond heard clucks and cackles from a fenced yard. Five scruffy chickens pecked beetles from the grass.

"How do we get them in the car?" he said.

Mia laughed. "We probably should have brought a sack. That's what chicken-thieves use, right? A big sack?"

"Um." Wind tousled the grass. "We'll just sort of drop them in through the sun roof, how about."

"Wow. We're going to die, aren't we?"

He hopped the fence. Chickens milled, pecking and cooing. He lined up behind a white one and leaned in for the grab. It squirted away, kicking dirt.

"I just want you to know you're being foiled by a chicken," Mia said.

"Let's see you do better."

"No, I think watching is more fun."

Another scooted away. Raymond adjusted his tactics, squatting down and leaning in as slowly as a stalking cat. Rather than striking, he just reached in and grabbed the body of a brown-feathered bird. It flapped its thick wings, yellow feet kicking, then settled down in his arms.

"Who's the king?" he said. "Now take this chicken and throw it through the roof of my car."

Mia grinned, grabbing the bird without incident, and deposited it through the sun roof. Raymond had a second waiting for her by the time she got back. They loaded up the others and turned home, birds clucking, whuffing their wings, scrabbling around the seats, stirring up a smell that was half sour and half pleasingly alive. At the house, Mia hopped out and opened the gate. He pulled into the garage.

"You definitely need a new car," Mia said.

He craned around. White liquid streaked his seats. "I look forward to killing them some day."

They transferred the birds into dog crates and carried the crates beneath the deck and scattered seeds in the crates.

"Now we just need a rooster," Mia said.

Raymond didn't know where everyone had gone or whether they'd ever see anyone else, but he didn't think he would mind. They ate eggs by the end of the week, the rich yolks sopping into their rice. Some days he didn't change out of his track pants. During the next hot spell, he and Mia didn't dress at all unless it was time to work, lying naked in the shade of the deck, her slim brown body filmed with sweat.

Once a week, they broke into a house and pulled dry goods from pantries and shelves, snagging batteries and books and clothing; they drove to movie theaters and collected cases of M&Ms and Coke and unpopped popcorn, some of which they planted to see what would happen. Beyond foraging, tending the garden, and their water-gathering, they had little work. With no insurance payments or oil changes, no junk mail to sort or Facebook to update, no jobs or dental appointments or dry cleaning, Raymond marveled at how little time it took to survive. The days stretched as broad as the ocean beyond their window. They surfed, went on walks, picnicked in the grass in the shadow of the lighthouse, fucked on the sand in the open sunlight. They napped and read and explored. One day, Mia surprised him with a carload of paints and brushes and canvases. He converted one of the empty bedrooms to a studio and started painting: the bay, the silent smokestacks of the power plant in Redondo, the misty hills of Malibu.

He was simply happy, and so was she. Find a partner. Find a piece of land and make it your own. That's all it took. This was more or less what people were trying to do pre-Panhandler, too, but that had been complicated by the pursuit of money, which was necessary to obtain all the things you couldn't do for yourself (such as, for almost every first-world citizen, grow your own food) and to support yourself into old, old age—80, 90, 100 years old!—in the midst of a world of 7 billion people, all of them seeking a plot of good land for themselves, with most of the best stuff already owned by a small fraction of humanity. No wonder life had sucked for most of them, self included. There just wasn't enough to go around. Not if a happy life required working toward watching a 59" 1080p HDTV after 27 years of retirement at age 92.

Not that returning to subsistence farming and dying at 64 would have solved all Western woes. Raymond recognized that much of what he and Mia had now was the result of the labor of millions who were no longer around to need it. He sure as hell couldn't have been able to forge himself a shovel, let alone build the batteries they used in their flashlights and radios. Some day, possibly within his lifetime, there would come a time when all these materials would be used up, leaving the next generations to relearn how to navigate by sea and extract metal from dirt. Their life by the sea would no doubt be much meaner if they had to grow enough not just to feed themselves, but to barter for all the goods they were currently lifting from the empty homes and stores.

Whatever, though. No matter how you broke down the causes and what-ifs — and he had all the time in the world to do that — he was happier than he'd ever been just gardening, surfing, fishing, foraging, and having sex. The only technological entertainment that entered the picture was listening to AM radio at night when the broadcasts were clearest and it was too dark to do anything else.

"And now," Josh Jones said, voice carrying over the wash of the surf and the warm, moist air of an early September night that would change everything all over again, "the report that will ruin whatever credibility I've built with you fine survivors of Southern California. I know you're out there. We dealt with way too many earthquakes, mudslides, floods, and fires to be done in by a silly old plague.

"To business, then. Really, I don't even know how to put this. Do I just come right out and say it? Because it's going to sound crazy. It's going to sound as if I am a crazy person, or at least a person who is capable of saying crazy things. Beautiful women — if there are any left in the world — will refuse to sleep with me. Dogs will laugh as I pass. Even the kindest of flowers will turn their heads in embarrassment. Maybe some of you out there are recording these broadcasts for posterity or because you know your kids won't be able to read. In that case, there would be a permanent record of my madness. I'll be mocked for generations."

"He sounds like he *has* gone crazy," Mia said.

"So you know what, I'm *not* going to say it. Not explicitly, anyway. I'm just going to tell you to go to your windows and look towards the ocean. It doesn't matter if you can't see the ocean because you were too dumb to move to Venice Beach after all its former residents checked out. Just go to the window, look west, and try to find a soft place to faint."

Raymond grabbed the radio and jogged upstairs, Mia on his heels, and opened the door to the deck. Above the dark bay, points of light hung in the sky on graceful strings, as if the stars had lined up and learned to dance. A great black orb drifted toward the city, blocking the stars behind it. Individual lights cruised below its mass. A low, penetrating whirr fought with the crash of the waves, a gusty roar like the wind of a semi on the highway. Against the dark background, the vessel was too high to get a good sense of scale, but its simple *presence* was enormous.

"Seen it yet?" Josh said over the radio. "Does that thing look human to you? I've seen just about everything human there is to see, and that does not look human to me."

Raymond dropped a step back. "What's he talking about?"

Mia raised her hand to her throat. "That thing is *huge*."

"First spotted in Japan a few hours ago," Josh said. "You might want to batten down the hatches."

"What the hell is going on?"

"The plague," Mia said. "It all makes sense."

II:

CONTACT

14

On Route 40 nearing Amarillo, Texas, Walt saw a mile marker for a town called Panhandle. Maybe that's why he detoured the opposite way just minutes later, angling south from the highway towards something called Greenbelt Reservoir. More likely he diverted because he already had a collapsible fishing pole and hadn't seen anything more exciting than a soaring hawk for well over a hundred miles, and if he didn't change it up soon, the boredom would do what the plague, riots, U.S. Army, and 1,500 miles of bandits and madmen couldn't: strike him dead.

The same green-yellow prairies and soft hills followed him south. He sweated lightly, then shivered as it evaporated in the cooling dusk. By nightfall, he still hadn't reached the reservoir, but a full moon lit the disused road well enough to continue. He would go on until he got tired, then camp and sleep a ways from the road; if the reservoir wasn't visible when he woke in the morning, he'd turn back and get back on track for LA.

He couldn't have planned it better. After another hour's walk through the dark grass, he crested a modest hill. Moonlight rippled on the surface of the wide, low lake. Birds cooed from shifting reeds. He descended slowly, smelling the mud of the shore and a humid sweetness he hadn't encountered since somewhere east of Oklahoma. The ground stayed hard until he reached the banks. The breeze was too soft to trouble the waters, but small ripples arose from breaching fish.

He spread out his blanket and unfolded his rod and dug out his jar of bait, ridiculous, garlic-stinking, nuclear-colored artificial marshmallowy goo that supposedly brought the fish leaping straight onto shore. He cast, somewhat poorly, then squinted at his bobber, losing it repeatedly amidst the black water.

Either the nostril-hair-withering bait lived up to its billing, however, or the fish had been screwing their fish brains out in the few months since there were no longer any humans around to catch them, because Walt landed two within twenty minutes. He cleaned them inexpertly, flinging the guts back into the water. He slipped the cleaned fish into a Ziploc bag and walked away from the green shore, flashlight in hand, to gather dry grass, twigs, and small sticks, which he tented on the bare ground and lit up with a faltering lighter. He'd shot enough small game along his walk to have picked up a couple pointed metal rods which he used to skewer and roast the fish.

He slept under the stars. That was nothing new. He slept outside more than most dogs. The constellations had grown familiar to him, though he didn't know what they were: the tiny kite, the squashed W. When he got up he ate some stale Rold Gold pretzels, then stashed the bag and pulled up a handful of cattails instead, stripping away the husk around the base and chewing up the clean, pulpy stems. Minnows flicked in the shallows, retreating when his shadow crossed them. Red-tailed blackbirds chirred from the reeds. For a while he simply wandered along the lake's edge, overturning stones, poking at waterstriders and snails with a stick, staring beneath the surface for trout. Flies buzzed disinterestedly. By noon, it was warm enough to drive him to peel off his shirt and wrap it around his forehead.

He suppressed the nagging feeling he should get back to the highway and on toward LA. A line weaved through the grass; he froze, waiting for the snake to slip away. Ahead, a short, flat spit of land projected into the lake. Weeds swayed in the shallow water between it and a minor island some thirty feet from shore. If he lived here, he could build a simple bridge to it, or find a rowboat somewhere and paddle to it at night to stay safe from animals and survivors. It was an idle thought. Still, he could swim there right now. See what there was to see. But he'd get wet. He might step on something sharp. Anyway, it was just a little circle of land. It wouldn't be any different from everything else around him.

He snorted, peeled off his clothes, stepped into some flip flops, and, otherwise naked, waded into the water. In the shallows, it was calm and warm. Slimy fronds waved around his ankles. Rocks ground underfoot. A school of minnows turned and beelined for the shore to his left. The water rose to his thighs; another step dropped him to his hips. Two more and he was forced to swim, the water warm around his shoulders and neck and frigid when his feet kicked too deep. A few feet from the island, he halted to paddle and extend his legs. Stones turned in the mud. He waded ashore and wiped the extra water from his body.

The air cooled his wet skin. He walked the perimeter to work off the water, turning over riparian stones. Worms squiggled into the mud. Nymphs waved pincers and paddled away. Waterstriders skimmed over the ripples. Red glinted from the mud. Walt poked it with a stick, dislodging a tarnished, algae-swamped Coke can.

Besides a bird's nest containing three ruffle-feathered gray chicks, the can was the most exciting thing he found. He pulled up two more cattails and ate the stems. Fish rose lazily. He swam back across and toweled and dressed.

It wasn't yet noon. He shouldered his gear and circled the lake until he found its source, a modest creek oozing between a jumble of smooth rocks. Trout as long as his palm swatted sunlight from their tails. He cast his line a few times, but the fish did little more than glance the neon bait's way. Light woods surrounded the stream, fuzzing the short hills. After a couple miles of tramping along the trickling water, he stopped to build a fire, fill a pan with water, and fish while he first boiled the water, then moved it off the fire to cool. He gazed at the hills where the creek must source. When the boiled water stopped steaming he refilled his empty bottles and started back for the lake.

He hadn't thought much in the hours since he'd been awake and moving. There'd been too much to see. Exploring the lake had reminded him of a real-life version of *The Legend of Zelda*, the last of which he'd played a couple years ago. It wasn't exactly the same, of course. The *Zelda* dungeons had a designed, logical procession to them. You went into one room to drain the water to reach the lower levels of the next room where you found the small key to unlock the door to the next room where you climbed across the vines on the walls to reach the grappling hook you needed to cross the chasm to reach the big key to open the door to the boss you defeated in order to increase your life meter and make you that much tougher for the next dungeon and the boss at *its* end.

He didn't know what the real-life equivalent of that would be. Something like searching the grounds of a nearby house to find the key to get into the garage to find the scrap wood he needed to build a raft to float to the island in the lake where he'd find the Coke can he needed to trick the baby rattlesnake at the foot of a tree to slither inside so he could climb up to the one branch suitable to make the fishing pole he'd use to catch the trout that would nourish him through the next leg of his walk. Faced with that, you'd just go smash in the window of a Big 5 instead.

But the feel of the worlds was the same. Walt was alone in the woods to explore lost lakes simply to see what was there and what he could do with it. A mundane find like snagging a trout or stumbling into a strawberry patch felt like a blessing. The discovery of a bottle of Ibuprofen or Jim Beam was an outright miracle. Even when there was nothing special to find, when the fish wouldn't bite or Busch Stadium was nothing but an empty crater of grimy seats and patchy grass, the finding of these places, the witnessing of their existence, was holy, in its way. Perhaps when he made it to LA he'd travel America's backroads, mapping lakes and rivers and woods for their own sake. He could go far south, too. Witness the old places, the temples and ruins and ziggurats enfolded in the jungles of the Yucatan.

Walt returned to the highway. He headed west. Some ways past Amarillo, tilted monuments jutted from the plain. He stepped into the wind-swept grass. Amid the dust and sunlight, cars rose from the soil at uniform angles. Each was wrapped in a skin of graffiti. Wind whisked through fenders and side mirrors. There was no sign of smoke or tilled fields in sight. Walt walked down each row of painted cars before doubling back to the highway.

He'd done a fair amount of exploring as a kid. A few blocks from his back yard, the fenced properties disappeared, replaced by forests on uneven hills and dark canyons laced with weedy trails. Squirrels barked from the boughs. Rabbits burst from the brush, kickstarting his heart. No doubt the land was owned by someone, but there were no fences. No signs. No shacks or roads or parking lots or barns. Walt didn't even know how far these backyard wilds stretched—he'd once followed the trails all the way to a two-lane highway, a walk that lasted until the sunlight gave no warmth and he worried his mom would be home from work before he returned. The sun set minutes before he slipped in the back door.

Another time, he cut west from the trails, hoping to reach an empty stretch of beach. A couple miles into his walk, he descended a slope into a shaded stand of trees. Water rested in the muddy footprints across the path. Overhead, a treehouse spread across the branches of the oak.

Walt stepped off the path. Horizontal boards were nailed across the trunk in an easy ladder. "JV + KM" had been carved inside a heart scratched into the bark. Above it was a word Walt had heard on the playground but didn't understand. Crumpled beer cans rested in the weeds.

Cold stole over Walt's stomach. This was a place where the older kids came. He knew they carried knives and drank beer. He didn't know what they'd do if they found him in the treehouse he desperately wanted to climb to. He'd be hurt and miles from home. He saw his bleeding face pushed into the mud and the treehouse took on a sudden weight of shadows and mystery, a violent unknown where strangers did bad things far from sight of their parents and police. Walt turned in a circle. The sunlight couldn't fight past the leaves. He turned and ran for home.

The Stonehenge of cars brought back whiffs of that same feeling. They had clearly been planted and painted as a whimsical gesture, as strange, stark art in the middle of an equally stark prairie. But whoever'd put them here was dead. They were now symbols whose meaning was lost, steel gravestones to an unknown intelligence.

A bend in the road eclipsed the upright cars. Days began and ended. Sometimes he didn't think of Vanessa for hours at a time.

Except when he ran low on supplies, he approached most cities by night; not all the bodies in the street were long dead. He liked the night better anyway. Late morning was the worst of all: though the heat was less than what would later cook the prairie, the heat of pre-noon was an itchy kind, a stifling closeness that woke you, dehydrated and cramped, through the walls of a tent that smelled like hot, musty plastic. It was a time for death and regret. Early afternoons were far better. He never felt bad for sleeping through their dozy warmth, and if the morning had been chilly, as they'd been back East, the sun's high strength was welcome. Late afternoon to dusk was a busy time, a time for assembling kindling, mending clothes, catching fish, and studying maps. It was productive and confident.

Sunset he didn't much care for, except after storms when the skies looked sharp and bright as shattered glass. Otherwise, they were too portentous, a bad, gusty border-time when it was too dark to work but too light to walk without fear of being spotted on open ground. Early night rarely saw harsh cold. It had an electricity to it, a charge that spurred animals and self to lean forward and cover ground. There was a foreboding to late night, when a weary brain saw looming strangers in place of mailboxes and heard lurking leopards in every shuffle of the wind, but the time made him feel like night's agent, too. Something to be feared.

But he liked the minutes before sunrise best of all. The sun wasn't yet visible, but its foremost rays were strong enough to clarify the shadows into grayscale reality. It was a vanishing time, just long enough to put away your knife and pretend you've been good all along. It was in the predawn that he most fully felt his survivordom. He felt more alone then than at 3 AM, but pleasantly so, the last witness of darkness and the first to touch the new day's dew. The time and the feeling it produced burnt off so quickly. Within minutes, the sun was up and you could forget at once there had ever been a buffer between night and day.

The miles rolled on and on, forgotten lands and leftover homes. Walt started smoking again. It passed the time. He spent entire weeks traversing the hard beauty of the grasslands, scrublands, and deserts of Oklahoma, Texas, and New Mexico. By that point, according to his maps, his trip was more than two-thirds complete. He didn't consider delaying. Instead, he perspired his way through a range of dry, yellow mountains, pausing to towel his sweat from within the shade of rest stops and under the sickly-sweet smell of pollen-swollen trees. On the far side of the pass, pines and green meadows carpeted the old stones. He knelt in the grass around a soggy-banked stream and stripped naked. Rather than the punishing, can-feel-the-UVs-cancering-my-skin burn of his trip through the desert, the day's sun felt simple and soft on his shoulders and face.

He soaped himself up, rinsed off, and sat naked on a rock to hack at his beard and hair with scissors, navigating through touch and his blurry reflection in the blade of a knife. Reasonably manicured, he lit a cigarette and sat back on the rock to dry himself in the sun.

Rocks clattered among the trees where he'd left his bags. He squinted through the sunlight. Smoke trickled from his nostrils, dry and sweet. The stream jangled among the smooth pebbles. Back near the trees, the rocks clicked again. Walt had left the guns with his bags. Stupid. Weak. He hadn't expected anyone else to be out in these wilds. Now he would pay for it. He reached for his knife.

The pines' lower branches waggled. Walt was struck with vertigo as the nearest tree appeared to lean forward. Brown-gray rods emerged above the waist-high wall of grass. Walt breathed out, smiling. Could he take down a buck with just a knife? His bare feet wouldn't be a problem. His soles were as thick as gardening gloves.

The antlers glided forward. Beneath them, what should have been a lean tan deer resolved into an angular, ridged mess of beaks, multi-jointed limbs, and hard skin the bright gray of wind-churned waves. Round, irisless eyes goggled from an oversize bulb of a head. The creature slid away from the trees on somewhere between four and eight legs—some also lifted from the ground to waver like antennae or a questing hand. It looked part crab, part squid, part dinosaur, part nothing. It paused, limbs lifted to the air, as if testing the wind.

15

"*What* makes sense?" From the deck, Raymond gestured to the huge dark wedge and its soaring strings of lights. "That thing? If I were to make a list of all the things that made sense, I would be dead before I got to the giant fucking mothership over Santa Monica Bay."

Mia hugged her elbows to her chest. "You think it's a coincidence that thing shows up just months after the plague that wiped us all out?"

"Maybe they're just passing through."

"If they want an inhabited planet, why waste soldiers and resources? Why not let a little bug do the job?"

Raymond rubbed his mouth. "If that's true, what do we do now?"

"We've got a car."

"The radio said it first showed up in Japan. We don't know if it'll stay. And unless Martha Stewart survived the Panhandler, I don't think we'll find a nicer home."

"We could die here."

"We could die anywhere. What if we go to Palm Springs and it turns out these things love high heat, golf, and pretty blue pools?"

"So we stay put," Mia said.

"We don't even know for certain they intended to attack us. Maybe this is a reverse *War of the Worlds* where they came to bring us peace and love and accidentally gave us space-AIDS instead." He gazed at the star-occluding ship rumbling toward the city. "I think we need to see what they do before we make any decisions ourselves."

"If they hover over here with one of those blue beams of death, you're getting the world's loudest I-told-you-so."

"Let's go inside. Put out the candles."

They locked the door, which Raymond found both absurd and comforting. Smoke wiggled from the snuffed candles. He and Mia stood hand-in-hand by the window and watched the ship drift to a stop over the downtown some twenty miles north. Smaller lights disgorged from the belly of the carrier and cruised over the dark buildings.

"Think one will blow up the Hollywood sign?" Mia said in something near a whisper.

"As long as they're here, I think I'd rather be where I can see them."

"When you put it like that, I think we should keep watch. Sleep in shifts."

"Let me guess," he said. "I get first watch."

"Well, it was my idea that's saving our lives here."

Raymond sat in darkness before the bedroom window overlooking the ocean. Mia slept soundlessly behind him. The massive wedge of the ship relocated somewhere around Venice Beach, hovering hundreds of feet in the air. Small vessels came and went in ones and twos, drawing slow loops around the cities or disappearing beyond the hills that ringed the valley. No more than six or eight of the smaller ships patrolled at any one time; sometimes as few as one streaked above the black streets. They left dark contrails, rumbling lowly, banking and climbing like standard jets. If they were capable of UFO-style zigzags or sudden bursts of eyeball-shattering speed, they weren't showing off.

"How's the Earth doing?" Mia slurred when he shook her awake five hours later. "Still existing?"

"Just a lot of buzzing around. Whatever they're here for, it's not to entertain us."

With Mia watching out, he fell asleep easily. A sky-shredding shriek woke him at dawn. A silvery plane streaked in over the water to the south.

"That's one of ours," he said.

"No shit. An F-16."

"Does this mean we still have a military?"

Two jet-sized triangles swung away from the giant black body of the carrier and raced forward on thin white contrails. As they closed, the alien fighters let loose a volley of compact rockets that tumbled away and then leapt forward as if stung. The F-16 pulled up hard, ejecting sun-bright flares that fell away on jagged columns of smoke. The rockets followed straight through the clouds. The jet curled off into a tightening corkscrew; as if they were tied to it on strings, the trailing rockets spun with it. Two collided in a white bloom that absorbed the missiles around it. Raymond wiped his eyes, blinking at the afterimage.

The alien vessels dovetailed apart. The F-16 slowed and swooped in behind the one that had vectored left. Missiles lanced forward. The alien craft banked hard, then burst in a shower of hot splinters. The boom reached Raymond a few seconds later, a deep thunder in his chest.

The surviving triangle swung in behind the F-16 as smoothly as if they'd choreographed it.

"They set him up," Mia said. "They were willing to lose one to take him down."

Electric blue light pulsed between the fighters. The F-16 crumbled. Flaming metal tumbled into the Pacific. Raymond didn't see a parachute. "Is that it?"

"Why send in a single plane? Feeling out their capabilities? Or did we just watch Maverick get blown up?"

"Identifying F-16s, talking tactics — what are you, Sun Tzu?"

"I used to paint miniatures when I was a kid. My uncle liked wargames."

"Weird." The motionless carrier threw its shadow over the beaches. Another blue triangle left a port on the carrier's smooth side and paired up with the inbound survivor. They curved over the bay, then turned south, shooting over the house in a window-rattling pass.

"So they're hostile," she said.

"Or defending themselves."

"They fired first. They killed us with a plague and then showed up with a battle fleet. You want to wait until they kick in the front door with their tentacles before you admit they're not here to make friends?"

He rubbed his stubble. "Yeah. All right. It doesn't look good."

The lines melted from her forehead. "So what do we do?"

"If we're going to leave, we need to be ready. That means putting together food. Water. Maybe some gas. And finding out about the highways. I don't want to peel out of here just to run into a permanent traffic jam on the 405."

"You really should have been an accountant."

"What kind of a thing is that to say to the man you love?"

"I'm just saying you're logistically-minded." She smiled and leaned in to kiss him. "Where should we start, General?"

The two fighters swooped in from the south and beelined for the carrier, startling him. "I don't really feel like driving around in broad daylight. Not when they've got a Death Star parked over Santa Monica."

"What, you don't think a car can outrun an alien jet fighter?" Mia flicked her thumbnail against her teeth. "So what if we forage the neighborhood on foot? We've got a lot of walking-distance homes we haven't been to yet. Then to check the highways..."

"What?"

"Just considering whether it's completely insane to grab a couple bicycles and check out the roads via velocipede."

He laughed huskily. "You're seriously proposing we run a bicycle ninja mission down the LA freeways while the Alpha Centauri Air Force buzzes the skies."

She lifted her palms up, then slapped her hips. "Don't think that *I* don't think this is incredibly, incredibly weird. It's just a whole lot less weird than it would have been six months ago."

He couldn't argue with that. Aside from a fat-bellied squarish vessel that disappeared into the rises of Beverly Hills that afternoon, the alien ship didn't do much more besides hang there exactly the way a brick wouldn't. That night, he and Mia dressed in black and jogged from the house carrying the revolver, a crow bar, a duffel bag, a siphon, and three red plastic gas jugs. Mia smashed passenger windows, popped gas caps. Raymond sucked gas into the jugs, wiping his tongue on his sleeve.

"We should have brought some god damn Scope," he whispered, tongue stinging.

"Keep sucking."

Dizzy, he sat on the curb while the gas drizzled into the jug. A point of light tracked across the misty skies. It had been a strange run: the dwindling money that had threatened to ruin their life together; the plague that had threatened to end their lives together; the gardening and foraging that had brought them closer than ever in this new silent world; now an alien invasion that threatened to—? That, he couldn't say. Maybe they were here to finish their eradication of humanity and he and Mia would die together in a flash of heat and light. Maybe they would round the survivors up and restrict them to subsistence on reservations. Or maybe, so long as the survivors left Earth's new arrivals alone, humans would be able to run free in the jungles, the mountains, the icecaps, whatever scraps of land the aliens didn't want.

Maybe it was just the gasoline talking, but Raymond was amazed by the idea that, barring complete eradication, people *somewhere* would adapt and survive. Despite the horror of the past and the chaos of the present, life went on. Cosmically, life in some form would always exist—if there were two sapient species, there were likely to be hundreds, possibly millions, condensing from primal sludge on far-flung worlds into beings capable of crossing the lightyears of vacuum that separated them from the others. Even if he was soon to be vaporized by one of these neighbors, he found it strangely comforting to know that uncounted species would continue to exist all across the universe until the day the last star burned down to a cold cinder.

He filled both jugs from a single Ford Excursion. At last there was some use for the things.

He waddled down the street after Mia, gas sloshing. In a white-trimmed Cape Cod manor, they found a basement pantry filled with cases of Sprite, bottled water, and modular transparent drawers of Wheat Thins, Ritz, orange peanut butter crackers, fruit snacks, granola bars, trail mix, dried fruit, snack-size Snickers, and bags of pretzels and Ruffles and Sun Chips and beef jerky.

"Mormons," Raymond said.

"What? How can you tell?"

"They're supposed to keep a year's worth of food in the house to help wait out disasters. Guess there wasn't much Jesus could do about an alien virus."

Mia tucked a black strand behind her ear. "Well, they can rest happy knowing they're still providing Christian charity. Start grabbing."

He managed to wedge a plastic drawer under each jug-laden arm and headed for home, sweating through the humid, neutral night. There, they stashed the goods in their garaged car and stood panting in the candlelit gloom.

"This'll take all night," she said. "We should just take the car over and load it up."

Raymond rolled his lips together. "I don't know."

"Because it'll waste gas? It's three blocks from here. We'll be fine."

"Not if an alien fighter jet decides we're stealing the food they rightfully earned via plague."

"You're no fun," she smiled.

"We'll compromise. I think there's a wheelbarrow in the shed."

The tire sagged, but the thing rolled. They bumped it up the steps to the foyer of the Cape Cod mansion and piled it high with drawers of food and cases of water. As they started down the sidewalk, a rising car engine blatted from around the bend.

"Get off the road," Raymond said.

"We already are."

"Leave the food." He grabbed her hand, rushed through the open iron gate of a white three-story Tuscan, and knelt behind a square stone pillar, dew soaking the knees of his jeans. A hollow keen skirled beneath the roar of the engine. Headlights bloomed in the fog up the street. A black Porsche swerved around the bend, slick with mist, and tore past their hiding spot, tail lights waggling as it skidded on the shoulder. Its engine faded.

"Yeesh," Mia murmured. "If you're going to drive drunk, you should do it in something less awesome than a Porsche."

She began to rise. Raymond grabbed her belt and forced her back down. "Normally when somebody's fleeing, it's *from* something."

The second half of his sentence was overwhelmed by a rising keen from up the street. A pale blue light burst through the fog some twenty feet above the ground. Raymond squinted in the glare. A truck-sized black oblong cut through the air, its edges ridged like a scallop. It hurtled past on a blast of wind and disappeared around the bend toward their house.

"Holy *shit*," Mia breathed.

"Let's wait a minute. It might not be the only one."

"Did that thing spook somebody into jumping into their car and taking off? Or did it see the car moving and fly in to run it down?"

Far down the hill, the night rang with the bang of high-velocity metal instantly becoming no-velocity metal. Screams filtered through the fog.

Raymond waited through a minute of silence, then rolled the wheelbarrow down to the house and pulled the garage door shut behind them. They lit a single candle apiece that night, whispering to each other in the shadows. The ship hung over the bay.

When they woke, it was gone.

They watched the skies from the window, then ventured onto the deck. With no sign of the carrier, its fighters, or the scout that had run down the driver of the Porsche, Mia watered the garden and fed the chickens while Raymond went inside for the radio and left it on the deck tuned to Josh Jones' station. It fuzzed and hissed. Raymond picked spinach and rinsed it in a bucket under the deck. He mixed pepper, vinegar, and crushed almonds and brought Mia a salad they ate in the sun.

"Maybe they don't like 72-degree days," she said.

"Or hovering-mothership ocean views."

"Where does that put us now?"

Raymond could only shake his head. His hands were sun-browned, rough-palmed. "They're crazy aliens. If we try to figure out what they're up to, we're just guessing, aren't we? For all we know, they didn't leave, they just flew a few miles up to drop a really big rock on us. The only thing we can do here is plan for the worst."

"That they'll come back, disintegrate me, amputate your limbs, and let their alien women repeatedly have their way with you."

"When does it start getting bad?"

She spritzed him with her spray bottle. "So we check the highways. See if they're traversable. Otherwise, business as usual."

"We'll check tomorrow night. Make sure they're really gone first."

Rather than surfing or going for a walk, he watched the ocean from their back yard, aware that if they had to drive away or the aliens came back with alien-nukes, he might never see it again. White foam lined the shore. Breakers rose and slapped the sand. Pelicans and gulls rode the winds and bobbed along the surface. The sea was both larger and smaller than his mental image of "the sea," with finite edges at Malibu on the north, the rocks beneath their house on the south, and the sudden straight-line terminus on the western horizon, which looked no further away than the green shores of Malibu. Yet he knew it stretched on and on and on, thousands of miles of unseen water, speckled here and there by islands you'd miss if you didn't already know they were there, so huge he could only see a bay-sized fraction of it at a time, and only then its wind-chopped surface. How long would he have to stare at the bay before he saw every drop of water circling through the Pacific?

"Well, hi out there, fellow incredulates," Josh began at 9 PM on the nose. "So the big news, in case you just awoke from a hospital coma, is an alien fleet rolled in, shot a few people, snatched a few others, and then left for more probeable pastures. Sources say they lit out for Las Vegas, but as we haven't heard from them in hours, I offer this as nothing more than rumor. Go nuts.

"Down to brass tacks and hard facts. If the military's out there preparing its inspiring resistance, all we've seen was a single F-16, possibly piloted by a madman, who managed to blow up one enemy fighter before being swallowed by the mighty Pacific. The good news: the bad guys don't have force fields or invincible polycarbon armor. They can be destroyed. Hypothetically, we can fight back.

"The bad news: they *do* have lasers. Or zappy light-things that resemble what we think of as lasers. They've got a big ship, too. A really, really, inconceivably huge ship. The silver lining is that as far as we know, there's just the one of these Imperial Star Destroyers. Which may be why it had to stroll off to Las Vegas itself to see what there was to see.

"Oh, right, and the other bad news: they're probably here to kick our ass. Hope some of you boys with crop dusters in the barns also have a few missiles stashed away in your grain silos."

Mia stood. "Let's go."

"What?"

"Josh said the ship's in Las Vegas. That means we can check out the freeways."

"Why can't that man just give us a damn traffic report?"

They drove down the hill in the black late-model Charger they'd stolen from one of the lots down in Torrance after deciding the increased fuel economy of a Civic hybrid wouldn't be worth the possible risk of not being able to outrun Mad Max-style attackers. Mia rolled down the window and leaned out her head to scan the skies. On the PCH, two men scattered in the headlights, bags bouncing heavily from their shoulders. After a few miles, the sprawling lanes of the 110 snarled with abandoned cars; at the edges of the Charger's headlights, a burnt-out trailer stretched across the road, packed in by the charred shells of sedans and SUVs. Raymond rolled to a stop, engine idling.

"That doesn't bode well for the I-5."

Mia nodded, frowning. "I don't suppose you ever took a whole lot of flying lessons you never told me about."

He threw it in reverse, did a head check, laughed to himself, then flipped around and, with a strange little thrill, drove the wrong way back to the onramp. Cool sea air flowed through Mia's window. The 405 stayed drivable all the way to Santa Monica, where one of its banking turns became tangled with shorn metal and fire-bubbled paint. Raymond clucked his tongue and got out on foot. His flashlight swept over bones and sun-tautened skin. The pileup was only a couple cars deep, but beyond, stalled and silent cars clogged the road like shiny boulders.

"Seen enough?" he said.

"The PCH runs north for hundreds of miles."

"You want to check every one of them?"

"Just the ones that lead out of here. If they're serious about wiping us out, the city will be the worst place we could be."

He backtracked down the highway and swung into Santa Monica, which he knew about as well as Bangkok. Figuring the streets he'd heard about before he moved to the area must go somewhere, he drove in widening circles until he intercepted Wilshire, then cut west among sand-colored apartment complexes, pink storefronts, and palm-lined sidewalks. A white sheet painted "HELP" flapped from the roof of a department store. He jagged the car around a wreck, glass crunching under the tires. On the corner, a man in a fur coat stared them down, ambling to the middle of the street as they drove past.

Wilshire flowed into the PCH. Dark cars angled the shoulder, but the road stayed navigable as the city sprawl cleared out into a solid row of beachside houses to one side and yellow hills to the other. He drove for three miles, headlights splashing the pavement, engine whirring through the emptiness.

"Pull over," Mia said.

He slowed, guided the car into the crunching gravel. "What do you think?"

"We could go right now. Just keep driving."

"Where would we go?"

"Somewhere with a stream. Or a lake. These days every house in the world is a mountain cabin without the mountain. Why not find a real one?"

He bit the skin inside his lower lip. "We'd lose the garden."

"Damn! If only plants could grow."

"Maybe all the sun and sea breezes have wiped your mind, but it's September. In places like mountains, that means it's fall. And you know what comes after fall?"

"Bourbon and eggnog?"

"Where are we going to find that? Or anything else we need?"

She cocked her head. "With all that food we found, I don't think we'll have a problem making it through a couple seasons."

"What about winter coats? Snow gloves? Axes or hunting rifles or great big piles of wood to burn when it gets cold?"

"So we'll stop by the first sporting goods store we see. We put our house together in like four months. Do you really think it would be that hard?"

He stared at the blank dashboard. "I like it here. I don't want to leave."

"Even if that means getting vaporized by aliens?"

"What happens when they come to the mountains? Do we go to the desert? The South Pole? The moon?" He ran his hands through his hair, clasping them behind his head. "How long do we run? Are we happy? If we're not, how do we find a place where we will be? I think if you find a place where you're happy, then you have to take risks to preserve it. Staying in the city's a risk. But so is lighting out for the mountains in the middle of the night when we don't know what we'll find there any more than we know what the invaders are going to do from here."

A slow smile lit her brown eyes. "I didn't know you felt that strongly."

"Do you really want to go?"

"I think we'd be safer. But I don't think we'd be happier."

He started the Charger back up and nosed his way across the median to the opposite lanes. Wet, cool air swirled through the windows. He would have missed that moist-salt smell, would wake every morning to the confused sense that something had been lost.

"Stop the car?"

He braced himself for another change of mind. Instead, she

asked him to get out, then took him by the hand and led him to the moonlight-lined beach, where she laid their clothes on the sand as a blanket, then unzipped his pants and straddled him. On the way home, he drove shirtless and shoeless.

"Apparently sin truly is reserved for humanity," Josh Jones reported a few days later, "because the aliens buzzed out of Vegas in just two days. Grapevine hears tell of men on the ground. Alien men, that is, or possibly women, or men-women, or cloaca-sporting lobster-monsters who find our human penises and vaginas so sickening they crossed the inky void just to stamp us out. In any event, these things are said to have lots of spindly arms and legs, with skin as hard and crusty as old sourdough. Supposedly they spent a lot of time going into hotels and coming out with corpses. Not mummy-bones, either—big wet fresh ones. Like going down to the farmer's market, you know, except instead of coming home with ripe red tomatoes, it's dead bodies. These ground troops have been seen in Vegas after the ship set sail.

"And speaking of sourdough, the mother ship was last reported lumbering west for San Francisco. Stay safe, friends."

Raymond and Mia resumed gardening and water-gathering and foraging. In concession, he took a trip to the REI, where they went in with flashlights and loaded up the car with parkas, sleeping bags, axes of various sizes, lanterns and replacement lights, freshwater fishing tackle with its bright pink PowerBait, jack knives and hunting knives and scaling knives. Every single rifle was gone. Brass littered the floor, spinning away over the hard white tile and brown stains of dried blood.

Josh's reports grew sparse. More house-to-house alien raids in San Francisco, then up to Portland, Seattle, and Vancouver, where fleeing motorists were destroyed by scalloped black fighters with platoons of alien infantry remaining behind to scour the cities. For several days, Josh had no news of the aliens at all: the carrier had disappeared somewhere over Canada.

Raymond woke two weeks after the carrier's departure to see it hovering above the bay. Lumbering, beetle-like vessels disappeared into the city while the wedge-shaped blue fighters circled overhead. After striking out at two more sports stores, Mia had ventured back to the former house of the Mormons. She'd come back with a pair of scoped rifles, a .45 and a 9mm pistol, and green cardboard ammo boxes that felt far too heavy for their size.

The morning of the aliens' return, she stuck the .45 in her belt and handed him the 9mm.

"Don't leave home without it."

That night gunfire crackled from the beach cities below them. Unseen ships keened below the cliffs. Fire blossomed a short ways inland, thick gray smoke angling into the sky. It burnt out by morning.

There wasn't much to do but watch from the windows. They held hands in silence. With warm afternoon sunlight banking off the waves, one of the heavy ships detached from the carrier and, flanked by two fighters, flew straight for the hills.

Mia pulled him away from the window into the lushly carpeted hallway, where they flattened their backs against the hall. The bass oscillation of an engine approached, climaxed, began to fade, then abruptly ceased.

"What's the plan?" Raymond said.

"Nothing to do but sit tight, is there? Unless you'd rather get blown up in the car."

"No. We can't afford the insurance bump."

He locked the door and drew the curtains. Hours passed with little more than the deep warble of the heavy vessel and the high whines of the fighters. Once, they heard the dry pop of pistols. With the sun hanging just above the horizon, an engine growled nearby. The staccato clatter of steps struck the asphalt.

Raymond parted the curtains. Up the street, alien foot troops fanned out from a boxy covered vehicle. Metal glinted in clawed limbs. While three took up position behind it, one of the beings strode to the picture window of the house two doors down and bashed the butt of a long rifle through the glass. Another team of four broke toward the neighboring house; behind them, four more trampled the overgrown flowers of the front yard on the way to their gates.

"Oh Jesus," Mia said.

Raymond's head buzzed numbly. "The panic room. Now."

He ran to the back bedroom and the painted steel door set into its wall. The handle wouldn't budge. From outside, metal groaned and clanged against the pavement.

"It's stuck," he said.

"Let me try." Mia bumped him out of the way and pulled with all her strength. With a frustrated shriek, she leaned on the brushed steel handle and rammed her shoulder into the door. "Did you lock this?"

"How would I lock it from the outside?"

"How should I know? I grew up in a trailer, not this ritzy mansion bullshit—" Downstairs, glass cascaded across the stone floors. A Y-shaped vein pulsed on Mia's forehead. She grabbed his hand. "Come on."

She raced for the back deck, closing the door behind them. A soft breeze countered the sunlight washing Raymond's skin. Below the deck, the yard terminated in a waist-high stone fence, cliffs and sea below. He bared his teeth. Even if they could leap clear of the rocks, the water would be no more than a few feet deep.

"Boost me up," Mia whispered. He goggled at her; she slapped him and cradled her hands in example. "Snap out of it and give me a boost!"

He laced his fingers together. She stepped in, steadying herself against the wall as he lifted her, forearms straining, her bare foot secure in his hands. She grabbed the lip of the roof and wriggled her chest and hips up over the edge as he pushed her feet up from below. She turned around and dangled her arm down.

Raymond crouched and jumped. Stucco scraped his fingers. His knuckles strained, supporting his weight as he kicked his legs against the wall. Mia clamped his forearms and heaved. The roof's edge sheared skin from his chest. He got a knee up and rolled on his back, panting. Mia pressed her body to the shallow pitch and army-crawled away from the edge. Muffled footsteps filtered from below.

16

Grass tickled the creature's cloth-wrapped abdomen. A flock of sparrows swooped over the creek. The creature spun, two noodly limbs shooting upright and tracking the vector of the birds' cheeping flight. Walt eased himself off the rock into the cold water. Slick rocks clacked under his soles. He crouched low, submerging himself until the rushing water soaked the back of his head, face upturned to clear his nose. He steadied himself against the rock with one hand and brought his knife to just below the surface.

Grass threshed. A three-fingered, stick-like limb parted the green wall at the bank of the creek. The creature glided forward, limbs splashing in the shallows. Rocks clonked beneath it. Walt's fingers tightened around the knife. The thing tapped the rock he'd sunned on with two brown-gray arms, planted them firm, and leaned its disclike body and bulbous, octopine head over the gurgling water. Walt took a good long look at the ridges of its neck, a supple thing that broadened to a fat stock where it connected to the body, which was shaped like one of the water-smoothed pebbles under his feet. A collar of fine fabric wrapped the base of its neck, flowing into a skintight blue wrap of its body with long holes on both sides to sleeve its several arms. It craned forward, slowly turning the two rubbery arms through a wide arc. The creek jangled.

The arms withdrew. The creature retreated from the rock into the grass and padded back for the clump of trees, disappearing from sight. Walt slipped from the cold water, sun beating his skin, until he could see the back of the creature's head. An instant after he'd risen, the being whirled and tore straight for him.

Walt shouted and warded one arm in front of him, knife hand close to his chest. The thing turned sideways as it closed, sticking a bushel of slapping arms and kicking legs between Walt's body and its head and two noodly arms. A leg struck Walt's shin. He grimaced and slashed at an incoming arm, flaying the tough skin down to its bone. Yellow fluid spattered the grass. The creature made no noise beyond the tapping of its feet on the stones. It picked up a rock in a pair of narrow claws and swung for Walt's head. He ducked, jabbing at its nearest leg. The thing reared up and bulled forward, knocking them both into the water.

The current pulled him downstream. The thing planted its thinner legs between submerged stones, poling along while its flatter tentacles threshed water. It closed on him in moments. He'd kept a death grip on the knife, which he waved in tight, fast flicks at a probing arm. A claw snaked in from the side and grabbed his wrist. Pain circled his arm as it crushed his tendons against his bones. He strained his trapped wrist closer to his chest, extending its arm, and slammed his other palm into its joint.

A nauseating crack shot over the burble of the water. The thing let go of his wrist and paddled backwards against the current, still silent despite its broken bone. Walt leaned into the stream, jogging forward in exaggerated strides to clear his knees of the water, and grabbed a trailing limb. He pulled down hard as he leapt out of the water, leveraging himself onto its back. His knife blade thunked against a hard skull. As arms whipped his back and clubbed the back of his head, he grabbed the creature's neck, dug in with his nails, and stabbed down hard into one wide, unblinking eye.

The thing bucked, spraying white slashes of water to all sides, flinging Walt back into the hustling creek. He tucked his head. His ribs jarred down on a rock, stealing his breath. He thrashed for his footing; before he could stand, the still-writhing body of the thing knocked him off his feet. He plunged under the water, taking an involuntary breath at the cold shock. For a panicked moment he couldn't tell which way was up. Sunlight. Air on his waving arm. He bumbled into a smooth, protruding rock, and, toes slicking over the moss, clambered his naked body up to its damp surface. He coughed, spitting water. Downstream, the slowly tumbling body lodged in the reeds at a bend in the creek.

Once he'd found his breath, Walt laughed.

He waded across the stream and dragged the corpse through the grass to dry land. There, he scanned a full arc of the light woods and meadows and the low mountains behind him. Wind shushed the grass. The stream tinkled. A bird chirred. He went back for his gear and dried himself off and put on pants and socks and shoes. He shouldered his stuff and lugged it back to the body. He laid a pistol on top of his duffel bag, spread out a tarp, selected a butcher knife and a paring knife, and rolled the creature's damp body onto the blue plastic.

He was no doctor. Despite the last few months of sporadic fish and game, he wasn't much of a butcher, either. But he was enough of a mathematician to add two and two, and either the thing in front of him had come from Earth or it hadn't; either some company had been so deep into biotech it was capable of creating humanity-erasing viruses and crab-hybrid monsters, or it had come from outer space, in which case he already had more than a few suspicions about the source of the Panhandler, too. (Though even then, there were other possibilities—if they were aliens, perhaps they were planetary vultures, and had swooped in after their monitors reported mankind was no longer an issue.)

Either way, he knew how to get to the guts of the matter.

He sliced the creature's clothes away from its body, set them aside, then stabbed the butcher knife down hard. Its skin was smooth but tough, resisting the knife like fingernails or hardened leather. Walt leaned into the blade. Clear and yellow goo slimed his hands. He sawed through the skin, knife jarring into unseen bones, some of which he was able to crack by leveraging his weight against them. Sweat beaded his brow and back. At a bone-free spot, he peeled back the hard skin and sliced it away from the membranes beneath.

The inside of the cavity looked like a mass of swollen spaghetti and meatballs colored the yellow of beached kelp and floating in a pot of watery yellow marinara. It smelled no better. He lifted out handfuls of rubbery tubes, knotted here and there by fleshy nodes the size of marbles and tennis balls. Snotty fluid glopped from his hands, pattering onto the tarp. Rubber gloves. He needed to loot some rubber gloves. The tubes and nodes hung by membranes from narrow bones.

Walt moved to the oversized head. Most of it was like the body, tough skin around fibrous lumps, but a third of the interior, including the eye sockets, was taken up by a bony ball punctured here and there by tube-choked holes. After two minutes of sawing at one of the sockets, his knife had only worn a small notch in the inner skull. He went to the creek, swooshed his hands around the cool water, and returned with a rock the size of two closed fists. The skull smashed on the third blow.

Beneath another membrane, he sorted through a pulpy, semi-solid mush of loosely connected gray-blue matter.

So at least it had a brain. All the rest of its organs, any lungs or kidneys or livers or spleens or anything like that, they were like nothing he'd ever seen before. He didn't want to believe it. Not that he didn't think they existed. He just didn't believe they'd possibly come *here*. But the nasty yellow muck he was covered in offered only one explanation: the thing he'd killed hadn't come from Earth.

Aliens, then. Aliens. Aliens with a bunch of small nodules instead of obviously vital targets. Headshots, he supposed. At least they had big heads.

He dragged the body into the creek and shoved it away with a long stick. The alien's clothing was spotted with pockets. He found a tin of dried, crumbling food with whiffs of salt and seaweed and rot. A pouch of water that smelled like a distant ocean. A blank pad that wouldn't respond to his touch or voice. A bag of metal balls inscribed with rings of pictographs. A gray, finger-sized tube with a small screen and what he thought might be a touchpad. And a hard rubber case filled with smooth, unyielding cards printed with shimmering figures and abstract icons. He ditched the food and water and added the rest to his bag. Whatever weapon it had been holding in its hands and claws had been lost in the water. He walked upstream and refilled his canteens and jugs.

This time, he traveled overland, paralleling the road from a distance of a couple hundred yards, skirting Albuquerque and the stretch of small towns that followed through the gently rising desert. Hostile aliens. Just that much more proof for how fucked up reality was. He didn't see how this changed his goals. Aside, that is, from the fact the invaders would probably nuke the shit out of the cities, or, if they were environmentally conscious, fire- or neutron- or unimaginably-advanced-alien-technology-bomb them. Then again, unless they were comically incompetent, they would have taken care of that before romping around the New Mexican wilderness. Whatever had happened to Los Angeles must have already gone down.

He tromped among the sage and yellow grass. As he descended from the foothills, the heat ascended. He napped under the shade of trees in a draw between two hills, troubled by flies, moving on in the just-warm dusk.

Aliens. Motherfucking aliens. As a kid, he'd immersed himself in Asimov and Heinlein and Clarke, all the classics, warm possibilities where the future was positive and our stellar neighbors meant us no ill-will. (Not that Heinlein, with his killer bugs and mind-controlling slugs, envisioned a hand-holding galactic UN. Still, beneath the warfare was the sense we would prevail, if only we tried hard enough and held true to ourselves as individuals and a people. Even in the barbarian-ravaged future of Asimov, the ingenuity of brilliant men carried the day.) He'd internalized this positivism—or they'd encapsulated his inborn instincts, who could be sure—but while these future-forward feelings lingered through high school, resisting the constant rot of fact and experience, this warmth had eroded during college like the wave-worn pilings below a dock, a process hidden from his higher mind. Even then, he'd paced the unsteady surface, ignoring the creakiness of the boards under his mental feet.

Vanessa's death had swept it away like a meteor-driven tsunami. In the psychological wreckage, the revelation of aliens, of other life, was nothing more than the ridiculous gilding of the absurd lily, the duh-duh coal brought before drooling, crazy-eyed Newcastle. When the social structure of the supposed greatest nation on Earth was one of under-your-nose slavery where 1% of the country owned half its wealth, what surprise was it that an alien race would want to destroy us for their own selfish ends? It was as natural as the dust around him or the dry, nostril-clogging pollen of the desert night. Of *course* the aliens wanted him dead. Who didn't?

In sharp contrast to this daily horror—and, in a way, making it all the worse for offering a glimmer of something better—were the balloon trips. The couple times a year when his parents took him up in the vehicles of their business were the only days he voluntarily woke before dawn. He sipped coffee from a thermos while his mom drove them to the grassy field where the first sunlight cast the surrounding trees in shades of gray. Walt shivered in his jacket while they filled the balloon with cold air from a fan. When his dad held the balloon's mouth clear while his mom finally lit the burner, waves of heat washed his hands and face. The bright Dacron swelled, tautening in the pink dawn until the fabric lifted clear, swallowing the sky overhead.

His dad said the same thing every time they stepped into the rickety wicker basket: "Welcome to the Cloudward Express, now offering one-way travel to Heaven if you lean too far over the side. All aboard!"

His dad had started saying that when Walt was just a little kid—possibly before he was born—but even once he'd grown old enough to consider it hokey as hell, he never rolled his eyes. The acts of preparing the basket and filling the balloon were somehow spiritual, a cleansing, fiery ritual that matched the red of the rising sun. And then the balloon lifted, lurching him up in a flimsy shower-sized basket held together by ropes and crowded with two other people going about the business of keeping them afloat, and if they let the bag get too hot, or he tripped over the side, he'd be dead just like that.

But he didn't care. Not when the green grass lay so far below. Not minutes later when the roads ribboned the woods and the houses clustered the roads and he could see the Atlantic like a field of glinting mercury. It was the stillness of it all, a long, centered silence broken by tweeting birds, far-off cars, his dad's sporadic jokes, and the occasional whuff of the flame, an interruption like a watchdog rousting from sleep before settling its head back between its paws. More silence, more stillness.

In these times, maybe two hours every three months, Walt felt a simple, fragile peace. Peace and an ache inside his chest: what made the time in the balloon so special and every other moment so hard?

Soon, the balloon began to descend. With the spell snapped, his parents chattered about what they had to do for the rest of the day, pinging him with questions about school and girls and his friends. He answered from that automatic place in his head, silently pleading for the balloon to rise again. A few minutes later, the wicker basket brushed the ground.

Three days and seventy or eighty miles from the creek in the woods, a keening whine pierced the sky. Walt hunkered in the yellow brush and set his bags in the dirt. He squinted at the blue sky, eyes watering, until he picked out a black speck curving through a wide circle miles overhead.

No real cover. Just scrubby green plants clinging close to the dirt and scraggly brown brush he'd lose a few layers of skin trying to hide beneath. He tucked in beside a dry, tangy shrub, resolving to wait until the flier headed away.

It banked through another circle. By the next circuit, Walt could no longer deny it: the ship was moving in a tightening downward spiral, a black oblong sweeping the desert for — what? Survivors? The person who'd killed the alien at the stream? How would they possibly know where to look?

His heart went cold. Too angry to swear, he unzipped the pocket of the duffel where he'd stored the dead alien's things.

17

Glass smashed inside the house. Raymond pressed his back to the roof, digging in his bare heels and pushing himself up from the ledge. Mia grabbed his wrist. A scout ship whined from up the hill. Beneath them, hard feet thunked stone and hardwood. Dishes shattered across the floor. The search moved with methodical swiftness, footsteps and the clatter of dropped objects moving from one room to the next. If the aliens spoke, Raymond couldn't hear them. Sweat slicked his palms and waistband, pooling in the small of his back. Aliens tromped up the steps, muffled by carpet, fanning into the bedroom directly beneath them. The soldiers paused.

With a soft rumble, the door to the deck slid open.

An alien clicked onto the wooden planks. It strode to the railing, scanning the silent yard with its oversized eyes, two thin limbs waving over its head. Raymond's foot slipped, scuffing over the rough roof. Mia's fingers clamped his wrist. The alien didn't budge. It raised a smooth, curved object like a buttonless remote to its head, one tentacle twitching near its waist, and eyed the rich brown dirt of the tilled and weeded garden. It put the remote away and walked inside the house.

The creatures thumped around for a while longer, opening doors and knocking things onto the carpet, then clacked down the front steps into the driveway. Mia scooted to the edge, legs dangling, flipped around so her stomach faced the roof, and dropped to the deck with a light thump. Raymond followed her down. She crept to the landing above the stairs. The front door hung open. Chairs had been overturned, closets opened, coats and shoes slung over the carpet. They retreated to the bedroom and hunkered below the windows beside the bed. Scouts whined across the skies. Troops clumped down the street. Once, gunfire crackled downhill, followed by a single sustained scream.

The sun sunk below the waves. The dome of its light retreated with it, shrinking into the blue, a wall of navy darkness advancing on its heels. At nightfall, Mia rose, knees popping.

"I need a drink."

"I might need two," he said. She bolted the front door while he mixed warm Jim Beam with warm ginger ale. He passed her a glass and sipped his, vaguely troubled. There were no ice cubes clinking around inside his glass. He still hadn't gotten used to that. They put the scattered coats and shoes away, cleaned up the stuffing ripped from the couch in one of the living rooms. The house carried an odd, tidal pool smell, like drying kelp and withered mussels. Mia spritzed lavender air freshener while he opened windows.

"Well?" she said as they sat in bed, curtains drawn. A single candle flickered near the door.

"Well what?"

"They just went house to house. You still want to stay?"

"Maybe they'll consider the neighborhood all clear."

"And maybe this was just a preliminary sweep and next time they'll come back with alien Rhoombas made to vacuum up blood."

Raymond didn't know what to say. If the aliens stayed, they'd be fools to stay themselves. Those things could come back any minute. Start dropping bombs. Chemicals. Leaving carried dangers of its own, but if they could get a toehold somewhere remote, a cabin in the Rockies, say, they'd probably be able to live for years without being discovered by the aliens. Possibly their entire lifetimes. The creatures hadn't brought a planet-wrecking fleet; he hadn't seen any superweapons; it even seemed plausible the combined military of Earth could have driven them back, if only every nation in the world hadn't been wiped out by the Panhandler. The aliens simply wouldn't have the resources to scour every last human from the planet. Not in this generation. So long as the survivors clung to their nooks and crannies, insect-like, and didn't try to bite or sting the new dog on the block, it seemed plausible they'd simply be left alone.

Deep down inside, he'd already made the decision to leave, but something was holding it back, like his intentions were a bubble trapped under tar. Inevitably, it would rise to the surface, but it was still working its way through the layers of his brain. He couldn't say when it would burst free.

Leaving meant giving up everything they'd worked for. Handing over the few scraps of green they'd collected from the soil, the few jugs of blue water they'd gathered from the sky and sea. Leaving would mean leaving their home, their last real link to the old world, to their old lives, a world capable of creating iPods and Charleston Chews and new episodes of *Lost*. Driving off into the wild yonder would mean accepting, finally, that it was all over. Whatever the future held, it would be nothing like the one he'd expected to live into old age with.

Dumb as it was, then, to want to stay in a place where alien beings were actively seeking to unroot the human remainders, he couldn't help it. He wasn't ready. His brain was still clearing the path for his emotions to follow.

"We'll stay prepared," he said. "If they leave again, we'll drive off. We'll head for the Rockies."

He meant it as a stall. As the virus had proved, everything could change in the span of days. The American army could arrive in force and blast the aliens into thundering rubble. The creatures could take a look around, consider humanity sufficiently ruined, and blast off to destroy another civilization in star systems unknown. Or announce the whole thing had been one big misunderstanding—who knew. Nobody, that's who, and that was the point. Whatever they believed today could be turned on its head tomorrow.

"What if they don't go?" Mia traced a smiley face in the thin condensation on her glass; he'd moved the whiskey and soda to the deck, where it had cooled compared to the warm indoors. "What if they keep searching?"

"Then we'll leave."

"Not by car. They're attracted to them or something."

"So we escape on bikes. Or via rowboat. Or use these big fleshy things dangling from our hips."

She took a drink, swished it around her mouth. "There's a bike store down on the PCH. Near the Thai place."

"I know. You've wanted one of those bikes ever since we moved here."

She grinned, swatting at him drunkenly. "A purple one."

"I want red." He tapped his teeth. "Now there's just the small matter of getting to them without being zapped into a small pile of ash."

Alien ships patrolled the skies from then on out, their low rumbles and high shrieks bursting the clear air by day and slicing through the hillside fog by night. He doubted they'd be able to pick out two people slipping through the night on foot to the bike shop — the things hadn't noticed the two of them hiding out on the roof, after all — but the possibility was paralyzing. As was holing up in their house all day, sneaking out under cover of dark to water the wilted bell peppers or pick a little cilantro to add flavor to food they could no longer cook over an open fire.

Drop ships came and went, ferrying soldiers to cities up and down the bay. Even after the carrier departed, the smaller craft remained, buzzing in and out of LAX, cleansing neighborhoods Raymond had never visited. Staying had been a mistake. The house, the yard, the garden, the ocean view, that wasn't what made their home a home. It was the freedom they'd had. The simple, unobstructed life they'd built for themselves. Cooped up and scared, they didn't have a home. They had a cage.

Like that, the bubble burst free. He was ready to leave.

A mountain in Colorado. They'd steal a couple bikes, rig them up with baskets loaded with as much food, water, and medical supplies as they could carry, and pedal out of the city under cover of darkness. Beyond the aliens' sight, they'd find a car and forage for supplies along the way. Grab a house in a town in the foothills of the Rockies, somewhere out of the way, of little interest to genocidists, and wait out the winter there, building up supplies, scouting the mountainsides for cabins, ideally near a stream or a lake where they could irrigate a garden and maybe even do a little fishing. Depending on the violence of the snows, they might be able to put in a bit of work on the cabin in the meantime. In the spring, they would move in and get to work chopping wood, planting seeds, digging a hole to store food and keep it cool. They weren't likely to be entirely self-sufficient by the winter after that, but they could augment what they grew and caught with preserved food rustled up from the town below.

That was the plan. It was a good plan. It was practical in a way that appealed to Raymond's sense of order, based on few assumptions (that the aliens wouldn't notice two people on bikes; that they'd be able to find regular supplies of gasoline along the way; that they'd be able to traverse a snowy mountain well enough to find a cabin before spring). It was elegant and flexible. Disasters could happen, of course, alien attacks or car crashes or blizzards, but these things weren't worth worrying about. They were too large, too total. Besides, they just weren't all that likely. Things normally went to plan, and when they didn't, they had a way of working themselves out regardless.

The one problem with the plan was he didn't know the way to Colorado. They had no maps besides one of the LA freeway system tucked into the Charger's glove box. The internet was long gone. He didn't even know, strictly speaking, where Colorado *was* —he knew it was one of those square states, but was it above Nevada? Under Wyoming? Somewhere to the north and east, that much he knew. And he supposed that was all he needed to know. Once they got out of the city, they'd head northeasterly, pick up maps at a rest stop or tourist center or glove box somewhere along the way. Things would work out. It made Raymond feel bad to think about, but there was simply too much stuff abandoned by the dead for him and Mia to starve along the way, no matter how many times they had to backtrack on their way to Colorado.

That left just one other hole: getting the bikes. Prior to being eradicated by disease, the citizens of the beach cities had been health nuts, cycling along the strand that bordered the beach, walking dogs on the esplanade sidewalks, sometimes combining the two, terriers and poodles trotting on leashes alongside muscly-legged men ensconced in their bikes. With near certainty, they'd be able to find a couple bikes in a garage somewhere down the street. But Mia didn't like the idea of breaking into random houses. It'd be noisy, attention-grabbing. Who knew how long it would take? Raymond nodded, citing the possibility the aliens had left monitoring devices behind, or traps, or other incidental viruses. They knew precisely where the bike shop was. It was no more than two and a half miles away. Walking the back streets, they could be there within 45 minutes, then bike back. The whole thing would be quick and simple and clean. Much more so than breaking into one garage after another.

They left for the shop that night, dressed in black, pistols in hand, a hammer and a pry bar dangling from Raymond's hips. A pair of binoculars swung from Mia's neck. They walked down the hill at a swift pace, swishing through the grass under the palms in the green strip that lined the road. Something rattled a can down the street, startling them. Raymond crouched beside a palm's rough, pinecone-like bark. Mia held her pistol to her chest. In the moonlight, a skunk hopped into the gutter, waddling, its brushy tail held high.

"I should shoot it on principle," Mia whispered.

"No way. They may be our last line of defense against the aliens. Bet you they've never even heard of tomato juice."

His heart rate calmed by the time the steep hillside street fed into the esplanade. Waves struck the beach in great and sudden bursts. Raymond frowned; out to sea, a single white light rose and fell on the dark water.

"Come on," Mia said.

Yellow two-story apartments fronted the road toward PCH. The lightest of breezes sifted the palms. Ahead, a row of silent people stood along the median. Raymond jolted, blood cold. The illusion quickly resolved into parking meters. A few cars remained untouched in their parking spots. How long it would take them to rust away in the steady daytime ocean winds? He stumbled on something light and clattering. Bones gleamed whitely from stiff clothes, connected by dry strings of flesh, the rest rotted away or eaten. It had no smell. He swallowed down his dinner of cold canned ravioli.

Six months ago, these few square blocks had been one of the most pleasant spaces in a city that was almost nothing but pleasant, a pedestrian-friendly collection of sidewalk cafes, shoe and dress shops, and quiet, tasteful bars. Walking down the sidewalk, Raymond had smelled pepper-roasted lamb, buttery calamari, the hot metal of the heating lamps the restaurants turned on to combat the evening breezes.

Friday afternoons, rain or shine, a farmer's market had opened on a side street, selling boxes of strawberries, lemons and limes and oranges, rich green spinach and bunches of dewy cilantro. One van sold potted avocado trees and fat-leafed dragonfruit plants. Mia worked part-time doing reception for a dentist down the block, and when Raymond drove over to pick her up in the late afternoons, sunlight pouring through his windshield so hard he could barely see the road, he'd park, feed the meter, and dawdle down to the market while he waited for work to let her go.

It amazed him they could sell heads of spinach for a dollar apiece, a bin of strawberries for two—less than half what he'd pay at the Ralph's or the Albertsons. As their money bled away, he paced their off-red deck with the half-rotted planks at the far end and willed the patch of yellow grass along the fence to morph into a deep brown field with tidy rows of leafy green. Meanwhile, the weedy stretch of dirt beside the driveway could be the perfect herb garden. It seemed possible, even easy, to grow their own tomatoes, basil, lettuce, and bell peppers, to halve their grocery budget to butter, eggs, and packs of chicken thighs. All for the cost of a few seeds and daily water.

Between the job hunt, fooling around with Photoshop on spec projects, and watching *Star Trek* streamed over Netflix, he'd never found the time. Instead, most Fridays he bought a twist of spinach for garlic mashed potatoes or a flat of strawberries for crepes, consoling himself with the thought that even two dollars saved per week would add up to a hundred by year's end. Every little difference mattered.

The market was gone now, a dark side street fronted by black-windowed apartments. Dry leaves and garbage littered the sidewalks of the cafes and salons. Metal tables and chairs sat in the open, dotted with heavy layers of rain-spotted dust.

They slunk along the road parallel to Pacific Coast Highway, meeting up with the main street the block before the bike shop. A tattered tarp fluttered over the lot. Dozens of bicycles rested in rows in front of the store, left out during the pandemic, dirt clinging to their stylish, colorful frames. They weren't even chained. Gaps in the rows indicated a few had been stolen, but most of the survivors, like them, must have been concentrating on food and cars and guns and medicine.

Mia wiped a clean line through the dirt coating a basketed bike, revealing a light purple paint job. She smiled and stage-whispered, "Regulators, mount up!"

Raymond found himself a red one, holstering his pistol. He hadn't ridden a bike since he'd gotten his driver's license over a decade ago, and he was afraid he'd spill into the street in a disaster of skinned elbows and torn jeans, but Mia pedaled off without hesitation. After an initial wobble, he rode smoothly.

Cool air whisked past his face, countered by the heat of his muscles. Mia leaned forward and turned off the PCH toward the empty cafes. The low slurp of rubber tires on asphalt was obliterated by the banging roar of sustained automatic fire.

Mia swerved in among the parking meters. "That's coming from the—"

Blue bolts flashed from the beach. A spray of tracers lashed the darkness. More gunfire kicked up, crashing over the surf, ricochets whining. Shouts and screams drifted on the wet air. Fifty yards from Raymond, a silhouette popped up from the stairs leading to the beach. Before the woman took two steps, a lance of blue light knocked her to the ground.

"We've got to get out of here," Mia said. "Like ten minutes ago."

The wounded woman's groan was riddled with pain. She rose to her hands and knees, a black lump, then collapsed back to the pavement.

Raymond gestured. "She's hurt."

"By the same laser that will hurt us if we stay!"

"We can't just leave her," he said. "Not when we can help."

He pushed off the curb and pedaled with all he had. Dead ahead, blue beams cleaved the night.

18

He flung the pad and the cards and the metal balls into the weeds. Above, the whining vessel banked, bleeding altitude. Walt stood in an open slope of gray dirt, yellow grass sprigs, and short green bushes. A series of bluffs staggered the flatlands a half mile away. The road lay a couple hundred yards in the opposite direction. No help there, either; more scrubby high desert bordered by dry mountains. No plants rose higher than mid-thigh. No buildings at all. Nowhere to hide.

The small black ship made a wide semicircle above the highway. Searching for their lost friend? Seeking vengeance on the one who'd killed it? Whatever the question, Walt's death was the answer. He ran for the tree-speckled bluffs, bogged down by the heavy bags bouncing on his back. Over his shoulder, the ship floated less than a mile above the road. Walt swore, skidding to a halt in a cloud of dust. He ducked the bags off his back, slung them behind a clump of bushes, and sprinted for the bluffs.

Stupid move, hanging on to the dead alien's stuff. He'd kept it partly as a trophy, partly with the hope that, with time and the right equipment, he could learn from it, spy on their communications network or track their movements or download some freaky alien porn to shame them out of the Solar System. Really, his thinking hadn't been practical at all, drawing from the primal instinct to take the possessions of those you killed. Possessions that had clearly included a tracking device of some kind. Assuming the aliens were capable of any emotion at all, Walt guessed their reaction to finding their friend's gear in a human's hands would involve powerful ray guns and attack-tripods.

After two thousand miles of walking, he was in willow-trim shape. He loped through the dust, breathing easily. Still, the bluffs stood impossibly far. The whining engines fell silent. The ship touched down on the road on insectlike legs. A portal rolled open. Walt stumbled, arms flailing, and put his eyes forward. If they caught him before he reached the low trees in the folds of the bluffs, there wasn't much he could do. He had a pistol belted to his hip and a jackknife in his pocket. That was it. That's what he'd have to defend himself against their guns or lasers or rockets or hypernuclear black-hole bombs. But it didn't matter: he would shoot at them until his clip ran out, and then, if he could get close enough, he would stab them, and if they took his knife he would punch and claw and bite their tough smooth skin.

Not so long ago, the understanding he would die would have caused him to question whether there was any worth to resisting a foregone conclusion. If his death were assured, better to subvert fate by taking control of the method, by *letting* the aliens shoot him, or better yet, by shooting himself, pulling the trigger with his middle finger.

Fuck that. If they were going to kill him, they'd have to root him out of the trees. Blow up the whole hill. Until the onset of the blackness, he would be shooting. Stabbing. Punching.

He charged across the desert field. At the road, four aliens milled around their ship, twiddling things too small to see. As if his looking at them had caused them to look back, one of the aliens stiffened in a universal posture of wary surprise and assessment. Walt spurred himself harder. He'd be at the scrabbly trees in less than a minute. By the time he glanced back, the aliens had left the road behind, running after him on smooth, many-legged strides.

Walt clattered into the loose rocks that blanketed the slope. It was steep going, and not far to his left the bluff simply rose in a sheer cliff, but here it was runnable, scablike swathes of broken rock between brambly green bushes and crumbly dirt. He leaned forward, balancing with his hand. The ground leveled into yellowing grass and pokey trees with pale green leaves. Another couple hundred yards on, the ground fell away at an unseen angle. Probably empty desert beneath. Walt pulled in behind a tree, gun in hand, and shrank against its thorny trunk.

Below, the aliens glided across the plain. They stopped at the spot where he'd tossed away the dead one's gear, then halted a second time when they came to his bags. While one stared motionless in his general direction, the other three spread out, poking among the dirt and the weeds. Walt panted, shirt sweat-stuck to his back. The nights had been cold lately — the signs for the previous towns boasted higher elevations than populations — but the days were still hot, borderline scorching. His mouth felt as dry as the bark scraping the side of his face. Far across the field, one of the aliens lowered itself and scuttled in the dust. A few yards away, a second reached down with a thick tentacle and hefted Walt's duffel onto its flat back. A third dangled his backpack from a sticklike arm. The group reconvened, waving their arms at each other in quick, flicking patterns as graceful as a swimming fish or a martial artist practicing his forms. With some consensus reached, they started back toward the road. A moment later, the one who'd been watching the bluff turned its back and followed.

Walt simmered as they hauled his things back to the ship. Had they taken his gear out of base cruelty, expecting him to now die in this dry place? Out of clinical curiosity, hoping to study his equipment and extrapolate the fundamentals of human survival? Out of a shrimplike fastidiousness that didn't allow artificial objects to lie in a natural setting? The fact he could only speculate, and therefore didn't know just how much to hate them, somehow made it all the more frustrating.

They took their sweet alien time getting back to their ship and even longer taking off. By the time the black vessel lifted into the sky, the sun was nearly touching the western mountains. Walt waited to move until he could no longer see the ship's dark oval or hear its high engines.

Not a single one of his things had been dropped or discarded. The only thing left behind was a bunch of shallow round holes where they'd tromped around. Yellow grass wavered in the waxing breeze and waning light. Already, the wind raised the hairs on his bare arms. He had no idea how far he was from the next town. They'd been few and far between lately, sun-withered things full of trailers and weedy lots. He passed just two or three a day, and they'd been thinning. Walt had the impression he was about to head into a true American wilderness where you might go dozens of miles without encountering a single home or gas station. He'd passed a small town earlier that day; if he backtracked along the road, he might be able to make it in five or six hours.

It would lose him a day of travel. Not that he had some neurosurgery appointment awaiting him in Los Angeles. Getting there in January would be no different from getting there in December. Did he have to keep going at all? Like pausing on a magazine ad before flipping to the next story, he entertained the thought of stopping, of finding a house back in the suburbs of Albuquerque and just...staying. But he knew he would hate it, rooting through the houses of the dead for boxes of Rice Krispies and rolls of toilet paper, returning home to watch from the window while the shadows stretched across the street. He had a goal in LA. He had a goal, and however arbitrary it might be, he was enjoying its pursuit.

He headed for the rising western road. He pushed harder than his standard pace, meaning to make the most of these last minutes of light; without the heavy bags, it felt easy, oddly fun, like leaving work early when no one will notice. He'd left his coat in the bag and the night was cool and getting cooler. The sun slotted into a notch in the mountains and sunk into another part of the world. He felt like a lone hunter, keenly aware that his survival was now on the line. He hadn't had such a strong sense of purpose in ages. Possibly, he never had—he needed to find food, water, and shelter, and the only way to do it was to walk on. Meaning through purpose: that was the lesson of the end of the world.

This feeling lasted until the cool became the cold of the high desert. Walt was tired and thirsty. He envisioned himself lying in the dirt beside the road, weeds prickling his bare arms, woken repeatedly by his own shivers, the gusting breeze, the furtive rustles of rodents seeking seeds. With no idea whether the next town was thirty miles away or just around the next bend, he began to make deals with himself, promising to lie down and try to get some sleep in another half hour, and when that half hour turned out to be a dull stretch of empty moonlit roadside, to go for another ten minutes, and when those ten minutes went by, just another five, because anyone can walk for five minutes—until finally, with an audible sigh, he dropped off the road into the dust, found a rock-free patch of dirt, and balled up, one arm pillowing his head, the other tucked inside his shirt for warmth.

His stomach gurgled. Whenever he woke, which was often, his tongue was so dry he had to wipe it around his teeth until it no longer felt like the arm of a desiccated starfish. After a little less than three hours, he was shivering too hard to go back to sleep. He got up, stretched, silently cursed out the aliens, and walked on, jogging intermittently once it grew light enough to see the road was clear. When it warmed up, he napped in the partial shade of a waist-high bush that smelled like pollen and dried-out sage.

The land rolled on, bristly yellow weeds over scabby gray dirt. Walt was already starting to think about slicing off parts of the bushes and gnawing them for moisture or trying to shoot a rabbit with his pistol and drink the blood. He should have carried three bags, not two, with the third a fanny pack or neck-pouch filled with the critical essentials: bottled water, high-energy food like fruit and nuts and dried meat, a couple of lighters and bandages, an extra box of bullets, and a thermal blanket. Enough to keep him healthy and focused for a couple days if he ever again had to ditch the rest of his gear.

Assuming he lived, he'd get right on that.

He hadn't even thought twice about drinking his own urine before he turned a bend into a spread of houses down the hill. An obvious main street, a tic-tac-toe board of side roads, a few splashes of persistent green among the shriveled yellow lawns and wind-driven dust. A place where a few hundred humans had once lived among the luxuries and conveniences of the era.

A 76 station waited at the edge of town, gas prices fixed at $3.19 for 87-grade. A dust devil twirled in from the neighboring desert, spinning itself out over the hot pavement. For a minute, Walt just waited, letting his senses sense and his instincts instinct. He crossed the lot and stepped inside.

The shelves had been emptied. Completely. The fridges, too, even of the rotting, clotted milk cartons he'd expected to find there. The trash cans offered the butt of a hot dog, now reduced to a foam of dry brown mold. The bathroom key was still under the register. Walt went inside the dark room to try the faucets just for fun. They didn't work.

A small local supermarket sat down the block, shopping carts rusting beside the cars, front windows smashed out. The front rows were just as empty as the gas station. He walked into the gloom of the back of the store, shuffling his feet, trailing one arm along the dusty shelves. Of the few objects he found — packaged rubber gloves, rawhide dog bones, boxes of toothpicks and straws — none were edible or potable. Something like frustration expanded from the center of his chest, squeezing his organs, but the emotion had a rawer, wriggling edge to it: the bone-deep animal panic that he might never taste food or water again. He found three boxes of something powdery, flour, possibly, or muffin mix, and shuffled for better light. Nope. Baking powder. Son of a bitch.

"Hold up there." A man's voice echoed among the scoured aisles. Walt dropped his boxes and went for his pistol. A hammer clicked. Through the sun-dazzle on his dark-adjusted eyes, Walt made out a man's silhouette, his arms extended, a pack clinging to his shoulders. "What do you think you're doing?"

It took two tries before Walt could speak around his dry throat. "Trying to find something to drink."

"You won't," the man said. "We took it."

"From the whole town?"

The man nodded. Walt could see a little better now, well enough to make out the man's brambly brown beard, his slight paunch, his t-shirt and cargo shorts.

"That seems excessive," Walt said.

"Not when nobody's making anything new." The man flicked his pistol. "Set down your gun and walk out the door."

Walt dropped his cocked elbows a couple inches. "I just want some water. Something to eat. Just enough to get me to the next town."

"Got anything to trade?"

He started a mental inventory of his packs before remembering he had nothing but his clothes and the contents of those clothes' pockets. The aliens had once more taken everything from him: first Vanessa, then his family and his friends, and as if that hadn't been enough, as a final measure they'd swung by in person to take away his food and his water, his sleeping bag and cookware and all the rest. He smiled. He knew he wasn't being personally persecuted, that he wasn't the human Job to their alien Jehovah, but he couldn't help feeling that way. Honestly, at some point it had crossed the line, become too much and too absurd to maintain his anger towards. He could still feel it there, deep down, but right now what he really wanted to do was laugh.

"No," he said. "Lost everything but what you see."

"Then put down your gun, walk out those doors, and get on down the road."

"How about you be a proper host and give me something to drink? That way I won't stink up your nice little town when my body collapses on Main Street."

The bearded man shook his head. "Don't make me ask a third time."

Walt squinted. The man's voice was young; eyes adjusting to the sunlight, Walt saw his face was, too. Not any older than himself. No doubt a local—no traveler would have pitched a permanent tent in this desolate place—one of at least two survivors, because he'd said "we," but no more than five, ten at the very outside, given Panhandler survival rates. Walt's gut said it was fewer. Possibly just the kid and his girlfriend. He had just enough to lose to be afraid to risk leaving this place in search of somewhere better.

A town's worth of food between two people. Laying claim to it by virtue of their ability to take it—so if they refused to share, with himself in danger of dying as a result, did that allow *him* to just take from them what *he* needed? He set this kettle of thought on the backburner—he did possess something he doubted they had, actually, way out in this nowhereland.

"I've got information."

The kid's pistol drooped fractionally. "About what?"

"The Panhandler. Where it came from."

"The Midwest, Iowa or somewhere. Some big pig farm where they grew piglets in vats."

Walt laughed. "I wish all we had to worry about were pigs. I've seen the truth, and if you want it, it'll cost you—" He did some quick mental arithmetic of what would get him through the next couple days. "To the tune of three bottles of water and four candy bars. Alternately, two cans of soup or ravioli, or one bag of potato chips. Family-size."

The kid shook his bearded face. "Two bottles of water, one Butterfinger, and one fun-sized bag of barbecue Lays."

Silly, considering the info he was about to pass on could save the kid's life, but unless Walt was about to cross into Death Valley (which he was pretty sure, but not absolutely so, was a ways into

California), it should be enough to keep him going. Anyway, giving up the info wouldn't cost *him* anything, and he really wanted water. He stuck out his hand.

"Deal."

The kid lowered his pistol. "Was it the CDC, then? Like the smallpox got out? Or mutated Black Death from India?"

Walt couldn't help smiling. "Aliens."

"Aliens?"

"Aliens. From outer space."

The guy's beard ruffled, his brows knotting. "Come on, dude. I'm serious."

"Same here."

"Yeah." The kid waved his free hand at the sunny street past the windows. "I don't see any Martians out there."

"Well, that's because you're kind of nowhere."

"How do *you* know, then?"

"I've seen one. It attacked me and I killed it. They look kind of squiddy and spidery. Crabby, maybe. Definitely something with a shell and little pinchy-claws and—"

The other man shut his eyes and waved his splayed palm, as if suffering a flutter of chest pain. "Stop it. Please, just walk out of here and leave town."

"Where's my snacks?"

"Come on. You don't know anything."

Walt regarded him silently. He had no way to prove it. No pilfered laser guns or floating holo-balls or stuffed severed heads. Nothing more convincing than his word. They'd had a deal and he'd told the truth. Somehow this felt more important than the fact that leaving without water could be a death sentence. They had a deal. The kid had broken their deal because why not? There was no one around to enforce it. It wasn't a covenant carved on stone tablets, the violation of which would result in a punishment of locusts and plagues. It was just a fleeting arrangement, something the kid could yank back if, in his own judgment, the rules no longer applied.

It wasn't much. The kind of snack you would pop down to the bodega for on a stoned afternoon. A few calories of matter and ounces of fluid. The kid probably had as much in his pack right now. If he and his girlfriend had really rounded up everything in town, they had enough to last for years. Likely it would go bad before they could consume it all. Yet the kid clung to it, likely from some combination of righteous principle (Walt had "lied" to him) and the baseless, instinctual terror of want that manifested itself in greed. The toddler's pout that it's mine and you can't have it. If the snacks and water in question just disappeared, the kid wouldn't miss them in the slightest. To Walt, it was the difference between reaching the next town or in collapsing in the weeds three days from now, gum-eyed, gazing at the faraway clouds.

"Give me what we agreed on," Walt said.

"If *you'd* done what we agreed on you'd be munching on that Butterfinger right now. Instead you try to feed me some cock-and-bull story about..." The kid mashed his lips together, fluffing his beard. "Invading ETs here for our Reese's."

"If I were a betting man, and I could trust the guy I was betting with to actually give me my stupid fucking bag of fun-size chips, I would bet they sent the disease to soften us up. You don't need to bring many tanks and shit when you can just wipe us out with galactic ebola."

"I don't want to hear any more of this stupid crap! Just get out and—"

Rage splashed Walt like a bucket of paint, shocking and vivid and total. He flicked up his pistol and fired into the right side of the kid's chest. The bang rang down the empty aisles. The kid spun, hands sprawling, gun skiddering away. He flopped on his face and gasped. As Walt walked up, he struggled to a seated position, left hand clamped to his upper chest, and kicked his heels at the floor, scooting away.

"You *shot* me!"

Blood pattered the white tile, coppery and hot. "And you might die. But you might not. I think that's pretty good."

"You shot me!"

Walt was almost annoyed enough to plug him again. "I heard you the first time, you god damn whiner. We're going to make a new deal right now. Is there food and water in your pack?"

The kid nodded, skin blanched beneath his beard. "The water and candy, plus some—"

"I'm going to take that and your gun. You're going to stay here and keep quiet for fifteen minutes while I leave town. Don't try to come after me. In exchange, I won't shoot you dead and go rape your girlfriend before I kill her too."

He'd been guessing about the girlfriend; the guy had *something* keeping him here, and Walt hadn't seen a wedding ring. Given the dread, hatred, and terror wrestling for possession of the kid's face, Walt guessed he'd guessed right.

"You leave her alone."

"I will. Now give me your pack."

The man gaped. Walt twitched the pistol. The kid winced and slipped the pack's straps from his shoulders. He held out the bag, left hand slick and red and shaking. Walt took it and backed off and crouched down to fight with the zipper. Metal-foil packaging, crinkling wrappers, ribbed clear bottles. Walt shouldered it and picked up the fallen pistol.

The kid stared at him, eyes bright with pain. "Don't you touch her."

"Don't worry," Walt said. "We have a deal."

He walked out the front door, half expecting a melodic beep from the dead sensor. Sunlight struck his skin. He jogged down the main street. He was thirsty as hell, but he didn't pause for a drink or a bite of the crispy Butterfinger until he was a half mile beyond the trailers and adobe houses shimmering in the still-hot autumn sun. He didn't see anyone on the road behind him. For a moment, he imagined going to a bar to meet the kid and his girlfriend, who would be a little chunky but pretty in an alternative way, a lopsided haircut and a nose with a strangely attractive lift to its tip, and they'd laugh over beers and argue but in a friendly way about Pynchon being over- or underrated and whether Nolan was the new Kubrick. He didn't think the kid would die of the gunshot; of infection, maybe, but not blood loss or internal damage. The pair had scoured the whole town. They'd have the antibiotics to get by.

Walt reached the next town in a little under two hours. He smiled wryly as he entered a mini-mart and loaded soups and soda and bottled water into the pack.

He broke into a silent two-story house, checked for bodies, then napped in the upstairs bedroom. At dusk, groggy, he found a backpack and filled it with a blanket, a can opener, a couple of cooking knives, a fork and a butter knife and a spoon, packets of kitchen matches illustrated with old presidents, two flannel shirts, a metal cup, some Band-Aids and Neosporin, a small and a large pair of scissors, some balled-up gold-toe socks, a couple of too-large shirts, and an unopened bottle of scotch. With the sun sinking into the mountains, he had a few slugs from a half-empty fifth of Jack Daniels, his elbows resting on the stone-capped island in the darkening kitchen. It didn't feel the way it used to. An empty habit. He left the bottle on the island.

Days came and went. He watched the skies, saw nothing but clouds. For all he knew the aliens had left. He crossed into Arizona. The days began to cool, the nights to freeze in the high hills; he slept in houses when he could find them. He saw some signs of others, smoke rising from chimneys, now and then a distant engine, but even fewer hints than before. Maybe the survivors were hiding. Maybe they'd simply run out of food.

More mountains, more desert, hours passed picking through houses, adding binoculars, a Swiss army knife, a lightweight sleeping bag, Bic lighters, gel ink pens, canned and packaged food, bits of wire and string, a replacement pair of shoes (keeping his old ones in the replacement duffel), a carton of Camels which he smoked as the mood struck him. There was an odd purpose in his exploring and gathering, a deeply-rooted need that left him serenely Zen-like. He entered houses looking for nothing in particular, picking through the dusty objects in drawers and closets, turning them over in his hands, contemplating their manifold uses, discarding the overspecialized and the no longer necessary, taking only the emergency and the everyday. Once, a rifle shot crackled over his head on his way through the middle of a town. He traveled overland until his water began to run down. He didn't resent the shot. A warning, no more. That was how you did things. Make your intentions clear, then follow through.

Somewhere in the desert, but a less-desert where green things were possible and scraggly trees grew in the folds of the hills, he stopped, stone-still, and reached for his binoculars. A mile off the highway, cone-like structures rose amidst the weeds and shrubs, steep and deep blue and thirty or forty feet tall, a few higher and thicker. Spindly-limbed things sidled among the tall cones, pausing to do things Walt was too far away to see. Hemispherical ground vehicles glided over the dirt on a blur of motion that could be treads or dozens of short legs. Perhaps a hundred or more of the cones, a couple dozen of the creatures, a handful of the cars.

It took Walt an embarrassingly long time to realize he was looking at a city.

19

Blue bolts licked the darkness, touching the clouds and disappearing as if they'd never been there at all. The shot woman lay facedown in the street, shins propped on the sidewalk. Raymond braked, the rubber of his tires grabbing hard at the pavement, and dropped to his feet. The air smelled like burnt hot dogs. The woman's eyes were shut. Her ribs swelled within her camouflage shirt. On her left lower back, a scorched hole exuded a wisp of smoke. The wound was dime-shaped and puzzlingly devoid of blood. On the beach eighty feet below and a couple hundred yards away, dark figures shouted and ran, lit by sporadic bursts of rattling gunfire and electric blue lasers. Armored aliens splashed along the tideline.

"Are you awake?" Raymond said over the hollers and bangs. "Can you move?"

She stirred, groping at the asphalt, lifting her short-haired head to blink at him. "Help me."

He'd let his bike drop to the ground. Mia sat on hers a few yards away, staring unreadably. He propped up his bike and gestured hard. Mia pedaled forward and pulled to a stop.

"Raymond. Aliens with lasers. We have to go."

"Help me get her up!"

She opened her mouth to say more, then gave one abrupt shake of her head and knelt beside the struggling woman. They hooked their hands under her armpits, guiding her to her feet. Raymond shouldered her weight. She groaned, face pinched.

"What now?" Mia said. "Think you can cram her into your basket?"

"Get on the seat," Raymond said to the woman clinging to his shoulders. She licked her lips and reached out with one hand, leaning clumsily for the seat. He helped her lift her leg over the bar, then, with Mia supporting the bike, knocked out its kickstand and jumped on. The woman wrapped her arms around his middle. A searing white blast rocked the beach below, followed by a huge, gut-thumping crump. As Raymond pushed off, wobbling, falling sand tickled his face and hissed on the sidewalk.

He biked for the hill, Mia just ahead of him. It was hard work, a strain on his thighs and his balance; if he hadn't spent the last several months gardening, surfing, hiking around, and hauling wood and water from place to place, he might not have made it. A man screamed from the beach, a long wail that penetrated the staccato thunder of gunfire. A blue line flashed over their heads. Raymond didn't risk looking back. A widely-spaced row of mansions appeared along the rising cliff, buffering them from the battle on the beach. Mia kept glancing back at him, face tight. A light fog enshrouded them. The sounds of battle became hollow, spectral, echoing in the cliffs, fighting with the thump of the surf. A deep buzz mounted to a crushing bass, then dopplered away. Seconds later, a string of explosions formed a constellation across the beach. The injured woman grunted. Raymond opened his mouth to ask if she was okay, but was silenced by a rolling wave of tremendous booms.

Things got a lot quieter after that. A few bursts of gunfire, a couple of shouts. Mostly nothing but the slow rhythm of the breakers folding over the shore. The silence was more frightening than the clamor and ruckus of the battle.

Mia unlocked the chained gates. Raymond stopped in the driveway. The woman was awake enough to dismount, eyelids fluttering in pain.

"Get inside," Mia whispered. "Get inside, get inside, get inside."

"We're getting," Raymond said. He helped the woman up the steps, then reached down for one of the flashlights they kept inside beside the door. With the light on, he froze, his mind clicking in dry little circles. He had no idea what to do, where to start.

"We should get her upstairs," Mia said, as if sensing his paralysis. "One of the spare rooms."

"Yeah." He pulled his head back to face the woman. "Think you can climb some stairs?"

"This is a nice house," she said in a dried-out voice.

"That's why we stole it."

Flashlight in his free hand, hugging her ribs with his other arm, he led her step by step to the second floor. Below, Mia rattled around in the closet where they kept their medicine. Raymond stumbled the woman into the room next to theirs and maneuvered her beside the bed. She went unconscious the moment she left his shoulder, thumping leadenly into the comforter, legs dangling off the bed's edge. Gingerly, he swung her feet up and rolled her on her back, then, after checking the curtains were drawn, went to their bedroom for candles.

Mia popped into the room with bottles and bandages just as he finished unbuttoning the woman's camo jacket. "What are you doing?"

Raymond gave her a look. "Not that. Give me a hand here."

The woman's smooth belly was unmarred. They stripped off the jacket, flinging it to the side of the room, and rolled her on her stomach. The wound penetrated some two or three inches into her back, black-fringed, just wide enough that Raymond could have stuck his little finger inside, a bizarre, sudden desire he quashed as quickly as he'd had it. There was almost no blood. Just erratic drops that slid through the invisibly fine hairs on her back.

Raymond sat back on the bed. "So, what? We just sort of clean her up?"

Mia pursed her lips and gave a little shrug. "Then slap a bandage on her. I don't really think it will matter."

He glugged rubbing alcohol on a fistful of cotton, breathing through his mouth to avoid its sharp smothering scent. "But she's hardly bleeding."

"What, you've never watched a medical drama? Shock? Infection?"

"We've got some antibiotics." He swabbed the edges of the wound, the hot red circle surrounding it. The task was both disgusting and automatic, the kind of thing that would make him shudder with revulsion if he gave it a moment's thought. Would they have been better off leaving her for a medic on the beach? Then again, everyone there had been blown up or driven off.

"Will they be the right kind for whatever infects her?" Mia patted a wad of cloth over the woman's back and, with Raymond holding her up by her shoulders, began winding a long tan bandage around her middle. "I just don't think people with big dirty holes gouged through them have very high survival rates."

He supposed she was right. If so, he thought the woman's death would be a failure, a nullification of whatever he'd achieved in getting her out of the combat zone. But trying to do what's right in the moment it's happening—isn't that all you can do? Mia clipped the bandage in place. He blew out the candles and went out to bring the bikes inside. Later, in bed together, the door open in case the woman called out, Mia touched his shoulder.

"That was a crazy thing to do, do you realize that?"

"She'd just been shot."

"I'm not saying it was the *wrong* thing to do."

"Oh."

"But if something had happened to you—what would I have done?"

"Grabbed a baseball bat and raced down to the beach to hit some alien-head dingers, I bet." He smiled over a small pang of annoyance. Nothing bad had actually happened. Instead, they might have saved someone's life. Now more than ever—cliched as he knew it was—that was one of the most important things in the world. Too much longer like this, and there might not be any of them left at all.

Her name was Sarah Campbell. She woke two days later, calling for water, sweating through her tank top. After they'd explained what happened and where she was, she told them about the attack on the beach by the Bear Republic Rebels, a resistance movement of soldiers and civilians based somewhere in the northern mountains. They'd come to Redondo to—well, she couldn't say; to find something, or to find something out, Raymond gleaned that much, but Sarah grew elusive whenever she began to approach anything like a fact about the mission. She was somewhat less vague about the BRR: a few hundred members and growing, some access to weapons and vehicles, in sporadic contact with several other cells around the world. All working towards the same rather obvious goal. So far, they hadn't had much luck.

"They've just got the one big ship." Mia gazed down at Sarah's pale, dirt-streaked face, her close blonde hair. "Why doesn't someone just nuke them?"

"They tried. Russia. The ship shot down the missile, then carpet-bombed St. Petersburg. Same deal in India. Not just incendiaries. Some chemical thing that poisons whatever's left of the rubble."

"But only after we strike first?"

"Seems so."

Mia frowned. "So we've got the choice of sitting on our thumbs and getting wiped out day by day and month by month, or taking a swing and getting annihilated all at once."

Sarah nodded, wincing. "Aliens seem content to kill us at their leisure so long as we don't try anything stupid. We need to start thinking sneaky instead of flashy."

"Are the Bear Republic Rebels accepting recruits?" Raymond said.

"Always."

He glanced at Mia. "What do you think?"

Sarah struggled upright. A waft of pus and burnt meat rose with her. "You don't want any part of that."

"Those things have been going door to door," Mia said. "The only way we stay here long-term is in a mass grave."

"Like it's any different if you try to fight back? Did you see what happened on the beach? The fucking hole in my back?"

"If you'd seen what's been going on *here*—"

"Look, it doesn't matter, okay? They blew up most of the airfields from orbit. Even the ones they missed, you think our pilots had a miracle cure? They're just as dead as the generals and the Marines and the guys who drove the tanks. Word is the enemy is setting up manufacturing plants. They'll wear us down until we're spraying AKs at their fighters like the god damn Taliban. Better to run off to the woods and live out our lives than get massacred like we did down on the beach." Sarah wilted back among the sheets, suddenly pale, sweat glistening on her brow and on her chest above her tank top. "You guys have each other, all right? You need to hang onto that."

"Speaking of which," Raymond said a moment later, "we've got some work to do. Just holler if you need anything."

"Thank you," she said softly. "And thanks. For picking me up."

"Didn't seem to me like I had a choice."

They didn't really have much to do—clean up the bikes,

maybe, but it was still too light out to risk feeding the chickens or tending the garden—but Raymond knew when a person needed some time to themselves. In the garage, he and Mia oiled the bikes amidst the soupy, clinging, asphalty fumes. Yellowish fluid grimed his fingernails. Mechanics had always made intuitive sense to Raymond, fitting as neatly to his stolid, careful mind as the bike's chains fitted to their gears. He wished he'd pursued such things years ago, learning to maintain cars and work simple machines, unknowingly preparing for this blown-out present. Could have earned them a good living in the meantime, too. If he'd had a few more years, maybe he could have made it as an artist and graphic designer, but there'd been no guarantees; given everything that had happened over the last eight-odd months, he felt regretful he hadn't been more practical, resentful that he'd chased his dream at the expense of their future.

Mia wiped oil from her fingers with an old shirt. "What do you think?"

"I think if these bikes get any greasier we can fry them for dinner."

"About the resistance. The BRR."

He sat back, sweating lightly. "You want to go?"

"It makes sense, doesn't it? If we're going to fight back, we have to do it now. Before they're settled in. While there's still enough of us to matter."

"Yep."

"Wait, you agree?"

"It's one thing to run off to the mountains when it sounds like everybody else has thrown up their hands and walked off. But if we ran and hid now—" He set down a wrench with a small metal click. "What if we wound up with a kid some day? Knowing it was just a matter of time before some alien ship spotted the smoke from our chimney?"

"You're cute when you're trying to predict the future." Her grin faded, gradual as a sunset. "Then there's Sarah."

"She can come with if she wants. If not, I don't see why we can't leave her the house."

"She'll need recovery time."

"You normally do when you're shot in the back."

"If we have to go before she's better, can you leave her behind?"

He cocked his head. "Let's do whatever we can to prevent

ourselves from having to answer that. Like getting another bike."

Mia nodded with a drawn-in little smile that told him she'd already decided for herself. Patrols buzzed the skies the next few days, pinning them inside until the middle of the night. Then they went to the yard to gather eggs and lettuce and slosh around water for the plants and dry corn for the chickens. Sarah slept a lot. Raymond spent some time thinking about how to get the BRR's exact location out of her despite her being dead set against ever seeing them again. The rains came back, dampening the October days, shrouding them in cloud and mist. Sarah began to walk by herself, to empty her own bucket by day and plod to the latrine in the corner of the yard by night. She showed no signs of infection. Once she was able to walk easy, and with the patrols diminished to a scattering of lone ships around the city proper, Raymond took Sarah out for a tour of the grounds.

She watched the chickens peck at the fog-dewed grass. "Where'd you find those guys?"

He gestured into the hills. "Up there somewhere."

"Suppose there must be plenty of loot out there if you look hard enough." She stretched. She'd taken a bath earlier, her first proper one since arriving. Her short blonde hair had feathered out a bit, buffeted by the unsteady sea breeze. Moonlight caught the freckles on her bare, toned shoulders. "And a garden, too. You two self-sufficient?"

"Some of the plants are still coming in," he said. "I think we would have been by next spring, summer. There'd be more than enough preserves to see us through then."

"Why in hell would you want to run off and join the army when you got a house and a garden above the sea?"

"Why are you so quick to run off after one setback?"

She gave him a hard-eyed gaze that looked for a second like it would lead to punching. That look burned off, replaced by a flicker of humorless laughter. "It wasn't the first." Her tone was worn-out, resigned. "You think anyone got off that beach? Besides me?"

He shook his head. "I don't know."

"Anyone who ran got hunted down. They always are. Only thing for us to do is melt into the wilderness and hope they'll let us live in peace."

"Well, no matter what Axl Rose says, this isn't exactly the

wilderness. We have to go."

Absently, Sarah stroked her upper arms. "That's too bad. You built something special here."

"It only took a few months of work. We can do the same somewhere else."

She gave him a long look, heavy with an emotional calculus he couldn't integrate. "You could, couldn't you."

While Sarah slept that night, Raymond combed the neighborhood until he found a third bicycle. He didn't see any sign of people or aliens during the hour he was out. On the way back, he heard the whine of a jet engine, but it was far off, obscured by the dark and the mist.

He woke to the sound of screaming. Sarah lay in bed, pale and sweating, the muscles of her arms and legs as tight as piano strings. He checked her wound. It had scabbed about an inch below her surrounding skin, but it looked no worse from when he'd helped change her bandage a few days earlier. Raymond gestured Mia out of the room.

"I think she's infected."

"Her skin doesn't look red."

"It could be something internal. Or in her bones. I don't know, I'm not a doctor-man."

Mia swept stringy hair from her face. She'd kept up combing it, but they'd had to ration their water more strictly since Sarah's arrival, and she hadn't bathed in days. "We've only got so much medicine."

"We've got boxes of it."

"Enough to last another forty years?"

He set his mouth. "If we don't give her anything and she dies, you get to haul her corpse out of here by yourself."

"Jesus." Mia laughed, startling him, "Did you ever think we'd be having a discussion like this? Threatening each other with dead bodies? What happened?"

"I don't know." He laughed with her in a way that felt very strange. They gave Sarah an antibiotic twice a day, parceled out painkillers. At night she staggered to the latrine and Raymond helped her back to bed. Mia set up three packs with food, water, meds, lighters, knives, extra socks and shoes, a knife and fork and spoon, lightweight blankets. She packed the pockets of three coats with extra gear—needles and thread, boxes of ammo, a small wrench set and spare nuts and bolts for the bikes, some string and wire and flashlights and matches.

Not that Sarah was in any shape to ride if something happened. Without speaking, he and Mia had agreed on that much. They hadn't again broached what they'd do if they had to leave and she couldn't. No use risking a fight over something that might never happen.

He began to hope that decision would stay hypothetical as Sarah's health picked back up. Over the next couple weeks, she was walking on her own, if weakly, and coming out to sit beneath the deck to watch them work the yard or to smile down on the dark waves. He asked her about the BRR on a few occasions, including where exactly they were located, but she brushed him off each time.

"I think you're nice people," she said over the ruffle of surf. "Fact, I know you are. Most people would have left me by that beach to learn who's better at scooping up dead meat: outer-space aliens or California sea gulls. You wouldn't give the BRR up to the invaders. Not like most."

Raymond sipped his water. "Then what's the problem?"

"You're good people. I can't help good people sign up to get slaughtered."

"Don't you think that should be our decision?"

She gave him another one of her long gazes, full lips parted, eyes flickering with a strange mercy quickly quashed. "Me and my boyfriend went into the movement together. Adam. Looked a little like you but more muscle. He'd been in the army—Iraq. 18 months. We lived in Bakersfield, which fell apart as fast as anywhere else. Didn't matter with Adam. He got us out before the worst hit and found us a farm by the hills. It's pretty dry there. I didn't see how we'd last any longer than it took the apples to rot off the trees.

"I think he could have done it. He'd done some stuff in Iraq, which is hardly any wetter—digging wells, outhouses, all the things you have to do to make living in a shithole a little less shitty. Anyway, it was just the two of us. You don't need a ton of good land to feed two people.

"We saw the ships a few months later. Don't know what they were doing way out in BFE. Checking out the old oil fields, maybe. They sure spent a lot of time poking around the derricks.

Their mistake. Third time they came by the same field, Adam was waiting for them. Mowed them all down with an M-16, then dynamited their ship. When another one flew in to see what had got the first, he and his buddy Chris took *them* out, too.

"Long story short, he talks me into joining this resistance group he's heard about on his ham, and the two of us and Chris drive off to this lake outside LA to find this group of ex-Marines and Navy and so forth. At first it's mostly scouting the aliens out, intel, and we can't believe the things we're seeing—groups of people rounded up and executed in the streets, others hauled off in these makeshift handcuffs for God knows what. Once we get a read on their movements, we start hitting 'em. Taking down their scouts. Adam booby-trapped their patrol routes with IEDs. Took out more than a few. Learned a few things, too. They look an awful lot alike, you know. Not just because they're fucked-up aliens. Their height, their features, their claws—hardly any difference from one to the other. Like they're clones, or hive-born.

"Then they started to crack down. Kicked our asses whenever we tried to penetrate the city. Somebody in charge gets a brilliant idea for an amphibious smash-and-grab down in Redondo. Me and Adam were on the same boat along with the rest of our platoon. Had an engine, but we paddled in to come in under the radar, so to speak. We got the salt-spray coming in with every splash and the waves weren't big but you feel every inch in your stomach. Whole place is dark. The breakers start to push us in hard and the next thing you know we're grinding sand. We jump out into the surf and rush up to the rally point at a lifeguard station.

"Only Adam doesn't make it. This blue bolt just cuts him down right above the tideline. His head, it makes this popping noise, and my face is stinging and hot and I'm standing there wearing his brains, his skull. I'm screaming. Everything's going to shit—lasers, bullets, shouting, aliens up on the ridge just wasting everybody. I don't even remember what's next. I'm running up the ramp, I'm up on the sidewalk, and one of those blue flashes lights me up, too."

She'd been gazing out to sea, to the constant wash of waves over sand. She turned to him now, fixing him with fever-bright blue eyes.

"If Adam couldn't make it, if he just dies there like he was nothing at all, what shot would *you* have?"

"Not much, probably." He didn't know what else could be said. They sat in silence until she started shivering. He helped her inside.

Maybe her infection broke. Maybe lifting Adam's weight from her shoulders made each step a little lighter. Whatever the case, within days Sarah was up and about on her own, if visibly thinner and paler. Raymond fed her more spinach with her salads, slaughtered one of the chickens and left the fat on when he cooked it. She began to smile, to help them weed the garden at night, sprinkling water on the peppers and lettuce and herbs, sweeping out the ground floor and the back porch without asking.

She looked good. On the mend. Strong enough to walk, if not to ride a bike for more than a few blocks.

Just when Raymond thought he might be able to talk her into leaving with them — to Colorado, if not the BRR forces — the aliens came to the base of the hills, spraying long plumes of fire from their racketing, hemispherical tanks. The world erupted in heat and flame.

20

He wanted to kill them.

Cold, cruel vengeance. To kill every living thing in that alien city growing from Earth soil. Walt imagined wrenching their tough-skinned limbs right from their sockets and snapping them over his knee. Stabbing their bulbous squid-eyes. Slashing open their bodies and watching their knotty guts and mucosal blood soak into the desert floor.

Not very wise, attacking a camp of hundreds by himself, armed only with a pistol and a couple of knives. Not very wise at all. But he wanted it so bad it felt as if he'd already done it. He spun through the possibilities—rush in, shoot as many as he could, steal a ship, blast off—but he wouldn't know how to fly it, would he, and they would just track him down and destroy him. Sneak in under cover of darkness instead, knife them in their beds (did they have beds?), skulk away. That one was at least plausible. He had the idea their eyes, for all their size, weren't so good. Before killing it, he'd crouched immediately below the one he'd fought in the stream, and it hadn't seen him until he moved.

Still, risking his life to kill a handful of aliens hardly seemed worth it. The blue cones in the distance could house at least a couple hundred of them, and with no sign of their scout ships, let alone the mothership or invasion fleet that must have carried them here, he had to guess Earth now housed several thousand of the creatures at the very least. Not worth it. If he still had the itch to stomp some aliens after he made it to LA, he had the feeling they'd be around.

He rose to a low crouch, meaning to slink along the brush and weeds until he'd cleared line of sight, when a large, dust-spewing version of the hemispherical vehicles trundled to the edge of the buildings, parked a short ways from a tall, spindly cone-tower, and disgorged 25-odd naked humans into the sunlight.

Walt sunk back down behind a prickly brown bush. He watched as, in what he took to be the universal sign of oppression, three aliens with rods or guns of some sort herded the people into a simple pen—he couldn't see the wires, and for all he knew the creatures used force fields to fence off their livestock, but it was a rectangle set off by a series of twenty-foot poles, anyway, and the captives stayed inside even when two of the aliens disappeared into the nearby cone-tower.

The humans milled about, some cupping their hands over their genitals, others not bothering. A couple of people tried to talk, but from what Walt could see, nobody was much interested in chatting.

The first person to sit down did so after just five minutes, easing himself onto the flat dirt. He was joined over the next few minutes by a couple of others. The bulk stayed standing for nearly an hour until, within the span of a single minute, all but three of the captives lowered themselves to the ground.

Walt sipped water, chewed some crackers. The late afternoon sun had been plenty warm while he'd been walking but was now wholly neutral. He'd spent enough weeks in these high deserts to know that, an hour after sunet, it would be downright cold.

Maybe the woman who started throwing rocks had reached the same conclusion. Maybe she simply didn't like being penned like a human chicken. Walt couldn't say. He just watched as the woman knelt, scooped several somethings from the dirt, and began hurling the somethings—rocks, most likely, but it was too far to see—at the tall poles.

The woman stopped a moment later and tipped back her head toward the blue cone-tower. She slung out her arms, waving violently, possibly shouting, then knelt for more rocks. When she resumed throwing, it was at the tower.

A blue line speared from the structure, so brief and faint Walt couldn't be certain he'd seen it. The woman crumpled straight down. Around her, the others leapt up screaming, crowding away from the sudden death.

The sun was most of the way to the hills before the aliens went in the pen to bring out the body.

Activity elsewhere in the city calmed down, the ground vehicles parking along the unpaved streets, most of the aliens dispersing into the steep, conical buildings. The people gathered into a huddle just before sunset. After, most of them filed one by one to a corner of the pen, where each squatted for a minute before drifting away to a seat in the dirt.

Walt already had his plan, so much as you could call it that. He watched through the settling darkness. A single light popped on from a high corner of the pen, casting the field in a twilight of long shadows. The rest of the camp or city or whatever the hell it was sat under a similarly half-hearted light. Lack of resources? Or already complacent that nothing and no one would be coming at them from the darkness?

Walt napped. He woke a couple hours later, watching the tower while his brain and body woke up. This time, he took his pack with him.

He moved past the camp, then cut across the open field, pausing at intervals to scan the grounds through his binoculars. No searchlights fanned out from above. No alarms wailed through the night. When Walt was within a quarter mile of the pen, one of the vehicles lumbered from the far side of the city heading for the highway. He dropped prone, waited for its bluish lights to swing onto the road and fade into the distance.

He crawled the last hundred yards on his belly. Dust swirled in his nostrils. Rocks jabbed his stomach. This close, he could make out the wires enclosing the pen, electric or something like it.

Everyone inside looked asleep. As he crawled up to the pen's edge, a young woman lifted her head, arms barred over her breasts.

"Who's out there?"

"Shut up," Walt hissed. "Put your hands above your head."

Hesitantly, she raised her hands, shivering. With her back to the light, it was too dark to get much of a look, but Walt smiled anyway.

"I'm kidding. My name's Walt. I'm—"

"What are you doing out there?"

"No time for questions. This fence—"

"I asked first. What are you doing here?"

"Getting *you* out of *there*." He pointed at the wires enclosing the grounds. "Is that electric? How does it work?"

"How should I know? For all I know it's sorcery."

Again Walt smiled. "How many of them are in the tower?"

Her shoulders rose to meet the edge of her dark hair. "Three? Nine million? I haven't been making them sign in and out."

That jibed with what he'd seen, though who knows what they'd been up to while he'd slept. "Listen. I'm an idiot, so I'm going to go inside that building and try to disable the fence. I need you to wake up the others and tell them to get ready to move. If any of them makes a peep, I'm running away without looking back."

She squinted at him, leaning closer to the wires, long legs silhouetted. With some will, he stopped himself from glancing at her crotch.

"Who are you?"

He put a finger to his lips. "Take care of business. I'll take care of mine."

She watched him turn away. By the time he crawled to the deep blue face of the tower, he heard her whispering to the others, shushing their confusion. He drew his longest knife, a Vietnam-era-type combat knife with a seven-inch blade and a broken compass in its pommel. The door was just a little too wide and a little too tall and sported a T-shaped handle on its right-hand side. Purely mechanical. It opened without trouble; either their door technology wasn't up to par with their interstellar travel, or they were way out in their version of the boonies. Walt supposed that sort of limitation explained why they'd only managed to kill 99% of humanity so far instead of the whole damn thing.

The door opened to a tight, spartan entryway with a bulky, fridge-shaped object to his right and a spiral staircase to his left. He paused, listening. An electric hum just soft enough to drive you crazy. Elsewhere, further up or possibly outside, the shuffle of a large creature's weight. Oddly gloomy, like the twilight of a theater before they turned the lights down all the way (an experience, some distant part of him registered, that he'd never have again). He stepped onto the stairs.

His foot missed. He fell forward, knee banging into the surface. He gripped his knife and froze. By the time he'd convinced himself nothing was on its way to investigate, he'd seen the stairs weren't stairs at all—just a long, smooth, inclined ribbon of some rubbery, sandpapery material that these things apparently oozed right up.

Between strings of mental swearing, he gave long thought to backing out the door and running west as fast as he could. He couldn't, of course. Someone in the pen would shout out at him, calling down the aliens. He should have thought of that beforehand. Everyone was in this for their own survival. Those human cattle in the enclosure out there, they wouldn't give a shit if he died running away. All they'd care was some coward hadn't died trying to save their own pointless lives.

He smiled, angry. This was why you never try to help.

There wasn't even a handrail. He planted one foot on the ramp, preparing to crawl, but found the hard, rubbery surface gripped his shoe as firmly as a handshake. He leaned up another step, then straightened until he was nearly upright. A strange vertigo hit him —his feet felt sturdy as roots, but his upper body felt dangerously unbalanced, as if he might topple over if he blinked in the wrong direction—and he lowered himself to a crouch. Above, the ramp spiraled along the wall all the way to a dim hole in the ceiling and an unseen room beyond. The center of the tower was empty, just disturbing, dizzying empty space.

He crawled up on an improvised combo of hands, knees, elbows, and feet, proceeding with the speed of a hungover turtle. Some fifteen feet up, the ramp flattened out, giving way to a short landing and an oval alcove set into the wall. A single glance at the recess told him all he needed: empty space, just large enough for one of the many-legged creatures to insert itself within, and two narrow windows facing black mountains and pinpricks of stars. And, a couple feet to the left of the windows, a rack of what were recognizably guns.

He picked one up. Pistol-like, with a short, fat barrel and a grip like the handle of a sword, a slightly flared cylinder with a round knob at the end. One button on either side of the barrel. Holding the grip, he could just reach the buttons with his thumb and forefinger. It was surprisingly heavy and he saw no obvious sign of a clip. He carried it in his left hand, knife in the right, and continued up.

More landings. More alcoves. He paused often but heard nothing beyond the background hum. He was more than halfway up the ramp and was certain he'd be incapable of safely moving up or down any faster than a literal crawl. If one of those things came in from down below or up top, he'd be a squatting duck.

His luck, if you could call it that—he didn't think any such term applied when you'd deliberately chosen to clamber around an alien guard tower manned by hostile monsters—held to the top. The ramp rose to a wide, round hole. Above, the same dim lighting showed little besides a wide window and a curved ceiling another fifteen feet up. No visible aliens. Walt straightened, inch by inch, until his eyes cleared the ledge.

The hole opened into the corner of a room as barren as the rest of the tower. Windows paneled a circular space some thirty feet across. One of the creatures was inserted into an alcove, its back to him, curled up more tightly than he could have imagined. Another stood twenty feet from the first in front of something that looked like a computer designed for slobbery dogs: its graphics were Atari ST-simple, and they changed little despite the at-times frantic typing, twisting, sweeping, and signing-like gestures of the limbs waving and poking at a combination of keys, trackballs, and empty spaces above gleaming black pads.

Neither turned his way. Guided by a growing hunch, he crept towards the one at the computer even more slowly than his scuttle up the ramp. The alien tapped and jabbed at its terminal. He drew up behind the alien, smelling its odor of fish oil and drying kelp. Its claws and tentacles twitched above the motion-pads, poked keys, massaged knobs. For a minute, Walt just watched its motions; he had every doubt he'd be able to replicate them and navigate the system, but who knew. Besides, there was something very sweet about this moment, of knowing the alien's fate while it remained clueless. He wondered if one of them had felt the same way when they'd unleashed the virus on Earth.

Fast as a viper, he raised his knife. The alien stuck up its two antennae-like limbs, swiveled its head, and fixed him with giant squid-eyes that looked like the perfect image of cartoon surprise. Walt barked out a laugh and slammed the blade down into its right eye. The knife plunged easily, sending a spray of clear, watery liquid followed by thick inky goop. The alien hissed and jerked away, limbs spasming, clubbing Walt's face. The knife slipped from his grasp, embedded in the creature's brain. It fell, tentacles slapping the rubbery floor, one bony leg sweeping Walt's feet from under him.

Feet thumped behind him. He reached for the knife waggling in the dying alien's eye but was driven back by a wall of writhing limbs. The alien from the alcove bore down on him, its eyes as widely, comically angry as the other's had been surprised. Walt leveled the alien pistol and jammed down the buttons, bracing himself for the bang and the kick. A beam of electric blue light appeared between himself and the alien. Skin crackled, sending fat sizzling into the air with the smell of fresh battered cod. The alien didn't make a noise as Walt waved the beam back and forth, severing limbs, slashing black gouges across its body and the pink, strappy thing it wore around its middle. It collapsed in an avalanche of charred parts that slammed into Walt and drove him back into the still-twitching body of the first.

Because there didn't seem to be anything else to do, he swore.

He arose from a mess of singed limbs and briny goo. The first alien hadn't sensed him until he'd jerked up the knife. The one by the stream hadn't noticed him until he'd moved, either. So they could sense bodily motion, but imperfectly. He remembered reading that sharks and some other species could sense the electrical charges of contracting muscles or something like that, but all the animals that could do that lived in water, which Walt was pretty sure could carry a charge much better than air. On the other end of things, he wasn't certain the aliens could hear at all. They seemed to communicate through motion, too, and they sure as hell didn't do any shouting or screaming when they died.

Walt shoved bits of dead alien away with his feet and turned to the computer. The screen meant nothing to him, abstract rods and squares and zigzag lines with no clear icons, pointers, or even text. Within seconds of fiddling with the controls, he was ready to walk outside and simply laser through the wires around the pen.

A pen that was rectangular. Just like the leftmost object on the screen. And the rods were the towers and the zigzags the mountains—could it be that easy? Experimentally, he moved his hand over one of the motion-pads, hoping to conjure up a pointer he could drag to the pen. Instead, the screen switched to a wall of glyphs which he couldn't turn back no matter how he waved his hands. After a minute of conducting an orchestra that wasn't there, he went to the hole, lowered himself onto the ramp, and scooted down to the ground floor.

He could hear the gasps from the pen as he walked outside,

hunched his back to shield the light as best he could, and simply lasered through the lower wires.

"You were in there a long time," the young woman whispered.

"Did you miss me?"

"Who would miss a failure?"

"Get the others over here," he smiled. She went and whispered to the crowd of two dozen, who ducked under the clipped, still-smoking wires and stood shivering in the night air.

"Now get down and crawl until we're outside the light," Walt whispered to the group.

"We're naked," hissed a stocky man with a hairy stomach.

"Would you rather get a thorn in your balls or a laser in your back?"

"Can't you steal a car?"

Walt raised the laser. "*Crawl.*"

They did. Through weeds and rocks and dust, through whimpers and soft yelps, pale asses bobbing in the moonlight. After a hundred yards, Walt stopped them and pulled out his binoculars. The camp was as still as it had been before he'd approached the pen. He rose to a stoop and gestured the prisoners on. Men and women rose and followed, knees and elbows rubbed raw and pasted with dirt. They ducked along with their hands splayed over their breasts and genitals, hissing through clenched teeth when their feet struck a stone; once, a young man fell and had to be helped along on the shoulders of two others. They reached the highway with no sign of alarm from the colony. On the blacktop, Walt dug out four bottles of water and handed them to the young woman and three others, watching with mild interest as each escapee glugged down as much as they thought they could get away with before passing it on.

"Well," he said, "good luck."

"Good luck?" the stocky man said. "With what?"

"I'm not your shepherd. Besides lying down in a big human bull's-eye, traveling in a group is the stupidest thing we could do. They'd find us in an instant." Walt waved at the dark hills. "I'm leaving. On my own. If you like living, you should do the same."

"That is insane." The young woman splayed her hands at the crowd, disregarding her nudity. "We're hungry. We're tired. We don't even have any goddamn clothes. They shipped us in here from San Francisco and I don't even know where *here* is. People are going to die. You can't just walk away."

"I got you out. You can figure out what to do next."

He turned away. When they followed, he jogged off the road into the cheat grass and brambles; their crunching bare-footed steps diminished. When he glanced back a couple minutes later, they were still standing there, silhouettes as straight and still as human cacti.

After that, he stayed well off the road, risking contact only to meet the demands of water and food. The land descended, mountains rolling down to hills, but stayed desert the whole way, mile after mile of yellow grass, spiky green-brown shrubs, and gray dust. According to the highway markers, he was nearly forty miles into the state before he realized he'd crossed into California. Other than a two-day stretch so hot he slept out the second afternoon in an empty rambler with all the doors open, the weather ranged from slightly warm in the day to slightly cool at night. It felt exactly as he'd always imagined California would feel.

He saw an alien jet once, streaking over the southern sky. He crouched among the weeds until the drone died away. Sometimes, he imagined at least a few of the prisoners had made it out. The girl, maybe — she'd been young, strong. Who knew.

Another set of hills rose to the west. By nightfall, he climbed up the highway, a patchy set of lanes unfurling along the sides of crumbling hills. Peaks swelled beside him, massive and silent in the darkness. Green weeds appeared in tufts beside the shoulder, then leafy plants, trees in the crags and scree. Dawn broke behind him and he moved through the brush, smelling the dew on the grass and the sweet-choking scent of flowering weeds.

After panting his way up an innocuous crest, he stopped cold. In the thin daylight, one vast cityscape carpeted the valley, too long and boundless to see its ends.

21

Down the hill, a crew of aliens fanned across the roads, metal glinting from their claws. Dome-like armored vehicles ranged ahead, squirting flame into houses and condos. Thick white smoke bellowed into the skies and was blown inland in streamers by the steady offshore breeze.

Raymond's voice was soft as church. "What the hell are they doing?"

Sarah turned from the window, giving him a steady eye. "Burning out the vermin."

"That's it," Mia said. "Time to go."

Sarah cocked her head. "You want to leave?"

"I have a thing about getting burned to death."

"They got an army out there!"

"And we'll have a barbecue in here if we stay."

"Mia's right," Raymond said. "We've got everything we need. We're ready to go. We can bike south along the coast and slip through Long Beach. Find somewhere the aliens aren't."

Sarah shook her head in wide, slow strokes. "Middle of the day? We go out there, they'll cut us down. We don't know they'll get all the way up here. Even if they do, we can hide in the yard, use those rocks by the cliff's edge—"

"You haven't been here long enough," Mia said. "They keep coming, keep rooting out the survivors. They're going to keep at it until the entire city's dead."

"And *you* haven't been out there with them. There's no surviving out in the open. We wait this out, they're not gonna bother coming back when they think they've burned everyone out."

"We'll stay," Raymond said. Mia's head snapped his way. "Until nightfall. Then we get away from monsters for good."

Sarah's blunt face went red from brow to chin. "You'll be killed! You think a couple of housemakers are gonna survive where a company of trained soldiers gets slaughtered like cows?"

"We're not going to try to fight them. Running's much easier."

"And what about me?" She twisted, clawing up her shirt to reveal the scabby hole in her back. "How far you think I can ride a bike?"

"You'll be okay," Mia said.

"What if I'm not? What if this thing tears open and I can't keep going?"

Raymond let out a breath. "Then we'll stop and get you patched up."

Sarah laughed. "While they're shooting us with fucking lasers?"

"We're going," Mia said, low. "If you don't want to come? You can stay. You can have the house. All yours."

"No." Her eyes flicked between Raymond's, her lips parted. "No, I can't stay by myself. I'll come."

"Good," he said. "Get together anything you want to bring with. We'll be in the garage."

Blue light flashed from a flaming cul de sac at the base of the hills. A tiny figure raced across a lawn, one hand clamped to their mouth. A thick blue beam winked on for a full second. As the figure's upper body fell to the ground, severed across the hips, their legs stumbled forward and tumbled into the grass.

Raymond turned away. Sarah stared after him as he headed down the hall, eyes so bright he was afraid her fever had resurged. That would explain her mood, too. He and Mia tested the bike's chains and wheels, doublechecked the supplies in their packs. They hadn't collected any seeds from the garden. The bell peppers would have seeds inside, but for most everything else, they'd be out of luck. How many details had they overlooked? For all their work and preparation, how much would they wind up wanting in the next few days and weeks? But that was just how things always went. You couldn't waste too much time worrying about being perfect. They'd done their best. They'd make do.

"Think she'll make it?" Mia said, as if running her thoughts down a parallel track.

He toweled oil from his fingers. "I think she has a better chance coming than she does staying."

She smiled with half her mouth. "Beneath the surface of that optimism lies something very, very depressing."

There wasn't much work to do: their bikes and gear were perfectly fine, and any other tasks, sweeping or weeding or washing dishes, all that felt pointless now. Raymond wandered the house, staring at beds and counters, opening cabinets and gazing at the dusty glasses, and finally, after a long look out on the fires creeping up the hill—he could smell the smoke now, he thought, though the wind continued to blow inland—he stood by the back window to watch the foamy, everlasting sea.

"You gonna miss it?" Sarah said from behind, startling him.

"Nothing's more peaceful."

"Those waves sure are pretty." She'd changed into a tank top, a smaller one of Mia's. She wasn't wearing a bra.

"Feeling okay?" he said.

She nodded at the garden, the ocean beyond. "You sure you want to leave? Think what you could build with another body around."

"We'll find that out some place that isn't about to be burnt to the ground." He scratched his neck; he should go shave. "Though I think we may wind up with the Rebels."

Sarah ran her fingers through her choppy blonde hair. "I'd better go get the last of my things."

He watched the waves until sunset, then went outside to free the chickens and feel the sea breeze on his skin. Smoke-scent mingled with seaweed and salt. Goosebumps flushed his arms. Quite suddenly, he remembered it was November, and most of the north would soon see snow. It was so easy, down here where winter meant cool rains that could be replaced by 70-degree sunshine as early as New Year's Day, to forget how cold it could be and how long it would last. If they didn't wind up with the BRR, they'd have to stay in the Southwest until spring. Waste a couple seasons somewhere temporary before finding themselves a new home in the mountains. Well, it would only be a few months.

Back in the house, there was a strange stillness to the air, an anticipation. The floor creaked under his feet.

"Raymond?" Mia called from downstairs. "Raymond, can you come down here?"

The beam of his flashlight wobbled as he jogged down the steps. Candles flickered in the garage. "Time to go?"

"For her," Sarah said. She clamped one arm around Mia's neck. The other held a pistol to the side of Mia's head. "You and me are staying right here."

22

Walt could hear it now, a steady sough that sounded so much like the wash of traffic he had almost convinced himself the next crest would reveal a coastal California that had never fallen to plague and invasion. Cars jamming along sunny streets. Taut-legged women in jogging shorts leading muscly, well-groomed pit bulls down the sidewalks. Men in sunglasses arguing breezily into their cell phones from behind the wheels of their red convertibles. After 3000 miles of walking, he'd find the one place in America that was still America.

But despite the cloudless skies, that false sound of traffic was punctuated irregularly by a heavy, crackling thunder. And the walls of nearby houses were scorched black or flattened in an ugly rubble of charcoal, jutting timbers, and gray, yellow, and black debris, things that had once been shoes and dishes and CDs and books and figurines, now nothing but torched, rained-out garbage. In his two-and-a-half-day march from the hills, he'd been shot at once, seen a handful of faces whipping drapes closed or ducking into doorways, heard the buzz and the whine of strange ships hurtling across the sky. This place was dead, too. A graveyard waiting for the last of its walking dead to wise up and bury themselves.

He wondered what Vanessa would think. It was exactly like and exactly unlike he'd imagined. The hills ringing the valley had held old ramblers and the 1960s' vision of the future. Descending brought him through miles of dirty streets and dirtier tenements, cars and buses damming whole blocks. At a glance, LA's middle had shown nothing but bilingual strip malls, grassless soccer fields, Spanish signs, and boarded-up taco shops, but there had been surprises, too: dirt lots packed with forty-foot stacks of pallets; iron grilles on the ground-floor windows of every home; bulk fabric outlets; three-story paintings of Jesus' face on the sides of warehouse walls.

And the highways—the fucking highways. Great gray ribbons of concrete soaring like bizarro Roman aqueducts. At one point, the highways were stacked four deep, one sunk into the ground, the other three crossing one on top of another until the last stood a hundred feet above the ground. Dogs gnawed bodies in the weeds. Stretches of the lanes were as blank as the desert roads; others sat clogged with vans and trucks and SUVs and sports cars, some torched black, leathery-skinned corpses sprawled on hoods and slumped behind wheels. Back in the cities, entire blocks resembled the burnt-out husks of a long-ago war, stray papers flapping in the breeze, glass glittering from porches and sidewalks. Other neighborhoods looked like model homes that had never seen a tenant.

After months of overland travel through woods, deserts, plains, and small towns, it felt nearly as alien as the field of blue cones where he'd freed two dozen people from the wired-up pen.

He knew Vanessa would have loved the weather, if nothing else. He hadn't been keeping strict track, but it was late October or early November and any kind of sustained walking left him dewed with sweat, morning or night. The skies were warm and blue. A bit chilly at night, but a light jacket was all he needed.

Two and a half days later, he could hear the wash and crash of surf.

Lines of tall palms fluttered in the constant breeze. Dead ahead, the sun gleamed hard and yellow, less than an hour from the horizon. He crested the hill. Half a mile away, a gap of silvery-blue sea glimmered between the beachside condos. Hacienda-style mansions squatted on the meandering residential roads to his right, a twin set of smokestacks rising some ways further. A couple miles to his left, a big hill or a small mountain rose in a round green lump, wreathed in sea-blown mist and the smoke boiling up from its base.

Something bad was happening over there. Logically speaking, he should have hidden for another hour until he could move with the relative safety of darkness. But the ocean was *right there*. He could hardly stop himself from sprinting, his pack thudding into his lower back, the sunshine soaking his skin but offset by that steady bay wind, a journey of three thousand miles reduced to a thousand final steps. He loped down the sidewalk, crouching down at intersections to watch for movement. Machines groaned a mile to his left. A single scream hung in the humid air, stopping as abruptly as an answering machine clicking off.

The strip of sea grew closer. Gulls screeched. Birds with wingspans as wide as his arms soared in twos and fours. Surf rustled and thundered. He could smell the sea more strongly than his own sweat now, a different scent from the beaches of Coney Island or Long Island—tangier, kelpier. He crossed another intersection, hand shielding his eyes from the onpouring sun, and reached the edge of what was once American civilization. A set of stairs led down to the sandy beach, flanked on one side by a blue Cape Cod-style home and on the other by a weathered apartment block with a rusty satellite dish sticking from its side. He jogged down the steps, stopping at the landing halfway down. The beach was cratered and scorched but clear of aliens or people. A rock jetty protruded a short ways to his right; further on, a wooden pier extended into the waves. South showed nothing but lifeguard stands and bathrooms on the way to a rocky beach set beneath sheer cliffs, all half-obscured by a light screen of smoke.

He headed straight across a bike path at the bottom of the steps. His shoes sunk into the sand. A tingling numbness swept over him. Ragged volleyball nets flapped in the wind. Spray speckled his face. Just before water's edge, he crossed a line of bulbous brown kelp, small white shells, and coin-sized lumps of what looked like tar. A fringe of gulls waddled away, murmuring squawks of complaint.

Walt stopped a couple feet below the tideline. Foam curled up the beach, bubbling away into the wet sand. At once he collapsed. For her, of course, Vanessa, the woman he would never see again, her megawatt grins and airy charm. But also for the knowledge— as sudden as his drop to his knees, as deep as the waters on the blue horizon—that whatever they'd had together had been gone long before the plague arrived. He cried for the complete and stupid loss of everyone and everything, of thousands of years of culture and growth swept away in the span of days. And lastly, for himself—not in self-pity, for he no longer felt any of that, but for his journey here, the sheer endurance and will of it, for the idiocy and impossibility of his nearly arbitrary quest. He'd fucking *done* it. He was here. He was alive.

He should have brought something of hers to give to the ocean. A picture, a necklace, a pair of her damn panties. She'd wanted to live here. Some part of her could have, and if he'd been a little wiser, he could have done more for her in death than he'd probably ever done for her in life. He sat back in the sand, disappointed in himself for the first time in a long time.

The sun hung over the horizon, round and red. It was suddenly cold. His shoelaces were bright blue.

Because they were Vanessa's. One of the pairs he'd brought to replace his on the road, which he'd done a couple weeks before losing his bags to the aliens. Hurriedly, he stripped off his shoes, tugged out the laces, stood, and splashed into the shockingly cold water until it swirled around his thighs. He balled up the laces and flung them as far as he could.

Back on the beach, he toweled off with a stiff blanket. He felt placidly empty. He thought about what he should do now. Automatically, he considered suicide. That had been the goal, anyway, to die somewhere along the reach of those endless highways. But the desire was no longer there. It had been burnt out somewhere along the way, as bygone and lost as the civilization of iPhones and stretch SUVs and high fructose corn syrup.

He supposed he should survive, then. Go see what there was to see.

He decided to watch the sun go down. It was his first glimpse of the Pacific, after all, and the ritual would put a hard cap on the trip he'd just completed. The sun sat a few degrees above the horizon, a red bloom amid the salty haze on the straight blue line of the sea. He sipped bottled water. The sand was still warm under him; the air was just now cool. Walt felt timeless, an anonymous, ephemeral witness to a process that had played out daily for billions of years, a cycle whose significance was clear even when its mechanics were misunderstood. (And if humanity survived now, isolated pockets in the unwanted jungles, deserts, and icy wastes, how long before they once more forgot the Earth revolved around this setting sun?) He could sit there forever, observing and confirming the process of tide and moon and bird and sun and dolphin, somehow *becoming* the world, as far removed from mortal fears and neuroses as the breakers rolling endlessly and unstoppably to the shore. The sun sunk halfway below the waves; was he far enough south to see the green flash of its final moment?

An explosion roared over the condos and the yellow grass.

He rose to a crouch, spell broken. Bits of debris and trailing smoke ribboned the air to the north. Screams and automatic weapons drowned out the waves. Another explosion ripped through an apartment building overlooking the beach, sending its face sloughing down the slope in a clattering thunder of stone, wood, and glass.

Walt zipped up his pack and ran for the bike path lining the bottom of the harsh hills, laceless shoes flapping on his feet. On the pavement, he stuffed his shoes into his pack and turned south for the tall green cliffs. Staircases and ramps punctuated the slope every couple hundred yards. No good; he couldn't be sure what was happening up in the streets. The smoke he'd seen while cutting across town roiled a handful of blocks inland from where the shore curved along the rising hills. He'd follow that curve, by night if he had to, until it took him to a place that wasn't on fire.

Engines thrummed above. The sun was minutes set by the time Walt reached the curve in the beach. The cliffs soared a hundred feet vertical, mounted near the top by spacious decks with long, red-timbered legs. The sand gave out to a rubbly carpet of sharded rock and browning kelp. Surf welled between the stones. In the sea's quiet moments, a sound like angry static drifted from the heights. He knelt to thread new laces into his shoes and started along the rocks, splitting his attention between his footing and for any possible passage up the sheer walls.

His foot turned on a slimy stone, spilling him into a damp and stinking mat of kelp. Thick black flies clouded his face. He struggled up, knees soaked, palms stinging. In the dimming light, he could see nothing but rocky shore and rising cliffs.

Ahead, the cliff jagged inward, slumping from a sheer incline to one that was merely stupidly dangerous. Fallen rocks piled around its base. Grasses, shrubs, and small trees poked from its pitched face.

The last of the daylight was slipping away. He could wait out the night down here, risking the tides and whatever the aliens were up to. Road-honed instinct told him it was something big. There might not be any city left come morning, and tucked away as he might be below the cliffs, if it spilled out to him, he'd have nowhere to run.

He started up the scree, planting a hand for balance. Smoke touched his nose. A third of the way up the climb, the rubble stopped, replaced by a fast rise staggered with flatter stretches. Walt leaned into the rock, planting each step, grabbing for the stumps of brush and trailing branches. Halfway up, he stopped on the flat top of a boulder to catch his breath. Waves rolled beneath him, dark and indistinct. He was already having a hard time seeing his handholds. Within minutes, he'd be groping along under the confusion of full night.

Foot by foot, he carried upward, fingertips bleeding, shoulders and biceps burning. Just below the top, the slope transitioned to a sheer cliff. Walt hung there a moment, squinting to left and right for an alternate route, but the nooks of the rock wall were blurred by darkness. He reached up and scrabbled for a hold. He raised his knee, planted his foot. The rock beneath him shifted and tumbled away, racketing down the stone rise. Walt's legs swung into empty space.

He gasped, sweat slicking the rock beneath his clenching palms. Above, a muffled gunshot clumped across the early night.

23

Sarah shifted her grip on the gun, teeth bared. Raymond's head buzzed so hard he thought he'd fall over. He blinked repeatedly, as if that would wash the nightmare away.

"Put down the gun," he said.

"So you can ride into a massacre?" Sarah smiled. "I shoot her now, at least just one of you buys the farm."

"And then you and I live here in bliss."

"That's right."

His face felt numb. "There is a problem with that plan."

Sarah squeezed the crook of her elbow tighter to Mia's throat. "What's that?"

"The part where you shoot my wife."

"Everyone loses people. You get used to it."

"Yeah, you seem to have come out with flying colors," Mia said.

Sarah ground the barrel of the pistol into Mia's hair. "Shut your fucking face. You're a dead person. Dead people don't get to speak."

"How do you think you'll get him to stay when *that* happens? Chain him to a bed and break his legs?"

"Shut up!"

"Maybe you just make great iced tea. And know how to make ice in a place where it never freezes."

The blood fled from Sarah's mashed-together lips. She stood across the garage just in front of the door, too far to charge. The other guns were with their packs near the middle of the room; much closer, but Sarah's index finger only had to travel a fraction of an inch. Raymond edged forward.

"You stop right there." Sarah pointed the gun at him, then quickly returned it to a spot above Mia's right ear. "You don't move. You move, and I stucco the wall with her brains."

He held up his hands. "Don't shoot. I'm frozen."

It was true. What was the logic? Did she truly believe she could kill Mia and then convince him to live with her in loving harmony until the aliens burnt the whole hill to the ground? The only thing that made sense was that Sarah had gone moon-barkingly, chair-eatingly crazy, that the months of watching everyone around her die, first to the plague and then to aliens, had broken her mind completely, reducing it to a howling, mad wreck. How could he try to reason with that? How could you talk an insane person into doing something sane?

"Maybe we don't have to leave," he said. "Maybe we can all stay right here."

"So you can tie me up in my sleep? Knife me?"

"Nobody's going to knife you."

Sarah jerked her chin at Mia. "She'll talk you into it. Then you'll make your little excuses, and be sad for a while, but you'll ride away and you'll forget me."

"Jesus," Mia said. "How about we take your picture and promise to pray to it every night?"

"Enough!"

"I saved your life." Raymond was on the verge of tears. He didn't understand how that could mean so little to her, how she could justify taking whatever she wanted without the barest shred of gratitude. "Doesn't that mean anything?"

"And now I'm gonna save yours."

She sneered at Mia, fingers shifting on the grip of the pistol. Raymond's heart disintegrated, floating away like cold mist. It hit him in a hot rush, questions and conclusions he'd only be able to sort out after the fact. His wife was about to be shot by a crazy person and he was utterly helpless to stop it. Not only that, but it was his fault—he'd saved Sarah, he'd brought her back here, helped restore her health, allowed her to stay although she was a stranger with no claim whatsoever to the life between himself and Mia. It hadn't occurred to him that the mysterious relapse of Sarah's fever had been nothing but a ploy to get them to stay at the house with her, to stave off discussions of sending her off on her own. Mia'd had some suspicions, vague as they were, but he hadn't even begun to question the unknown woman in their home. He couldn't or wouldn't see the bad in a person, and now Mia would die.

Yet he couldn't have just left Sarah on the sidewalk above the beach to bleed to death, either. What *should* he have done? Made her leave as soon as she was able to walk? Snuck out with Mia in the middle of the night? How would he know to do these things without the foreknowledge of what was happening right now? Maybe any notion of power or control was just a laughable illusion — 21st century humanity had been wiped out by a plague it could never have suspected. He and Mia had weathered that, had built themselves a new life amidst the wreckage, but now that was going to be blown away, too. It had all been a sad delusion.

Sarah pointed the gun at his legs, frowned, and pulled the trigger.

The bang was impossibly loud, tearing through the garage with a force as terrible as the bullet plowing through his left thigh. The impact staggered him. He banged into a toolbox and fell hard on the concrete floor. The pain hadn't yet hit. Instead, its threat waited in his nerves like the afterimage of lightning in the seconds before the thunder strikes.

"Not going anywhere now, are you?" Sarah said. She swung the gun back Mia's way. "Not once there's nothing to leave for — "

Mia darted forward, grabbing Sarah's wrist and jabbing her stiff fingers at Sarah's eyes. Sarah shouted and cringed back, hand to her eyes. Mia hammered her wrist into Sarah's forearm. The gun jarred loose. Mia punched her in the nose; Sarah yelped, stumbling back into the bikes. She tumbled down in a crash of metal.

Mia picked up the gun and pointed it at Sarah's teary face. "I don't know who the fuck you are. I'm not sorry I won't find out."

"Don't shoot!" Sarah thrust up her hands. "I'll go. I'll leave right now. I'll — "

Mia pulled the trigger. Sarah's body flew back into the toppled bike. Her arms flopped limply, elbows bent like a butchered chicken. Mia righted her aim and fired three more times, hands bucking.

"Are you okay?" Mia leapt over the boxes of food and jugs of water, kneeling beside Raymond and his blood-soaked thigh. "Don't move. I'm going to find one of those blood-tying things."

"Tourniquet."

"Don't move."

She rushed into the house. Raymond clamped his palms to the wound and tried not to faint. It hurt now, a knifing burn; the bullet had passed clean through his muscle, and blood dribbled from both holes. Mia returned with a handful of rags, a fifth of Grey Goose, and an abbreviated extension cord, stray wires poking from the end where she'd chopped it short.

"You cut that up?" Raymond said. "What if we need to plug something in out back?"

"Take off your pants."

He unbuckled and unzipped, breath hissing into his lungs as he peeled his jeans away from his leg. "You killed her."

"I fucking did."

"I mean, you *killed* her."

She splashed vodka over the bullet holes. He arched his back in pain as she swabbed blood. "Honey, she shot you. She was about to kill me."

"I know." He *did* know. He did know that. Something was wrong. Besides the hole in his leg. And the corpse sprawled over the bike. Those were obviously wrong. This wrong was a different wrong, like remembering a memory but maybe that was just something you dreamed or got told. He frowned. Mia taped the rags around his leg and he screamed. She knotted the cord around the top of his leg. The pain brought him around. "How are we going to leave?"

Mia tucked a sweaty strand behind her ear. "The alien army down there will be a strong incentive to figure that out. Drink this."

He swallowed from the bottle of water. Room temperature, but it tasted amazing; he drank half the bottle in one long chug. "I'm sorry. I should have known."

"Rest here. I'm going to check the window. Maybe we can wait another day."

She left him with his pain. He sat up, panting. He willed himself to stand. He owed it to Mia. If he couldn't move, she'd have to go without him. He grabbed hold of a shelf of oil cans and pesticides. It was his fault. If he was able to weather the fire, they could arrange a place to meet—Angels Stadium, any landmark south of LA. Leaning into the shelf, he pulled himself to his right foot, sweat popping along his hairline, pain throbbing through his thigh. They could do it. She could take a gun and he could hide in the yard and follow her after the flames were gone. From there, take a car to Arizona or New Mexico, just the two of them, and wait out the winter. Just the two of them. He stood, quivering.

Mia popped through the door. "We need to leave. We can walk the bikes if we have to. We just have to outpace the fire."

Raymond grabbed a five iron from a dusty bag of clubs and caned his way to Sarah's body. He knelt, grimacing, and rolled her body off the bike. She was warm and yielding. Hot blood soaked his palms. Mia crouched in front of the garage door, grabbed the handle, and rolled it up with a hollow rumble.

On the other side, a man stood in the night, short and lean and blank-faced behind his patchy beard. He raised a strange pistol to Mia's face.

24

Walt scrabbled his toes against the cliff face. Beyond its edge, another burst of gunshots clapped its approval. Walt's biceps shook, his fingers stiffened. The pack pulled on his back like something alive. He lamented never lifting weights.

He wouldn't let go. He wouldn't fall. Arms jittering and burning, he hauled himself straight up, feet groping. A rock loosed, kicked down the cliff. Dangling from his taut right arm, he reached with his left and dragged himself another foot up the stone. His toes found a ledge. He rested there for some time, waiting for the burn to seep from his arms. When he resumed, the climb was surprisingly easy, the cliff yielding hand- and toeholds so readily it was like it wanted him off just as much as he did. The slope leveled out. He crawled the last few feet on his belly, rolling into the overgrown, dried-out grass of a dead person's back yard.

Gunshots. Possibly gun shots fired at a god damn alien. He could smell the smoke with every breath. Orange fires lined the dark neighborhoods a few hundred yards downhill. Spotlights blazed on windows and doorways. Gouts of flame spurted from hemispherical tanks.

The shots had come some way to his right, further out along the curve of the point. Walt jogged out to the sidewalk, passing an Italian-style home with vacant, broken windows and a wide-open front door. The neighboring joints looked worse, if anything; weedy, yellow yards, shattered windows, broken-down fences, loose papers flapping in shrubs and iron grilles. Southern California looked like shit.

Ahead, a dusty car sat in the driveway of another monstrous

home ripped from a Tuscan fairy tale. Green things grew in the side yard, sprouting from rich brown soil in neat leafy rows. Curtains shaded intact windows. Hard to tell in the darkness, but those windows didn't look too dusty.

He opened the iron gate and crept into the driveway, laser pistol in hand. Voices from the garage—a woman and a man. No sign of aliens. Walt turned for the street. The garage door cranked up. He whirled, sighting his pistol at a thin, pretty young woman whose olive hands were painted with drying blood.

He glanced at the youngish blond guy with a bloody bandage around his leg, then back to the woman. "Did you shoot him?"

"No!"

Walt flicked his gun at the stretched-out blonde woman with the holes in her face and chest. "Did you shoot *her*?"

"Of course I did." She glanced at the corpse and snorted. "My husband rescued her from an alien attack on the beach. She was part of a resistance movement. The rest of her platoon got killed on some mission. Maybe that drove her crazy. Maybe she was crazy before. Either way, things got all *Single White Female* in here. After she shot my husband, I shot her." She cocked her head. "Who the fuck are you to care, anyway?"

Walt met eyes with Raymond, who was pale with shock or bloodloss or both. "That what happened?"

"She wanted to kill my wife and stay here with me. She was nuts."

Walt considered the bloody mess that had once been a fit young woman. She was now quite dead. Of course, if everyone who'd killed another person deserved execution, Walt himself would need to be hanged, electrocuted, gassed, and guillotined. There was the matter of whether they were lying about the particulars of the woman's death, but he didn't think so. The man had been undeniably shot. The dark-haired woman had a righteousness to her. A clarity, too. Anyway, who gave a damn?

He lowered his gun. "Okay. Let's load up the car."

"Can't," the woman said. "They can sense cars. We're leaving on bikes."

"Bikes," he smiled. "Why didn't I think of that."

The man, Raymond, glanced to his wife. "I don't know."

"Me neither." She turned to Walt, fixing him with a crossbow stare. "Who *are* you?"

"My name's Walt. I'm from New York. We have to go."

"So take one of the bikes. We've got a spare."

He waved the pistol. "This thing shoots lasers out of it. That makes me like God from the Third Testament where all He does is kill aliens. Only this God doesn't know Beverly Hills from Bakersfield."

Raymond's mouth parted. "What?"

"You can come with us tonight," the woman said. "Once we're out of here, so are you."

"Agreed." The couple had pretty much everything ready: the bikes, packs of gear, a sort of trailer, hitched behind a purple bike, loaded with water and blankets and more backpacks. The woman belted on a pistol. Walt threw his leg over the bike with the trailer.

She stared him down. "That one's mine."

"Just trying to help."

"Help different."

She kept one eye on him as she gently helped Raymond lift his wounded leg over his bike. The man shut his eyes, breathing hard. Mia smoothed sweat from his brow. Walt smothered his frown. She'd stay with her husband, he saw, even if it meant stopping altogether, dying in the same blast from an offworld weapon.

"Where are we going?" he said.

The woman's attention stayed on Raymond's wavering effort to keep himself balanced. "South."

"Where south?"

"Not-here south."

Raymond hopped from the garage on his good leg, bike wobbling beneath him. "We should have stolen a tricycle."

The woman smiled and walked her bike beside him. Walt trailed, gun in hand. As they crossed the driveway to the street, Raymond glanced back at the house with wistful near-regret. A look like leaving for college for the first time. Like wandering through your back yard and discovering the grave of your first dog.

An explosion kicked up downhill, fierce and close enough for the shock to strike Walt's skin. Raymond inched uphill, one hop at a time. Walt moved beside him and supported his handlebars.

Even so, Raymond had to rest less than half an hour later, dropping off the road into the scrubby grass that fringed the cliffs. Mia gave him water, some crackers. Walt watched the silent road, ready to race off if more than a scout appeared. If worse came to worst, he'd leap off the cliff and see what happened.

The aliens stayed downhill, torching the million-dollar homes with all the patience of incoming tenants who plan to stay for the next ten or twenty million years. Raymond declared himself rested a few minutes later. They made good time then, aided by the road, which first flattened out and then ran downhill. The road angled into a sharp point; at sea's edge, a dark tower rose into the night. A light flickered through a window at its peak, disappearing a second after Walt saw it.

He reached for his weapon. "We could rest here."

"I don't think so," Mia said. "It's a dump."

"And I hear it's haunted," Raymond laughed.

Walt rolled his eyes. Couples. Like their histories were so much more special just because they'd had someone to share them with. They moved on, stopping a quarter mile or so down the road at a railed overlook. Walt could no longer smell smoke, just the salty sea, the sweat griming his clothes, the sweet-sick scent of weeds blooming across forgotten yards. For a while after that, there were no houses at all, just empty slopes and the rolling road. Besides the beach, it was the first open and undeveloped land Walt had seen in days.

Raymond stopped in front of a steepled church, leaning over his handlebars. "I think that's all I've got."

"It's okay," Mia said. "We're far enough for now."

The church's front doors were locked. Walt walked to the neighboring field, picked up a rock, and threw it through the door's window. He swept broken glass with his foot while Mia helped Raymond inside. She returned to help him wheel in the bikes, storing them in a kitchen at the back of the church, then hauled the packs to an upstairs office with a couple of couches. Raymond lay on one, shoes off, scanning his leg with the help of a flashlight.

"How's it look?" Walt said.

Raymond made a face. "Shot."

"Guns will do that." He grabbed a pillow from the other couch and dropped it to the floor with a dusty plop. The blankets from the bike-trailer had the same smell as the couples' house. Wordlessly, Mia spread a blanket on the other couch and sat down to shuck off her shoes.

Raymond watched him make his bed. "You said you're from New York?"

"Yeah."

"How'd you get here?"

Walt pointed to his feet. "Those guys."

Mia narrowed her eyes. "You walked. For thousands of miles."

"If you only do one thing all day long, you can get a surprising amount of that thing done."

She smoothed hair away from her forehead. "Why?"

"Because there is a lot of time in a day."

"Why'd you walk from New York to LA?"

"Oh. To kill myself."

She laughed through her nose. "You didn't do too hot."

"My life has not been an unqualified success."

Her smile melted, replaced by something he couldn't read. Raymond clicked off his flashlight, ruffling into his blankets. Walt was suddenly conscious of the man's breathing, of Mia's, of every shift among their bedding, however minor. He raked up his blankets.

"I'm going to find a couch somewhere."

Mia shifted on her bedding. "I was going to suggest the same thing."

Walt squinted, found the flashlight, and wandered down the hall, boards squeaking under the thin carpet. In another office, he locked the door and curled underneath a desk. He fell asleep before he'd decided where to go next.

In the morning, he climbed the steeple and surveyed the hills with his binoculars. Smoke rose inland. Black specks keened from the north. He climbed down to poke around the church, but found nothing more interesting than a couple of basement vending machines which he broke open for a breakfast of peanut M&Ms and Coke. He'd never really liked Coke. After months without anything like it, it tasted ambrosial.

Footsteps creaked overhead. He found Mia right before the front door.

"Some scout ships out there," he said. "Don't go far."

"I don't need to run a marathon to take a piss."

He handed her a can of Coke when she got back. "You should tow Raymond in that bike trailer. He keeps bouncing his balls around like a bunny with a stroke, your kids will be senile before they're born."

"We're not having kids."

"They can't hear, either," he went on. "The squid-crabs, I mean. The scrabs. No, that's terrible." He licked his thumb, wiped Coke from his lip. "But they can sense motion. So if you're stuck in an elevator with one, fart all you want, just don't try to exit before them."

"They can't smell, either?"

"No, the sound. Possibly they can't smell, but a lot of ocean creatures seem to do nothing *but* smell other things. I expect their sense of smell is at least adequate."

She gave him a look like he'd asserted he could speak to housecats. "Are you being serious?"

"I've killed a few of them," he said, swinging back to things that might be relevant.

"How?"

"Stabbed two through the eyes. They have brains and they don't like being stabbed in them any more than we do. Lasered a third. They have distributed organs or something like it, though. I get the impression it would take a lot of bodily damage to take them down; explosives would work, shotguns probably, too. Swords. I expect swords would be great. I had a sword for a while, but I had to leave it behind when they hunted me down after I killed the first one."

"You know a lot about them." Mia popped her Coke with a pleasant hiss. "Where are you going now?"

"I had been thinking south. I think there are interesting things in the south." He shrugged. "Do you know where the rebels are? The ones the woman who shot your husband was rolling with?"

"She said they lived at a lake outside LA. The only place I know like that is on I-5 on the other side of the mountains."

"There, then."

"You want to fight back."

He shook his head. "I have to."

Mia nodded slowly. "Before last night, we wanted to go there, too. Maybe we could go together. It'd be safer."

"You mean than for you to try to make it with a husband with a hole through his leg."

"And for you to actually find the place instead of winding up in a Mexican whorehouse."

"That doesn't sound so bad."

"These whores have been dead for eight months. After bleeding out of every orifice."

"All right." Walt crumpled his empty soda can and chucked it to the floor. "We're all going to die, you know."

Two weeks later, Walt sighed down at the lake. Flattened patches of canvas flapped by its shores. Outhouses stood at two corners of the camp, doors hanging open. Though Walt could see wheel ruts all the way from their place on the ridge, there were only three cars, two of them burned.

Raymond eased himself from his bike trailer and leaned against its side. "Think the aliens got them?"

"Don't see any bodies."

Mia tipped her head. "Maybe they took them. Like the prisoners you found in the desert."

"Don't see any signs of explosions, either. Aliens roll in, I don't think these guys would just throw up their hands and say 'Well, you got me.'"

Raymond poked his makeshift crutch at the dirt. "So what do we do now?"

It had been hard for Walt not to get his hopes up the last couple weeks. There sure wasn't much else to do. He'd taken point on their bike-mounted march across the suburbs of Long Beach and Anaheim, but didn't encounter anything more frightening than a starving black labrador. Raymond slept a lot. Mia asked him a lot of questions about his trip and the aliens, which he'd mostly answered except when he didn't feel like it. When Raymond was awake, he readily accepted Walt's orders and asked a lot of questions about Walt's trip, too, though he had the impression it was more about hearing about rescues and escapes than Mia's specific inquiries about where he'd first seen the aliens and what the government had been trying to do in New York before he escaped. He liked them, in a vague way—they clearly loved each other—and hated them for the same reason.

Smoke rose from Los Angeles County. They crossed the mountains to the east. Walt's impatience rose with the smoke. Its particles contained timbers and curtains, roof-tar and bedsheets, but also, no doubt, the aerosolized remains of human beings. Every day it took the three of them to reach the rebels was one more day they wouldn't be helping to kill the beings doing that burning. The ones who'd seen Earth, decided they wanted it, and kicked over the anthills of humanity. The ones whose plague had taken her away.

Up on the ridge above the lake, he couldn't help wondering that if he'd biked by himself, freed of Raymond's trailer and regular need to nap, whether he could have caught the resistance before they slipped away.

"Just one thing we can do," he said. "Get down there and find out where they went."

A short ways up the hill, a dirt road branched off the cracked highway. Walt drew his laser and walked his bike down the switchbacking dirt, Mia and Raymond behind him. Besides the lake, there wasn't much to see: collapsed tents, a firepit, outhouses that still stunk vaguely of shit, a pile of fish bones by the shore, a long stretch of picnic tables. A simple wooden shack roughly near the center of the abandoned camp. Shaky, prophetic, all-caps graffiti blazed from its side, bright red words about angels and end times. Suspecting the shack had been the command post, Walt creaked open the door. The front room had a lightweight desk with empty drawers. The back room held a cot and a bucket. The cot was empty; the bucket wasn't. Walt scowled and went outside. He and the couple wandered the grounds, poking around under the tents, occasionally calling each other for leads that wound up false—a paperclipped set of marching orders that turned out to be from April, before the aliens had arrived, and a string of penciled numbers that turned out to be the scores from the last ten Super Bowls (Raymond, a fantasy football player, had cracked that one). If there was any sign of where the rebels had gone, Walt couldn't see it.

The sun hovered above the peaks a couple miles away. Once it disappeared, the night would come fast. Back beside the wooden shack, Walt knelt to inspect a scrap of paper. One side was blank. The other showed a stick figure of a man with enormous balls.

"If our time weren't worthless, I'd say we were wasting it." Walt crumpled the paper. "We don't even know if they left us a sign."

"Well, they wouldn't leave anything the aliens could figure out," Raymond said. "What kind of sign could only a human understand?"

Walt sat back on his heels. "Culture."

"Culture?"

"*Simpsons* quotes. *Star Wars* references. Cave paintings of a guy with a mustache bellowing about soup. Anything *we'd* get that *they* wouldn't." He cocked his head, reached for the crumpled sketch, and smoothed it over his thigh. "Is this a Jackie Treehorn reference? Where did Jackie Treehorn live?"

"Who's Jackie Treehorn?"

"*The Big Lebowski*. Come on, he's a known pornographer."

"That guy. Um." Raymond pressed his fist to his forehead. "Malibu."

"Where's Malibu?"

"Just north of LA."

"Could the rebels be there?"

Raymond squinted one eye until it was nearly closed. "If they like getting incinerated by raging fires. It's like right there."

Walt turned the sketch one way and the other, looking for letters hidden in the lines of the sketch, for numbers or coordinates embedded in the curly hairs on the figure's testicles.

"What are you doing?" Raymond said.

"Malibu, then. It's the only lead we've got."

"You guys seen this graffiti?" Mia called from outside. "This is some prophetic shit."

Walt met the other man's eyes. Together, they rushed from the shack. Walt circled the building, reading out loud the messy red paint sprawled around three of its walls: "IN THE REALM BETWEEN ANGELS AND GIANTS / SAINT STREISAND AWAITS THE COMING / OF A RED DAWN ON THE WRONG HORIZON."

"Obviously," Walt said.

"Giants and Angels," Raymond said. "Between San Francisco and Anaheim."

"Well that fucking narrows it down."

"Saint Streisand?" Mia laughed. "Who's the superfan?"

"Saint Barbra Streisand?" Walt glanced at Raymond. "That mean anything to you?"

Raymond tipped back his head, lips parted. "Santa Barbara. It's a city up the coast a ways."

"So what the fuck does—"

"*Red Dawn*." Mia's eyes flared with comprehension. "The Patrick Swayze movie where the locals fight off the Soviet invasion."

They stared at each other in the fading sunlight. Walt dropped the sketch in the dirt. "Well, that was easy."

"Why did they fly out here at all?" Mia said. "It's so much *effort*."

Raymond peeked under the bandage on his leg and frowned. "Could be for water. Look at them. They crawled out of an ocean or a river somewhere."

"But water's everywhere. There's water on the moon."

"Not the kind you can swim around in."

"If they can fly all the way here, I think they can melt a few blocks of ice."

Walt tapped out a cigarette, flicked his lighter. The cherry glowed orange in the darkness of the park. The smoke chased the scent of trees and weeds. They'd been on the road three days and he expected they'd reach Santa Barbara sometime the next day. For better or worse. For all they knew the rebels had moved on again, or been wiped out, or the graffiti on the shack had been nonsense, some war-crazed trauma victim's idea of a joke. Walt inhaled, smiling. He supposed that *would* be funny: scrawl some gibberish on a wall, let travelers try to make sense when there was no sense to make. Watch from the hills while they rolled out on a wild goose chase. If their search for the BRR didn't pan out, maybe he'd give that a try himself.

Mia gave him a look. "I still can't get over that.

"Over what?"

"You survive the Panhandler, and what do you do? Start smoking."

"I already smoked."

"You'll regret not quitting next time you have to outrun a bear."

He let smoke trickle out his nostrils. "Bears have to eat, too."

"They don't have to eat *you*."

Raymond popped a big blue antibiotic. "Not so long as you can outrun me."

Walt flicked ash. "It doesn't matter. The aliens will get me sooner or later."

"You don't know that," she said. "There aren't enough of them to police the whole planet. You could hide in the mountains. That's what we're doing if we can't find the resistance."

"The thing is I'm not going to leave them alone."

Mia considered him across the moon-bleached blackness. "Why do you think they did it?"

"Water," Raymond said.

Walt glanced into the patchy black woods beside the clearing. "Why do you think?"

"Just to kill us off." She leaned forward, conspiratorial. "They wanted to take us out before we could become a threat. There's no other reason to come all this way when other resources must have been so much closer. Is there?"

"There are a million possible reasons. I doubt they'll ever bother to explain."

"Don't you want to know?"

He stubbed out his cigarette. Tiny orange embers blinked away. "What would it change?"

"Don't you sound tough."

"Well?"

Mia sat back, staring into the space between them where they would have lit a fire if Walt hadn't ruled it out. "It would make sense. The plague. The invasion. The extermination. It would all make sense."

"How the hell can the end of the world—"

Behind him, a man cleared his throat. Walt spun, the cool smoothness of the alien pistol appearing in his hand. Three silhouettes stood twenty feet away, assault rifles glinting in the thin silver moonlight.

Walt rolled his eyes. "Haven't we all seen enough guns already?"

III:

LIFTOFF

25

"Are you the resistance?" Raymond said.

"Get on your knees!" A bear-shouldered man rumbled forward, gun out, barely a toy in his swollen arms. A thick gray mustache carpeted his snarling lip. "I said get *down!*"

Raymond lowered himself to the damp grass, bracing his knee. Mia reached for his hand. Walt stayed on his feet.

"We look like aliens to you?"

The hulking old man raised his elbows as if to jam the barrel of his rifle into Walt's face. "I'll have all the time in the world to read your guts you don't kneel down right now."

A tall, thin man stepped next to the first, glasses winking over his cadaverous cheeks. "Otto, you really think they'd play dress-up just to fool you?"

"They must first know us before they can destroy us."

"They have bombs for that."

The grass soaked Raymond's knees. His leg throbbed. "We're looking for the Bear Republic Rebels."

The third figure edged forward, nearly as thin as the tall Asian man, a bony, bright-eyed woman in her mid-30s. Her dark hair was bound behind her head. "Are you soldiers?"

"Who isn't?" Walt said.

Mia lowered her hands fractionally. "We found the sign. It said the resistance was here."

"What sign?" Otto said. "Did they send you here?"

"I can barely walk." Raymond undid the lace keeping his slit pant leg together, exposing the blood-spotted bandage. "I don't think 'they' would send a crippled guy to take you down."

Walt shrugged. "Unless that's a cunning ploy to lower their guard."

The tall man rolled his eyes. "Don't encourage him."

Otto snapped away his gun. "You'd be better off if you *were* on their side. You won't find nothing here."

Raymond rose, teeth gritted. The tall, gaunt man was David, the woman Anna. They led the newcomers down a path through the woods. A mile from the road, collapsed tents lay beneath the leafless branches. Cold ashes waited in the dark. Dew gleamed from a flipped Jeep. Under the scent of moisture on fallen leaves, a faint whiff of feces clung to the night.

Walt laughed. Raymond eased himself to the ground. "What happened?"

Anna's eyes, so wide she constantly looked like she was preparing to sit down to her first meal of the day, went rounder yet. "Well, they disappeared!"

"We think they left," David said. "I don't see any bodies, for one."

"Because the squids took 'em." Otto wiped his glasses on his shirt and gazed into the black woods as intently as if they'd caught fire. "They're here for meat. Our meat."

Mia crinkled her brow. "That's a long way to go for sausage."

Walt gazed at Raymond. "Remember that next time you're thinking of taking a solo trip to Alpha Centauri."

"Hilarious," Mia said.

"Shit, he could be right, though. I busted out a bunch of people they had penned up like pigs."

Otto snorted. "A little elf like you led an alien jailbreak?"

Raymond expected him to come back with withering bluster, but Walt just stood there. Raymond rubbed his leg. It hurt in that dull but insistent way that was somehow more aggravating for the knowledge it wouldn't fade soon.

"Have you been here long?" he said. "Is it safe?"

"Nowhere ever has been," Anna said.

"A few days." David caught Otto's eyes. "What do you say? Mind if they split the camp with us?"

Otto laughed, a phlegmy chuckle of Marlboros and old wars, and swung his chunky hand at the field of musty tents and dented, empty cans. "You sure we got space?" His gaze honed in on Walt. "No. You want to sleep, find some place that isn't next to me."

"We're not going to hurt anybody," Mia said, puzzled.

"At least not from this planet," Raymond said.

Otto lifted half his mustache. "Look, you came out here to go stomping around with the rebels. You see any rebels here? Any flags? Jets? Choppers? Tomahawks? You got nothing for you to stay here."

Raymond stood, leg shivering. "*You're* here."

The old man snorted again, then shook his head. "It's a free country. But you so much as look my way while you think I'm counting sheep, I'll put one between your baby blues."

"I'm glad we could be reasonable."

They had their choice of tents, but Raymond had to sit and rest his leg before he'd finished hammering the second stake. He watched with jagged annoyance while Walt took over—it seemed like he'd never have another moment alone with Mia again; he estimated he'd last another two or three nights before he'd have his first wet dream in years—but as soon as the tent was up, complete with its moist-tent smell, Walt set off to find another for himself. Raymond crawled through the flap and struggled off his shoes. He was suddenly exhausted, unable to stand, barely capable of nodding when Mia asked if he was tired. She began to unroll their blankets, but he couldn't bring himself to help.

David boiled coffee in the morning while Otto patrolled the fringes and Anna tried to coax a squirrel from a tree with a handful of peanuts. The other two were still in their tents. Raymond and Mia had quit building fires at the house once the aliens got too serious and the coffee was the first he'd tasted in weeks. He lifted his mug, a dirty white thing printed with music notes and a smutty one-liner about piano teachers, then sipped.

"I think those things flew all this way for dark roast."

"I had to crush the beans with a hammer." David nodded at the sock he'd used for a filter. "Don't worry, it was clean. In a relative way."

"Who ever thought brewing coffee could be such work?"

"It's remarkable how fast it all went away. How long would it take you to learn how to build a car? I can conceive of living in a cave rather than attempting to set a foundation. A cave!" David laughed, wryness shot through with wonder. "If we didn't have those damned crabs kicking over our sand castles, I think it could be honest fun to try to piece it back together."

Raymond rolled coffee over his tongue. "Think we could do it?"

"Sure. We can still read, can't we? If our visitors up and left this afternoon, I can envision running water within a year."

"I'd kill for that."

David leaned forward, elbows on knees. "Don't try to fight some silly war. You have a beautiful young woman. Find someplace to be with her where nothing will interfere."

He nodded but said nothing. Part of him wanted to do just that. If Colorado was a dream, it was one that could be willed into reality. If the aliens were having that much trouble quashing the cities, how long would it take them to win over the wilderness? Did he owe it to his species to help fight? How did you measure that responsibility against the responsibility to keep those you love happy and safe? He suspected this wasn't a question for the head. Instead, it was for the heart, the guts, any of the squishy things below the brain.

The coffee was cold when Mia woke, but he poked up the fire. Her eyelids fluttered at the roast potatoes and rosemary.

"Let's go for a walk," she said once she finished eating.

"My leg hurts."

"Exactly. We'll stop when it gets to the bad kind of pain."

He found a long, sturdy, and reasonably straight stick. The woods smelled like pine needles and a coldness that might never come. Mia matched his erosion-slow pace. Birds cheeped from the branches. After a few hundred yards, he was hot enough to ditch his flannel. After a half mile of knotty woods and open grass, the pain forced him to sit in the sun on a broad, flat boulder, where he knuckled the muscles around his throbbing wound.

"What do you think we should do next?" he said.

She grinned. "You ever done it in the woods?"

When they finished—he'd stayed on his back, which felt like it had a couple new scrapes, not that he'd noticed while he was cupping her breasts and she was grinding him into his discarded clothes—he thought until he remembered his question. "About the Bear Republic Rebels. Now what?"

Her chest rose and fell under his flannel. "I don't see any rebels to do anything about."

"They could have relocated. Gone out on a mission."

"And they could all be feeding alien larvae."

"I'd like to stay," he said. "Just for a while. If they haven't come back in two weeks, we'll decide from there."

"Okay." Her voice was dreamy. He let his eyes rest along with his leg. He never slept so well again.

Otto rarely offered more than a handful of words, but made no further demands for them to move on, either. Walt passed the time lugging in water from a stream beyond the hill, gathering edibles with Anna, who was some kind of botanist, and keeping watch over the trailhead to camp. David brewed his coffee and combed his radio dial for anything besides static. After Raymond's fourth afternoon of limping through the woods with Mia, he returned to find Otto sitting in front of their tent, a cigar squiggling smoke from his lips.

"You're working hard. That's good. But you're going to get hurt. That's not so good."

He swept his forearm across the sweat on his hairline. "We'll be okay. Mia's keeping her eyes open."

"You need to find a woman who can build a set of crutches." Otto nodded at a pair he'd leaned against the tent, stripped blond pine branches knotted together with fibrous white twine. "See if those don't help the leg."

Raymond sat down to inspect them. The wood was smooth, the bonds tight. "Thank you."

"If you're gonna be here, you need to be healthy. You hunt?"

"When I was a kid."

"Well, start reminiscing. The winter won't kill us, but three straight months of baked beans sure might."

Otto shoved off, knees and knuckles popping, and shuffled in the direction of the trailhead. Raymond watched until he disappeared around the bend.

That night, they all ate together for the first time, gathered around the fire as it roasted potatoes, cucumbers, tomatoes, and red bell peppers from an overgrown garden a couple miles up the road. David cooked them on a fine mesh screen, fastidiously speckling them with pepper and flaky rose sea salt, then forked the slices out on paper plates and topped them with a chutney mashed from garden mint, cilantro, and chilies. Raymond dug in while it was hot enough to burn the roof of his mouth, leaving small strips of skin he wiggled free with his tongue.

"I've been thinking about this for a long time now," Walt said when they'd been reduced to licking tomato juice and salt from their fingers, "and what I can't figure out is how the three of you came to form this little A-Team."

Anna straightened her dark ponytail. "What d'you mean?"

"Daffy scientist, dapper, epicurean survivalist, and grizzled old gun-lover. It's like you met on a reality show."

"You think I'm daffy?"

"Don't be offended by a snap judgment. It's true of anyone who cares about squirrels."

"My story's same as yours." Otto's plate was crumpled on his belly. "Met these two here trying to find the army. They broke down up north. Couple of geniuses who'd never seen a fan belt before."

David folded his paper plate in half three times, then dropped it into the fire. He used a rag to wipe down his knife and fork. "I was a history professor at Pomona with a mildly successful blog about pre-modern technology and solutions to problems we no longer have. It was a curiosity, then, or a hobby for green advocates who'd rather spend their money on iron cookware and goose farms for fletching than they would on alternative energy, but now the wind farms are powering nothing and I know how to boil leather, so there's that.

"My Sasha and I both proved immune to the Panhandler. We had a cabin in the mountains where we lived while the violence boiled off into steam and the stovetop patina of the dead. We spent some time discussing the ideal place to relocate—right where we were, where we had the advantage of familiarity? Canada, for the isolation? Central America, to avoid winters and achieve a yearlong harvest? An island in the Gulf seemed attractive, too, but neither of us knew much about nautical matters.

"Ultimately, we decided to travel to Eastern Washington. It's relatively isolated, it's a desert clime with mild winters, and despite the summer heat, which frankly sounds barbaric, you can make good work farming due to volcanic soil and the Columbia River, which, we predicted, would also once more become a potent source of salmon. So. The truck was loaded. Routes were mapped. Food canned and tubbed. Gas siphoned.

"I-5 is an interesting route, if you've never taken it. The interior of northern California is positively Mediterranean, if lacking a gorgeous blue sea or the centuries of cultural tradition. But the olives are just as green.

"We were attacked outside Redding. Mountain town, very pretty. Sasha died on the highway. We were holding hands and she fell into the weeds. The shot entered the back of her head and one look at the remainder told me enough. I ran into the woods. I lived there like a native until it got too cold. I supposed I'd come south for the weather, but really I was hoping to run into my attackers. Motorcycle people. They wore orange. I saw no sign of them. I detoured to Monterey to see whether the aquarium still had any minders—she'd been a marine biologist, Sasha, relished our trips there. She loved to roll her eyes at the guides."

In the silence, a log crackled, startling Raymond. David stared at his hands. Anna gave him a gentle smile.

"I was working for a Monsanto team up north," she said. "Altering seeds. It was reeling, dizzy stuff. We made DNA sing and dance and sprout horns. If I still had that team, these aliens would be toast. Chomped up by fifty-foot carnivorous corn cobs. I'm not kidding. Well, kind of. I wasn't surprised by the virus or the invasion. I think I'd been assuming the agricultural conglomerates would take care of the apocalypse within the next decade themselves.

"I don't know why I headed south? Mexico, I think. Oaxaca. Pictures of the cliffs. And then Chichen Itza. I thought if I saw those ruins I could understand our own. I took Highway 1 because what's the hurry? The ocean's nice." She nudged David's hunched shoulder. "I bumped into this guy staring at a bunch of dead fish."

Mia dug a seed from her teeth. "What about you, Otto?"

"Already told it."

"Come on, there's no TV out here. I'm dying."

"Kids didn't take to the sickness," he said simply. "Figured I'd go to Alaska. Always wanted to live there before I had my girls. But when I found these two outside Monterey without a rifle, sidearm, or spitball gun between them, well, it seemed like murder to leave."

Raymond couldn't tell if there was an edge of annoyance to David's smile. Anna's seemed wholly pleased. "So you three?" she said. "Let's don't stop story hour here."

"Well, we inherited a house in Redondo Beach," Mia said.

"And were about to lose it," Raymond smiled. "Or be forced to move out of, anyway."

"Then, you know, the world ended."

"And after our house burned down, we realized all those much nicer houses on the hill didn't have owners anymore. So we moved into one. We had a garden, a system for water. It was really nice."

"Then we looked outside and there was a mothership hovering over the bay." Mia laughed, sobering up as she checked off the alien sweeps and their measures to clear out the city, the botched raid by the Bear Republic Rebels, how they'd taken Sarah into the house. "She shot Raymond as we were trying to flee. We bumped into Walt in the street on our way out of town. That was just, what, two weeks ago?"

The faces around the fire turned toward Walt. "I walked there from New York." He tossed his paper plate into the flames. "It took a while."

"You *walked*?" Otto said. "From New York City? Has the East Coast not heard about cars?"

"It made sense at the time."

The fire coughed sparks. At the time, Raymond thought, it always makes sense. Even here and now, camped out with strangers waiting for an army that might not exist, forced into the wilderness by aliens and plague, it made sense, in its own particular way; he knew the chain of events that had brought him here, could see the shape of several routes from here. But should they have moved into the house on the hill? Should they have gone to Alaska? Mexico? Eastern Washington?—well, no, he'd driven through the place enough to know that. But the point stood. It would be cliched to think that, no matter how narrow the rapids ahead looked, he had a million options at any point in time, but the truth was he *did* have a million options. Some better than others, no doubt, but he couldn't know which for sure until he gave them a shot, and if he found himself in the midst of a bad current, he could switch course at any time. A million boats could clog any river. All he had to do was jump to a different deck.

In a literal sense, though, he had a bullet-shaped hole through his leg that was still on the mend. So he hobbled through the woods on his crutches, Mia handing him bottled water when they stopped. Walt, ever restless, announced he was heading back south for a few days to seek out sign of the BRR. The others lodged no complaint.

Even as Raymond was living those days—smelling the pines, feeling the grit of the trail under his feet, the sharp yet sweet pain in his thigh when his weight landed too strongly—he knew they'd be ones he looked back on with no second guesses about what other boats he could have taken instead. They were simple and clear and good. They reminded him of the first days Mia had moved in with him in Seattle to his dingy apartment shared with two male friends and a small German Shepherd, none of whom ever raised a finger to clean. It was dirty and they had no AC in the summer and Raymond supplemented his job cataloguing books at a bookstore with food stamps, but his friends were right there and Mia liked them and he knew the neighborhood. The two of them had to stretch $180 to cover a month's groceries, and he knew if they were still living that way in their 30s, something would have gone terribly, dreadfully wrong, but at the time, it was a perfect balance of work, sleep, sex, vodka, video games, art, weed, sobriety, and movies, with just enough nights out at the bars, restaurants, and parks to keep from getting cabin fever.

The culmination of this period, which had lasted two years until he and Mia moved into their own apartment minus roommates and dogs of any kind, had come on a Fourth of July weekend when his roommate Matt talked them into driving to the lake and barbecuing in the heat beside the dazzling cool water, where they ate beer-marinated bratwurst and passed around fifths of Dr. McGillicuddy's Fireball Whiskey while playing a strange game involving golf ball bolas and PVC pipe wickets. In the morning he and Mia had dismissed their hangovers with a puff of smoke (but not too much to drive) and he'd taken her down to a motel on the Oregon Coast, which she'd somehow never seen, and it was rainy and windy and cold, but they poked at sand dollars and crabs on the shore and ate seafood caught that day and then went back to the seaside motel where they'd screwed so hard he was surprised the headboard hadn't pounded down the walls and bucked them right into the neighbor's room.

That was it, one weekend, a stereotypical summer holiday with his friends and one more day spent on vacation proper, but the memory was so clear to him he could have narrated every detail on command—how the sun had disappeared in mist as they crested a ridge past Portland; the scallops at dinner at a restaurant where the carpet was so worn it was shiny; the dirty word they'd found carved into a colossal and wave-worn trunk washed up on the sand; the color of the mugs—white outside, teal inside—at the coastal-hipster coffee-and-sandwich place they'd walked to before driving back north. Two days that felt endless because each moment was so rich it could have fed a full day of its own. He and Mia had had that time together in the house on the hill before the aliens arrived, and now, walking and screwing and chatting in the quiet, cool woods outside Santa Barbara, they'd found it again. That was what life was about. Building times so good they felt like forever.

A week later, Walt came back from LA with two more alien lasers, a pack full of bows and arrows, and an idea. He plunked down by the fire. Otto, upset that Walt hadn't properly identified himself before he drew down on him at the trailhead, was mollified when Walt handed him one of the short-barreled foreign pistols for examination.

"Don't suppose you found this piece in a Hollywood pawn shop."

Walt shook his head. "I lifted it from its former owner, who made no objections to me taking it after being very thoroughly shot."

"Just how thorough?"

"Skull like a bowl of gazpacho."

"I take it that's a soup."

"You take right." He leaned in toward the heat, face yellowed by the firelight. "I found a way to fight back."

Otto nodded, the stubble on his neck rolling. "Nuke 'em. I know where three silos are in-state."

"We can't nuke them," Mia said.

"Says who? Now's not the time to be worrying about a few flipper-babies."

Raymond frowned. "They've tried. We heard about it on the radio. Everywhere they've launched a nuke, the aliens knocked it down and leveled the place."

"Did Americans try?"

"Not that I know."

"There's your problem."

"It's not nukes," Walt said. "It's the opposite. I don't know how many of those things there are—five thousand, ten—but I know how many there aren't."

David ran a thumb along the wrinkles below his jaw. "Guerrilla warfare. The tactic of occupied lands throughout history."

"They can't fly in reinforcements overnight. If we can kill them one by one, until they don't have the men to crew their ships, we can beat them."

"This plan," Anna said, "sounds like it could be rephrased as 'choke their rivers with our dead.'"

Walt laughed. "I'm not asking anyone to come with me. You don't have to decide right now. What I'm telling you is I'm going to go back to Los Angeles to kill as many of those genociders as sneakily and evilly as I can."

Otto stood, as if ready to ride off on a stallion then and there. "They killed my daughters. I been waiting for some army, but if I haven't seen it now, I doubt I ever will."

Raymond glanced at Mia, who was already searching for his eyes. "I don't know about us. We'd need to talk."

"I'll go," David said. "All the knowledge in the world is no use if you're disintegrated before you can teach it to the children."

"Um," Anna said.

Walt hugged his knees to his chest, his face still and distant as the full moon. "Take your time. I'd like to radio around. Spread the idea. See whether anyone else is already trying it and what they've found out. Should take me a couple weeks before I'm ready. Do whatever you think's right."

Raymond shifted, thigh jangling with a sudden shot of pain. A new boat floated down that river.

26

Smoke tumbled from the chimney of the false hacienda, rising in a pillowy white language even aliens could understand: *humans live here*. Down the block, Walt shied his left arm away from the thorns of the brush he was hidden beneath and listened to the keen of the coming ship. Could be in for a bombing. That would be some bad luck. Have to scrap the whole campaign, at the very least resolve for a longer slog than his most patient projection. If they couldn't count on luring the squids out to play, whittling them down could take years. Years Walt may well wouldn't see; his spot was just thirty yards from the hacienda's front door, and if the bombs came largely or sloppily enough, his last moments would consist of the transition from being Walt into becoming a foul-smelling mist of vaporized guts, carbonized bone, and superheated shit.

Well, he'd find out soon enough.

Something hefty and ceramic crashed from the second floor of the house where Walt crouched in the shrubs. He scowled. While Walt was out roving and broadcasting, Mia had trained with the others at camp, ranging from competent to natural at everything she tried, be it firing pistols or bows, building and lighting fires quickly, or hiding in just the right place to have full coverage of a park trail while remaining nearly invisible. But first time in the field and she was smashing vases like an epileptic steer. He turned over the idea of walking out on the group and continuing on his own. Then again, no need to decide while he was still waiting for the bombs.

The engine-noise swelled until it was ready to jiggle the

windows from their frames and his teeth from his jaw. Through the thick screen of branches, the scalloped black oblong of a flier descended vertically, disappearing behind the clay tile rooftops a couple blocks away. Dust plumed above the houses, dispersing in the faint wind. At once, the keening snapped off, leaving Walt's ears ringing with the tiny wail of a muted TV.

Three aliens rounded the corner, carrying weapons in claws and tentacles, dressed in their perverse pink straps that reminded Walt of a pandering anime character. He had the sudden urge to laugh. Less than a year ago, he'd had to worry about taking out the trash, given himself ulcers over whether an unknown young stage actor had the kind of abs that could shatter an already-cracked relationship. Now, he was hiding in a bush with a laser pistol in one hand and a grease-blacked katana in the other while a team of human-hunting alien seamonsters slapped their way down a sunny Los Angeles suburb. Why ever plan for *anything*?

The three beings crossed the lawn of another Spanish-style manor three houses down, sticking near its front as they advanced towards the smoking chimney. When they reached the neighboring house, one squid posted up behind a pillar and aimed its guns up at the blank windows. The other two crossed an overgrown, yellowing side yard for the porch of the smoking house.

Up and across the street, a flock of pigeons burst from a third-story window. The aliens whirled. From the window above and behind Walt, a needle-pointed arrow slashed the air, thunking through the closest alien's skull. Yellow fluid splashed the porch. A second arrow pierced the body of the posted-up squid before it could return fire, crumpling it in a sprawl of squiggling limbs. Blue lines appeared between their claws and Mia's window. Under the brush, Walt took aim and lased through the neck of the unwounded squid. The arrow-wounded survivor rose, uttered a noise exactly like a human gasp, and turned its weapon on him.

Another arrow knocked it back down, jutting from one of its many armpits. Walt fired, singeing its face before it yanked itself away from his beam. A return shot scorched the thorny brush three inches to his right, clogging his nose with thick wet smoke. His next shot missed. An icy heat licked across his left forearm; his hand jerked reflexively, firing wild. He smelled burnt hair and sausage. The alien picked itself up, guns leveled. An arrow hissed between them, piercing its throat and pinning it to the patchy yard.

Walt rolled out from under the bushes. Laser ready, he jogged up to the pinned body. Yellowy, mucosal blood guttered from its wounds. He raised his katana and struck off its head.

Down the street, Otto kicked open a front door and sprinted around the corner where the flier had touched down. Walt severed the heads of the other two creatures and knelt for their guns, carefully tapping the pads he'd discovered that sent them into a safety-like sleep mode. Across the street, the door creaked open.

"Don't have *too* much fun there," Mia accused, bow slung over her shoulders.

He flicked his sword, slinging gore. "Enjoyment in one's work is one of the keys to a fulfilling—" A gut-shaking explosion downstreet made them both wince. Greasy smoke uncoiled over the rooftops. Otto's shoes smacked pavement. Walt grinned, slung the pistols into his pack, and sheathed his sword. David wanted to study the aliens' gear, so Walt knelt to gather it up, disabling the tracking devices with a sleep mode similar to that on the guns— they'd hunted him down in Arizona because he hadn't seen a simple on/off switch. "Don't even think we needed the pigeons."

She jerked her chin at his forearm. "Are you hurt?"

He glanced down at the raw spot. His skin was pinkened, an uneven line of hair obliterated or reduced to small black curls. "Like the wise man said, pain don't hurt."

"God, I miss movies." She glanced at Otto as he pulled up beside them, panting. "Did you blow the ship?"

"To seven different hells, girl."

"Bikes," Walt said. "Gloat later."

They were near the crest of the hill before they heard the far-off whine of another flier; by the time the bombs fell, crumping, as removed as the howls of a wolf, they were more than a mile away. Walt pulled off the road anyway, holing up in a shoe store in a busted-up strip mall.

"Question," Mia said in tones that would have passed in a library. "Did anyone think that would go that well?"

Otto shrugged his bearish shoulders. "We got surprise, planning, cunning, homefield advantage. Can't ask for much more." He twitched his gray mustache, considering. "Besides a column of armor and some Warthogs up high."

"That went about as well as a monster-fight can go. It was like we had the cheat code for *Contra*."

"Well, the next level of a video game is always harder than the last." Walt had a bad feeling as soon as he spoke the words; absurdly, he remembered playing *Battletoads* as a kid. Specifically, the level where his toad-warrior mounted up on a hovering scooter and he had to dodge upright obstacles that resembled giant sticks of original-flavor gum. They came one after the other, faster and faster, until his scooter was speeding so fast it inevitably resulted in his craft being smashed and his froggy body being flung to its death on the far side of the screen. By the end of the course, reflexes were simply not enough. The only way to make it out the other side was to know in advance the location of every single stick.

That was a video game. You could memorize it. It didn't adapt to you. Eventually, if you played it enough, memorizing each of its obstacles, you would beat it, no matter how many times your toad died along the way.

He glanced at Mia, the contrast between her delicate face and the taut muscles beneath her sun-browned skin, and thought, suddenly, of kidnapping her, conking her out and running away to live in an igloo to train penguins to bring them fish through the winter.

"What are you smiling about?" she said.

"Alternate realities."

This, too, was truer than the glibness that had spurred it. No matter how fast the obstacles came or how often they changed, he couldn't stop playing when the game was the only chance he had to see every last one of those things dead. As for Mia and Raymond, he was less certain. In a small, strange way, he'd been disappointed when they told him they were in with his mini-resistance. He'd wanted them to go somewhere—the Caribbean, Brazil, the outlands of Patagonia. Anywhere but LA.

Instead, Raymond said they'd given it a lot of thought, and at the end of the day, they'd decided living like there's no future would only guarantee it. Or something equally hokey and cliched, who could remember such things? He'd even tried to talk them out of it, told them they didn't owe him, humanity, or anyone else a damned thing, that when happiness slows up enough for you to catch it, you grab it with both hands and lock it in your closet. Mia had just given him this look that only a woman can give a man and told him he'd watched too much *Die Hard*. Well, what can you do. You can't force a person to not go ambush nightmarish killers from beyond the stars.

After the success at the house, they repeated their trap in a Beverly Hills radio station, replacing the smoking chimney with a broadcast signal and the pigeons with two goats they found cropping the grass of an elementary school. They roamed through and lived in the subway tunnels—that LA had a subway was both news and hilarious to Walt—camping in the cavernous gloom at the base of the stairs, retreating to the platforms with candles and flashlights to sleep, stirred at night by the skitter of rats and the sudden panic that they lived in a concrete cave that smelled like mold and stagnant water and that if their lights burnt out they'd have to stumble through total darkness while their hands trailed along the cold tile walls. But it was safe, inasmuch as anything was these days. Anna watched from a rooftop of an art deco apartment, binoculars clamped to her eyes, walkie-talkie in hand, while Walt led David and Mia to plant two IEDs—David and Otto had combined forces to gin these up—at the entrance to the Staples Center, where they'd seen pairs of squid visit for reasons that probably had nothing to do with basketball.

And then, like that, the missions dried up. Not for want of waiting or watching. That, aside from occasional midnight scavenger runs from the tunnels, was essentially all they did. But because the aliens disappeared. Not the ships; those still scorched the sky on a daily basis. Their base at LAX was only growing, too. Walt spent long hours watching the creatures erecting their cone-houses and milling around, but he couldn't think of a way to tackle the airport that wouldn't result in a lemming-like display of self-destruction. It was the foot patrols which had stopped. The only time when the aliens were vulnerable to six people on foot armed with hand-lasers and equally silent bows and arrows.

"They got wise," Otto said, a dim hulk on the candlelit subway platform. "They may look like dog vomit, but they ain't dumb."

Raymond paced the edges of the light. His limp was almost gone. "It was working, wasn't it? So what do we do?"

"Draw 'em out."

"How's that?" Walt forked up a cold meatball. "Parachute naked into LAX?"

"I thought you were the idea man, idea man."

"If they've wised up to us picking them off, they'll wise up to us drawing them out to pick them off."

Mia tugged her blanket around her shoulders. "Do you think we should stop?"

"I say we bomb *them*," Anna said. "See how *they* like it."

Despite the darkness, Otto squinted. "Push came to shove, I could fly us a helicopter. Doubt I'd even have to remember how to land it."

"Are those automated now?" David frowned. "I didn't think autopilots had progressed past in-flight duties and...oh. You're laughing."

"Other ideas?" Walt said.

"Sabotage?" David said. "It would require access to their ships."

Anna rubbed her nose. "Poison them. Just poison the shit out of them."

"With what?" Otto gestured to the empty rails beyond the light. "You got a spare truck of Martian Big Macs down that tunnel?"

"Did we conclude they eat people? We can find corpses, fill the corpses with poison, and leave them in the open. The rest takes care of itself."

"They're not going to eat bodies off the sidewalk!" Mia said. "Would *you*?"

"I prefer my meat freshly killed through humane methods. But these creatures appear crustacean in nature, from which we might conclude they are not only carrion-eaters, but — "

"We don't know they eat people," Walt said through a mouthful of marinara. "Think better than you're thinking right now."

"Why don't we keep doing what we're doing?" Raymond glanced around the candlelight. "I haven't even gotten out there yet. How do we know the patrols won't come back tomorrow?"

Otto palmed his gray stubble. "The fact you want to go to war tells me you've never been in one."

"You have?" He raised his brows at Otto's nod. "Which one?"

"Which one you think? I look young enough to have been plunking camel jockeys? I'm talking about the jungle. Churned clay. Socks that never dry out." He drew a long breath, puffing his chest. Walt should have guessed he was a Vietnam vet, and a specific kind at that: he who thinks final authority in all matters rests with those few who'd been at Khe Sanh or Hamburger Hill.

"I'll tell you something," Otto went on. "One day I'm on recon with a roughneck named Samms. The sun's starting to go down, which you don't like, because it's still hot as a dog's mouth and meanwhile the night-bugs are starting to make so much noise you couldn't hear a Panzer brigade sneaking up on you. The shadows, too. Fronds that could be men or their guns. You see everything and nothing and the only reason you don't head straight back with a false all-clear is the guilt of walking the others into the unknown.

"We reach the edge of a clearing, Samms and me, and the sun comes back. It's yellow on the green grass and the brown water. Down the way, a dozen VC with AKs are yelling at unarmed civilians and kids. I don't understand a word of what the civilians are saying back but you can tell they're scared. That break in the voice means the same in any language. It's open field between us and them and Samms and me know we can't get any closer without getting plunked.

"They're arguing for a while, the soldiers and one rice-skimmer, and then one of the men with the guns gets bored and he shoots the farmer. We're far enough away it's a second between when the farmer drops into the muck and when we hear the report. The other civilians — there must be forty of them, fifty — take off across the sopping fields. Mud's splashing their knees. The soldiers just stroll after them like they just finished a nap. No hurry at all. After the civilians have made a hundred yards, we see why.

"Across the field, there's a barb wire fence. The woman and the kids are streaming into the fence and they're screaming and tearing themselves apart trying to squirm to the other side. Caught in the spikes, the soldiers walk right up to them and shoot them dead. Less than a minute after the first farmer got shot, the field is quiet and the barb wire is heavy with the bodies."

Otto leaned back from the circle of candlelight, shoulders sagging like a weary bear. "Samms and I had tried to help, we'd be two more bodies in the field. Samms knew it. I knew it. But every day since I know I should have tried. I should have given everything to stop those monsters at the wire."

Walt scowled down the gloomy tunnel. The old man was ready to die. Probably, he was just as ready to seize command if Walt decided to turn back or if the aliens persisted in staying beyond their reach. He supposed they were all doomed anyway; whether they died tomorrow or two years from now, there was no stopping the enemy. Otto was too war-sure. David, too theoretical; Anna, too scattered; Raymond and Mia, too—domestic. They'd killed a few aliens together, sure, but it was too fantastical to go on.

Something was coming. After moving in together after college, Vanessa had adopted a six-week-old chihuahua, an all-black female with floppy bat ears and round black eyes. He'd resisted the move, as much as he could—she'd brought it home without a word of warning, walking through the door with a velvety little thing that could hardly run without falling down—but had wound up serving as its primary caregiver on the long nights while she auditioned, rehearsed, then unwound in a Village bar. That meant housebreaking. He laid down newspapers, even the diaper-like puppy pads that were supposed to convince dogs to go in one spot, but on countless occasions he looked up from a Mets article on his laptop to find the little dog squatting on the middle of the carpet, urine dribbling from its vagina, its black eyes so blankly stupid he wanted to crush the thing in his hands until it stopped squealing. His anger was so thorough, so mind-erasing, he had to count out loud until it boiled away.

Here they were, six little puppies piddling across Los Angeles. The force that smashed them would be furious.

It began to rain. It continued to rain. It rained until water spilled down the subway steps and sluiced onto the tracks, forcing them deeper into the tunnels. They jugged all the water they could, took impromptu showers with soap and shampoo looted from the smashed-out CVS on the corner. David constructed an elaborate filtration device from charcoal, sand, and a trash can with a drain punched through its side. Anna wandered back from a midnight run to Home Depot to seed carrots and lettuce in the sidewalk planter. Otto watched with mustached disapproval from the bottom of the steps where he spent every waking minute ensuring he'd see the aliens before they saw him.

Walt doubted the man had to worry. They hadn't seen alien foot patrols for three weeks. Even the aerial presence had lessened, as if the invaders were equally discouraged by the ceaseless rain. Walt had waited for them to relax their guard or for another strategy to emerge, but there existed a hypothetical point where waiting would backfire—when reinforcements would arrive from the stars, or the aliens began breeding, or humanity simply lost the numbers and will to fight back. He wandered the platforms, flashlight in hand, in search of ideas. Instead, he turned a corner and found Mia hastily wrapping a towel around her lithe, damp, candle-shadowed body.

Water dripped from her dark hair. "You'd think I could find some privacy in the LA subway even *before* everyone else died."

"Didn't know this was the ladies' room."

"Now that you do, will that make you more or less likely to come back?"

"I'd rather not start making enemies with humans, too."

"Sounds smart." She slicked back her hair, pattering water on the concrete. "What are you doing down here?"

He kept his eyes on her face. "Thinking."

"Well, sorry to interrupt you."

"Who says I stopped?"

She smiled, eyebrows puzzled. "When I start shivering in a few seconds, it's cold, not because—"

Footsteps rasped down the platform. Adrenaline jolted through Walt's solar plexus—he envisioned driving his flashlight into the alien's throat—but then a candle wobbled into view, followed by Raymond. He frowned at Mia's towel, the bucket of soap and water.

"Need a hand?"

She glanced over her shoulder. "He got lost."

"I know where I am," Walt said. "It's just not where I meant to be."

"Okay," Raymond smiled, confused.

Walt waved and turned down the tunnel, afflicted by the sudden need to jerk off. It was past midnight, but Otto was still on watch behind the newspaper dispensers he'd fortified at the base of the stairs. Rain punished the streets. Through the screen of mist, the mile-wide lights of the mothership hung to the west, implacable behind the black swirl of clouds. Walt went behind the counter of the CVS, where he had just enough light to complete his business, then went back into the tunnels to tell the others the ship had come back.

"About time," Otto said.

David ran his finger down the ridge of his ear. "What does this change?"

"I'm sure they'll be texting me that info any second," Walt said.

"I'm ready to go," Raymond said. "Just let us know what we need to do."

What they needed to do was watch. That was the whole strategy: minimize risk while grinding away. In that vein, they watched from the rooftops in the foggy night, rain thumping the tarps they carried for cover, and returned to the tunnels half an hour before dawn. Otto took the bathroom mirror from the CVS, carefully smashed it in half, and left the shards at the top entrance, standing the largest piece upright. He settled in down the stairs and watched the reflected street through his binoculars. Late in the afternoon, he woke Walt from a platform nap. The patrols were back.

"They can track cars really well," Raymond said. "We can drive one a few blocks, pull over and set up down the street, and see who comes out to play."

Otto smirked. "Good luck finding a battery that isn't deader than Ethel Merman."

"Who?"

"Could work," Walt said. "Any idea how big the blast radius is on their bombs?"

"Under a block." Anna sketched an intersection in the dust, circled a quarter of it. "I spent a while in San Francisco on my way down. Ran with these soldiers for a week or so. Crazy crew. When they weren't having orgies on top of Coit Tower, they were strolling over the hills with SAMs on their shoulders. Eventually, they all got killed, mostly in bombings that were hot and awful, but wouldn't frizzle your hair from a block away."

"Still a variable," Walt said. "A bad one."

"We haven't done this before," Raymond said. "They'll think we're from out of town."

He didn't like it. He didn't trust cars. Maybe that was just the New Yorker in him. "Find something we can drive."

Otto insisted on aiding Raymond's search, likely because he'd die of withdrawals if he didn't get behind the wheel and under the hood of something stat. He returned equally proud and ashamed of his find: an old-model Tempo, paint flaking from its roof, hood, and doors, one of which was crumpled by a generous dent.

Otto toweled oil from his knuckles. "Your power locks don't power, your automatic seatbelts would earn you a ticket in 48 states, and from the rattle I'm guessing your catalytic's been taken behind the barn and shot years ago. But it runs."

He'd jammed it in neutral so they could push it down to Santa Monica Boulevard without turning over the engine and risking an early visit from alien fliers. The rest of the team gathered up lasers and bows, taking pistols, swords, and hammers for emergencies. Once they were ready, Walt ran them through the plan a second time: David in the crow's-nest, spotting. Himself and Mia holed up a few blocks down, lasers ready. Otto and Anna another block further. Raymond, driving, would roll past, park three blocks past Anna and Otto, and run back to join them. If nothing came by to investigate within twenty minutes, they'd relocate their shooters down the street and try again.

In the street, the rain sifted down in tiny specks just like it had in New York, like dust in an afternoon sunbeam, the kind of more-than-drizzle that would take forever to soak your clothes but leaves your skin slick and cold in seconds. Despite that and the late December date, it wasn't truly freezing. Winter and midnight and the worst LA could offer was a chill. These people hadn't known how good they had it.

A scout ship keened from miles away, lost in the charcoal skies. They took turns pushing the car, two on the bumper with one at the wheel. The remainder watched the clouds and the street. The gutters were clogged and gray. The ankles of Walt's pants grew sodden, clinging to his legs.

They double-parked beside a blue Civic with a skeleton behind the windshield. David started up the stairwell to an office roof. Otto jogged off to scout the street. The dome light flipped on when Raymond opened the door. He stopped halfway into the seat, teeth clenched, leg jutting from the car.

Mia started forward. "Let me help."

"I've got it." He didn't have it. He struggled and wiggled, hanging from the door frame, but when he tried to swing his leg into the car, he closed his eyes and went pale. "Give me a minute."

"Hell no." Walt leaned in to pull him from the car. "You can't be gimping it up if they send a jet on the way. Driver's got to get out of the blast radius the instant he shuts off the car."

"Or she," Mia said.

Raymond stumbled from the car. "No way."

"Like it's so much safer to hide in the rain waiting to shoot

Cthulhu's bastard sons with a laser gun?"

Raymond glanced at Walt. Walt shrugged. "If there were kids here, I'd let the kids fight, too."

"I don't like it," Raymond said.

Mia reached for his elbows. "If we can't do this all the way, we shouldn't be here at all."

Raymond leaned in close to her and said something too soft to hear. When they broke, Mia slung herself behind the wheel and poked at the controls until the wipers swished rain from the windshield. She turned the key. The engine kicked over, idling with a metallic rattle. Exhaust wafted into the dank air. Mia turned off the car. Walt could no longer hear the keening of the scout. The dark, rain-slicked streets looked alien, a gray netherworld from a primal past or an exhausted future. He suddenly wanted to leave. The street, the city as well. His skin prickled.

Otto ambled back to the group, rifle pouched in the crook of his arm. "All clear."

Walt gazed down the street, waiting for a sign that wouldn't come. If he'd been on his own, he would have walked away.

"Walt?" David said over the walkie-talkie, infuriating him instantly—they were reserved for emergencies, who knew whether the aliens could pick up their signal. "I think something's coming."

Clouds flowed inland, black and thick. At first Walt thought his ears were making up the sound, giving themselves something to hear besides the spatter of rain from the eaves of empty bars and Thai joints and dress shops. Then a ship slashed below the clouds, furls of vapor trailing in its stream. Down street, it braked sharply and turned on its tail.

He blinked. "Run."

"Get away from the car!" Mia turned the key, gunned forward on screeching tires. Raymond cried out. The car jolted forward and the alien vessel screamed back to meet it. Light flared from the ship's belly. Mia dove from the car into the street, rolling on the wet pavement, elbows raised to shield her face.

The street ahead became a white sun. Walt lost himself in heat and light and sound.

27

Raymond's ears rang. His head thumped. His skin stung. His nerves were a burning web of numb fire. Smoke hazed the street. Bits of falling rock clinked on pavements and parked cars. Someone was screaming. He couldn't feel his feet. A round, smoldering crater bridged the street ahead. The car was gone. So was Mia.

Someone grabbed his arm. Walt. "Come on!"

"Where's Mia?"

"It's making another pass. We have to go."

Raymond staggered forward, but Walt's arm clung to him like a wet rope. "Okay. I'll just get Mia."

That rope-like force tugged him back from the crater. Mouth gaping, David spilled from the office doors into a scree of shattered glass. Anna goggled at the sky. Otto gave them a blank look and sprinted down the cross street. Walt pulled Raymond after the old man.

Otto swerved alongside the shelter of the buildings. Raymond's leg ached. He still couldn't see Mia. Puddles splashed around his shoes. A jet hummed way up in the sky. A human jet? Why would a human jet have bombed them? Were they killing everything that moved? His left cheek was warm and tingling. He tasted briny metal.

His existence seemed to blink off for a few minutes. Then he was down in the dark, candles flickering over the grimy tiles of the subway, seated on the platform. He stood, leg twingeing. Otto muttered with Walt across the way. Raymond limped toward him. The skinny stick of shit barely had time to flinch before Raymond punched him in the eye. Walt's head snapped back. Without a word, he bounced to his feet, jabbed Raymond in the nose, and doubled him over with another strike to the stomach. Wheezing, Raymond plowed his shoulder into Walt's midsection. The thin man jolted into the concrete.

"You dumb shits!" Otto's heavy hands pawed them apart. Walt wriggled against the old man's granite grasp, eyes fiery windows in the blank wall of his face.

"You killed her!" Raymond bucked his shoulders. "You put her in that car!"

"I sure did."

He blinked. "Then you killed her!"

"Aliens killed her."

"On *your* orders."

Walt just nodded, eyes dimming. Water trickled down the tunnel. Raymond tensed.

"She saved us," Otto said in his ear. "Do you understand that?"

"What are you talking about?"

"The car was the target. She hadn't hauled ass away from us, we'd all be belly-up."

"I watched from the roof." David's eyes were sunken, dark. "I didn't think any of you had survived."

Otto's hand was hot on his shoulder. He would have killed Walt if that grip weren't there, leeching away his rage, a meaty, dangling lamprey. Raymond's knees went out. He sat down hard, a tangle of legs. His howls echoed down the empty tunnel. Anna's eyes bulged. Otto shuffled. Then Raymond was crying too hard to scream, his ribs bouncing against the cool stone, tears and snot slicking his tipped face; soon, he was too tired to do anything but lie still and breathe and breathe and breathe.

By the time he finished they were gone. Raymond relit a candle and rose, shaky and strangely relaxed. His feet moved on their own. Otto and Walt murmured to each other down the platform; further below, he heard snoring. He watched himself walk up the dust-colored steps past posters of dead rappers promoting vodka and of movies that had never made it to public screens. The air was thick like a bathroom after the hot showers he no longer had. He smelled mold and washed-out urine.

The mouth of the exit was as gray as the walls. He snuffed his candle and swayed up steps still moist from the rain. A weak breeze touched his face. The street was silent, the rain finished. Broken windows gaped blackly from offices and banks and ground-floor restaurants. The city was nothing more row after row of useless, walled-in spaces. A sodden bee's nest lost under a board in a vacant field.

He wandered in a way he hadn't wandered since he was a kid. Black hills bracketed the city to the north. Soaked paper stuffed the gutters. Crashed cars rusted in intersections, the desiccated bodies of their drivers as broken as the windshields and hoods. In an alley between a tattoo parlor and a waffle house, a child's body lay under the tires of a smashed van, its leathered skin rain-soaked, its long black hair a snarled lump. When they'd moved into the house in Redondo, the basement had been filled with two generations of belongings. Box after box of his grandma's clothing scraps, patterns, zippers, and lace fringe, all yellowed and crusty. A wheeled chair, its vinyl seat hard and brittle. Tubes of paint with age-spotted labels, paint caked inside. A box of broken desk lamps with two-pronged cloth cords. Mason jars of loose screws and bolts and washers. Envelopes of undeveloped film with expiration dates in 1935, the blank photo paper separated by black tissue that shredded to the touch. All of it—every magazine, plastic bag, and screwdriver—coated in a tactile layer of dust and grime, yellow and gray and greasy. Things no amount of cleaning could make proper. Nothing could be sold or salvaged. The only thing to do was pile it up and set it on the curb.

In Los Angeles, yellow buildings rested in gray streets. It didn't matter what happened to it now. There was nothing left worth saving.

Raymond wandered until his feet blistered and his leg throbbed. When he returned to the tunnels, even Otto was asleep. In the morning, they gazed dumbly into their cans of cold beef stew.

David cleared his throat. "I think it's time we talk about where we go from here."

"Talk away," Walt said.

"I've been thinking about the structure of LAX. Specifically the sewers. If we can find a map, or devote the time to mapping them ourselves, I don't see why it would be impossible to gain entry to their local base of operations and...well, explode it."

"Start planning."

"I'm quite serious."

"Then start planning. In the meantime, we'll keep looking for chances to pick them off."

"We're not going to kill an alien invasion two and three at a time." Anna's voice was low and hard as the platform. "We'll be dead before spring. And they'll still be squirming in their towers, spawning, squirting their sperm over the Earth."

"At this point we're cavemen," Walt said. "What more can we do?"

"We can nuke them," Raymond said. They all turned his way. He hated the pity and patrimony in their eyes. "The big ship is back. It just takes one big missile."

"Boom," Anna said.

David blew into his knobby hand. "At this point, it does make for an attractive possibility."

"To prompt those things to blow up the city," Walt said. "Along with us and everyone else who's hiding in it."

Raymond rolled on his back and smiled at the black ceiling. "Where are the nukes, Otto?"

"Don't tell him."

"Otto. Where are they?"

"It won't help. It'll just get people killed."

"We're all going to die, Walt. Bombed in the street. Shot on the beach. Burned in our homes. We'll starve and we'll freeze. We'll nod out behind the wheels of cars and beside the road when we just can't go on. We'll die alone, or we'll die telling someone we love them. What does it matter? We're all dead. You can die here, setting traps for the things who killed our whole species before they set one tentacle on the dirt. Or you can die trying to kill them all. To make sure no other human feels what we've felt."

Droplets tickled down the tunnels. Otto's mustache twitched. "Vandenberg. Right north of Lompoc. Not far out of Santa Barbara."

Raymond wanted to rise that moment and walk out of this hell. Leave Walt to the creatures. But some dull, pedantic quarter of his mind informed him he didn't have the time or the energy. He wanted to run. He wanted to scream. He wanted to sleep until everything on the surface wilted to dust.

"God damn it." Walt's lighter splashed his face with quick orange light. Tobacco mingled with the mildew of the subway. "If you want to go, then go. Disappear. Don't put the rest of us at risk."

"Fuck you, Walt," Raymond smiled. "Who's coming to Vandenberg?"

Anna tipped back her chin, mouth pursed. "Staying here is stupid. I'm not getting *bombed*. That's for Arabians."

Raymond laughed at the roof. All this and still the old bigotry. "David?"

"She was your wife, wasn't she?" David said.

"She was."

"Sasha was mine. I'll go."

Raymond chuckled again. Walt was about to be as alone as he felt. "Otto? You want to show us the way?"

The old man hunched his heavy shoulders. "No, I don't think so. Don't think I will."

"What?"

"I get why seeing what you seen gets you ready to take out the knives. I don't blame you. She was about my daughters' age, you know." Otto smoothed his gray mustache with downward strokes. "No matter how big a boom those missiles make, I don't think it's gonna wake any of them back up."

"Fine." But it soured him, reduced his victory over Walt to a trivial, meaningless moment. Raymond was sick of his emotions pinging around like a ball-bearing on a concrete floor. "I'm going to sleep. We'll leave tomorrow night."

He half expected Walt or Otto or both to try to talk him down, to physically stop him. Walt just watched him rise to gather his gear. Otto looked at his own hands, turning them over each other, rough skin rasping. Raymond brought his things to the lower platform and clicked off his flashlight. On the cold stone, he shivered.

The ache in his leg fueled his march toward the hills. The mist returned, fogging the windshields of the silent cars, sliming him with clammy dew. Their feet scuffed the dark sidewalks. Raymond had two moods now. Despair came with no warning, rogue waves of helplessness that sucked him out on a rippling tide. When it receded, he was left with a dry and pulsing rage. That fueled him, too. He carried one of the laser pistols in hand. He hoped he'd finally get to use it. Aliens. Looters. It didn't matter. Just one thing prevented him from making some extra noise and light right there in the street and killing whatever crawled out to investigate: getting to Vandenberg, and smashing that mothership out of the sky.

Like the night before, Walt hadn't offered any serious resistance. Just talked some bullshit about how they'd need keys and codes and electricity and the whole thing would be a stupid waste. Raymond figured those bunkers were built to last a long time. Their own generators. There would be overrides, backdoors into the system. For all Walt knew there was a big red button Raymond could mash down with his fist. If it really needed some special key or code, a general, colonel, or buck private would have stayed there till the bitter end, bleeding out every orifice, but still waiting for the president's command to rain down hell on whichever country had unleashed the virus that had killed America dead.

Walt had laughed at that ("Nobody's going to iron their uniform and run up the flag while their wives and mothers are coughing blood"), but Walt thought everyone else was just as amoral as he was. There were those who remained devoted to their duty no matter how dim the candle got. If just one soldier had stayed true to his responsibility while the rest of the world scattered and died, Raymond would free the Earth from the monsters who'd wrecked it.

As they headed west, art deco highrises shrunk to apartment blocks and the shells of sushi-fushion joints. Surf rumbled ahead, hollow and rhythmic. Beyond the sand of Santa Monica, waves foamed in the clouded moonlight. The lights of the ship hovered in foreign constellations. At the first sight of color to the east, Raymond pulled them off the PCH down a curling, palm-lined street, where they holed up in a clay-tiled hacienda the size of a high school gym. Out back, the pool was half full of green sludge. He slept in a dusty canopy bed and was awakened twice by the rumble of engines from the highway.

David and Anna heard them, too, and readily agreed to stay put until nightfall. Raymond watched the street through the curtains while they discussed trajectories and targeting. The sill was cold against his elbows. He remembered holding Mia.

They returned to the road with the return of the night. The upscale density of Santa Monica transitioned to stark houses on dead lawns. A short hill rose just past the highway. On the other side of the road, cream-colored manors on stilts crowded the black sea.

Ahead, chaotic thrashing broke the metronymic wash of the waves. White spray drifted on the buffeting sea wind. Raymond hunkered down beside a damp white wall and peered down an alley between two houses. Past the sand, dark shapes fought against the breakers, leaping and plunging, jerky yet graceful—and all wrong.

He got out his binoculars and leaned into the night. Three of the creatures stood on the beach, silent and still. Past them, dozens of others tumbled and tussled and grappled. At times, they fell without being touched. One lashed the water with its tentacles, splashing everyone near it.

One of the three on the beach waded into the water. By the time it reached the pack of swimmers, their heads bobbing and disappearing in the swells, the sea reached only to its swollen carapace.

Raymond lowered his binoculars. "They're children."

28

"We should have killed them."

Otto glanced at him over top of his glasses. "Unless you had a Stinger in your back pocket, I'd say that jet was a little out of range."

Walt poured a bottle of rain water over his hands, scrubbing sweat and grime. "Raymond. The others."

"I don't know who raised you, son, but unless it was a Khan, you don't kill a man because he disagrees with you."

"If they launch that nuke, they'll kill anyone who's left here."

The old man spat on the platform. "They won't be launching a nuke any more than they'll call the squids over for a handjob. An ICBM is not a video game. Why d'you think I told them where the damn things are in the first place?"

"What do you think the army was doing when the bodies were clogging the street?"

"The hell should I know? I took the president off my speed dial when I discharged."

"In New York, the military rounded up the survivors for lab rats. The normal protocols got chucked into the East River the moment the dead outnumbered the living."

Otto eyed him through his thick and scratched-up lenses. "Yeah, well I don't see you hunting Raymond down and slinging him over the hood of your car. What's going through your crooked mind?"

"We destroy the mothership first."

"Just blow it right up."

"To bits."

"And you've got an idea how?"

"Yeah."

"To smash it all to hell."

"It's not to invite them over to watch the Jets."

Otto laughed, a honking, hooting laugh that should have been paired with a hat slapping a knee. "Then why the *fuck* have we been shitting in these tunnels all winter?"

"Because," Walt said, "it's a terrible plan."

"Quit making me thrash the bush here."

He sucked in his cheeks. "We capture one of their jets, load it up with explosives, and fly it to the carrier."

"You're talking about that movie. With the guy who talks too much."

"No, Jeff Goldblum uploaded a computer virus to alien software. We're going to upload a plane full of bombs."

Otto tapped his thick finger into Walt's chest. "And they blew up the White House, those disrespectful sons of bitches. *Independence Day*. You think the squid blew up the White House, too?"

"I don't think they gave a shit."

"Never bought that myself. I think you stick a word like 'psychological' in front of 'warfare,' you're losing sight of the real objective."

"So you think it'll work?"

Otto hooted again. "Hell no, you idiot. But what else do we got?"

Walt hadn't expected any other answer. He didn't know how they'd get a ship. After failing to make more than the scantest progress with the alien computer in the desert, he didn't see how they'd possibly get one of the jets off the ground, let alone handle it well enough to thread it inside the carrier's belly without ruining a bit more than its paint job. It was all stupid, frankly. Cruelly, horrifically stupid. They ought to just leave. Shoot themselves. Worst of all, the idea *was* inspired by *Independence Day*, the brainchild of the guy who'd directed the fucking *Godzilla* remake. All the dozens of sci-fi books and movies he'd absorbed over the years—his favorite hangover treatments had been lemon-lime Gatorade, darkness, and a flick like *Omega Man* or *ID4* or *28 Days Later*—and the best he could do was rip off one of the most widely-mocked solutions in the history of the apocalypse.

He supposed that was the truth of it. Any species advanced enough to reach Earth would be so overwhelming that the only thing to do was hide until you died. Even this lackluster bunch — capable of mustering just a single carrier and a few thousand troops instead of the tens or hundreds of thousands you'd need to occupy (rather than annihilate) a planet, bearing technology which was human-superior but nothing unimaginable or godlike — had easily quashed everything the survivors had thrown at them. The outcome, except possibly the moment before the first nuke had been launched, had never been in doubt. This wasn't *Die Hard*. It wasn't *Star Wars* or *First Blood* or *Red Dawn*. There was no victory. If there was a point to fighting back, it was for the simple joy of hurting creatures who'd hurt them first.

He knew of worse ways to pass the time.

"You know those mines you rigged at the Staples Center?" he said. "You know how to make anything bigger?"

Otto chuckled. "You kidding? When the Y2K or Peak Oil hits, you want a bomb, you got to know how to build it for yourself."

Otto squinted from behind the BMW whose trunk he'd keyed with "BUY AMERICAN" while Walt was scattering tracking devices across the parking garage. The old man's glasses glinted with a stray glimmer. It was nearly pitch black down there, musty with old rain. Silent shells of cars waited in the darkness for drivers who'd died months ago. Horror movie stuff. Walt shivered, then rolled his eyes. *Real* monsters were on their way, and he was still spooked by the make-believe ones.

They'd spent two days preparing. While Otto put together explosives of all different size and shape, Walt had planned and scouted. Lure in a flier, kill the crew, try to figure out how to fly the thing before anyone noticed it was missing. Meanwhile, if Raymond had risked pulling a car off the side of the road, his crew could already be balls-deep in a nuclear bunker, smoking cigars and running the final check before sending their missiles winging to LA. Walt should be treating every moment as if it were his last. He should be thinking poignant thoughts and writing them down to enlighten and shame alien scholars sifting through the ashes of the civilization they'd destroyed. He should at *least* be praying for forgiveness from Vanessa for not being more of a man, from his parents for not calling more often, from Nate in 3rd grade whom Walt had jump-kicked in the stomach after Nate intentionally booted a kickball over the fence.

But they were all dead. They couldn't hear him. These were apologies he should have made in the moment they happened, not after months of the distanced hindsight and soothing regrets that make every man's intentions as pure and bright as a glacier. In this world, the world of scared truths, Walt's last words might be no more than a tacit agreement with Otto's somewhat obsolete message about supporting the local economy.

Out in the mist, an engine wailed, faded, wailed, faded.

"Circling," Otto said. "Ideally not so as to find the best angle to open the bomb bays."

"They'll come down."

"Says who?"

"When one goes missing, others come. They care about each other. That's how we're going to kill them."

"You should have worked for Nixon, boy."

The engine keened closer until grit and scrap paper blustered against the narrow windows near the garage ceiling. The ship touched down. Its engine spooled to silence. Walt could hear his own blood in his veins. Feet and claws stomped the street, became muffled, then returned twice as loud at the top of the ramp to the basement garage.

Two of the creatures slapped down the slope. Pale light fanned from metal handhelds. The looted tracking devices continued their noiseless broadcast. The soldiers raised their rubbery sensor-arms, turning them slowly through the gloom. They glanced at each other, flashed hand signals. One gestured up the ramp. The second plodded forward. Walt grinned and brace himself.

Orange light flared from the front columns. A nauseating bang shook dust from the ceiling. Twisted metal shotgunned the parked cars. Walt's guts splashed inside his ribs. He rushed through the dust, laser and sword in hand. Yellow remains smeared the ramp, bubbling, slipping down the concrete in the stink of burnt powder and vaporized flesh. Otto ran beside him, chuckling, holding up his pants with his free hand. In the street, swirling lights painted the apartment complexes around the landed flier. A blue beam flicked above Walt's head.

He dove behind a Porsche. Otto flopped in beside him, popping up to exchange lasers with the soldiers around the plane.

Walt dropped flat and sent beams slicing beneath the undercarriage of the Porsche. An alien fell, tentacles flailing. Another volley and the tentacles relaxed across the pavement.

"Got to kill that crew before they start blabbing," Otto panted.

"Give me one of those pipe bombs."

"You aren't gonna hit them from here, Johnny Unitas."

"Light one up and hand it over before your fat heart gives out."

Otto's salt-and-pepper mustache twitched with laughter. Walt poked around the car to pepper the squid moving from the flier's wheels to the cover of an SUV. In the whirling lights, their octopoid, deepwater bodies looked like something from a dream that can't be wholly forgotten nor remembered. A laser appeared between the aliens and the Porsche's headlight cowl, sizzling the orange paint. Walt ducked.

Otto passed him a shockingly heavy metal rod with an honest-to-god fuse hissing from its end. Feeling like a cartoon, Walt said, "Cover me."

The old man swore, dropped the laser pistol, and unslung his bolt-action rifle. He triangled his elbows across the Porsche, aimed, and squeezed off a round. He'd fired a second before Walt rolled out from the car, ducking alongside the line of parked Lexuses, Hummers, and Nissans. The rifle bellowed over the crackle of blue bolts. A beam caught Walt on his pack, melting the plastic into the shoulder of his jacket. A rifle round clanged into the hood of the distant SUV. The aliens flinched back. Walt's fuse had nearly disappeared into the bomb's rounded end. He skipped forward, planted, and slung the fizzling pipe end over end toward the cluster of soldiers.

It fell from the whirling light, rattling across the asphalt. Walt crouched behind a van and pressed his palms to his ears. A shot echoed between the apartments, followed by a second. Adrenaline tingled across Walt's gut. Otto must have botched the fuse, the chemistry. This was it.

A metallic bang splintered the night. Shrapnel pinged into car doors, shattering windows. The van rocked against his back. Walt stood. A blinding light burned from the side of the dark oblong flier. At first he thought it was a weapon, but then there was light and noise and force and darkness.

And Otto stood over him and he could smell blood. and burning and plastic and smoke and his ears keened and the sidewalk under him swelled and rippled, carrying him nowhere. Otto was saying something. He said it a few times more before Walt understood.

"Sure," Walt said, standing to prove it. His knees buckled. Otto grabbed his arm with tough, knotty knuckles.

"That doesn't look like any fine I've seen."

"Well, see it." He frowned. "Where did the ship go?"

"Davy Jones' of Mars."

"Those aren't words."

"Come on, kid."

"We have to get the ship." A craggy heap of metal smoldered where the ship had rested. It must have taken off, but he couldn't hear it. Just the ringing in his ears. The crackle and whip of flames. And Otto chuckling ruefully.

"Oh, you got it. Now lean on me. We got to be gettin' ourselves."

Walt tried to resist, pawing at the smoke as if waving it away would reveal the flier, but Otto pulled him along like a leashed beagle. By the time the keen of a second ship whined across the skies, Walt understood. They were already a mile or so from the explosion, but he mumbled something about holing up in a nearby boarded-over Thai restaurant to wait out the search. Otto helped him through a gap in the boards, then grabbed a newspaper from the table by the front bench and swabbed dust from a booth.

"Well, shit." The big man eased himself into the padded seat. "It was a good idea, kid."

"It was an awful idea."

"Don't see anyone else doing any better."

"Can't try the tracking devices again. They'll just bomb us. Then bomb our bombed-out craters."

Otto retrieved a red handkerchief and swabbed his sweaty face. "It ain't the end of the world. If Los Angeles is about to get turned into a silicon parking lot, you don't need a Ph.D. to know you might be better off hitting the trail."

Walt leaned back into the squeaking plastic seat, sighing with something a lot like relief. It felt good, in a way, to be done. Not just with this campaign. It had been a long time since he'd wanted to die in LA. If he left—and the fact that, one way or another, the city was about to be destroyed made that "if" something of a nondecision—he couldn't imagine himself rejoining the fight in San Francisco or San Diego or wherever the hell else there were still people trying to do something about the uninvited guests. He could no longer pretend resisting would do anything for the survivors or the ghost of Vanessa or even himself. It would simply be suicide in another form, a helpless admission of a lack of imagination. He supposed he'd like to watch the city blow up before moving on. That would probably be pretty spectacular. The hills would probably be far enough away to be safe. Or get up above it all somehow, watch from the skies. If they noticed, there would be worse ways to die.

He went very, very still.

"I changed my mind," he said. "I'm going to die after all."

Otto's brow wrinkled. "Look, I don't see how's there any reason to stay. You're young. You go be a pirate or some such."

"I have a better idea. In that it's much, much worse."

29

"That's it, then," David said under the sound of the surf. Down the beach, alien children tumbled in the waves. "There's no hope. They'll outbreed us."

Raymond rubbed his mouth. "There's always hope. All we have to do is get to the nukes."

"They could have these creches everywhere."

"And if we take out their carrier, they won't have anything to defend them with."

"You propose we stay the course," David said.

"Let's get out of here before they see us."

Anna wagged her head. "We can't leave."

Raymond frowned. "It's dark. We'll just cross the street and sneak north."

"Those are *monsters* in our *ocean*. If you see a monster, you don't say 'Oh, I hope the water's not too cold.'"

"What are you talking about?"

"We should...you know." She mimed a machine gun with her hands, made a "sh-k-k-k" noise down in her throat.

He cocked his head. "They're kids."

"For now."

"No, that makes sense," David said. "Every day they continue to grow, they will become that much more threatening to whoever eventually contends with them."

Raymond glanced between them. "What if we get hurt? Who will get to the missiles?"

"What's going to hurt us?" Anna said. "I count three adults and a whole lot of nothings."

"*Kids.*"

"So what? You find a baby rattlesnake in your bed, you grab the biggest boot you got. You think after we kill all their parents, we can just hug them up and say 'Hey, now who wants some s'mores?'"

Raymond was struck with sudden mental vertigo. Who *were* these people? "We don't know how those things think. We can cross that bridge when we come to it."

Anna laughed, cold as a Northwest rain. She kicked to her feet and sprinted from the alley onto the dry sand. She whooped and drew her laser. David glanced at Raymond, eyes wide as hubcaps, and started after her. Blue light streamed between her and the whirling adults. They fell as fast as she could press the button. Amidst the breakers, the children froze, silent as always, all the more terrifying for having no voice. Raymond raced after David, slowed by the sand.

"Stop it!"

Anna charged the nearest child, black hair flapping behind her. Her laser knocked the youth into the surf. David shot, too, screaming, not as a battle-cry, but something wilder, the scream of a man falling off a ledge. Electric lines criss-crossed the beach, lighting up those long, bug-eyed faces, their whipping tentacles and quivering claws. Raymond slowed, drifting to a stop beside a clump of stinking kelp. Anna whooped, surf splashing her knees. David held his gun in both hands with his elbows tucked tight against his belly. The last child ran parallel to the water, glancing behind itself, Anna high-stepping at its heels. She drew close enough to grab it, then shot it down.

Bodies bobbed in the waves. Others twitched on the tideline, cold water foaming over their punctured shells. Limbs rolled in the shells and seaweed. Raymond felt thrilled and sick and frozen. His leg throbbed. David blinked by the water, clearing his throat. Anna shot the last corpse again, then turned and strode back down the beach.

"Let's get the fuck out of here," she said. "It's starting to stink."

"I believe our first order of business should be to restore power." David snuggled his blanket over his shoulders, cheeks gaunt in the blue-gray dawn. "That in hand, all our subsequent actions require all the less labor."

Anna poked a handful of almonds into her mouth. "Yeah, if that includes one damn big electric fence. Once those things are out of here, it's the *people* who'll come back."

"Well, security will have to be accounted for, of course. I suspect we won't be lacking for bravos to fill out that niche."

"I say that's our numero-uno. Find some guys we can trust, set them up with some lasers, and we're gold."

"We won't be dealing with peasants used to cleaning themselves with their own hand. I think the best way to forestall *internal* dissent is to reinstall the basic comforts—light, plumbing, refrigeration."

"Which we just hand right over to the first pack of assholes with AKs."

"I suppose we'll have to divide our labor. Know anything about windmills, Raymond?"

He glanced up. He'd barely heard their conversation. After the beach, they'd marched miles up the road, finally stopping at the first threat of dawn to hunker down behind a stand of trees. He'd tried to focus on his feet, counting steps, playing games where he pushed off with the balls of his feet rather than letting them roll forward into the next step, but his mind kept coming back to Mia and the beach. Seeing those things die had been marvelous and hollowing, like the invasion of Afghanistan after 9/11: justified, even righteous, but also sickening, because any way you sliced it death was death, and some of those who were about to suffer deserved it far less than others.

He didn't know for a *fact* the young ones were innocent. Maybe they tore their way out of their dying mother at birth, or survived the first few weeks through cannibalism. Maybe they were already being trained to enslave and slaughter the human survivors. In any event, they'd grow up, in all likelihood, to finish the genocide or at least accept the fruits of its happening. Part of him was filled with a vicious joy to see their goopy blood boiling away from the holes lasered in their hides and faces.

But the beach hadn't been a battlefield between uniformed soldiers. It had been something *they* would have done. Now those kids could never grow up under *human* rule, a benign captivity where they lived among Earth's natives, but with the back-bending shame of knowing what their parents had done before being defeated. That would have been the best punishment of all.

"What?" he said.

"Do you know anything about windmills?" David repeated patiently.

"Why would I know anything about windmills?"

"Life teaches a person all sorts of interesting things. If I had the proper clay, kiln, and plants, I could craft you a set of dishes right here. Complete with glaze."

"I don't know anything about windmills."

"Ah. We may need windmills to power our initial infrastructure before we get the old gear up and running."

He stared at David, those sharp cheeks, the quick intelligence in his brown eyes. Was he insane? Already they were talking as if the aliens were incinerated on the wind and not occupying the ruins of the world's greatest cities. As if another week from now, two at the utmost, they'd all be back to playing Xbox and ordering General Tso's chicken for delivery, thinking back on the last ten months as a hiccup, an eye-rolling yet adventurous detour when we all had to shit in the woods and eat out of cans. Without warning, Raymond found himself crying, heaving sobs that bobbed his shoulders.

David glanced from him to Anna, alarmed, then patted his shoulder.

"I don't think we should have elections," Anna said. "Those never really worked."

He was woken more than once by the rumble of ships hunting for those who'd killed their babies. By afternoon it was silent, and Raymond agreed when Anna stated it was probably safe enough to continue north. Privately, he didn't think this was true—he thought the aliens would keep searching for a long time—but a part of him longed to be spotted, to be vaporized and blown out to sea before he knew what had happened.

He walked. When the others rested, he did too, his mind throbbing with his leg and his feet. They slept sparingly. Pelicans drifted on the constant seaside wind, the great big Vs of their wings throwing fast shadows over the sand and sidewalks. He stared out to the west, pinpointing the precise place the sky merged with the sea.

The road curved west. Mountains sprung up to the north, folded brown ridges and green foothills dense with brushy chaparral and open grass. Past the sickle of yellow sand, the ocean was so blue he could almost forgive the invaders for wanting it. Midafternoon, he shed his jacket and walked in shirtsleeves, the sun and sea air drawing a light sweat from his skin. Palms swayed above the clean glass and red roofs of a college that was all the prettier because there was no one left to use it. The dumb chug of a lawnmower wafted from the city center.

Their water was low, so when they set camp in a beach gazebo, Raymond offered to go forage. Night settled on Santa Barbara like the evening's first drink. His breath hung in the salty air. He walked fast to stay warm. The ARCO off the highway was dead empty, rats rustling in the wrappers, napkins, and smashed glass. The Rite-Aid was bereft of water, candy bars, toilet paper, soap, contact lens solution, even makeup. He wasn't surprised. Gas stations, grocery stores, pharmacies, those were the obvious survival caches, the first place looters would look. Raymond clicked off his flashlight and headed for the Spanish-style church on the corner: it would have snacks and water and canned goods in the basement, the stuff of picnics, socials, and charity.

The bell tower projected from stark white stucco walls. The doors groaned, huge old oak lined with iron. He held his flashlight up and away from his body. The light splashed over a dried-up fountain, dusty benches, and a foyer with a coat room to one side and an office to the other. The main chapel held row on row of cobwebbed pews. It smelled like dust and dried-up water. His footsteps echoed through the arched whale-belly space. Something scraped in the darkness. He flicked his light over candle-packed cupolas, the stage and its dusty podium.

Another scrape behind him. He whirled. The flashlight beam glared from a machete and two hard eyes. He was too frozen to scream.

"Who are you?" Her blade was cocked back, ready to strike his bare neck.

"I'm looking for water."

"Mine is mine."

His laser hung from his hip. "I didn't know anyone was here."

Her fingers curled around the handle. "No one does."

"Wait," he said. She was no more than 14, and under the dirt and darkness on her face may have been younger yet. Her blonde hair was hacked short, sprouting in greasy twists. "We're going to destroy them."

"The angels?"

"The aliens. The ones who gave us the disease."

The girl slipped forward half a foot, keeping her soles close to the floorboards. "You'll die. That's all."

"Then let me die trying."

"My dad showed me how to salt meat. To smoke it over a fire and dry it."

A wave of hot prickles tingled over Raymond's face. "Let me go. I won't hurt you."

She raised the thick blade. "I know."

"The thing on my belt is a gun," he blurted. "It looks like a Nintendo controller, but it's killed people. Humans. I don't want it to kill any more."

Her nostrils flared. She shifted her grip on the tape-wrapped handle. She slid back, feet rasping, disappearing inch by inch into the blackness beyond the flashlight. He shifted the beam but she was gone. He sidled for the door, reaching for the laser pistol. At the door, there was a moment he had to glance down to reach for its handle, and he was certain it would end, then, the cold bite of the jungle-knife's steel smashing through his throat. Then he was in the street, where palm fronds whispered and bugs piped from rotting wood.

He found bottled water in the back of a garage and returned to the gazebo. Anna and David were asleep in the blankets, his arm slung over her chest. Raymond stared into the night.

The road carried westward, a warm corridor between the mountains and the sea. Days later, at Lompoc, a sign pointed them toward the base, and they followed that road over low hills and the shrubs and the grass, smelling pollen, salt, and a cold that never quite came no matter how late the hour.

He expected bunkers, silos, flat pavements, barb wire on concrete ramparts. Instead, Vandenberg's main presence was a big white building block, one face painted with a giant American flag, which stood across from a factory-like jumble of curved pipes and liquid reservoirs, all massive. A huge scaffold rose from the flattened top of a hill. Narrow roads ringed the site, turning off for scattered outbuildings. Waves washed the shore a hundred yards away.

Amidst the scaffolding, naked missiles waited in the sun.

30

"Well, kid," Otto said, gazing at the blue and yellow cloth, "I'm damn sure glad my friends are too dead to witness this sorry business."

Walt laughed. He couldn't help it. He'd been laughing since he thought of it: their superweapon, a wad of circus-colored nylon. A basket that had once carried wealthy lovers in the sunrise above the California coast would instead lift as many of the highest-yield, lowest-metal explosives Otto could rig up. It was perhaps the dumbest idea Walt could have thought of, and back in the Thai restaurant where they'd waited out the enemy jets, Otto had said as much.

"You think they don't have radar? Only chance we got is if they're laughing too hard to shoot straight."

"Balloons don't always show up on radar. Depends on the equipment. The weather."

"These are an advanced species that smashed us like a wine glass at a Jew's wedding."

"Wrong. It doesn't have to be a wine glass."

Otto scowled, hunched over the booth's table. "Why don't we steal a fighter jet instead? Crash it into the carrier's bridge?"

"Because," Walt said, stepping to the boards across the windows, "I don't know how to fly a jet."

"You do a balloon?"

"My parents owned them. We take it up at night, up high, then drift down, as slow as we can. They hunt by movement. Maybe their sensors do too."

"And if they do see us, what then? You gonna bail out the

side?" Otto shook his shaggy head. "Falling from a mile up, the ocean's like concrete. The sharks will spread what's left of you on their toast."

"Probably. So the fuck what?"

Otto spread his thick, callused hands. "I'm just getting this out here so I can scream I told you so on the way down."

That had been that. On the spot, Walt had checked the restaurant's voluminous yellow pages—if this thing worked, they'd have to establish Phone Book Day—and found a purveyor of hot air balloon rides a ways up the coast. He'd returned to the tunnels for supplies and struck out the next night while Otto stayed behind to build more things that went boom (he claimed he'd manufactured his own C-4 when his platoon ran out in Vietnam) and try to scout out the structure of the monstrous ship hanging over the bay.

It took two days to find the balloonery. Two more to make sure all the equipment was available and working and then get back to Otto. Another three to load up their wagons—literally; they'd picked up little red wagons in a Toys "R" Us, thinking they'd be easier to move than wheelbarrows and more stable than shopping carts—and roll up the coast to the hills. They spent one last day preparing, testing and setting up the gear, going over Otto's dozens of sketches of the gigantic ship's external geography and hypothetical interiors. That evening, with the balloon spread on the grass, its deflated nylon envelope tethered to the ground, Walt waited for the night to deepen.

He kept one eye on the sky, waiting for the meteoric streak of the ICBM that would spell the final death of the city. Otto said Lompoc was some 150 miles upstate, the air force base just past that. It had been more than a week since the others had left. Even if Raymond and company stayed on foot, they could be there by now, making the final calibrations before turning the key.

"Will you quit the skygazing?" Otto groused. "You'll get your chance to kill yourself soon enough. No way they figure out how to get a missile off the pad, let alone aim the damn thing."

"About as likely as taking down a mothership with a hot air balloon."

"You're darker than a snake's asshole, son."

A mist had rolled in with the night, blocking out the stars. He would have liked to see them one last time. The clouds had their silver lining, though. He wouldn't have to rig up anything to conceal the burner's flame.

"I'm going to miss it," he said.

"Shit."

"This isn't a 'wax nostalgic because I'm about to die' thing. I didn't get enough time. I was afraid for so long."

"Yeah, well, life ain't fair, is it."

"Obviously not."

Otto squinted up at the clouds. "You had another eighty years to live, what would you do?"

"I would walk around," Walt said. "Catch fish. Build fires. Go swimming. Sail. Watch stars. Fry mushrooms. Read books and throw them away."

"Simple life, huh? What if you break your leg fifty miles outside Vancouver? Or you get to be sixty and your knees start barking any time you walk further than the corner? What do you do then?"

"Die."

Otto grinned. "Me, I was looking forward to a couple decades of couch-side NFL Sundays and cold Millers."

"If you can build bombs, you can brew your own beer." Above, silent black clouds drifted inland, bound for mountains and rivers and deserts. "I wouldn't wait to do what I want to do or for things that are wrong to get better on their own. You keep moving forward. Every day, you walk on."

Otto nodded. Walt watched the clouds. Finally, it was time.

He lugged out the fan—gas-powered, fortunately—and started it up, packing cold air through the balloon's mouth. The envelope rippled, slowly swelling. Otto leaned into the bulging nylon, smoothing it against the light wind. After ten minutes, the envelope was plump, approaching round. Walt slid on his gloves and flipped on the burner with an airy whump. Flames shot for the balloon's open mouth. Heat reached Walt's face. The envelope tautened, began to bob from the ground. Finally, it rose, righting the wicker basket with it, tugging its tethers.

He helped Otto load the basket with blanket-wrapped blocks of what the old man had assured him was C-4. He frowned at the burner. Well, whatever. Waking up in the morning was a risk, too. Otto handed him a pack of laser pistols and bottled water and rope and thick plastic hooks. Walt waved him in. The old man climbed into the basket with knees bent, hands outstretched like he might fall overboard at the slightest sway. Walt smiled and cast off the lines.

He opened the burner. The basket lifted, rocking faintly. Otto hunkered down against its wicker wall, knuckles tight on the lip. The balloon lifted into the darkness. The field fell away.

Otto swallowed. "If I jumped out right now, think you could rig this stuff on your own?"

"Quit barfing and try to enjoy yourself."

They were high enough to see the ship now, a great disc of lights and bays half-hidden by the low marine clouds. The wind blew from the sea, nudging them inland, and Walt took the balloon higher, hunting for a stream that would take them out to sea. The air cooled. An enemy jet lifted from LAX, blue lights winking. It soared and banked north. Towards them. Walt hung there, hand on the switch of the silent burner.

"Should have brought parachutes," he said.

"I'd prefer a rocket launcher."

The vessel tracked closer, rumbling below the clouds. It would be on them in a minute. Walt's stomach sank. He'd wanted to set foot on the carrier, at least. Get off a single bomb. Show them they weren't untouchable. Otto put his hand on his shoulder. Walt nodded.

The jet curved out to sea, lifting toward the waiting carrier. Walt laughed and hit the burner. It roared, spouting flame into the waiting envelope. Sea-mist pickled his face. Gauzy clouds wrapped them up, freeing Walt to rise and rise until he found the stream.

The balloon slowed its inland drift, swayed. He cut the burner. The balloon eased toward the shore.

Toward the waiting ship.

31

Three metal spears rose sixty feet from the tarmac, sleek and cold and massive. Scaffolding buffered the rockets, one side of the support structure a blocky rectangle taller than the missiles themselves, metal steps like a fire escape running up its side, the second section standing there like a metal power pole, wires dangling between it and the rocket. The weapons looked more than ready to down an alien ship. They looked ready to end the world.

"Amazing," David said.

"I thought they'd be underground," Raymond said. "In Wyoming."

"They must have brought them here during the virus. Ready to strike down the perpetrators."

"It'll just take one," Anna said. "What do you want to do with the other two?"

Wind ruffled the grass. The afternoon warmth had leeched away, lost as the sun dropped into a half-haze of spray and what might soon be clouds. Unseen, a red-tailed hawk shrieked across the hills. It felt unreal, something from a dream, a half-remembered story told to him while he was high.

"Let's move," Anna said. "Split up and secure the grounds."

Raymond straightened. "I think we should stick together. It isn't that big."

"You got lungs, don't you? Something happens, make them shout."

He glanced to David for support, but the man was already fumbling his laser from its improvised holster. Anna worried him.

Her assumption of leadership was a disaster in the making: she was impulsive, angry, enthusiastic to the point of being crazy. They could easily have been killed during the beach massacre. Vandenberg *looked* empty, but right there nuclear missiles sat out in broad daylight. They were power incarnate. The kind of thing that would attract survivors and occupiers alike.

With sudden clarity, he knew he should shoot her. It was what Walt would have done. There would be no arguing her around. But too much of him simply didn't care. Of *course* she was crazy, a ready murderer, maneuvering to seize power even in situations, like their hypothetical future society, that didn't yet exist. That was just the way things worked. That's what Mia's death had revealed to him. People could be killed at any time, be it on purpose, accidentally, or through cosmic indifference. No dream was guaranteed — most would fail, no matter how hard you worked. Everything decayed, and too often, people were actively helping to make things break down that much faster. All you could do was get away. That's what he should have done. He should have gone to Colorado with Mia. Built his own little corner of the world with the person he'd loved.

He stalked off across the grounds. Jeeps and massively long flatbed trucks sat empty, dirt caking their windows. An assault rifle rusted in the weeds. Birds twirped from the tall white radar stand, nests woven into the crotches of its metal joints. He walked to the curve in the road and stared out to sea. It was just as empty, wasn't it? He turned to brush dust from the window of a metal shack, peering inside at dark computers, radios, and desks. When he finished his sweep, he reconvened with David and Anna at the metal doors of the big white block that seemed to serve as the command station. David strained against a metal bar he'd levered under the handle. Anna stood back, arms folded. The door rattled; David fell away, panting.

"Let Raymond give it a shot," she said.

"There's something at the bottom." Raymond pointed to a flat white strip glued across the door's lower edges. "Let me take a—"

"You just have to lean into it." Anna took the rod from David and bore down. The veins in her forehead squiggled under her skin. The door popped open, juddering, the white strip snapping free. Its broken edges glittered with bright metal. "Told you."

Dust and death wafted from the dark entry. They fetched

flashlights from their packs. David tried the lights to no luck. Down a dusty hallway, another set of doors stood closed, sealed by some kind of magnetic lock that now lacked the power to keep them out. The corridor opened to a wide, spacious room that had been emptied of all equipment and furniture. On the floor, bodies lay in two rows. Desiccated skin hung from the bones. Brown stains spread beneath the remains. There was little smell.

Further on, the computers were black, lifeless. Raymond didn't know why he'd expected any different. He was about to sit down there in the middle of the floor when David found the stairwell to the basement. The man nodded, cheeks wrinkling around his small smile.

He had the generator on in minutes. Lights flickered, blinking over the dust griming every chair, keyboard, and monitor. On the top floor, the Pacific sunset streamed through the dirty windows, illuminating two dried-out bodies in uniforms, a fallen pistol, and a pair of keys glinting from the room-wide terminal.

David reached for one with a single finger, withdrawing as soon as he made contact. "Oh my."

Anna stared at the controls. "Is that all we need? Can we do this?"

"I'll have to get into the software. We have no idea where those things are currently aimed—China, I'd expect, perhaps North Korea. The targeting will have to be reconfigured entirely."

"That's not telling me the answer to what I asked."

"This is military software. It may have military-grade encryption. I won't know until I dig in."

"Start digging. I'm going to get on the radio and see if the ship's still there."

Raymond honked with laughter. "We don't even know if it's still in LA?"

"So what? The 'I' in 'ICBM' doesn't stand for 'in-state.'"

In the orange glow of the waning sun, he laughed again. Had the plan really been so threadbare? What if the keys hadn't been here? The generator hadn't worked? What if the mothership had since left for parts unknown? Rolling around on that dingy subway platform, this had been his big bright idea? At the time, lost in the fog of the bombing in the street, it had felt foolproof. Now that he was standing in the control room, hours or mere minutes from a launch, he didn't see how they'd even made it this far.

"Oh." David leaned over his monitor. The text was too far away for Raymond to read. "There's no security at all."

"This is strange," Raymond said.

"What's strange is those nukes weren't launched just for the fuck of it." Anna pointed at the two withered bodies. "That's why they're dead. One of them wanted to."

"You weren't here."

"When you remove all other explanations, the one that remains must be correct."

David clacked keys. "I don't know what I'm doing. With a few hours, I may be able to rectify that."

"Take your hours. I'll be on the radio." She strode from the room. Raymond drifted to the window and stared out as if he were keeping watch. David didn't seem to notice. The window faced west and the sun was on the sea and sinking so fast he could see it moving through the mist. It seemed like it should hurt, staring at it like that, but it didn't. The sun slipped away. He blinked against the greenish afterimage floating across his eyes.

"Can you really do this?" he said.

"Perhaps if I didn't have to answer questions about whether I can do this."

"Oh."

"Sorry, I'm all frizzle-frazzled here." David shook out his fingers, breath whooshing. "I don't tell missiles when and where to explode. I code websites about pre-Elizabethan leather-tanning."

Raymond stared out to sea. "Will we have to shield our eyes?"

David swiveled in his seat. "Does it look like you can see Los Angeles from here?"

"From the launch."

"The launch. I wouldn't think so."

"I'd like to watch it. It should be remembered."

David hunched over his keys. Clouds massed, thick and gray. The light flowed off to the west. Anna returned some time later, yanking him away from memories of trying to find Mia purple shells along the beach.

"They're still there," she said. "If you can trust somebody from Salt Lake City, anyway."

"Mm," David said.

"How's it coming in here?"

"Along."

"Good. Goodness." Her protruding eyes settled on Raymond. "What are you doing for the cause?"

"What am I doing?"

"You look like you're reading over David's shoulder. Nobody likes it when you read over their shoulder."

"What else is there to do? Should I sweep up?"

"You could be looking for food and water. There must be some. I bet they have some very nice guns, too. Do you think the batteries in this alien shit will last forever?"

"I'm going to watch the rocket launch," he said. "The Twinkies and M-16s will still be there in the morning."

She cocked her head and stepped forward. "What, does your leg hurt?"

"Get out of my face."

"Did you watch the sunset, too? I bet you did. I bet you sat here and thought poetry to yourself."

"Get out of my face. Step back and stay back."

"Or do you miss your girlfriend? Need some alone time to go wet those cheeks?"

Heat blasted through his nerves. He hooked his fist straight into her jaw. Anna's head snapped back, eyes wide and wild. He swung again, clumsily — the last time he'd been in a fight had been in a snowfield beside the middle school gymnasium — but with all the horrid power of his fury. His third punch knocked her to the linoleum. Her lip dribbled blood. The skin around her left eye was pink and already starting to swell. Raymond forced his foot to stay still and not smash into her teeth. If he started, he wouldn't stop until he saw brains.

"I'm going to walk outside and watch the rocket go." His voice shook. "Then I'm going to walk away. If you come after me, I'll jam my thumbs into your froggy eyes and scoop them into the dirt."

Anna gagged sticky blood into the dust.

"Bye, David," he said. "Good luck."

The man gaped at him, hand pressed to the base of his throat. "Are you sure this is the right idea?"

"Never."

He got his pack. His feet echoed in the stairwell. The night was cold. He put on his coat and walked up a short slope to the parking lot, where he sat down on one of the low concrete spot-markers. The missiles waited on the pad, sixty-foot silhouettes, monuments to a dead people that would soon be used to end another. He zipped his coat up to his neck. The wind ran in the grass. His nerves fluttered like he'd had too much coffee. He watched for the front door to open, fanning light onto the dirt, but Anna stayed inside.

He had no way to know how much time had passed when he heard the rumble; he'd broken his watch sometime in the city and hadn't bothered to replace it. Clouds filled the sky from edge to edge, dark and low. He *thought* it might be thunder, but thunder faded. He widened his eyes as far as they would go, as if that would wipe away the clouds and splash sun across the sky, and then he saw the lights: a pair of blue dots inbound from the southeast, sweeping in over the hills.

His stomach coiled. He bolted for the command center. At the top floor, Anna scuttled back from him, knocking down her chair.

"They're coming," he said. "They found us."

32

The ship thrummed in the night, undershot by a deep whine that could shiver the bones from your body. Walt flipped on the burner, maintaining altitude, but he could still feel the noise in his ribs, sharp as an icepick and chthonic as a cavefish. Otto retreated from the basket's edge to hunker down and swab mist from the lenses of his binoculars.

"It's dank as a submarine's basement."

Walt glanced over the side. "Anything?"

"All the clouds you could ever want to wear."

"Keep looking. If we're going to get splashed across its side, I'd like a moment to curse a few people first."

Otto shook his head, mumbling, and scooted back to the basket's side, where he nudged his chin past the wicker edge and clamped the binoculars to his eyes. "We even close?"

"Getting there. I'm about to start easing us down. Try not to piss yourself."

"This mist, you couldn't even tell."

Walt kept one hand on the vent's control line, trying to feel a descent he couldn't see. Between the cold and the clouds sucking up the heat, he doubted he'd need the vent at all. A minute later, he waggled his jaw, popping his ears.

"See anything?" he said.

"Nothing count?"

"Nothing is something."

"Then I see something."

"Good."

He continued to let the balloon sink of its own accord. They were higher than the ship, he knew that much. He thought they were on top of it—it was a big enough landing zone, that was for sure, and the droning, penetrating hum of its engines and systems sounded more or less straight down, which was something. A something a lot like Otto's, maybe, considering that maneuvering a balloon that's the passive reactant to heat and winds is clumsy in the best of circumstances, let alone when you can't see a damn thing, you're probably fifty pounds past your recommended weight limit, and the continuing existence of humanity is at stake —but still. Something.

His ears popped again. He glanced over the side, saw nothing but darkness and swirling particles of water. He could definitively feel their descent now. He reached for the burner to slow their fall.

Otto craned over the edge, too excited to remember to be afraid. "I got something!"

"What kind of something?"

"Oh, I think you probably ought to take a look for—"

The basket whammed into solid metal, throwing Walt against the covered bundles of C-4. He struggled to his feet, hip and knee stinging. The balloon's envelope sagged downward, pulling sideways, scraping the wicker basket over the solid metal beneath.

And to all sides, too, a flat stretch that quickly disappeared into the mist. Not much question of where they were. Not unless somebody had just replaced the ocean with a million billion tons of black metal.

The basket skidded over the hull. Walt heaved bundles of explosives over the side. They landed on the ship with muffled thumps. Otto shook himself and pitched in. A sudden gust yanked the basket hard. Walt glanced up at the bobbing envelope. He'd intended to deflate it, reduce the risk of it falling past a window, but there was no time. He vaulted over the basket's edge. His feet hit, sliding on the rain-slick metal. His elbows banged into the hull. He clawed and scrabbled and then there was nothing beneath him but mist and open air.

He dangled from a smooth metal bar, legs penduluming in the gap. The balloon skittered away, sinking behind a drop in the ship's hull. Walt strained his arms, lifting one elbow onto the slippery surface, but his other hand slipped loose, dangling him from one awkward wing.

A rough, heavy hand grabbed his upper arm. Another took

hold of his collar. Otto hauled him bodily to solid ground. Behind him, a rift yawned across the deck.

"You son of a bitch," Otto panted. "You trying to leave me all alone up here?"

"Just impatient to get inside."

"Well, on your feet, then. We got a bread trail to follow."

The hull extended to all corners of the compass, a flat black range interrupted without earthly reason by open gaps and fat, ten-foot-high triangles that may have housed delicate equipment or may have been bolted on just to look scary as hell. Not that there were any visible bolts. There were hardly any seams, either, as if the whole goddamn half-mile vessel had been poured into a single mold. Otto stooped for a cloud-sodden canvas bundle of C-4. Another rested in the gloom twenty feet on. They found five of the six packages and spent fruitless minutes circling for the last before Otto pulled up and gazed over the metallic horizon.

"We could spend all day up here, kid. What we've got will either dunk this bird or it won't."

Walt tapped his toe against the solid hull. "Having my doubts on that front."

"Yeah, well, that ain't all we got in store for these assholes, is it?"

"I've got my doubts about that one, too. Any clue which way the engines are?"

"Figure we walk far enough in one direction, we'll learn soon enough."

The ship vrummed up through the soles of his shoes. He saw no windows or portals of any kind. A blustery wind came and went, misting his jeans and jacket. He would have said it felt like the surface of the moon, but as far as he knew the moon didn't make a rubbery clank if you stepped down too hard. Moonside visibility wasn't restricted to thirty feet in front of you, either. They shuffled forward, skirting the holes and unclimbable rises. Massive cupolas cast blue towers of light into the skies, spaced widely enough to leave whole sections in near-total darkness.

The wail of an incoming flier cut over the ship's organ-rattling hum. Walt shrunk against a house-sized black block. His fingers were stiff with cold; he kept one hand in his pocket for warmth while keeping the other out to ward against falls, switching them every few minutes. After a while, his mind gave up any notion of trying to make sense of where he was or what he was doing, settling into an alert blankness. He walked.

Without warning, he stood on the edge of a steep downward arc. Beaded mist trickled down the slope.

"Fifty/fifty," Otto said, jerking his chin right and left. "Bet you that's the best odds we see from here on out."

Walt cupped his hand over one ear, then the other. "I can't tell."

"Well, don't look at me to hear the way. I've logged a few thousand too many hours behind a black powder pistol."

"Okay." It felt and sounded like there were engines to all sides, but in another sense, that made his choice all the easier, because what did it matter if he was wrong? "I never much liked the left, anyway."

Walt started right, skirting the abrupt curve into blackness. The going was smoother along the rim, less fraught with sudden pits, but the clouds stopped him from any sense of how far they'd gone and how much might remain. One step after another, rubber squeaking on metal. They stopped to catch their breath and sip bottles of water. They hadn't brought any food. Walt hadn't expected to eat again, and he began to regret he hadn't taken along what would once have been a simple treat, a bag of M&Ms or a Peanut Butter Cup, as a sugary memento of everything that had been lost. He could have sat dówn on the hull with it and eaten it and for a moment he wouldn't have felt so cold or forlorn.

He carried on. A steep ridge peaked from the surface, forcing them inland. Had he already seen that trio of bulges off to the right? The ship was circular; could they have already have completed a full revolution?

The hull's thrumming swelled. Ahead, the mist glowed like moonlight. The steep curve led down to round nozzles jutting from the ship's side, monstrously wide, steam boiling in their glaring light. Walt laughed.

"Those things are volcanoes. We'd need to be supervillains to take them down."

Otto swabbed moisture from his brow. "I know a crank like you's popped a balloon or two in his day. You put a crack in the side of something that big and nasty, it'll do the rest of the work for you."

"Balloons," Walt said. "Thanks for putting it in a language I can understand."

He walked on. Once the first engine was directly downslope, Walt stepped out of his shoes and lined them neatly on the edge. He unshouldered his pack, unzipped his coat, peeled off his shirt.

"What the hell are you doing?"

Walt squeaked his bare foot against the damp metal. "If I start to slip, my skin's going to stick to this a lot better than my clothes."

He dropped his pants and, down to his threadbare black jockey shorts, laced his shoes back on; his clothes might not have much stick, but against the wet surface, his rubber soles clung like a terrorized cat. Otto knotted the slender rope. Walt slid it over his shoulders and tightened it around his waist. The cord was light, thinner than his pinky.

"If I slip, this thing is just going to tear me in half, isn't it?"

"Naw." Otto gestured at the featureless metal plain, void of anything to hitch the other end of the rope to. "You fall hard enough to do that, you'll just pull me right off the edge." He plunked down. "Good thing I'm fat."

Walt emptied his pack of everything but a heavy bundle of C-4. "Just slap it right on?"

"Just slap it right on."

"If anything goes wrong..."

"Yup."

Walt exhaled and lowered himself to the surface. It was witheringly cold, a sharp metal bite against his skin. He crawled feetfirst down the slope, lowering himself on his side whenever he threatened to slip, stabilizing himself with the full surface area of his arm and side and legs and shoes. He could support his own weight until halfway down the curving slope. Welcome warmth rose from the engines. The rope strained around his hips. As the hull steepened, he slid down on his butt until it bumped against his heels, then lay flat and stretched down his legs for another scoot. It was exhausting and freezing and painful and slow, but it worked, and he wormed his way down, two feet at a time, until he stood on top of the giant nozzle's base, heat rolling over him in drowsy waves. He unwrapped the explosives and mashed the white, clay-like material into the crease where the engine protruded from the hull. Once his hands were halfway warm, he started the climb back up.

"Get it?" Otto said when he emerged minutes later.

"Got it."

"Wish someone could see this," the old man grinned. "Doesn't much matter, I suppose. Homer himself wouldn't have words."

Walt caught his breath, then jogged in place until the feeling returned to his hands and knees. The remaining engines were a monotony of scooting down cold, clammy metal. When he finally finished, he flopped down on the hull, his ribs swelling like a landed dolphin's. Otto draped his clothes and jacket over him. His hands and shoulderblades burned where the skin had rubbed away. His toes were soaked and stiff and his left pinky toe pulsed like it might be broken. His head was too heavy to lift from the metal.

"You got it in you?" Otto said softly some minutes later. "I can head in myself. Leave you with the detonators."

The very question brought him back, marshaling his anger, his defiance, his existential need for revenge. Within a minute, he was sitting upright. He stood to put back on his clothes. They were nearly as clammy as his skin, but the leather jacket felt like steel mail on his shoulders.

"Waiting on you," he croaked.

Otto's groundside sketches of the ship made it easy business to reach the metal spire that marked the spot below which the landing bay doors took in and let out the jets, fliers, and dropships. Walt expected another grueling descent from the top of the hull to the bays, but Otto's crude maps didn't show the spiral ladder that led straight down to a platform clinging to the ship's dark side. They got out their pistols and entered a manual door. The well-lit tunnel led to a scaffold high inside the quiet bays. Below, landing strips led out to the cold and misty air. They huddled on the scaffold, watching. Walt didn't know the time—2 AM, 5—but the bays were empty as a midnight alley, and in the course of five minutes of waiting, a single crewman had strolled across the dim runways.

"Any further in, we're liable to take a laser to the noggin," Otto said.

Walt nodded. "Fuck these guys."

Otto dug out the detonator, clicked a home-built cap off the simple switch. "Fifteen minutes." He laughed, deep chuckles that bunched his sides. "For all the good that will do us."

He flipped the switch.

33

Anna advanced on Raymond, all fear of him forgotten. "You brought them."

"How the fuck did I do that?"

"They weren't here until you went outside."

"Neither were the clouds. Did I bring those, too?"

David turned from his computer, eyes darting between them. "Did they follow the radio signal? Is the radio still on?"

Anna's eyes widened. "Of course not."

"We must have tripped a tracking device. We have to find it!"

"David!" Raymond shouted. The gaunt man spun to face him. "It's too late for that. How long until the nukes are ready?"

"I'm trying to refine the target coordinates. Hypothetically, they can be launched at any time."

Raymond crossed to the south face of the sprawling room and pried open the blinds. The blue lights blinked beneath the clouds, tracking closer.

"Keep working. We'll try to hold them off as long as we can."

The wild light receded from David's brown eyes. "Sir."

Anna shook her head hard. "You have to launch now."

"We have a single opportunity for success! If I miss by a fraction of a mile, all will be lost."

"What if they bomb us?" She pointed repeatedly at the alien vessels closing on the base. "What then?"

"That depends on where their bombs detonate. If it's on the building itself, we will be vaporized. If it's an air burst—"

"Then we're stupid fucking corpses, and stupid fucking corpses can't launch missiles. Now turn those keys."

Raymond started back across the room, hand dangling near his gun. "Wait. Keep working. If we see their missiles launch, if they start circling, you turn those keys."

David rolled his lower lip between his teeth, gaze flicking between Raymond and Anna. He nodded. "If you see anything at all—"

"I'll say the word."

Anna's face blanked. She wandered to the southern windows. The jets careered closer, lights brightening, then swung out to sea, slowing until Raymond could hardly believe they could stay aloft. David's fingers clattered over the keys. The two jets turned straight for the base. Raymond held his breath. Rather than the blue triangles of the fighter jets, these two craft were fatter, almost lumbering, flattened ovals nearly the size of passenger jets. The vessels sunk lower and lower, glided past the shore, hung in the air above the far end of the landing strip, and began to descend in a dark swirl of dust.

"I'm going downstairs," Anna said. "I'll fortify the doors."

Raymond exhaled. "Good luck."

"Lock the doors behind me."

He nodded. She drew her pistol and ran down the stairwell. Raymond clicked the lock, wedging an office chair beneath the door handle. Anna's footfalls faded away. He bent his knees and grabbed hold of a filing cabinet. Metal squealed across the tile. David glanced sideways, annoyed, then returned to his monitor. Raymond shouldered the cabinet in front of the doors, swept a desk clean, then flipped it on its edge and shoved it some twenty feet from the entry, broad side facing the doors.

Out the window, white lights flooded the tarmac. Dust blustered away from the grounded vessels. Aliens descended short ramps, waggling claws and tentacles in the pale spotlights.

Straight below, a dark figure raced from the base of the command center, hunched down in the night. Anna rushed into the lee of an outbuilding, paused to peer at the aliens, then bolted north for the open fields.

"God damn it," Raymond murmured.

"What's wrong?"

"Get ready to wrap it up. We don't have long."

An open buggy bounced down the broad ramp. It hit the pavement and peeled out, veering north. Four aliens jounced from its back. A fifth manned a spindly turret mounted at the nose. Raymond pressed his face against the cold window, breath fogging the thick glass. A floodlight spilled from the buggy's front, silhouetting Anna as she sprinted across a dirt road bordering the airfield. Her tiny figure stumbled. She picked herself up, firing a spray of blue lines over her shoulder. The buggy's turret opened fire. Thick, strobing light seared across the cold field. Anna's upper body tumbled away from her churning legs.

The buggy swung to a halt, dust whirling in its floodlight. The grounds were still. An alien leapt down, padded over the dirt, and fired three blasts from a hand laser into the dark grass. It remounted the vehicle. The buggy circled back, rendezvousing with a squad of creatures just beyond the nearest outbuilding.

Raymond resumed piling chairs, desks, and computers against the doors. With the room's furniture all but completely rearranged, he bunkered up behind the upturned desk, sweating, chest heaving. Several stories below, a loud bang rattled through the building.

David stood, cracking his knuckles. "I suppose that's my cue."

"Is the missile locked on?"

"Well, you have to ask yourself, exactly where is their ship? Right over the bay, yes, but we can't say for sure. I checked with the network's satellites, but they're all dark." David rubbed his nose. At the bottom of the stairwell, the doors burst in with a metallic clang. "I decided to get creative. Why launch one missile when we've been graced with three? Assigned each a different airburst coordinate, varying the heights and X-Y plots of the bursts, should allow us to cover quite a lot of ground. Or air, as it were."

"Meaning?"

The man shrugged his narrow shoulders. "If they're anywhere in that bay, they are not going to be very happy about it."

Raymond let out a long breath. The air tasted sharp and piercingly sweet. He crossed to the control board, its knobs and flat screens. The two keys waited in their steel circles beside unwinking red lights.

David reached for one. Raymond gripped the other. The cold metal seemed to cling to his fingers. Appendages smacked up the staircase. Through the eastern windows, the rockets sat ready on their pads.

"The true ultima ratio regum," David said. "Ready?"

"Fire away," Raymond said. David began a countdown. Beneath the count and the tentacles hammering against the doors, Raymond tipped back his head and whispered, "I love you."

They turned the keys.

The missiles were silent. Raymond tried and failed to twist his key further. "What's the matter?"

"Is your key turned?"

"As far as it goes." The doors thunked, rattling against the mounded files and desks. A chair jarred loose and crashed against the floor. "Are all the...buttons pushed?"

"They're pushed." David blinked peevishly at the board. "Perhaps I missed something. A last level of security."

Another barrage of blows assaulted the doors, the hardest yet. At once, the aliens stopped their attack, leaving Raymond and David in thudding silence. Raymond didn't know whether to laugh or scream.

"It was a trap," he said. "Why would they do that?"

"Eh?"

"You really think those things would leave functional nuclear missiles two hundred miles from one of their main bases?"

"I hardly think they know the location of every warhead on Earth. Anyway, what would be the point?"

"David, they're aliens. The thrill of the hunt. Religious ritual. Maybe it's a super clever plan to draw out the most cunning and ambitious survivors. Whyever they did it, they left everything we needed to hope—and now that it's time to launch those rockets, they're standing there like dead trees."

"How...how *rude*."

Rude. Perfect. Like life is a job at a call center and every day brings nothing but threats, complaints, and insults from strangers who don't give a shit about you. That, ultimately, was why Raymond couldn't feel particularly angry or frustrated or tragic about their failure. Mostly he just felt forlorn. If it's all rudeness, the only thing is to find a few people who love to know you as deeply as you love to know them. To cling to, enjoy, and protect each other. The callers on the other end sure the hell won't. He hadn't known Walt, not really. He sure didn't get to know Otto or Anna or David—not unless being aware the former professor could give you a dozen different recipes for stewing mutton counted as knowing him.

Searing light flared from the top of the doors, tracing a white-orange line through the metal. Molten droplets hissed on the desks below.

He'd taken a gamble with them because he couldn't face how hopeless it all really was. They'd been conquered. By aliens. That was it. Time to pack up the blankets and go home. Time to light out for Colorado with the one person left alive who cared whether last night's dreams were good or bad.

After cutting horizontally through a foot-wide stretch of door, the blinding force cut a sudden line straight down.

He'd chosen to chase delusions of glory. The weed-dealing. Security for Murckle. The commando nonsense in the city. His reward was to die beside a stranger. He couldn't argue with that. He had his pistol in his hand. He didn't intend to use it.

The arc light cut 90 degrees again, tracing the third edge of a square, then jogged up, completing the shape. The smoking metal square jangled against a file cabinet. A fist-sized ball hurtled through the hole in the door.

Raymond closed his eyes and remembered a 4th of July weekend when he and Mia watched the moonlight on the waves of the Oregon coast.

Light filled the room.

34

Cold wind stirred the cavernous landing bay. Eighty feet below and two hundred feet away from their place on the catwalk, a conveyer hummed into life, drawing a dark, pilotless jet into a massive tunnel and the storage cells beyond. White lights blinked alongside the tarmac, leading the way. Two of the creatures stood near the slowly moving vessel, exchanging gestures Walt could barely see. He leaned forward. To the right, another spiral ladder descended to the bay floor; the catwalk continued across the walls, disappearing into shadow.

"Given how fucking ludicrous this is," Walt whispered, "I don't think any strategy is off the table."

"Bridge is front and center," Otto shrugged. "Literally, I mean. I figured we'd just mosey on that way."

"Through a foreign ship a half mile wide."

"All roads lead to Rome, don't they?"

"Shit." Walt glanced down the catwalk. Mist gleamed on the metal. "Suppose we'd better stay out of sight as long as possible."

He crouched forward, gaze switching between the far-off aliens and the web-like walkway ahead. There were no handrails, probably because those things didn't have hands, but the path was at least wider than human-normal, nearly six feet across, and Walt was able to largely pretend there wasn't eighty feet of open air between him and the runways below. Otto shifted behind him, shoes squeaking. The conveyor finished hauling the jet into the depths of the bay. The two aliens followed it out.

Walt hurried on. A black door opened off the catwalk, tall and ovoid. A recessed silvery circle sat in its center at neck height. Walt pushed the circle. The door cracked down the center, the two halfs retracting into the walls. Beyond, lights flicked on noiselessly, dim but more than enough to make out the rounded, high-ceilinged hallway that extended for dozens of feet before gradually curving out of sight.

"Pray we don't run into Darth Vader," he muttered. He stalked forward, pistol in hand. Doors passed on either side. The tunnel unfurled further and further, curving leftward with each step. Behind them, the lights faded to nothing, leaving them in a perpetually advancing circle of illumination and granting Walt no way to tell how far they'd traveled.

"You tell which direction we're headed?"

"Starting to get off track," Otto murmured. He tipped his head at one of the featureless oval portals. "Want to see what's behind door number three hundred?"

Walt shook his head and continued on. Too easy to get lost down a rabbit hole, to stumble into the main barracks. Their only hope of reaching the bridge was, like Otto implied earlier, to follow the big roads—which, of course, meant risking run-ins with anything else putting them to use. If so, no big loss. Alive or dead, the bombs would go off in another twelve minutes.

Finally, the tunnel branched, a six-way intersection with a steeply pitched hexagonal ceiling. Glyphs played on its high walls, providing useless instructions. Walt glanced at Otto, who pointed down the rightward-veering branch. This kept on like the previous tunnel until suddenly widening into a bright lobby. To one side, windows overlooked a wide and dark room, sparsely furnished with perversely tree-like metallic chairs and stands with as many limbs as the aliens themselves. Walt skirted past. Far down the curved tunnel, lights flicked into being.

"Back," Walt hissed. He jogged back to the lobby, Otto beside him, and knelt beside the doors to the gym-like room. Otto extended his weapon. The soft smack of feet and treads filtered down the hall. The light followed, first as faint as starlight, but quickly advancing to something he could have read by.

A pair of aliens padded into the lobby, lightly dressed in glyph-marked straps. Their fat, ovoid heads swung toward the two humans. Surprise flashed in those watery, oversized squid-eyes. Walt opened fire.

Otto's target dropped in an instant, smoke curling from the

dime-sized hole between its eyes. Walt's leapt back in a confusion of limbs, yellow fluid pattering from a scorched hole beside its mouth. Walt fired off five more shots as fast as the pistol would let him. The thing dropped, tentacles flapping against the smooth floor.

The hallways were dark at both ends. Otto gestured toward the gym. "Try the doors."

They opened easily, swinging outward in conventional fashion, so long as you overlooked the apparent total lack of hinges. Otto grabbed hold of a mess of limbs and dragged the body for the doors, the alien's tentacles still twitching, claws opening and closing dumbly. Walt went for the other body, stashing it beside Otto's in the corner of the room of metal trees.

"Ought to pick up the pace." Otto palmed viscous yellow blood onto the thighs of his pants. "Right now surprise is the only advantage we got."

Walt didn't argue. They jogged onward, dogged by the lights, soon passing another vast room thoroughly filled with stools and roundish things that could have passed for tables. At its far end, creatures stirred in dim light, metallic bowls flashing in their tentacles. The windows to the cafeteria began at knee height; Walt flopped to his belly and wriggled along, Otto army-crawling behind him. When the tunnel once more narrowed around them, they rose and hustled on.

Past a pair of retracting doors, the tunnel expanded into a massive hangar of wide-open spaces and canyons of freestanding shelves forty feet high. Black machinery rested in the walls and dangled from ceilings too high to see. Metal clicked on metal. A hundred yards down an alley of shelves, an alien carefully selected a steely rod from a drawer of identical pieces. Walt aimed his pistol and edged on. The alien didn't turn.

Emptiness, stillness, and desertion, as if the ship were a closed museum, a place that no longer was. It could have housed tens of thousands, even millions, but Walt had seen no more than a skeleton crew, the ushers left to sweep the stadium after the game has finished. Were they that low on manpower? Were these creatures interstellar Pilgrims, a handful of outcasts gone far to sea for a new home? No reinforcements, then, no swarming billions with lasers clamped in their claws and knives clenched between their beaks. Just a small sect with a good idea: let the virus do the fighting for us. Bound by strict scriptures and baffling beliefs. And when they'd arrived and found a few of the locals still kicking — now what?

At once he was convinced it was true. It would explain so much: their lack of a cohesive plan. Their inability to finish the job. Their hesitance to just bomb the hell out of anything left. And why he and Otto had been able to plant bombs on the engines and slip inside their floating fortress. They just weren't that *smart*. Certainly no smarter than most of the humans through the history of their own invasions. That understanding filled him with a cold and questing fury, and when he and Otto reached a round hub of identical doors, digital glyphs shifting above each one, he knew precisely what to do.

"What do you think you're standing around for?" Otto said.

He turned in place, slowly scanning the readouts above the doors. "A guide."

"We got about two minutes before the engines go, son. After that, it's apt to get messier than a pet store Dumpster."

He continued turning. He didn't have to wait long. Piping lit around one door, outlining it in soft blue; the glyphs above stabilized, flashing twice. The doors opened, revealing a roomy and well-lit pod and disgorging a lone alien into the round hub. Its sensory forelegs reared in surprise. Walt shot it through the throat. It gurgled yellow goo onto the rubbery floor. Walt shot it in the head, kicked it back into the pod, and stepped in behind it.

"What the hell?" Otto hissed.

"This place barely has a crew. The only ones here must be going somewhere important."

"Or straight to the barracks."

"Or the bridge."

"Or the shitter."

"Shut up." The doors glided closed. Hammocks webbed the high walls. Walt snarled his arm into the lines and braced his feet. The pod accelerated at a shallow downward angle, lurching his stomach. Otto swallowed and burped.

The pod jolted, lifting Walt's guts. Otto glanced at his watch. His brows and mustache jumped. "Well, that would be the bombs."

"Did they work?"

"Let me just ring up one of the engineers here," he scowled.

"How in God's name would I know that?"

The pod slid to a swift but smooth stop. The doors parted. On the other side, a waiting alien hopped back in horror. Otto bullrushed it, laying into it with his pistol. A second being scurried into the short, curved foyer. Walt dropped it with a quick blue pulse. Otto gritted his teeth and ran right, Walt on his heels.

He found himself on the upper terrace of a vast, stadium-style auditorium that led down like a giant's staircase to an oval command center of officers and computer banks. The far wall was a single transparent pane, huge and perfectly clear. Beyond, whitecaps surged inland, washing Venice Beach. Black mountains rose behind the silent corpse of the city. The scene tilted subtly downward, as if the ship were a rollercoaster just past its zenith.

Inside the auditorium, dozens of aliens throttled the space above their control pads, gesturing furiously to each other, signing orders with flailing limbs. Others rushed for the elevator-pod. An eerie silence hung over the chaos, as if Walt were watching through soundproof glass; no yelling, no alarms, just the clicking of their ball-shaped keypads and the thump of their feet on the spongy floor.

Otto flanked left along the smooth blue wall, gunning down a pair of creatures on their way to the elevators. The flash of his pistol spurred a score of sense-limbs to leap upright. Other creatures stayed bent over their controls. Otto fired, aimed, repeated. Walt sprayed blue light at every alien in easy range and ran along the upper tier toward more of the unarmed crew. They splayed shot in their seating-hammocks, limbs coiling and flopping. Others ran down the broad circular tiers, sprawling over spindly desks, collapsing them. Something small and silver blurred from below. Otto hollered and poured back fire.

At the end, a half dozen of the things clustered together at the very lowest terrace, tentacles intertwined, clutching and plucking at each others' leathery bodysacs, limbs held before them — warding, pleading, praying. Walt strode down the tongue of carpet, pistol extended. He didn't begin firing until they were close enough to touch.

The bodies of captains and admirals dropped no different from the others, mucosal blood slopping together. Monitors flashed soundlessly. Walt panted, wide-eyed, the world literally tipping beneath him.

He found Otto seated halfway up the wide steps, one bloody hand held to his glistening belly. The old man grinned, eyes pinched. "What are you staring at? You ain't finished yet."

Walt nodded. Like a Luddite god, an avenging aspect of the billions of dead, he circled the bridge, shooting every monitor, black box, and control pad he could see. Plastic smoke curdled in the air. Sparks spritzed from shattered circuits. Otto hadn't moved from his seat on the steps.

"What the hell are you waiting for? Get out of here!"

Walt gestured for the window, now half filled with the black waves below. "The ship's going to crash!"

"I can't think of a better reason to abandon it."

"What about you?"

"Don't give me shit about how you can't leave me behind. I'm an old man with a gut wound. I've got less chance than the Cleveland Browns."

"Save your breath," Walt said. "I just reached the same conclusion."

"You son of a bitch," Otto laughed. Blood seeped from his side. "Get somebody to write me a song or something. Anyway, another few weeks, you're gonna be hurting for things to do."

"It was fun, Otto."

"You have yourself a boy and you name him after me. That won't be any possible unless you quit this sewing circle right now."

Walt grinned. He turned and ran up the terraces, swerving around toppled desks and smoking hardware. Yellow blood oozed down the tilted floors. The elevator door closed automatically behind him. He could hardly feel its angled ascent. The silence inside pressed on his ears like swimming to the bottom of the pool. Three aliens waited at the far end. One managed to squeeze off a shot before he cut it down.

He sprinted through the huge warehouse, shoes banging, and down the curving tunnels past dark windows. Many of the doors now hung ajar; aliens scrambled down intersections clutching strange, spiky tools. He shot anyone who gave him a second look. Most failed to see him at all, or deliberately ignored him, rushing instead for whatever repairs or escape pods they expected would save their lives. Walt was back on the catwalk above the landing bay in five scant minutes. Below, jets taxied from storage, cramming the runways in the rush to launch. Engines blared, painting long shadows from the harsh white light of their boiling engines. His feet clanked on the metal walkway. And then he was through the last door, the last tunnel, standing in the cold wind on a thin platform overlooking the calm waters of Santa Monica Bay.

He laughed all the way down.

EPILOGUE

He had it all. Canned ravioli. Bags of spaghetti. A pot and a bowl and a knife and a fork. Lighters, matches, flint. The alien pistol and a hunting rifle with two boxes of bullets. A blanket. Leather gloves. Extra shoes. Three pairs of socks. Fishing line and hooks. A flashlight with a spare pack of batteries. A bigger knife and a second small one because you can never have enough knives. Needles and thread and a lightweight rope. A change of clothes. A box of Butterfingers he'd found in the back of a liquor store. Some aspirin and generic antibiotics and a bottle of Famous Grouse scotch and a bag of Bali Shag with an extra pack of rolling papers. That was it. It was enough to carry. Anything else he needed, he'd find it along the way.

He'd woken up high on a beach amidst dead fish and great bundles of kelp rotting in the morning fog. He smelled horrible; he'd vomited at some point. He tried to stand up and passed right back out.

His next try, Walt wobbled to his feet and climbed uphill. The afternoon sun warmed the sand. He soon fell to his hands and knees, crawling until he reached a street where the houses hadn't been leveled by the ship-borne wave. Behind him, its ruined engines bulged above the ocean, still smoking, faint white plumes mingling with the sea's own mist. He smashed in the window of a pretty blue Cape Cod house and shuffled over the creaking floorboards until he found bottled water in the moldy fridge.

Two days later, frame-rattling explosions jarred him from bed. Smoke grimed the sky above the airport. He went back to bed. In the morning, the skies were clear.

He got his act together, spent a week gathering up his gear. By then, he felt strong enough to go for runs along the beach, adding weight to his pack every day to rebuild the strength he'd lost recovering from the crash. He took the pistol with him; the smoke of campfires rose from the hills and beaches now. Once, the crack of a rifle had echoed down the streets. He didn't feel forced out by these new neighbors. He'd never been the LA type anyway.

Elsewhere, it was still winter. He headed south, sleeping under stars that no longer looked so far away. He figured he would stop in a place where it was nice to fish. San Diego was on fire. He went around it.

On a dry Baja beach, he caught four fat, green-silver fish with scalloped fins. He roasted them on sticks, skins and all. After he ate the first, a man appeared up the beach, waving his hands over his head. He was young and sunburned and hungry. So was his wife. Walt offered the kid a fish. It turned out they had beer, Negra Modelo in thick-bottomed brown bottles. He was named Vincent, his wife Mickey. College kids in a past life.

They talked for a while about where they were headed (them: Panama; him: somewhere), where they'd come from (Idaho; New York), what they'd seen recently (a pair of aliens hunted down with dogs and rifles; lots of sand).

"Yeah," Mickey said, tugging the strap of her tank top, "but like how did it even come to that? I mean, did you ever think we'd be taking them down with *dogs*? Did like one of them get drunk at the wheel *Exxon Valdez*-style?"

"Oh, that?" Walt said. "That was me. Me and this Vietnam vet named Otto. He was probably an asshole in the Bush years, but he was a cool guy when I met him." He sipped his beer. "We landed on the ship with a hot air balloon. Blew stuff up until the thing went down."

"And then what?" Mickey said. "You hang-glidered to safety?"

"I jumped. From what I remember, it was fun."

Mickey laughed, white teeth flashing in the firelight. Vincent smiled and put his arm around her shoulder. For a moment Walt bristled, ready to protest, to insist it *had* happened, that they weren't laughing at a tall tale, but events which had, for the second time in the last year, cost the lives of everyone he knew. But if he'd heard his story from a stranger, he'd laugh· too, wouldn't he? A handful of nobodies couldn't save the world. No doubt a hundred better stories had already cropped up around the globe.

But he wouldn't change his. He owed that much to those who'd been with him.

Walt left before they woke. It was the wind that spoke to him now, in whispers and urgent hisses; the sea that murmured to itself like it had forgotten something from a list. He walked when he was ready and slept when he was tired. When he had nowhere else to be, he sat beside the waterline and watched the sun go down, listening to the wash of the sand. He thought he heard names, sometimes, but then the waves receded, a scrub of foam and salt, snatching them back before he could be sure.

He decided to walk to the end of the southern world, the cold hills of Patagonia, where no people had lived even when people lived everywhere. Maybe the breakers would speak clear names there. Maybe he would find something to make him stop.

He intended to live along the way.

ABOUT THE AUTHOR

A lifelong fan of fantasy and science fiction, Ed's short stories have appeared in a few dozen magazines and anthologies. Along with writing fiction, he works as a movie critic, which is awesome.

Born in the Northwest, he's since lived in New York, Idaho, and most recently Los Angeles. As is required for all authors, he has a fiancée, two dogs, and a cat.

He blogs at http://www.edwardwrobertson.com